WELCOME TO THE FAE WORLD

WINTER FAE QUEEN

USA TODAY BESTSELLING AUTHORS
LEXI C. FOSS & J.R. THORN

Editing by: Outthink Editing, LLC

Proofreading by: Jean Bachen & Katie Schmahl

Cover Design: FrostAlexis Arts

Cover Photography: CJC Photography

Cover Model: Danielle Elwood

Interior Male Character Art: Covers by Julie

Published by: Ninja Newt Publishing

First Edition

eBook ISBN: 978-1-954183-82-7

Paperback ISBN: 978-1-68530-062-3

"OH, HELLO!" I GUSHED. "AREN'T YOU just the cutest thing?"

The seal cocked its head, watching me with dark brown, liquid eyes.

"Oh, yes, very handsome indeed," I cooed, wanting to approach it and bend down to stroke my fingers through its pretty fur.

"Artica…" Kalt warned.

I grinned at him, turning slightly to study his expression. "What? Do seals play pranks, too?" I teased out loud before facing the beautiful creature again.

Except it was no longer there.

Instead, a tall, toned, and *completely naked* male stood in its place, whipping back long, luxurious brown locks that dripped with icy water. "You hear that, Kalt? She thinks I'm cute," he murmured, irises twinkling, his words smooth as velvet with the sexist accent I had ever heard in my life.

Holy lickable Festivus… balls.

My voice caught in my throat as the walking sex-on-a-stick sauntered toward Kalt and me, his sultry eyes never once leaving me.

"Artica, this is Norden," Kalt said with exasperation as he pinched the bridge of his perfect nose. "And yes, this seal does play pranks. So keep your distance."

"Naughty ones, I might add," he amended with a panty-melting wink as I struggled to keep my eyes above his waistline. I didn't really care what kind of pranks he played, as long as he kept *talking*.

The male with ripped abs and skin faintly glittering with sea salt didn't stop his advance until he was up against me, so close our breath mingled. He smelled of the winter ocean mixed with notes of nutmeg.

I inhaled him, my gaze flickering between those eyes of melted chocolate.

"Have you brought a female candidate for our triad, Kalt?" he asked as he tilted his head, his voice lilting playfully. "Her affinity for ice is... *alluring*." He traced his lower lip with his tongue. "I can almost taste her compatibility. Color me intrigued."

Can't. Breathe.

How was I supposed to accomplish my work around here when *seals* could turn into sexy-as-sin men with voices that set my veins on fire?

Then his statements finally sank in.

Triad?

Winter Fae were known for their mate-circles of three males and one female.

Had Kalt joined a triad while working here?

And... and were they looking for a female to join them?

I nearly squealed. *I volunteer!*

"For the thousandth time, I'm not in your triad, you incessant selkie," Kalt snapped, melting all my hopes and dreams in a breath.

Well, icicles.

For the dreamers in the world, this one is for you.

WINTER
FAE
QUEEN

WINTER FAE QUEEN

The Royal Water Fae I'm in love with just hired me to be his intern.

Oh. My. Fae.

I only applied for the job because of a dare, and now I'm packing my bags for the North Pole.

No big deal. I can totally be professional. I haven't seen him since the Academy anyway. Maybe he's gotten fat from all the Winter Fae sweets

Except, no. Kalt hasn't gotten fat at all. He's still perfectly chiseled and even more gorgeous than I remember. And worse? He has two equally hot friends.

A royal elf named Lark.
And a sexy-as-sin selkie named Norden.

I am so screwed. And I mean that literally because the elf and the selkie seem to think I'm their mate. Only Kalt completely disagrees.

Oh, and not only am I dealing with these three hotties, but my water magic is also on the fritz. I accidentally stirred up a snowball fight in the middle of Santa's workshop, then ice tinsel started shooting from my fingertips like confetti.

It's a problem.
One I'm not sure how to solve.
So, yeah, wish me luck! And send warm vibes. I really need some help melting all this snow...

Winter Fae Queen *is a quirky paranormal romance featuring a Water Fae from the Elemental Fae universe and her three potential mates.*

INTRODUCTION

Welcome to the Winter Fae Kingdom. It's filled with sugary delights, joyous elves, sexy selkies, gorgeous Winter Fae Royals carrying large packages, and enough mystical energy to inspire belief throughout the entire Human Realm.

Artica's story is deliciously sweet and guaranteed to warm even the iciest of hearts. It's also a standalone featuring a happily-ever-after ending.

However, a word of caution: Artica's males are hot enough to melt ice and frequently do so when they play with each other in the bedroom. After all, Winter Fae culture requires a triad of three men who believe in and cherish each other just as much as they love and worship their female mate. It's how the Winter Fae thrive.

So grab a snowflake and hold on tight.
You're about to slip and slide into the Arctic Circle.
Where you'll meet beings inspired by beliefs.
Who just might inspire some holiday cheer...

PROLOGUE
PRINCE LARK

C oronation.

A joyous time meant to inspire smiles and love and holiday cheer.

Of course, every event here has that impact on life at the North Pole. But I don't feel cheerful at all. In fact, I am downright dreadful.

Why?

Because I've only found one of my mates.

Well, technically two. However, the second continues to deny what we both know. Which doesn't bode well for the festivities to come.

So I'm infusing a bit of Winter Fae magic in the air in

an attempt to draw out more potential mates. It's a tug of belief mingled with a sensual appeal that should draw compatible souls to the North Pole.

I just hope I'm not too late.

And that they don't deny me the way the Water Fae Prince has.

The whole point of my existence is to *believe*, thus I'm choosing to believe now. To believe that mates are out there. That they will love me. Join me. Form a joyous union in the aura of the Winter Fae Source and indulge me in a beautiful happily-ever-after.

Otherwise, my kingdom will fall.

And the spirit of the holidays will tarnish with it.

No more festive cheer. No more celebrations. No more mystical beliefs.

A heavy burden for just one to carry, but I was born into this role for a reason, and I won't let Winter Fae kind down.

All I need to do is *believe*.

And believe, I shall.

Welcome to my world.

It's frigid on the outside but warm on the inside. Filled with more love and joy than a single heart can contain. Which is why I need three.

Three mates. Three loves. Three believers.

To continue the holiday tradition.

To ascend.

To become the icon the Human Realm needs—the Winter Fae King.

ARTICA

"Snowflakes," I cursed, stuffing my blouse into my skirt as I ran through the Water Quad of Elemental Fae Academy.

Late! Late! Late!

Why did I have to take a nap in the middle of the day and nearly sleep through my afternoon classes? Oh, right. I'd stayed up all night obsessing about today.

The irony.

"Icicle," I hissed under my breath as I burst through a group of attractive male fae, their hair frosted with ice to celebrate today's special occasion. Normally, I'd stop to ogle them— blame my sex drive that was overactive even by fae standards—but lately I only had eyes for one fae in particular. Too bad he was off playing emissary at the North Pole right now.

It didn't matter. I'd never see my dream-date again if I missed all the best assignments because I'd stayed up all night thinking about him.

And his internship.

Oh Fae, what if Kalt actually picks me?

I'd only applied because of a stupid dare, and now I couldn't even sleep without seeing his face.

Running around a corner, I spotted a decorating committee of Water Fae cheerleaders too late. Their perfect blue eyes went round with alarm as they froze in their various positions on a ladder. I slammed into them, sending them toppling down like a deck of cards. They squealed as they fell, letting go of a string that had been holding up a banner.

It fluttered overhead like a bad omen, the rainbow letters the last thing I saw before it folded over me.

Internship Assignment Day!

More like doomsday since I was most assuredly going to be assigned an internship in the Hell Fae Realm at this rate.

Or worse, the Shifter Realm.

I loved animals, but those dogs needed to learn some damn manners. My professor would assign me to them just to "teach me a lesson."

The mere thought of it made my skin itch. I'd been mauled by a pack once, all of them tugging at my clothes while teasing my inability to shift.

I'd secretly feared their kind ever since.

Wolf shifters. Ugh.

Yep. Totally my fate.

All because I'd overslept.

Toppled a team of cheerleaders.

And wrapped myself up in a banner.

"Fluff!" I screeched as I tried to swim out of the suffocating cloth.

The bell rang, signaling the beginning of the end for me. *Shifter Fae, here I come*, a darker part of me thought. But the lighter side refused to give up.

I gathered the invisible water droplets from the air, forming them into a blade.

"No weapons!" a girl shouted, but I really didn't give two ice cookies about rules right now.

My makeshift blade sliced through the fabric, shredding it with a distinct *rip* before it fell away, and I marched toward class.

"Hey!" one of the girls shouted. "You're paying for that!"

Flipping her off, I dove into my classroom and slammed the door behind me, leaning against it as I heaved for breath.

Had I made it inside before the bell had stopped ringing?

Professor Elway sighed and pushed his glasses up the bridge of his perfect nose. "Not a great day to be tardy, Artica."

I should have been groveling with my apologies, but I couldn't speak. My eyes were glued to the popsicle-melting physique of Kalt, the Elemental Fae Emissary to the Winter Fae Realm.

Who was supposed to be at the North Pole right now.

Except, he was right here, perched on the edge of the professor's desk, fully witnessing me undress him with my eyes as all the unruly memories of my dreams came back to haunt me.

Holy frost-cicles.

Instead of chiding me, he seemed to be sizing me up as he propped one leg on a chair. He dangled something between his fingertips. I tilted my head at it, guessing it was a package from the North Pole based on its shiny red paper and silver bow. My treacherous gaze drifted to his other, more *sizable* package, causing my chest to go tight.

I suddenly felt as though I'd eaten too many spiced coldberry biscuits.

Stop staring at him like an unwrapped gift on Fae Festivus.

I forced my gaze away from Kalt's, um, *gifts* and met his unblinking gaze.

Ice blue.

So pretty.

Except the stern line of his jaw suggested he wasn't all that pleased with me. Probably because I'd just been ogling his crotch.

I hoped he was thinking of a punishment for my tardiness, one just like my dream involving lots of frosted cream and Festivus garlands that ended in us both naked and panting and—

What in the fae is wrong with me?!

I swallowed past the lump in my throat as I tried to freeze out the inappropriate thoughts, but damn, Kalt was distracting. His snow-white hair flowed evenly over his shoulders, framing a face made from marble. His frigid gaze seemed to pierce right through me, holding an edge of arctic ice that made his eyes glitter like glass.

Well, apparently time at the North Pole has upgraded his sex appeal from come-hither to holy-Festivus-balls-I-want-to-lick-him.

He shifted as I stared, his hard muscles rippling underneath a silk shirt open at the collar, hinting at the hard lines I wanted to run my tongue over.

"Artica!" Professor Elway snapped, and I realized he'd been talking to me for quite some time.

Jolting up straight, I grimaced. "Y-yes?"

His nostrils flared. "Take. Your. Seat."

I blinked at him a few times. "Y-you haven't given out assignments yet, right?"

He glared at me. "No. So if you'd like to be considered, I'd recommend not making me repeat myself."

Praise the Source!

Nodding, I ducked my chin to my chest and hurried to my seat, desperately hoping no one had seen me drooling over the very lickable Water Fae I had been crushing on for ages.

When I took my seat and risked a glance, I found Kalt still watching me, and I melted on the inside into a puddle of Artica-shaped goo.

"Now that we're all here," Professor Elway began, looking pointedly in my direction. "Most of you probably remember Prince Kalt. He graduated not that long ago, and he's offering one of the more glamorous internships for this Festivus season."

Several of the females in the class shifted.

Or maybe just me.

But yeah, we all knew of Kalt.

Perfectly chiseled, handsome, sexy Water Fae Royal with a penchant for ice.

Mmm, yes, please.

"Prince Kalt is here to escort the lucky Water Fae selected for the Winter Fae internship back to the North Pole. As I'm sure most of you already know, an intern is needed there immediately due to Queen Claire's successful Interrealm Fae efforts and our emissary's hard work."

I sucked in a quick breath.

If I somehow miraculously won the internship, I'd leave today. *With Kalt.*

Professor Elway continued. "Now, according to Internship Day tradition, selections will be revealed through an interactive project. But there's a catch." He produced an array of frozen trinkets.

I sat up a little straighter in my chair.

"These baubles have been magically frozen with your assignment etched into the crystal inside. However, they have fragile interiors. Damage them, and you'll never learn what your assignment was, and your chance at the internship will be forfeited." He eyed all of us seriously. "You must successfully use your abilities to adjust the water element inside."

Kalt nodded beside him. "I froze them myself."

Oh, even his voice makes me melt. All accented and deep and sighhhh.

"Indeed," Professor Elway murmured, his voice not nearly as sigh-inducing. "And one of the trinkets has your internship inside it."

Kalt dipped his chin again in confirmation. "I received too many qualified applicants. We'll use ice and water to decide on a victor."

"A suitable assignment," Professor Elway agreed. "So you all will select a bauble at random to learn your internship assignment. Only one of these is tied to the North Pole. All the others will automatically read your essence and provide your internship location accordingly. Assuming you melt it appropriately."

His blue eyes glittered as he evaluated the class.

"Well, good luck, then." Professor Elway sent the trinkets to gather in a basket on his desk beside Kalt. "Come select a bauble."

Several fae leapt forward at once, making my heart stutter.

The internship with Kalt was now based on luck.

And I wasn't exactly a lucky fae.

Case in point, the banner incident.

Well, maybe I'll be selected for another internship with Queen Claire, I thought hopefully.

I approached the desk with Juniper—a classmate I'd shared most of my classes with over the years. "Are you nervous?" I asked her softly as we lined up to pick our frozen trinket. "Because I'm nervous."

She shook her head. Juniper was a gorgeous Water Fae with blonde hair and sea green eyes. As usual, sprigs of holly were in her hair. She'd fit right in at the North Pole. "I know exactly where I'm going," she said. "And if I somehow don't get what I want, then that internship will just suck dragon balls."

I laughed at her determination. Juniper didn't fear anything or anyone.

But this task didn't have the same meaning to her as it did to me.

If I selected the right bauble, I would be working with *Kalt*.

Which meant I needed to think positively. Happily, even. Just like a Winter Fae.

Juniper selected a trinket with her long, manicured fingers.

Snowflakes. Cupcakes. Sugar cookies. Elves. Oh, my... I repeated to myself as I carefully retrieved one of the icy knickknacks. *Okay, Artica. You've got this. Winter Fae, here we come.*

I lifted my gaze to Kalt, still perched on Professor Elway's desk beside the basket of baubles, and startled when I found him staring right at me with those icy blue eyes.

Totally deserve that look after ogling him so openly, I thought, my cheeks heating.

Dropping my attention to the ground, I rushed by him and took my seat to concentrate on my task.

Okay. I can do this.

I was a talented Water Fae with an affinity for ice.

Just like Kalt.

That was how I knew of him—he'd been the head of

his class in my younger years, and I'd fallen in love with his impressive abilities. He also possessed a genuineness about him that I enjoyed.

And he was pretty nice to look at, too.

A giggle bubbled in the back of my throat, but I forced it back. *Focus.*

Juniper sat next to me and immediately went to work.

Where did she want to go, again? I couldn't remember. But I hoped it wasn't the North Pole. Except *everyone* wanted the North Pole internship.

Hence Kalt's statement about having too many applicants.

Not surprising, really.

The Winter Fae were notorious for their jolly personas, and everyone seemed happy there. Even the Human Realm had legends about the North Pole's inhabitants.

Santa, elves, reindeer, Festivus cheer—or Christmas cheer, as some humans called it—all of it stemmed from the Winter Fae. Except Santa wasn't some old fat guy, and not all elves were waist-high.

No, some of the elves were Royal Winter Fae, and *hot*, from what I'd heard. I'd climb their chimney any day.

Overseeing toy-building, candy-making, and royal balls? Straight up my alley.

I hummed some Festivus tunes in my head while I worked, determined to infuse my jolly essence into the trinket. Then I carefully used my magic to experiment with the water inside.

The fragile element was a rod of ice shooting through the center. Inscribed along it appeared to be writing. Break the rod, ruin the inscription.

All right.

I just needed to shift the mixture of ice and water

around so the ice was behind the inscription and the water was at the front. That way, I could actually read it.

But the bauble had been enchanted to make things a little more difficult than separating liquids from solids. I bit my lip. This was like playing with those dumb little handheld games where you tried to use water to hook rings on tiny spikes.

My senses prickled, drawing my attention back to Kalt.

He drew his fingers through his long white hair as he studied me, his icy gaze holding a touch of warmth. Or was it interest?

Maybe I imagined it.

But nope, that smirk... that smirk was real. He even had little dimples on his cheeks.

I almost dropped the precious frozen sphere. Because *Fae*, he was gorgeous.

And distracting.

Sooo distracting.

His gaze didn't waver from mine, and if I stared back at him for half a second longer, I'd likely combust. Glancing down at my bauble, I ignored the warmth crawling up my neck, only to freeze as Juniper gasped.

Oh, no...

She just won the North Pole internship, didn't she?

Heart sinking, I glared at my bauble, still working on clearing up the inscription to make it readable. Maybe I'd win something for second place. Impress Kalt enough for him to need two interns or something.

Not likely.

But I refused to give up. Who knew what Juniper's inscription said? It might just be the internship she actually wanted.

Focus, Artica.

I can do this. I can do this. I can do this.

The ice shards behind the rod shifted with my magic, ever so slowly revealing the inscription beneath.

North Pole. My jaw dropped. *No fluffing way...*

My eyes snapped up to Kalt. He smiled, setting the butterflies in my stomach loose.

Juniper leaned toward my desk, eyes narrowing as she read my bauble. "Holy Fae. North Pole? Is that what you wanted?"

"Yes!" It was an effort not to squeal with excitement. "What did you get?"

Juniper tilted her trinket so I could see it. *Fortune Fae Academy.*

"That would be my second choice," I said honestly. "All those hot Alphas!"

Juniper smiled, but I caught the glint of jealousy in her eyes as they flickered toward Kalt.

Back up. He's mine.

Not that I had any right to claim Kalt. But I still felt protective over him now that I was officially his intern.

Professor Elway swept between our desks, looking at our baubles. "Congratulations to the both of you," he said, his voice upbeat. "Juniper, you're going to love the Fortune Fae. It's always a learning experience to see how their Omegas peer into the future."

"Right," Juniper said slowly, tearing her gaze from my crystal orb to stare at hers. "Sounds... fascinating."

"It is!" Professor Elway gushed. "They have unique mating circles consisting of Alphas, Omegas, and Betas. It must be an incredibly alluring society." His tone turned serious. "Which is why more interns than I care to admit have rejected the Water Source to become Fortune Fae themselves."

That caught Juniper's attention. "Really?"

He nodded. "If I had to guess, once one witnesses such

a mating dynamic, it's very tempting to want to experience it for yourself. Females will typically become Betas or Norms, but you'll still be able to look into the future. It can be addicting, or so I hear." He shook his head. "But we all have fates and roles to play. There's no changing that."

Juniper nodded, her eyes bright with interest.

I thought of the few Fortune Fae I'd met and how romanticized their society was. The professor had a point. It didn't help that everyone there was alluring in more ways than one…

My eyes flicked to Kalt, who *still* stared at me.

Don't overthink it, Artica. It's because I picked his bauble.

Which totally sounded dirty in my head.

I'd absolutely played with his *trinket* more than once in my dreams.

"Besides, you wouldn't want to be mated to a Fortune Fae Alpha," the professor went on, clearing his throat. "I hear they do something called 'knotting,' which I will not elaborate on further in the classroom. But they're aggressive and powerful, so I'll leave it at that."

Any trace of disappointment melted away from Juniper's expression as she tapped her lip. Professor Elway chuckled before leaving, his job seemingly done.

Juniper leaned toward me. "What do you think knotting means?"

I bit back my laughter. "Um… I think you're better off not knowing."

"It's a sex act, isn't it?"

My cheeks heated. There was little I didn't know when it came to sex acts in the fae realms, given my extreme curiosity that often landed me in trouble.

Although, this particular act was one I'd learned about during my internship with Queen Claire. One of her friends had been, um, vocal about her recent heat experience. And I'd heard everything through the too-thin wood of Queen Claire's office door.

I'd promptly read up on the activities and how dangerous knotting could be for a non-Omega Fortune Fae.

But if Juniper really wanted to witness it… "You could probably ask for a demonstration. You know, for educational purposes of Fortune Fae biology." I had read about the mating courtyards that the Fortune Fae often used, which would be perfect for a presentation.

Her face reddened into a blush as she giggled behind her hand. "Seriously? That sounds amazing."

"Shit!" someone in the back of the class yelled.

Juniper and I both turned. A Water Fae stared glumly at his frozen bauble, which had cracked into two.

"We can't all be successful," Juniper said. She gave me a warm smile. "Congrats on the North Pole, Artica."

A shimmer of excitement skated up my spine. "Thanks. I'll try not to freeze my butt off."

"Unhappy with your selection?" a deep voice rumbled beside me.

I twisted in my seat, staring at the sculpture of Kalt's flawless face.

My brain short-circuited.

Because wow, so, so pretty. Even better than my dreams. Like perfection personified. And—

He raised a pale brow, some of that perfection melting into an expression of impatience.

Because he'd asked me a question.

Unhappy with your selection?

Fluff. "No!" I blurted. "I mean, yes. As in…"

He tilted his head, pinning me with his icy stare.

This male would be the death of me.

I sucked in a breath. "You can't possibly understand how ecstatic I am."

His lips curved upward. His arm brushed my shoulder as he reached for my bauble and plucked it off my desk. Examining it, he nodded. "And here I thought you didn't even want the job... what with it being a dare and all." He held up the trinket. "Nice work. You'll be perfect for the North Pole."

Glazed ice crept up his fingers and along the sides of the sphere, covering it entirely until it glimmered like a diamond, then exploded into glittering snow.

My lips parted, watching the flakes swirl into nothing.

But wait... how in the fae did he know about the dare?

Kalt's palm appeared before me. "Shall we go grab your things?" he asked, distracting me from my thoughts. "We have a long afternoon and evening ahead of us, as I need to bring you up to speed immediately."

Or rather, freezing my ability to think of anything other than the fact that Kalt had just offered me his hand.

Like a date.

Except, not a date.

An internship.

But his hand...

I set my palm against his soft skin, allowing his heat to bleed into my skin as he pulled me from my chair. *I'm going to the Winter Fae Realm.*

To work for Prince Kalt.

Oh. My. Fae.

I didn't need to be a Fortune Fae to know that everything in my life was about to change.

KALT

E lemental Fae Academy brought back so many pleasant memories.

Playing water tag outside.

Enjoying a good game of ice pistols with the Fire Fae.

Studying for fae politics classes—which I now realized were a joke. Sure, understanding the history of fae kind helped in certain situations, but my job as an Elemental Fae Emissary to the Winter Fae was all about schmoozing and networking.

Especially when fae from other realms appeared, which happened often now that the Interrealm Fae agreement had been signed.

The Winter Fae possessed a great deal of concealment magic, thus making them a necessary stop for certain fae wishing to visit the Human Realm. Not all required it, of course. Midnight Fae and Fortune Fae often walked among mortals without notice. But certain Shifter Fae needed help disguising horns and hooves.

And then there were the Hell Fae. Many of them were humanoid in nature. Some… were not.

Regardless, while customs varied, they all enjoyed the same sort of kiss-ass treatment—a methodology not taught in any of my classes here at Elemental Fae Academy.

Artica would be fine.

Assuming she could focus long enough to remember her manners.

She'd been adorably flustered upon entering the room earlier, her pretty blue eyes sizing me up with obvious interest. Just as she always had when I'd entered a room.

A childhood crush that never seemed to die.

Something I rather appreciated now.

Because Artica had grown up into a beautiful Water Fae with curves that tempted my ice magic out to play. I'd caress her skin with gentle snowflakes, then soothe the frigid burn with my tongue in the next instant.

Except, no, I wouldn't. Because she was officially severely off-limits as my intern.

A good thing, honestly, as Lance would flame my ass if I touched her. They were friends, and Lance was practically family to me since his brother, Titus, and my cousin, Cyrus, were both mated to Queen Claire.

"This is me," Artica announced as we reached one of the residences of the Water Quad. "Um, do you want to stay here, or…?"

Her cheeks reddened beautifully, making me grin. "I'll follow you up." Mostly because I rather enjoyed her frazzled state.

While she might have applied to my internship on a dare, she'd actually been one of my primary candidates. Not because of our link through Lance, but because of her high scores and cheerful energy. She would fit in nicely at the North Pole, something the magic in the baubles had proved.

Prince Lark—the future King of the Winter Fae—had bespelled them for me, saying the best candidate would select the right trinket.

I'd felt the truth of that when Artica had picked her crystal orb. My water magic, coupled with Lark's familiar energy, had flared to life beneath her fingertips, telling me immediately that she had the winning bauble.

All she'd needed to do was master the ice enchantment inside to reveal her fate.

And only the destined candidate could do that.

There was another test in my pocket, just to be sure, as I didn't want to bring back the wrong Water Fae. But I almost didn't need it to be certain of Artica's appropriateness for the role.

A fact that proved even more true as we approached a decorated dorm door covered with real snowflakes and bright red flowers blossoming with earth magic. I arched a brow. "A little early for Festivus decorations, isn't it?"

About six months early, to be exact, since it was technically summer here in the Elemental Fae Realm. Same with the Winter Fae Realm. Not that it stopped the elves from keeping it cheerful year-round.

"It is *never* too early for decorations," she countered, her smile stunningly beautiful. "But if it bothers you, I don't recommend coming inside my room."

Oh, I'm definitely going in your room, I thought, too curious to stay in the hallway like a gentleman. "If it bothered me, I wouldn't be able to stand living among the Winter Fae," I told her instead. Then I nodded to her door. "Let's see what you've done to the place."

She nibbled her lip, then shrugged and used her water element to create an ice key to open her door.

Both my eyebrows hit my hairline at the winter wonderland inside.

Frost decorated all her furniture and a potted fir tree in the corner. Icicles and snowflakes adorned the green ends but hung off of them enough not to freeze the pines, and the dirt appeared freshly watered.

"Queen Claire loves Christmas trees from the Human Realm, so I, uh, made one." Artica shrugged, then went to her closet to begin packing while I studied the other decorations in the room.

This had to be Prince Lark's wet dream come true.

He would enter this bedroom, fuck Artica into that mattress, and never let her go.

An image that should not appeal to me at all. Because I was *not* in his triad, no matter how many times he bloody said it.

And I should not be fantasizing about another fae fucking my intern.

Thinking about myself taking her was one thing, but picturing Lark doing it? While I watched? Entirely another.

He was a friend. A political advantage. A *coworker*. A future king.

Not my... whatever this is...

"Kalt?" Artica asked, a note of hesitation in her voice.

I realized then that my hands had curled into fists, and I'd frozen beneath some sort of leaf hanging from the ceiling. Turning slowly, I found Artica right beside me with wide eyes.

"Sorry," I said, striving for the first excuse I could think of for my strange behavior. "Your room reminded me that I need to decorate mine at the palace. Prince Lark is a fan of the... holidays."

"Prince Lark," she repeated. "A Winter Fae Royal?"

"Hmm," I hummed in confirmation. Her application had confirmed her interest in fae politics, as she'd taken several of the same courses as I had.

"Oh, this is exciting," Artica said, clapping her hands together. She started to pack again, only to stop and look back at me. "Also, I was trying to tell you that you're standing under a mistletoe."

I blinked. "What?"

She pointed over his head. "That's a mistletoe."

I took in the leaves above my head and the little bell beneath them. "Like the human tradition?" I'd become well acquainted with the mortal holidays during my time with the Winter Fae. They were the ones in charge of spreading cheer and holiday magic to the children of the human world, which made understanding their traditions rather important.

Elemental Fae resided in a realm away from the humans.

As did many others of fae kind.

Winter Fae were different, as their livelihoods were literally dependent on the cheer of mortals throughout the festive season.

Hence, I'd needed to brush up on my understanding of the mortals rather quickly, something Queen Claire had assisted me with since she was a Halfling—part fae, part human.

"Why do you have a mistletoe in your bedroom?" I asked, not giving Artica a chance to confirm that this was a human tradition, because I already knew it was.

"In case a handsome fae comes to visit," she replied dreamily. Then she froze, her eyes widening. "Oh, but I didn't mean, that is, I... well... it's..." Her cheeks turned that delicious shade of pink again, reminding me of strawberries—a human fruit I very much enjoyed.

"Because standing beneath it means I owe you a kiss," I said, fighting a grin as her face turned a darker shade closer to red. "Right?"

She appeared ready to faint.

My lips curled. "Come here, Artica." I was enjoying this far more than I should, but she wasn't technically my intern yet. Besides, she sort of qualified as an old friend via her relationship with Lance.

"It's… it's just a silly tradition," she mumbled.

"A tradition that Prince Lark takes very seriously," I told her, meaning it. "He would be most displeased if he learned his Elemental Fae Emissary ignored a mortal belief. Now come here."

Her lips twisted to the side, but she seemed to find truth in my statement. Which meant she understood the importance of human traditions to the Winter Fae.

We might be in the Elemental Fae Realm, but that didn't really matter now that we were both politically tied to the Winter Fae Realm.

May as well get her used to this now, I thought as she stepped toward me.

"Close your eyes," I whispered to her. This was so inappropriate of me as her new boss, but she was the one with the mistletoe, not me.

And I could say she wasn't my official intern until I tested her with the gift in my pocket.

That would be the final token of her employment.

Until I gave it to her, she wasn't technically working for me.

Yes, this logic worked.

Except an honorable part of me argued that I was just making up rules, so rather than press my lips to hers, I brushed a chaste kiss against her warm cheek.

It both fulfilled the mortal superstition and made our embrace friendly rather than intimate.

Her long blonde lashes fluttered as she opened her eyes, a hint of wonder mingling with disappointment.

She'd wanted me to truly kiss her.

Because of that damn crush, I thought. As the first cousin to the Water Fae King, I often developed admirers. But Artica had always been a bit different, her fascination with me more innocent and childlike.

It made me not want to risk hurting her.

Unlike so many others, she didn't throw herself at me. She just worshipped me with her eyes.

And there was something exquisitely beautiful about that.

"Finish packing," I told her softly. "I don't want to miss dinner tonight with the Winter Fae."

She swallowed. "Right. Yes." She continued gathering her items while I casually stepped out from beneath the mistletoe—I wouldn't be falling for that again.

Yet a tingle of energy settled over my skin, urging me to move beneath it once more, like Prince Lark himself desired more magic.

An impossible notion.

One that was definitely in my head.

Because the damn Winter Fae Royal kept saying I was part of his *triad*.

The Winter Fae typically formed a triad of three males who then hunted for their fourth mate together—a female.

Once the circle was complete, all the members of it actually transitioned into Winter Fae. Which meant that most Winter Fae were not originally born of winter magic, just married into it. Thus, they weren't considered abominations in the eyes of fae kind. Similar to how

Fortune Fae were fae that rejected their Sources to become seers.

However, Prince Lark was a true Winter Fae Royal because he'd been created by a circle of Winter Fae, meaning he'd been born a Winter Fae. He possessed pure Christmas magic as a result, and not only that, but his father was the reigning monarch. Hence, he would soon take the throne.

And he was convinced that I belonged in his triad with him and Norden, a sensual selkie who adored the idea of me joining them.

Agreeing to it meant giving up my identity as a Water Fae Royal, and I hadn't even properly mastered that yet. So how could I become a Winter Fae? Let alone join the triad of the future Winter Fae King?

Shaking my head, I focused on my current task of preparing Artica for her internship. Which included giving her the package from my pocket.

Another test.

But a different one from the baubles.

This one... was a test from Prince Lark himself.

I started to pull out the small package, when Artica asked, "How did you know about the dare?" Her attention was on her suitcase, but her mind clearly remained focused on me.

"Lance," I admitted, amused.

"Oh." She cleared her throat. "What, uh, did he say exactly?"

"That he dared you to apply because of your affinity for ice. He also said you'd be an ideal candidate for the Winter Fae Realm and that I'd be sorry if I didn't hire you." Lance knew about her crush on me but had still insisted on her being the right fae for the job.

A glance at her resume had confirmed it.

As had her quickness with the bauble.

And her festive bedroom.

"Everyone wanted the internship," she said, peeking at me before quickly returning her focus to her bag. "That was the only reason I didn't immediately apply."

A lie.

She hadn't applied because of her crush on me.

Which was fine.

"I'm glad he dared you to do it," I told her honestly. "I agree that you're an ideal candidate."

Her back straightened, her blue eyes finding mine again. "You do?"

"Of course I do." I leaned forward a little. "You didn't really think the trinket was a test, did you?"

It was a secret I shouldn't divulge, but I couldn't afford to have an unconfident intern at my side. Not with everything happening with the Winter Fae Coronation and Queen Claire's Interrealm Fae activities.

"Those baubles were bespelled by Winter Fae magic. Only the fae best suited for the job could select the Winter Fae trinket. Which I already knew was you from the applicant pool." I waggled my brows at her. "Good thing you made it to class, almost on time."

Her lips parted, the plump formation drawing my attention to them automatically and gifting me with visions of just what she could do with her mouth.

Something I should *not* be thinking about.

But I preferred it to the image of Prince Lark fucking her on the bed.

Of course, now I was imagining her mouth wrapped around his—

Fae bells, I'm losing my mind to the fairies, I thought, blowing out a breath and shaking my head again. "We should go." Because I really needed to take a nap or something.

No, wait.

It's the gift, I realized, slipping my hand into my pocket and ignoring how tight my pants had become while standing here.

Artica's gaze dropped to my waist, her eyes widening a bit.

Probably because she could see exactly why my pants were suddenly tight.

But I distracted her with the package, lifting it between us.

Her eyes slowly followed, her brow furrowing.

"Lance told me to keep an eye on you because you're a troublemaker," I teased, partially telling the truth. He'd claimed that Artica could be a bit clumsy, but the fault only made her more endearing. "So I brought you a welcoming present." More like Prince Lark had forced me to bring it. However, that was neither here nor there.

"Is it a leash?" she joked. "Or maybe a shock collar?"

I chuckled. "Not quite, but it does go around your neck." I handed it to her. "Open it."

A hint of water magic touched the air as Artica calmed the flush in her cheeks, making my lips twitch at the sides. She really did blush a lot, so I supposed that was a clever trick to help calm her body temperature.

She tugged at the bow, carefully unwrapped the shiny red paper, and discovered the box inside. Her nimble fingers popped the top open, revealing the gleaming crystal inside.

Her eyes widened. "A snowflake necklace?"

"Not just any snowflake," I murmured, taking the chain from the box to deftly wrap it around her neck. That pretty blush appeared again, warming my fingertips as I clasped the ends at her nape.

Fortunately, we weren't under the mistletoe again or I'd be tempted to truly kiss her.

An urge I really needed to ignore.

Along with about a dozen other ideas floating in my head.

Prince Lark had probably bespelled the package to seduce me, too. Which would explain all these inappropriate inclinations.

Swallowing, I focused on the pendant at Artica's throat, needing to explain the enchantment of the gift. "The snowflake will never melt because it's infused with my magic"—something Prince Lark had insisted on, saying he needed my affinity for ice to freeze the pendant in place— "as well as North Pole magic."

She lifted a finger to graze the glittering edges of the frosty flake. "It's beautiful."

"Yes." *Focus on the necklace, not on Artica,* I told myself, clearing my throat. "So anyway, as I said, it's an appropriate gift for a troublemaker, as it's a wishing charm."

Her eyes flew up to mine. "A wishing charm?"

I nodded. "If you ever find yourself in trouble, just touch it and make a wish, and the snowflake should help you out."

She stroked the pendant again, her expression wistful. "How many wishes does it have?"

I grinned. "As many as you like, and as long as they're within reason of the charm's capability. It can grant minor wishes, but there's a recharge period, and it can only recharge when you're in the North Pole since it has to draw on Winter Fae magic to function properly." It also had another feature to it, but we'd address that later.

"Wow," she breathed. "Th-thank you, Prince Kalt. Or, um, *Emissary* Kalt?"

I snorted at the titles. "No need for formality, Artica. Just Kalt is fine."

"Okay." She didn't sound all that okay. She sounded breathless, like she was about to pass out.

"All packed?" I asked, trying to distract her from whatever whimsical thought had given her that dreamy expression.

"Um, yes?"

"You don't sound sure."

"I... I don't know what I need," she said slowly. "How cold is it there?"

"Cold," I admitted. "But there are enchantments, and you'll have additional items in your wardrobe to help you fit in."

"Fit in?" she repeated.

"You'll see what I mean," I promised her. "So are you ready?"

She glanced at her bags, then nodded. "Um, yes, I think so."

"Good, because they'll be offering dinner soon, and trust me, you don't want to miss it." I considered her for a moment. "Mist or portal room?" I'd misted here earlier, a talent very few Water Fae possessed. But as a royal heir, I had the gift in my blood.

Artica's expression told me her choice before she even voiced it. Because pure joy and excitement radiated from her. "Oh, mist, please."

My lips curled. "Good. I prefer it to portaling." I held out my hand. "Ready when you are, Artica."

ARTICA

Holy frost balls, that's cold.

Even with Kalt's body heat—something I'd very much enjoyed about the misting experience—I froze almost immediately upon arrival. So much so that I'd missed an introduction to whomever Kalt had handed my bags off to.

It was a quick "hi" and "bye" experience that I'd barely heard beneath my frozen hair.

Because a blouse and a skirt were *not* enough warmth for this chilly realm.

Something Kalt could have warned me about.

Yet he seemed fine in his dress pants and button-down shirt, so maybe it hadn't crossed his mind.

I shivered as icy snow crunched under my boots—the only appropriate part of my attire—while Kalt led me along the Arctic beachfront.

It would have been romantic, if my lips weren't frozen.

As a full-blooded Water Fae with an affinity for ice and cold, I would eventually adjust to the extreme temperature after enough exposure. Which was probably why Kalt didn't react at all to the chilly climate.

For now, however, I created an insulating barrier that hovered just over my skin, except for the part that still held Kalt's hand.

I didn't care if my fingers froze off.

Kalt was *touching me*.

And I wanted that to last as long as possible.

Which ended up being only a half second longer because he released my hand and murmured, "You should finish insulating yourself. It'll take a few days for you to acclimate to the cold."

Suppressing a frown, I did as he instructed.

If this was going to work, I needed to screw my head on straight.

He was my *boss* now, so I had to stop sighing and ogling him, at least when he was less than a foot from my side, as he was now.

My fingers went to my new necklace.

The only one to ever give me jewelry before was my mother. Until Kalt. And this wasn't just any necklace, but a wishing charm. *That's pretty romantic, right?*

Sighing at my impossible mind, I tried to appreciate where I was—in the gorgeously enchanted North Pole.

Blue skies, tranquil waters, and icebergs dotted with penguins, encompassed most of my vision. For some reason, Kalt hadn't taken me directly to the palace, opting instead for me to freeze upon arrival.

Perhaps he was testing my mettle against the cold.

"So you said the baubles weren't really a test," I hedged, wanting to know more about that. "That you'd already chosen me for the internship, or knew it would be me. But how did you know that?"

I spoke while altering the frigid breeze around us to

wrap it around my body, leaving a layer of still air just over my skin. It was a trick I'd taught myself to keep myself warm when I didn't want to bother with heavy coats during trips to colder realms. Making the air currents move around my body was excellent insulation that kept the cold at bay.

Kalt glanced down at me, his lips twitching. "Because of tricks like that. You've never been instructed on how to insulate yourself, yet you know how to. Water Fae have different ranges of their talents, and some are more suitable to work with Winter Fae than others."

He created a small ice sculpture in the palm of his hand to demonstrate—an ice dragon.

I formed a sculpture of my own: a Pegasus.

He smiled with approval.

"Our affinity for ice is ideal for the North Pole. Queen Claire's Interrealm Fae relations are a challenge, one I can't tackle alone. That's why you're here. You're the best suited for the job I have in mind."

I clamped down on the overwhelming urge to grin like an idiot at his words.

"The Winter Fae talents are key for fostering relationships among the realms because of their Winter Fae concealment magic. They help other fae hide among humans, which further strengthens the alliance Queen Claire is trying to build across the fae kingdoms." His gaze turned distant. "Who knows? One day, we may all need each other's help. Which provides motivation for us all, hmm?"

My lips curled down.

Because that last bit sounded a bit ominous.

I made a mental note to ask Juniper about the latest multi-realm prophecy from the Fortune Fae. It was often impossibly cryptic and littered with doom and gloom, but if it had Kalt concerned, then that won my attention.

"I think kindness is also a motivation," I said softly. "For us all to get along, I mean."

He nodded. "Kindness is a crucial ingredient in the Winter Fae culture. Another reason you're well suited for this job."

We slowed as we approached a bunch of fae—who I assumed were Winter Fae or some kind of wintry being that resided in this realm—gathering what appeared to be long shards of ice along the shore.

"What are they doing?" I asked.

"Collecting belief crystals." He slowed to a stop and scooped a shard off the frozen ground, turning it over in his hands.

I frowned. "It looks like regular ice to me."

He grinned, those delicious dimples reappearing and causing my stomach to do backflips. "Give me your hand."

Heat rushed to my cheeks as I obeyed, lifting my hand, palm up, for him.

Kalt's warm fingers cupped underneath mine as he pressed the crystal against my skin. A small rush of adrenaline shot through me as my fingers closed over it. Something about this crystal had me excited. Giddy, even.

What's happening?

"Now, Artica. Do you believe in the North Pole?"

My hand tightened around the crystal. "Of course I do. I'm here, aren't I?"

His smile lit my soul on fire. "Turn around."

Spinning on my heel, my eyes widened and a gasp escaped me.

Shimmering on the top of an icy hill was a giant, colorful palace that definitely hadn't been there before. Domes in the shape of Human Realm Hershey kisses—a delicious treat that Queen Claire had introduced me to last year—crowned the spires, each of them striped in red and white. And there were several towers that twisted like piled-up frosted fae meringue pointing toward the cloudless sky, too.

"How…?"

Kalt plucked the belief crystal from my hand. "You've just powered up the crystal with your belief. Belief is valuable here, Artica. It powers the Winter Fae Source."

"Oh." I stared at the Winter Fae palace, taking in its sugary grandeur.

"You can close your mouth now."

My jaw snapped shut. "The North Pole has an invisibility shield?"

"It's all part of their concealment magic, not necessarily invisibility. If you didn't believe the Winter Fae Realm was here, then you wouldn't be able to interact with it or see it. Perhaps that defies the laws of human physics, but magic, especially of the Winter Fae variety, doesn't like to follow the rules. Did you expect anything less?"

"I guess not." Kalt began walking again, and I followed alongside him, wondering how he could tell the belief crystals from the regular ones. "What enemies do the Winter Fae have?" I found it peculiar that they needed to hide in such an inhospitable realm. I doubted that humans often came here.

"Not many," Kalt admitted. "Although, it's best to be prudent when it comes to humans. Their curiosity often ends in violence, and this isn't the only place in their world that the fae want to live."

I nodded, aware that the Fortune Fae and Midnight Fae often frequented this world.

Elemental Fae, less so.

Because we didn't particularly care for what the mortals did to their surrounding environment.

"Queen Claire wants the Winter Fae to help create similar shielding for other parts of the Human Realm," Kalt continued. "To successfully hide fae activities, I mean. I've actually been working on a deal with Prince Lark to expand the Winter Fae Source abilities to other regions. It's something I'm hoping he'll enact once he ascends."

"Really?" That sounded exciting. "Queen Claire will love that."

"I know." He flashed me a cocky grin that reminded me a bit of his cousin, Cyrus, the current Water Fae King.

Except Kalt wasn't nearly as intimidating as his cousin.

King Cyrus often visited Queen Claire. And, well, I usually hid or ran away when he arrived.

But Kalt had a friendliness to him that made him somewhat more approachable. Or he would be approachable, anyway, if I wasn't so in love with him.

However, this opportunity might be just what I needed to get him to notice me. Especially if I helped him achieve his desire to extend the abilities of the Winter Fae Source.

That would make it clear that I was something more than just an eager student.

Someone who could be trusted and respected.

Someone who was mate-worthy of a powerful emissary like Kalt...

"You're going to help me with admin work, making sure things run smoothly," Kalt added, his hasty tone suggesting I'd just turned all starry-eyed on him.

Yes, off to a fantastic start, Artica, I chided myself.

Then his words registered, making me frown. "Admin work?" I repeated, my excitement dampening as I shifted backward, trying to give him some space.

He grabbed my arm in response, yanking me forward

again, causing me to nearly lose my balance and topple over. His hand grabbed my hip, holding me upright as his gaze went to the ground beneath me.

I shook my head, needing to clear it, confused and flustered by finding myself in his arms.

Then I noticed the puffy snow around my ankles.

"What's... what's wrong?" I asked, unable to hide my bewilderment. *Mmm, coconut*, I thought, inhaling his sweet scent. *Yes, I would like a taste very much, please.*

Kalt waved a hand, and a patch of snow crumbled away, leaving a gaping hole drilled into the ice. "Abominable snowman trap," he said, a hint of amusement in his tone. "They're mostly harmless, but they love their pranks."

I blinked, my coconut daze lifting as I peered into the hole scant inches from my booted feet. "Where does it lead?"

"Likely to an ice cave filled with sticky maple syrup. Not even a shower will save your hair from that." His tone suggested great displeasure.

My eyebrow inched upward, curious as to how he knew all this.

"Not that I know from experience," he clarified, clearing his throat. "Anyway, you'll need to watch your step while you're here. The Winter Fae and the native North Pole species can be, well, unpredictable at best. While they often only want to have fun, they have powerful magic at their disposal that must be respected."

"Another reason for my necklace?" I guessed.

He dipped his chin. "It will absolutely come in handy eventually."

Which meant he knew about my clumsy habits. That was what he'd really meant by calling me a troublemaker.

Lance enjoyed teasing me for my ability to always land myself in trouble—usually literally.

"I'll watch my step," I told him, noticing that he hadn't released my hip yet. Actually, I was pretty much still snuggled up in his arms.

Visible air plumed in front of me as I released a breath.

I could get used to this.

A magnificent seal suddenly hauled itself up onto the shore, and Kalt released me as if I'd burned him. What would have normally been disappointment quickly disappeared as my eyes locked onto the chocolate coat of the stunning animal, my heart soaring at its twitching whiskers.

"Oh, hello!" I gushed. "Aren't you just the cutest thing?"

The seal cocked its head, watching me with dark brown, liquid eyes.

"Oh, yes, very handsome indeed," I cooed, wanting to approach it and bend down to stroke my fingers through its pretty fur.

"Artica..." Kalt warned.

I grinned at him, turning slightly to study his expression. "What? Do seals play pranks, too?" I teased out loud before facing the beautiful creature again.

Except it was no longer there.

Instead, a tall, toned, and *completely naked* male stood in its place, whipping back long, luxurious brown locks that dripped with icy water. "You hear that, Kalt? She thinks I'm cute," he murmured, irises twinkling, his words smooth as velvet with the sexist accent I had ever heard in my life.

Holy lickable Festivus... balls.

My voice caught in my throat as the walking sex-on-a-stick sauntered toward Kalt and me, his sultry eyes never once leaving me.

"Artica, this is Norden," Kalt said with exasperation as he pinched the bridge of his perfect nose. "And yes, this seal does play pranks. So keep your distance."

"Naughty ones, I might add," he amended with a panty-melting wink as I struggled to keep my eyes above his waistline. I didn't really care what kind of pranks he played, as long as he kept *talking*.

The male with ripped abs and skin faintly glittering with sea salt didn't stop his advance until he was up against me, so close our breath mingled. He smelled of the winter ocean mixed with notes of nutmeg.

I inhaled him, my gaze flickering between those eyes of melted chocolate.

"Have you brought a female candidate for our triad, Kalt?" he asked as he tilted his head, his voice lilting playfully. "Her affinity for ice is... *alluring*." He traced his lower lip with his tongue. "I can almost taste her compatibility. Color me intrigued."

Can't. Breathe.

How was I supposed to accomplish my work around here when *seals* could turn into sexy-as-sin men with voices that set my veins on fire?

Then his statements finally sank in.

Triad?

Winter Fae were known for their mate-circles of three males and one female.

Had Kalt joined a triad while working here?

And... and were they looking for a female to join them?

I nearly squealed. *I volunteer!*

"For the thousandth time, I'm not in your triad, you incessant selkie," Kalt snapped, melting all my hopes and dreams in a breath.

Well, icicles.

My fingers went nervously to my neck as I sighed.

But a selkie? I'd never met one of those. I wonder if all his people have that gorgeous accent? Oh, I wish I could hear him say my name. I bet it would sound so sexy on his tongue!

"Artica..." Norden immediately said, and I went rigid.

Snowflakes. Kalt had given me a *wish-granting* pendant, and I'd just used it to make a naked selkie say my name. *Cream puffs, this—*

"Artica," Norden repeated, enunciating every consonant so slowly that I couldn't help my shiver of unrepressed delight.

Because sigh.

I could listen to his voice repeating my name for the rest of my life.

Kalt frowned, his gaze dipping to my fingers on the pendant, and I dropped my hand to my side.

"I think Prince Lark would love to meet her," Norden continued, his words nearly a purr.

"P-Prince Lark?" I asked, twisting toward Kalt, who stood entirely too close behind me.

Being wedged between these two was going to be the source of all my fantasies tonight.

"Yes," Kalt said, setting a protective hand on my shoulder just as Norden licked his lips again, his eyes raking up and down my body.

"Hmm, and our prince is in need of a princess," Norden purred. "You would be a delectable candidate."

Kalt frowned. "Aren't you supposed to find multiple candidates for the Crystal Princess role?"

Norden shrugged, his gorgeous locks sliding off his shoulders with the graceful motion. "Our prince can be picky. I will only choose candidates who are compatible." He grinned at me. "And I know compatibility when I see it." He brought my fingers to his lips, grazing my skin with a delicate kiss. "If you would permit it, I could introduce you to the prince."

Heat bloomed on my cheeks, not just from his words but from his touch. I had no idea what a Crystal Princess was or why this sexy selkie thought I was a candidate, but I didn't want to refuse him.

I mean, yes, please. I'll happily do whatever you need, I wanted to say. But my throat and mouth failed to work. Probably because I'd forgotten how to breathe.

Details.

Norden chuckled. "Bashful little beauty, isn't she?"

Kalt didn't comment, his face expressionless. But a hint of ice encircled his eyes, giving his irises a silvery gleam.

Is he angry? I wondered.

"Well?" Norden prompted. "She's your candidate."

"She's not my candidate," Kalt replied through his teeth. "But I'm not going to deny a meeting with Prince Lark."

"Mmm." The selkie's eyes sparkled with delight. "I thought you might feel that way, Frosty."

Frosty? I nearly asked.

Then Norden brushed his warm, lusciously soft lips across the back of my knuckles again, distracting me. Despite the frigid air, he seemed to exude warmth and heat.

"I love your eyes," he said softly. "They remind me of ice crystals only found in the deep sea. And your hair..." He hovered his touch over a curl draped across my shoulder.

I didn't dare move. If this gorgeous being wanted to touch me, I wasn't going to stop him.

"May I?" he asked, surprising me with his tender request. Most Water Fae would just stroke my hair without a second thought. But that was because our kind typically showed affection through touch.

"Norden…" Kalt warned before I could speak.

"It's okay," I managed to say, my throat still tight and my lungs burning with the need to properly breathe. "Go ahead." And now I sounded hoarse.

Very sexy, Artica, I thought at myself. *You certainly know how to woo a man.*

Of course, his curiosity could be entirely innocent, for all I knew.

Minus the candidate commentary that I don't understand.

Norden brushed his fingers over the lock of hair, and a visible shiver swept through his body. I didn't dare look down to see if other parts of him were reacting to our nearness, but based on the low groan he just released, I realized he might have a bit of a, uh, *hair fetish.*

I spared a glance at Kalt, who rubbed a hand over his face.

Norden's mouth parted as he lifted his hand to inspect the strands. "This is like the rays of sunlight when looking up from beneath the waves."

Kalt groaned behind me. "Enough of your flattery, selkie."

"What? Afraid she'll warm your frozen heart, Frosty?" Norden taunted.

I made a mental note to ask Kalt later why Norden called him *Frosty*.

"Your smarm is nauseating," *Frosty* deadpanned.

But I didn't want him to ruin the moment or scare this charming male off, because I rather liked the worship in his gaze. And his accent, mmm, I wanted him to speak again.

"So, what exactly is a selkie?" I asked, voicing the first question that popped into my head. Norden was obviously a shifter of some kind, but much better mannered than the ones I'd met before, even if he harbored a weird hair fetish.

"A seal shifter," Kalt explained. "One who is compatible with North Pole magic, so he can do more than shift." He glowered at the selkie. "I've yet to see his magic be used for anything productive, but Prince Lark has a certain weak spot for his charm."

Norden flashed me a grin that made my knees weak.

His long hair had dried quickly, and I reached for a strand to see if it was as soft as it looked.

I mean, he'd touched my hair. It only seemed fair that I could touch his back, right?

I stepped forward, my hand hovering near his silky locks, like he'd done to mine. "May I?"

He blinked, glancing at Kalt, who had frozen at my words.

I'm beginning to understand the nickname, I thought, waiting for Norden's response.

He gave a small nod, his lips curling a little. "Anything you desire, *Artica*."

Oh, there were a lot of things I desired in this situation, but I'd stick with stroking my fingers through his mesmerizing strands.

His chocolate irises swirled temptingly as I threaded my fingers through his matching hair, the strands tracking all the way to the middle of his back.

"Wow," I breathed, lost to the soft texture of his beautiful mane. "You must use a lot of conditioner for it to be this *soft*." I was hypnotized by the texture, reveling in the way it ran through my fingers as I combed the long lengths.

Well, maybe we both had a hair fetish, I marveled.

Norden chuckled, pure delight gracing his handsome features.

I glanced back at Kalt. "Seriously. Have you touched his hair? It's like a cloud and a waterfall mingled to create heavenly silk."

Kalt gaped at me as if I'd grown two heads. His gaze dipped to the place where I curled my fingers through Norden's incredible locks.

"No…" Kalt said evenly. "He doesn't let *anyone* touch his hair."

"You *may* be allowed when you admit to being part of our triad," Norden murmured with a wink.

Kalt groaned. "Don't you have somewhere else to be?"

"Not really." Norden finally took a step from me, and the arctic air slammed into my face as a result. I quickly insulated myself again. "Lark told me to go for a swim while he dealt with coronation details. It sounded boring, so I obliged. But now I'm hungry."

His gaze locked onto mine, causing my heart to stutter as though I'd missed a step on a set of stairs.

"There are rules here, Norden," Kalt chided. "Flirting is fine. But no touching unless you're officially courting her. That includes her hair." His eyes narrowed. "She doesn't know your kind, selkie. You might as well have put your hand between her legs."

My jaw slackened at the harshness in Kalt's tone.

But his words only made the corners of Norden's lips quirk up, mirth swimming in his eyes. "Whatever you say, Frosty. Just remember, you approved her introductory *meeting* with Prince Lark. *As a candidate.*"

He turned around and dove back into the water, giving me a view of his perfectly sculpted ass before he vanished under the waves.

I blinked. "What… what was that?"

"Your first lesson in local politics," Kalt said, brushing his shirt as if to remove invisible dust particles. "I suggest you don't touch his hair again."

Was that a note of jealousy I sensed?

"So it's all work and no play, huh?"

Kalt fixed me with a stare that just made him one hundred percent hotter.

Or *icier*, as it were.

But no one did the frost glare like Kalt did.

And that just made my heart soar a little more for him. Because sigh.

"Trust me, the North Pole is going to be more fun than you can handle," he promised.

I took that as a personal challenge.

We'll see what this intern can handle, Prince Kalt.

I glanced at where Norden had disappeared through the icy surface. Not only was he an intriguing shifter, but he was also the mate of the Winter Fae Prince himself.

If a selkie was that hot, it made me wonder what his mate would be like.

And why doesn't Kalt want to join their triad?

That had to be a big deal, considering Prince Lark was the future King of the Winter Fae.

I almost asked, but Kalt was already trudging back through the snow behind me.

"This way, little intern," he called back to me. "You'll stoke Norden's already large enough ego if you stare after him too long."

And that's a bad thing? I nearly asked. Instead, I trailed after him and said, "He seemed nice to me."

Kalt snorted. "Of course he did. He's been assigned to sniff out all the eligible Crystal Princesses for Prince Lark." He glanced at me, his expression giving nothing away.

"And you're the first and only female I've seen him interested in thus far."

That made me shoot up an eyebrow. "Really?" I wasn't sure if that was a good thing or a bad thing. "Uh, what's a Crystal Princess?"

Kalt grinned. "Probably more than you bargained for when you took this internship."

"That doesn't answer my question."

"No," he admitted, his lips twisting. "The Crystal Princess eligibility is, well, it's complicated. But it has to do with the upcoming coronation and Prince Lark's triad. Sort of like a courtship."

I chewed on my bottom lip. "And this... this complicates things, right?" Since he clearly didn't want to be in the triad, and I came here to be his intern, not a Crystal Princess.

He shrugged. "Not exactly. I want to build strong relations between the Elemental Fae and the Winter Fae. Your agreement would show good faith between our races."

My brow furrowed. "So you want me to accept?" Meaning he was all right with me being courted by other males.

Because he's not interested in me at all, I realized, my heart prickling with ice.

It wasn't like I didn't know that already.

But this... this sort of proved his lack of interest entirely.

"You accepting would allow us more meetings with Prince Lark," he murmured. "Which could help further the agenda of establishing Winter Fae sources throughout the realm."

Right. Because that was his primary goal here.

Just as it should be mine, too.

"Would I be committing to anything?" I wondered out loud. "By agreeing to the courtship?"

His shoulders lifted and fell again. "Winter Fae mate-bonds work differently than ours, but the bonds still work both ways. They've been trying to push me into their triad for months now, but a permanent bond hasn't formed, so even if they have a thing for Water Fae, it's safe to say that you won't be committing to anything you don't want to."

So you're not willing to join their triad, but you're perfectly fine with me setting myself up as a candidate, I thought, frowning. *I see.*

Well.

Unlike him, I wouldn't mind a little romance.

And if Kalt didn't want me, why would I deny the sexy selkie who clearly had an interest?

Which, wait, hold on... "Norden called me your candidate." And he hadn't meant for the internship. "You said I was chosen as your intern because of my talents for ice and my ability to do well at the North Pole..." I trailed off, my mind processing the statements in a brand-new light. "You brought me here because you knew I would be a potential Crystal whatever."

Kalt's glassy eyes glimmered with mischief, clearly not aware of how wrong this was. "I can't say I'm opposed to Norden's interest in you, but there are many other tasks for you to perform as my intern." He waved toward the snowy path. "Starting with attending dinner with me."

My brow furrowed. *Like a date?*

No. Like work.

As a potential princess-crystal-whatever for His Royal Highness.

I narrowed my gaze, uncertain of how I felt about this development.

Part of me wanted to argue, to snap at Kalt and call him out on his high-handedness.

But a tendril of Norden's addictive nutmeg scent curled around me, calming me slightly.

Maybe I imagined it.

Maybe I didn't.

However, I instantly felt lighter. Giddier. Happier.

I was literally walking into the happiest place in the Human Realm.

Embrace it, I told myself, sighing. *Embrace it, and let the Winter Fae internship truly begin.*

LARK

S *leigh bells.*

Dismissing Norden had been a colossal mistake. Coronation preparations served as a cruel reminder of just how screwed I was, and only my selkie mate seemed to be able to distract me from the approaching deadline of *life*.

Without an established triad, the Winter Fae Source might not accept me. My own death didn't concern me. The fate of my people was what mattered.

And Norden.

Leaving him would... hurt.

He'd been my best friend for years, making him an obvious candidate for my triad and my bed. Our compatibility was unprecedented.

Just like my compatibility with a certain Water Fae Royal who continued to ignore my summons.

My jaw clenched.

Triads and mate-circles were all about *belief* and *love*, two vital components to Winter Fae kind. So if I couldn't complete this monumental task, then how could the Source trust me to be the king of magic fueled by belief?

My mood darkened as a cluster of cheery miniature elves native to the North Pole prattled on about the decorations, which would be pointless if the Source struck me dead the moment I accepted the crown.

And what then? My people were counting on me. There were no other suitable heirs to the throne, and the Winter Fae could be thrown into chaos. A fact my father loved to remind me of, yet he'd insisted on retiring anyway.

Hence the coronation planned for my thirty-second birthday on July twenty-fifth. A young ascension, as my father had been forty for his. But he said it was time.

Because he *believed* I was ready, therefore I must be.

Except I wasn't.

I hadn't even successfully formed my triad yet.

Fudge.

A particularly slim elf named Holly chattered happily away about ribbons, glitter, and candy canes as her recommendation for the central pieces. Clearly oblivious to my mood. Which made sense. Winter Fae Royals were never unhappy. We were meant to lead, to spread jovial energy, hope, and *love*.

There's that word again.

"Blue candy canes, not the rainbow ones," Holly clarified, marginally softening my mood. She sat in the middle of my suite, surrounded by confetti and other samples of coronation supplies, all of which suited my usual tastes.

The elves who worked for the royal family knew my preferences by heart, and they also knew how seriously I took my responsibility to the crown.

"Although, I'm not sure about gold or silver glitter

beverages, Your Highness," she continued, picking up a champagne glass.

I slowly lifted a glass of spiked hot chocolate to my lips —a gift from Norden before I'd dismissed him. He'd added a hint of peppermint to it, making my lips curl.

At least one of my mates believes in me, I thought, sighing.

"What do you think?" Holly pressed, referring to the glitter beverages.

"Hmm, gold," I said, rubbing my fingers together. A steady stream of golden glitter liquid filled the glass, prompting "oohs" and "aahs" from the elves.

"Excellent choice! This is why it will be a lovely coronation. You've thought of every detail," Holly gushed.

Yeah. Every detail except for the ones that mattered, like a mate-circle worthy of the Source.

"What about sprigs of mistletoe hung around the doorway?" she pondered. "We've grown fond of that human tradition."

I tilted my head. "A bit much, don't you think?"

"Yes, yes," she said, scratching away in her notepad.

"I think that's a delightful idea," a voice with a sinfully sexy accent said.

My muscles immediately tensed.

Norden. Right on cue.

He must have sensed my misery through our link.

"I don't need mistletoe to kiss you," I said, not moving as he walked up behind me and placed his hands on my shoulders. He pressed his thumbs against my back, rubbing the tense muscles with slow precision.

"Mmm, but I love the excuse to kiss you when you're not in the mood for it," he whispered against my ear.

Holly lifted her pen in the air. "Mistletoe around the throne, perhaps?"

I sighed. "So fae can line up and kiss me right after I'm crowned? I don't think so."

My ascension to the Winter Fae throne was not about to be overshadowed by a winter wonderland orgy.

Although, Norden would be perfectly happy with that.

"You're taking this coronation too seriously," Norden purred.

I most certainly wasn't. Aside from the very likely scenario that I would probably fail and die—a very good reason on its own to take my coronation seriously—was the fact that several species and kingdoms would be in attendance for this ceremony.

I had the Elemental Fae Queen to thank for that added pressure, and our little Interrealm Fae alliance.

"Holly, remind Norden who's on the guest list," I practically growled.

The small she-elf flipped to another page in her notepad. "The Winter Fae court and their mate-circles, of course. The Arctic selkies. Head elves. Representatives from each of the other fae realms, including but not limited to the Elemental Fae, the Midnight Fae, the Fortune Fae, various clans of Shifter Fae, perhaps even the Hell Fae, and…" She paused, her eyes roaming over the notes. "Your father, mother, and their triad."

"Ah," Norden said lightly, moving his hands from my shoulders to my neck, swiping a thumb along my jaw. "You want to impress your parents with your ascension."

"I want to *survive* my ascension and not be the reason that the North Pole implodes on itself," I corrected. "Everything has to go smoothly—and that means no public displays of affection to distract me."

Norden lifted his hands from me and came around to the front of my chair, smirking. "Not even small, quick kisses?"

"You don't have that kind of control." Once Norden set his dick on something, he didn't stop until he was satisfied—and it took quite a lot of effort to satisfy a selkie.

Perhaps, right now, his brand of foreplay was the distraction I needed to calm my agitation, but on the day of my ascension, I would have to be entirely focused—something Norden needed to understand.

"Don't be such a frozen flounder." Norden moved toward the giant ice jacuzzi I kept in the corner of the suite nestled between two large windows that faced the sea. Since he often preferred to shift and wander about naked, I indulged in a view of his tight ass before he lowered himself into the water that I kept at his preferred, optimal temperature.

Which was sub-freezing.

He sighed and sank into the water that drifted with ice, admiring the new additions to my suite. I'd been personally working on the mural of an underwater ocean scene, one that Norden had described to me in detail.

Since I couldn't join him on his underwater adventures, I would bring his world here.

I was quite proud of the painting. Norden's lips ticked up into a grin when he spotted the new shipwreck I'd added with seals dancing within its shadows. The humans often hit icebergs and lost their lives attempting to learn more about this unforgiving landscape. I couldn't blame them, not when my world held sensual mysteries like the selkie who'd been the first to join my triad.

He glanced at me, his molten chocolate eyes seeing straight through to my soul.

Reminding me again that I'd at least won over one heart who truly believed in me.

Just need two more...

"I never mentioned an octopus," Norden said, pointing at the small addition to the corner.

"It's *my* mural," I quipped while Holly fussed with her notebook, turning the page and cursing when confetti spilled everywhere.

Norden, no doubt, thought that I'd tailored my suite to *him*, but I'd had a love of water and the sea for as long as I could remember.

It was probably what had originally attracted me to him.

My fellow Winter Fae only reminded me of the frigid responsibilities and rules that sucked all the fun out of the royal magic. High elves and worker elves catered more toward the fun-loving joy that gave the Winter Fae magic its power but weren't typically compatible with the Winter Fae when it came to mates.

Norden, though. He was a selkie, and responsibility was a foreign concept to him. He lived in the *here*, the *now*, and moved with the current instead of against it.

I loved that about him. A creature of the sea who could take me away from the pressure of the throne. It was why I'd claimed him the moment we'd both reached the appropriate age.

I wouldn't play the game of my ancestors. I didn't need to court my triad or my future queen.

I simply *knew*.

Just like I *knew* Kalt, the Elemental Fae Emissary, was also meant to be mine.

I just had to win him over, a task that was proving far more difficult than Norden.

My love for water was likely why Kalt appealed to me. The Water Fae Royal would also complement our triad with his political prowess, and he would help balance Norden's complete lack of regard for responsibility.

When I took the crown, the distraction my selkie could offer would have its place, but I would need to run a kingdom, too.

Unfortunately, Kalt wasn't willing to accept his place quite yet.

Something my father assured me was typical.

Very few Winter Fae were actually born. And those who were, were always male.

Like me.

All the other Winter Fae were more or less turned through their mating circles, thus allowing a great influx of power in our realm.

My mother was actually a Midnight Fae. My father was a true Winter Fae, hence my lineage. And the other two members of his triad were Shifter Fae.

My Midnight Fae mother had not wanted to mate my dad, stating the sun burned her eyes and was unbearable here during the summer months. Such as right now when the sun shone literally all day and night.

But he'd eventually won over her heart and her belief in his magic, and they were happily bonded in their circle today.

I wanted that. My triad. My female. My circle.

If only Kalt would comply.

My jaw ticked at his insolence. His body responded to mine. I'd felt his compatibility the moment he'd entered my domain.

I'd even felt him when he'd returned from his realm today, and the connection had felt stronger than ever, as if amplified twofold.

Mine.

Norden glimmered with particularly ripe sexual energy, so I suspected he'd run into the Elemental Fae Emissary, too. Because he sensed the connection as well.

Holly cleared her throat, then added a high-pitched "ahem." I dipped my head to encourage her to continue.

"Did we decide no on the plum pudding?"

"Oh, come on, Lark," Norden said from the jacuzzi. "No kissing *or* plum pudding?"

"You don't even like plum pudding."

"I like the way it sounds." He grinned. "I could lick it off of you after the coronation."

Fine. If I survived, we could celebrate however he liked.

I sighed, reaching for my hot chocolate again. "Yes to the plum pudding," I said dismissively. "Are we almost finished?"

Holly checked over her notes. "I believe we have everything we need to get started."

"Good." I stood, stripping off my shirt. All this coronation talk was striking a chord with my nerves, and with Norden's return from his swim, I wanted a distraction.

"You're dismissed, unless you want to see something more festive than you bargained for."

Some of the elves tittered, while others groaned. "Here we go again," one mumbled.

"Hush!" Holly said, waving a frantic hand to silence the others. "Enjoy your... festivities, sir."

I smirked as she led her entourage out the door, shutting it behind them.

Water splashed as Norden stood from the jacuzzi. "One day, they *will* want to see just how festive we can be," he teased.

"Done with the jacuzzi already?"

"For now." He stepped out of it and grabbed a fluffy white towel, wrapping it around his waist. It hugged seductively around his hips but didn't hide his erection.

He lazily walked up to me, and I caught how dark his eyes were. That meant only one thing.

Norden was in the mood for a rough fuck. Something had awakened his primal instincts, and I didn't think it was me.

Hmm... "What has you so worked up?" I asked.

"A certain Water Fae." His irises glittered like chocolate diamonds. "Kalt has returned with his new intern."

My interest was piqued. I'd helped Kalt bespell some random ice crystals with Winter Fae magic in hopes of drawing out a potential mate from the Elemental Fae Kingdom.

If the Water Fae Royal didn't want to be mine, maybe someone else did. Which would explain my connection to him because perhaps he knew my true mate.

There'd been several key candidates, but only two he'd been seriously considering.

Both of them had been female.

However, my spell would have attracted either a male or a female, leaving me in open suspense as to whom he'd actually brought into my realm.

"Male or female?" I wondered out loud, needing to know.

"Female."

Interesting. Typically, a Winter Fae couldn't court a female until his triad was complete, but that didn't make it impossible.

That said, if Norden had met her and she'd satisfied his selkie's tastes, it would've worked him up.

Although, anything that moved would likely satisfy him.

"And she's pretty, I assume?" I hedged.

"'Pretty' is an insult," Norden said, kneeling in front of me. "She's... perfection." He began undoing my pants.

Even if he was just trying to placate me, I wasn't going to complain. "We must keep her."

"Keep her?" I asked, raising a brow. "I tasked you to find Crystal Princess candidates for the coronation. *Plural*." Which meant he couldn't keep the first one he met.

Kalt's orbs weren't the only items I'd bespelled with Winter Fae magic over the last few weeks.

I'd sent trinkets all over the kingdoms, trying to draw out compatible mates.

And the purpose for working with Kalt's magic had been to see if there was a candidate somehow linked through him to me.

Norden grinned, the sensual delight in his warm eyes suggesting I had underestimated his desire to find us a queen. Not candidates. But a single female.

"You know how difficult it is to court a female without a complete triad, Norden." I preferred to take this step by step, even if time was of the essence. At this rate, I couldn't afford a mistake.

And a triad was far more successful with a solid foundation in place *before* choosing a female.

It was important that all the males agreed on a chosen mate. I would never force a member on my triad who didn't belong.

Something that Kalt often pointed out, of course. Except I knew he belonged, even if he wasn't ready to admit it yet.

My instincts couldn't be wrong here.

He belonged with me.

"She just might convince Kalt to finally join us," Norden said, not exactly reading my mind but knowing me well enough to guess at my thoughts. His perfect hair slid over his shoulder as he canted his head while staring up at me. "Do you want to know how I know?"

The silky quality of his voice pulled at my groin, a fact he more than noticed as he slid my pants from my hips. "How do you know?" I asked, my voice gruffer than the last time I spoke.

"Because I made him jealous," Norden murmured, tilting his head the other way.

I frowned at the purposeful movement, then noticed a slight unevenness to his hair. Just a single tendril of silky brown strands that didn't quite line up with the others. Something I knew *never* happened. The man spent hours brushing his hair, constantly grooming and perfecting every layer.

He couldn't stand having a single strand out of place, hence why he never let me touch his hair.

But... that strand... that strand was telling.

"Did you...? Did you let her *touch your hair?*" I asked, unable to hide the shock in my voice.

He just grinned and curled his fingers around my shaft, giving it a harsh tug.

Glittering fae, I breathed, finally realizing what had him so worked up.

Not only had he met a compatible female, but he'd also let her *touch his hair.*

"Norden." His name left my lips on a groan as he took my cock into his mouth, his tongue swirling over the tip.

Fuck. He let a female touch his hair. And now... Frozen fae... I couldn't think when he did that with his mouth, and he damn well knew it.

He took me to the hilt, proving his lack of a gag reflex before gently pulling back, his dark eyes glimmering with a mixture of pride and expectation.

He'd clearly made his choice.

Just like I'd done with him and Kalt.

An immediate decision driven by instinct, and perhaps a hint of *need*.

"I take it you requested a meeting?"

He hummed his affirmation, the vibration setting my insides on fire.

"And Kalt approved?"

Norden confirmed with another deep-throating suck that went straight to my balls.

"Fuck, Norden," I growled, his skilled mouth making me so damn hard that I nearly came without much provocation.

But he pulled back from my groin, his irises swimming with dark intent. "As you wish, my prince. Fuck me into oblivion. Then we'll go find our mates."

I wrapped my palm around the back of his neck, careful not to mess up his hair, and pulled him to his feet. We stood evenly together, our dicks touching as I tugged him flush against me. "Have I told you lately that I love you?"

"Not this afternoon, no," he replied, his own palm finding the back of my neck. "But feel free to whisper it against my throat while you drill into me."

This male.

This devious fucking male.

"On the bed, selkie," I demanded.

"Of course, my prince," he murmured, his eyes grinning. "Make it rough. I'm in the mood to *bark*."

ARTICA

I couldn't stop thinking about Norden. The frosty scenery didn't help matters. I kept expecting him to appear or slide down a snowbank to play at my feet.

A completely presumptuous expectation.

But he was so unique and beautiful and *soft*.

Oh, and naked.

Very, very, very *naked*.

Mmm, I just wanted to curl my fingers through his hair while he kissed me. I bet he was the *best* kisser.

Heat crept up my neck. *Stop thinking about the sexy selkie.*

Yeah, because chiding myself *always* worked.

My lips twisted to the side. *Maybe he enchanted me? Like literally? A prank, perhaps?*

"Are selkies always so, uh, sensual?" I asked Kalt, hoping to find out more about their natural gifts and penchant for mischief. This could all just be an elaborate ruse.

Or related to my *candidacy*.

My mood plummeted with the thought.

Because Kalt had brought me here to be a candidate for another man's triad. There really was no louder way to say, *I'm so not into you.*

"Yeah," Kalt replied, not to my thought. Although, it sort of felt that way with the timing, but he couldn't read my mind, so it was his response to my question about selkies and their sensuality. "When they're courting a potential mate, anyway," he added as he led me around the wall of the palace.

Courting. I liked the sound of that. Even if it hurt a little that Kalt had set me up for it.

Although, Norden clearly didn't mind the setup.

So why should I?

I should embrace it.

Enjoy the moment. Live in this happy realm and indulge in whatever could happen.

Maybe it would make Kalt jealous.

Ha. A laughable notion. *But one worth considering*, I decided, recalling how he'd reacted to the selkie touching my hair. *Hmm...*

My musings were cut off as we entered the gorgeous courtyard. Pine trees waved on the breeze, covered in icy beads and frozen icicles. Giant snow globes glittered with golden statues beyond it, framed by a never-ending snowfall drift throughout the grounds.

Oh, and there were *actual* real live gingerbread men sweeping the doorsteps to their small gingerbread houses.

"Wow," I breathed. "This place is stunning."

"It is," Kalt agreed, taking a moment to soak it all in. "I won't be staying long after the coronation, so I'll try to enjoy it while I can."

I raised an eyebrow. "You're leaving?"

He nodded. "Yeah. I think so."

"But Norden's courting you, too, isn't he?" I hadn't

asked about it earlier, but I felt a little bolder now that I'd been labeled a candidate. What about Kalt? Shouldn't he also be agreeing to meetings? "I mean, the Winter Fae Prince wants you to complete their triad, right? Wouldn't that help Interrealm Fae relations?"

He frowned and I winced.

"Sorry, that was… I didn't mean to overstep." Although, he'd technically overstepped by setting up this courtship thing. So why did I have to go through it alone? Why didn't he join, too?

Or better yet, why doesn't he just join the triad and make me the middle of a Kalt and sexy selkie sandwich?

Because, I mean, yes, please.

He cleared his throat. "No. Well, yes, you're right. It would help ally the Elemental Fae and the Winter Fae if I accepted their proposal." He palmed the back of his neck, his gaze on one of the gingerbread men sweeping a porch. "But it's different for the male triad. There's no true courtship. If I agreed, it would be a permanent bond. And there are no other candidates Prince Lark is considering for the male role."

"That's sort of a compliment, then, isn't it?"

"Yes, but it's an unwanted one," he replied.

I frowned. "Do Winter Fae bonds not work the same as ours?" Because Elemental Fae bonds required compliance from both parties to engage in each of the four levels. The first two weren't even permanent, allowing the bond to fade.

Very unlike Midnight Fae bonds that were dictated through male biting and unbreakable after the first bite.

Also unlike Fortune Fae bonds that were founded on dubious consent. Or non-consent, really.

I couldn't see Winter Fae bonds working like either of those. The fae here were too chipper for forced bonds.

Kalt shook his head, sending his long white hair cascading over his broad shoulders. "Winter Fae bonds exist on belief. Meaning I would need to believe myself worthy of Prince Lark's triad. And I would also have to choose to believe in him more than my Water Fae heritage may allow."

"To switch Sources," I translated.

"More or less," he replied, his lips flattening. "I would still retain my affinity for water, but I would be a Winter Fae instead of a Water Fae Royal."

"And you don't want to give up your royalty status."

"Well, I would really only be trading one for the other. Prince Lark's triad would be considered royalty." His brow furrowed. "But I'm not interested in becoming a Winter Fae."

"Hmm," I hummed, not exactly believing him. He wasn't telling me something. However, I couldn't exactly push. "So the Winter Fae Source is powered by belief, which trickles into the mating bonds."

"Yes," Kalt confirmed. "Which means that if I failed to believe in any way, including failing to believe in myself, the Source could reject Prince Lark at his coronation, and the fallout would inevitably ignite a war between our kingdoms."

I winced.

Right, that would be bad.

"Yet you set me up to be a candidate," I pointed out.

Kalt glanced at me, his gaze lowering to the pendant resting near my breastbone before looking away. "It's not as risky for them to court you. The belief only needs to be on the triad's side, and you can choose to stay or to walk away. I would not be afforded the same choice."

My lips parted, his statement registering deep inside me.

I hadn't considered the idea that I could... *stay.* I mean, yeah, I'd been intrigued by the idea of being courted, but I hadn't truly pondered the notion of it becoming a reality.

Just fantasized a bit about the selkie and Kalt turning me into an Artica sandwich.

Totally innocent compared to accepting the reality of a mating bond with three males and becoming a Winter Fae.

Which was exactly why Kalt had refused the triad—he would have to accept that reality.

Me accepting the courting was as simple as that—agreeing to allow a few males to try to seduce me.

Very different concepts and responsibilities.

"Once a selkie sets their eyes on someone, they're relentless," Kalt continued, leading me onto a path made of gumdrops. "They can also become aggressive. So be careful."

"I can take care of myself."

"I'm sure you can, but that pretty face is going to make you a target around here."

My soul sang at his words.

He thinks I'm pretty.

I decided to milk it.

"Just pretty, huh?"

We reached a wrought-iron gate shaped like candy canes, and he paused, turning to consider me. One of his hands folded around mine. "Beautiful," he said softly.

And just like that, I forgave him for the whole setup thing.

Yeah, I was easy.

But the love of my life had just called me *beautiful.*

Sighhh.

It would be frowned upon to kiss my boss on the first day of the job, right? my inner fae deviant whispered.

Right, the practical side replied.

Except the way the snowflakes fell on his hair and lashes, how angelic he looked here in the Arctic… *Double sigh.*

He released my hand and opened the gate, ushering me inside to a small courtyard with snow and ice sculptures. Past that was an entry point to the palace.

"You must be hungry," Kalt said, walking forward to open the door for me. "I'll take you to the cafeteria where we'll have dinner. We'll save the grand tour for tomorrow."

"Okay," I agreed, still exhausted from not sleeping last night. But being here beneath the bright sunshine and surrounded by snow was certainly one way to keep me aware and awake.

Of course, Kalt's presence helped, too.

Because now I didn't have to dream about him. I could just glance over to see him. All that Water Fae Royal glory. Sculpted cheekbones. Chiseled jaw. Arched white eyebrow.

Stop staring, I told myself. But I found myself saying, "You're handsome, too, by the way," instead.

I clearly lacked all self-control and reason around this fae.

His dimples flashed, his icy gaze twinkling. "Let's focus on food."

Not exactly the reply I wanted, but all right. I could sate the hunger in my stomach since I'd not eaten all day. Then maybe he'd let me lick him for dessert.

He wanted me to be *courted*, not necessarily *chosen*.

That meant I still had a chance. Maybe. Probably not. But I was hanging on to the miracle! Besides, this place was all about believing, right?

He escorted me down a long hall and then through a set of large double doors.

Where I stopped in my tracks.

ARTICA

C*afeteria* was much too boring a word for the large room in front of me.

It was like I'd been dumped into a Human Realm Christmas movie.

A network of string lights hung from the ceiling with frozen orbs floating among the twinkling strands, amplifying the overall lighting of the grand hall. Buffets stretched along the back walls, the tables stuffed full of items. And a bar took up the space to my left—the floors, benches, and tables seemingly carved out of ice—with most of its occupants being small elves.

On my opposite side, there appeared to be some sort of festive activity going on. *Ride-a-Reindeer.* The goal seemed to be a steering lesson of some kind, but the animal looked more content to just buck the elves off his back instead. Maybe it was more of a training exercise than a game?

But the table nearby was definitely for fun. Cookies and various frosting colors lined the top while several of the elves all competed in some sort of decorating contest.

Then ate the results for fun.

"*Fae*," I breathed. "This is where you *eat*?"

"Yeah, uh, I know it's a bit much by our standards," Kalt said as he ran his fingers through his hair. "But it's pretty normal for this realm."

"It's incredible," I gushed, stepping farther inside to take it all in. My stomach rumbled as the alluring aroma of cinnamon, oranges, and warm spices hit my nose.

I did what any sane fae would do—I went straight for the buffet.

And frowned at what I found.

Cakes, pies, puddings, cookies, tarts, sweet breads, candy canes, chocolate, pastries, and more treats lined the table, but nowhere was there any savory food.

Like dragon steaks. Or mouseberries. Or shroom sandwiches. Or salad patties.

Nothing that I would actually consider a meal.

"Um, did we miss dinner?" I asked as Kalt reached my side. "These are all desserts."

"No, we didn't miss anything. While you're at the North Pole, this is what you'll find for every meal— breakfast, lunch, and dinner. The Winter Fae love their sweets." He grabbed a wrapper from the section labeled *coconut taffy*. "Your jaw is hanging open again."

I closed it, uncertain of when it'd hung open the first time. But it had probably done so several times today, starting with when I'd found him sitting on Professor Elway's desk. "But there's nothing hearty and warm? Not even soup?"

I could really go for a big bowl of orc stew right now. Mixed with codberries and violet greens. *Mmm.*

Not piles of sugar and confections.

Kalt reached past me and scooped up a mug of cider,

handing it to me. "This is probably the warmest, heartiest thing you'll find here."

"I don't know if I can live off dessert."

"There's a restaurant near the veil in Greenland that serves international cuisine," he murmured. "When you're really homesick, we can go there for a treat. But it's important to try to acclimate as much as possible while we're here, which means eating in the common areas with the beings of this world."

I considered that for a moment, my chin dipping in a weak nod.

His lips twisted into a wry grin. "Plus, there's a little bit of Winter Fae magic in every dish, which will restore your energy. It makes the sugar pretty much secondary to the infusion of magic." He nodded toward the buffet. "Go ahead. Try it. You'll see what I mean."

Inhaling the spicy apple scent, I carefully lifted the hot beverage to my lips.

Delicious warmth ran through my entire body, spilling down to my toes. "Mmm," I hummed, taking another sip. "Okay, maybe this won't be so bad."

I took my time browsing the offerings at the table, selecting a fruit tart and a braided sweet bread before sitting at one of the many tables scattered around the "cafeteria."

Kalt sat across from me with his own plate piled high with cookies and more taffy. I raised my brows and he shrugged. "The coconut taffy is my favorite, and the cookies have pumpkin in them. Have to squeeze in some vegetables where I can, and the pumpkin ones also seem to offset the taffy's effects."

"Effects?" I repeated, curious.

He shrugged. "Winter Fae magic can be infectious. While the food is nourishing, there can be some side effects involved. It's better to just accept it." When I stared at him, he grinned. "As long as I'm not risking war between realms, I *am* capable of having a little fun, Artica."

I knew that.

I'd seen him have fun at the Academy.

But it was nice to know the male I'd observed still resided beneath the formal emissary exterior.

Smiling, I made a show of biting into my fruit tart. *Oh, flaky-butter perfection, this is good*, I thought, moaning as I sensed the surge of magic fluttering through my veins.

Yeah, fun sounded like a great idea.

Kalt passed me a blue-striped candy cane. "The ones that aren't red are enchanted. Why don't you see what this one does?"

I stared at it distrustfully. "Pass."

"Come on." He waggled his brows at me. "One makes you fly for about ten seconds."

I nibbled my lower lip, considering.

Flying certainly appealed to me a bit.

"All right." I broke off a piece of the candy cane and placed it on my tongue.

My eyes widened. I'd expected a blue raspberry flavor but instead experienced a tropical mix of pineapple and coconut. I sucked on the candy as Kalt watched me expectantly.

"Well?" he prompted.

I shrugged. "Must be a faulty stiiiiick..."

But on the word *stick*, my voice pitched an octave higher and I held the vowel out much longer than necessary, almost like I was...

Singing it.

"Oh, no," I said, and it came out as a warbled tune. I clapped both hands over my mouth.

Kalt burst into laughter. "A singing enchantment!"

Snowflakes. No, no, no.

If Kalt heard me sing, I'd *never* win him over. He'd probably even tell Norden I was too defective to be a candidate, then send me back to the Academy.

But I couldn't help it, and *Kalt* was the one who'd made me eat it. So, really, it was his fault my fantasies would never come true now.

Maybe I should punish him by singing.

He obviously deserved it.

"Tell me about your day, Artica," Kalt murmured, unable to fight his grin.

I frantically shook my head.

He leaned over his plate of food, mirth sparkling in his crystal-blue eyes. "One thing you'll learn quickly around here is that holiday cheer is king. You can't fight it. Might as well embrace it."

Sure, whatever *that* meant.

"I haaaate si-nging," I ironically sang.

"Better learn to like it," Kalt said, enjoying this entirely too much.

"No, you don't understand. I was teased foooor it. It's traaaaaumatic." Whatever I was singing, it was most definitely in a minor key and didn't sound too terrible, despite my memories of the last time I'd tried to sing.

Of course, that had been many years ago when I'd been a faeling with my underdeveloped pitch, so perhaps my tune had improved since then.

"You have a beautiful voice, Artica. Don't hide it."

I looked past him to the ice bar over his shoulder. Several elves stared at me, eyes bright, grins wide.

"Sing!" one cried out in a squeaky voice.

That started a chant.

"Sing, sing, sing, sing!"

"Oh my Fae, *okay*," I sang, my voice jumping to a much happier tune.

A cheer went up, and Kalt leapt to his feet.

"What are you doooooing?" My voice held an impressive vibrato as he pulled me from my seat and swung me around into his arms.

"Dancing," he explained.

Whatever had been in that taffy had loosened Kalt up, but he embraced it, just as he'd told me to do.

We were in the North Pole now, a place of joy, laughter, and endless desserts.

The elves laughed and joined us on the cafeteria floor, and a small elf band started up a jazzy number.

Oh, fluff. I was now starring in a Christmas-themed musical. *Not* what I expected to do on my first day.

"I'll ask again—tell me about your day," Kalt demanded, twirling me.

When I returned to his arms, I opened my mouth, and—

"I almost didn't go to class
Was gonna sit around on my ass
Because of a bet
This is what I get
The most magical internship—"

"O-of the year," I stuttered out in what was supposed to be my soaring final note. I cleared my throat. "Well, frost. Enchantment's worn off."

Kalt nodded at the dancing elves, the happy music floating in the air. "They don't care. This is what the North Pole is all about, Artica. Welcome to your first taste of holiday cheer."

I became overwhelmingly aware of how I settled so perfectly in his arms.

Swallowing, I tilted my head up to look into his eyes.

"Lance might have dared me to apply, but only because he knew I wanted this internship. However, I'll admit, this is nothing like I expected it to be."

"Is that a good thing or a bad thing?"

My lips quirked. "I'm still deciding."

He shook his head. "You're as bad a tease as Norden," he accused, chuckling when my cheeks heated in response to hearing the selkie's name. "Want a drink? I promise it won't make you sing again."

I nodded eagerly and he led me to the bar, where the elves were shooting drinks into mugs to the beat of the music, singing along to a tune I didn't recognize. Could have been a song from the Human Realm or something from the North Pole culture.

"Please tell me they have regular alcohol here," I begged as we settled on a pair of stools at an ice table near the bar. The effects of the desserts were starting to wear off, leaving me with a mixture of embarrassment and sobriety that only alcohol could remedy.

"You're in luck. Although, I will fully judge you if you don't stay on theme and order a spiked cider or eggnog."

I stuck my tongue out at him, then quickly retracted the movement, realizing how childish it made me appear. "Oh, that was…" I cleared my throat. "Yeah, not sure where that came from."

Kalt pinched my chin, forcing me to look at him. I sucked in a quick inhale. "It's the holiday spirit, Artica. It's impacting you, just like it does everyone here. I can normally keep my head, but it's difficult. There's no reason to apologize for Winter Fae magic winning us over."

A giggle bubbled up in my chest, but I held it down.

Kalt's hand cupped my jaw for a moment as his gaze dropped to my lips, then returned to my eyes. "Part of being an emissary is blending in. As my intern, you have my permission to experience the holiday cheer any way you want."

Even if it means kissing you?

Because I *really* wanted to kiss him.

"Within reason," he added as if reading my mind. He dropped his hand from my face.

I nodded, trying to recover from the heat blazing through my body. "Of course." I stuck my tongue out at him again, this time unapologetically. "Now, where's my alcohol?"

Kalt ordered me an eggnog first, followed by a "sugarplum fairy" martini with cranberry juice and vodka. Meanwhile, he enjoyed two rounds of coconut juice with clumps of taffy and rum.

I studied him over the lip of my martini glass. "You really like your coconut taffy, don't you?"

He didn't answer, just took a long, measured swallow.

I had no business being so turned on by a man drinking his coconut taffy rum.

We sat in content silence for a few moments as the elves sang and danced in the background, many on the tops of tables.

"About the triad thing..." I began, still stuck on something about the situation. "If the only issue is your, um, belief, couldn't we remedy that?" If I managed to convince Kalt to establish a permanent alliance between the Winter Fae and our kind in the form of a mate-bond, it could do some real good for our kingdom.

And if I wound up between a selkie and the fae of my dreams by chance, I wasn't going to complain. I hadn't met Prince Lark yet, but if he was anything like Norden or Kalt, I was sold.

And if it didn't work out, I could still walk away.

However, based on Kalt's expression, I could tell that

he intended to walk away from it all. Yet the hint of hesitation in his icy gaze suggested that it was the last thing he wanted to do.

Trying to keep this as professional as possible, I maintained a stern expression as Kalt glared at me. "I mean, I may be a candidate," I went on. "But that doesn't mean anything at all. I'm just one of many. While you have no competition, right?"

His jaw ticked.

"It's one thing if you don't like them," I continued, aware that I was pressing a button that would probably destroy all the joy we'd discovered today. But it was a fair discussion to have, considering he'd brought me here and *approved* of me qualifying as a mate candidate.

So we would discuss his own candidacy, too.

Quid pro quo, as it were.

"But if you do like them," I went on, "it would be a positive alliance between our realms."

A Water Fae Royal mating a Winter Fae Prince? That sort of bond would absolutely bolster the Interrealm Fae dealings between Queen Claire and the Winter Fae.

So much so that I would almost be able to accept Kalt ending up in a mate-circle that didn't include me. It would break me into a million pieces, but if that was the price for securing an alliance between our faedoms, I'd accept it.

"I already explained the risk, Artica," Kalt said, setting his drink to the side. "Belief isn't something that can be manufactured. It's unpredictable and unreliable. I'm not saying that I *don't* believe in myself, but the possibility is there. And I would never do anything to destroy the work we've accomplished so far with the Interrealm Fae efforts."

I waved a hand dismissively. "Yes, I get that, but you're thinking too hard about it. Maybe it's not about the belief in *yourself* but about how much the other members of the triad believe in you." Norden had certainly appeared confident in the connection, which left the Winter Fae Royal. I tilted my head. "What's he like? The prince?"

Kalt frowned. "He's... he's a broody asshole," Kalt finally said. "But he takes his responsibilities just as seriously as I do. Cyrus adores him. And, I'll admit, we've grown close over the last few months. We're similar in a lot of ways, to the point where I could definitely see him becoming a best friend over time."

I was startled by his admission. "If you're already that close, or have the ability to be that close, then what's so wrong with joining his triad? Is the risk really that bad?"

"Very inquisitive, aren't we?"

I lifted a shoulder. "You brought me here to be a candidate. I'm allowed to ask questions."

"I didn't..." He trailed off, sighing. "I knew there was the potential for you to be a candidate because of the Winter Fae magic involved with the selection process. But I chose your application because it was good, Artica. Not because I wanted to add you to some sort of princess contest. Well, not entirely for that, anyway. But maybe a little bit."

He winced, the guilt written into his features.

Because yeah, he absolutely brought me here to be a candidate.

Which was fine. I had no problem being courted by a sexy selkie and a prince. That was, like, a dream, right?

"It's okay. I'm over that part." I fluttered my fingers, demonstrating my dismissal of that previous annoyance. "But I want to understand why *you* won't join his triad. Because, on the off chance that I'm seriously considered as more than a candidate, I need to know what I'm getting myself into."

There. That was well stated. And beautifully mature, too.

He studied me for a long moment. "Mating is permanent."

"Yes, I'm aware."

"I'm not ready for a permanent situation."

My eyebrows rose. "Well, you have no problem committing to your job."

"That's entirely different." He folded his arms on the ice table, the chatter from the bar behind me seeming to dim into the background at having him so near. "I'm not ready to mate yet."

My heart squeezed in my chest, the words a pang I didn't want to experience.

"Not that it's any of your business," he added.

"You technically messed with my mating ability by bringing me here when you knew I'd likely be a candidate," I pointed out. "Something I could argue is none of *your* business, either. Yet here we are." I mimicked his position. "All to align fae affairs, right? To bolster our relationship with the Winter Fae?"

His gaze narrowed to icy points. "You make it sound like I'm using you."

"You are to an extent," I told him. "But I'm okay with it." I meant it, too. I would do whatever it took to help secure this alliance for Queen Claire. And if I ended up in a sexy selkie's bed while playing politics, I would not complain.

Because clearly Kalt had no interest in *anything* regarding a relationship with me or otherwise.

"Look, I'm not a risk-taker, regardless of how small the risk might be, and I'm not suitable for royal duties, no matter how much my cousin or Prince Lark tries to convince me otherwise. There's a time and a place for everything, and now is not my time."

He went silent as if he'd said too much.

I realized now that Kalt had made a point to avoid the Water Kingdom. While he wouldn't ever be king, there were plenty of royal duties he could have undertaken as a Water Fae Prince. Instead, he'd jumped at the chance to establish Interrealm Fae relations when Queen Claire had founded the initial efforts.

"I want to make a real difference, Artica," he went on, his words as cold as ice. "I can't do that if I'm tied down to a mate-circle or if I make decisions with my emotions rather than with my mind. Too much has been happening. The gates to the Hell Fae Realm have been reopened for the first time in… a very long time."

Yes, I'd heard about that. The Hell Fae King was planning something big, but no one knew what yet. And he wasn't sharing details.

"And the Sources have been misbehaving," Kalt went on. "The prophecies coming from the Fortune Fae are all filled with a common message that something is coming, something that'll impact *all* the realms, and the fae need to be ready for it. We all need to be on the same side when it hits, whatever *it* is."

Okay, that part, I hadn't heard about yet.

"I'm willing to sacrifice a lot for the fae, but I can't do that if I'm in a mate-circle. Because then it wouldn't just be myself I'm sacrificing, Artica. It would be those I cared about as well."

Ah, and there's the real reason he won't commit, I marveled, awed by his dedication to his cause.

He didn't just want to help Queen Claire in her efforts. He wanted to lead the charge.

And he couldn't do that if other lives were tied to his.

He retrieved his drink and downed the rest of it. "You're souring the festive mood. You should eat another candy cane."

I clicked my tongue. "How about *you* eat the candy cane this time?" I asked, allowing the distraction. Given everything he'd just divulged, he'd earned it. And I had a lot to think about now.

His lips curled, but his dimples didn't show. "Fine. Go grab one for me."

I narrowed my eyes. "You know, I think I will."

Finishing off my martini, I stood from the bar and sauntered off toward the buffet table, enjoying the slight buzz from my drink. I found jars of the multicolored candy and hesitated, my hand hovering. Green or yellow? Maybe orange? I already knew what the blue ones would do.

My lips curled at the idea of seeing his reaction to whatever I picked.

Maybe I'd grab one of each and see which one he was most scared of.

I returned to the bar with a pink, yellow, orange, green, and purple candy cane.

He eyed them. "I'm not eating all of them."

"No. Just one." I held up yellow, carefully observing his reaction. "This one, maybe?"

His expression didn't change. Not in the slightest. He reached for it, but I yanked it away.

"Hmm. Maybe not."

"Artica, what are you doing?"

I answered by holding up the orange candy. "This one."

His eyes narrowed. "Just give me a damn stick already."

"Well, which one do you want?"

"I don't care. Green."

I finally allowed myself a giggle. An evil, maniacal one. I set the green one far, *far* away from his reach.

"I see," he rumbled, sitting back, amused. "You're trying to give me one I don't want. Clever, but it won't work."

"Noooo."

"I know what they all do, and I don't have a preference."

My spirits flattened a bit. "The blue one was your least favorite, wasn't it?"

He winked.

He's ruining all my fun.

"Tell me what they do," I said.

"I think I'll let you discover that for yourself."

I pouted. "You're no fun."

His eyes turned sultry as he smiled.

I considered the candy canes, then picked up the purple. "I've made my final decision. This one."

He frowned, but took it and bit off a chunk, crunching on it. I waited, eager for him to jump up and do a jig or grow an extra pair of arms or something.

Torturous seconds passed.

Nothing happened.

Wait, no. Goose bumps spread across his skin, his hairs rising in response.

"So... what did it do?" I asked.

"Dulled my magic for about sixty seconds. I have about forty magic-less seconds left to go before I can insulate myself again."

I crossed my arms. "That's hardly fair."

He chuckled. "Yet I would hate to have a full minute of being powerless when I really needed it." He chuckled. "Norden used this one on me once. I won't be caught off guard again."

"Hmm. I suppose it does open up some opportunities..." I twirled a lock of his snow-white hair around my fingers and used my magic to shoot ice right up to the root.

He grimaced. "You'll regret that."

"Oh, will I?" I reached for my martini, then realized it was empty. "Should I keep taking advantage of the final twenty seconds?"

He caught my hand in his before I could reach another lock of hair. My breath caught as he stared intently at my face. "Ten."

I used my other hand to blow him a kiss, shooting powdery snow into his face.

The elves in the bar who'd been watching us burst into laughter.

He sighed, dusting snow off his nose. "I suppose I deserve that."

"I suppose you do," I said smugly.

Frost skirted from the hand he was holding all the way up my arm. I jerked back, shuddering at the bone-piercing chill.

He smirked. "Time's up."

"Yeah, yeah, I got that," I said, rubbing warmth back into my arm.

A group of elves wandered over, singing a lively tune. Little hands plucked at my clothes, pulling me off the stool. "What's happening?" I asked, rounding on Kalt.

"They want you to join them. It's a good thing. Means they like you."

The elves dragged me onto the cafeteria floor, and the magic here—holiday cheer or whatever—fully took over, making me giddier than ever.

I danced and sang with the elves, swaying my hips and spinning until I was dizzy.

All the while, Kalt watched from the bar, an absent smile on his face.

Yeah, I was really going to like it here, but I was going to need to do something about Kalt's predicament.

He didn't deserve to be alone, not when he hadn't listed a single reason against joining the prince's triad other than political ones.

The gleam in his eyes said that he was holding himself back from happiness for the sake of the realms.

But something was missing, and if I tried hard enough, I'd convince him to do what was best for all the kingdoms… and what was best for himself, too.

No, not if I tried, I corrected myself as I brushed my snowflake pendant with my fingers.

If I *believed*.

KALT

Artica was going to be the death of me.

I thought about her as I entered my chamber and went straight for the shower. I'd sent her off to her guest room down the hall, still giddy and slightly inebriated by the North Pole beverages.

I had fun today, probably more fun than I'd had in a very long time.

Something that would prove to be a problem if I wasn't careful.

Turning on the water as hot as it would go, I stripped and braced myself under the steaming stream. I hissed in a breath, the scalding heat hitting my icy skin and melting my magic faster than it should.

Ugh, I needed to get that female out of my head.

And Norden.

And Prince Lark.

Frost.

Thinking of the three of them stirred an array of

goose bumps on my arms that quickly subsided in the warm water.

I'd somehow managed to engage Artica in the first level of Water Fae bonding. Yet she hadn't seemed to notice, her mind too inebriated to sense the connection.

But she would certainly feel it tomorrow.

An initial courtship bond.

All because of that damn mistletoe in her dorm room, followed by her snowy kiss after at the bar. Or maybe it was the latter that had done it alone. I really wasn't sure. However, at some point, my soul had expressed an interest in hers, and she'd responded immediately with resounding acceptance.

Which didn't surprise me.

I knew how she felt.

But I shouldn't have allowed things to progress that far.

We'd just been having too much fun.

Similar to what had happened my first night in this infectious realm.

Prince Lark and Norden had cornered me that evening, offered me a welcome party that had almost ended in a fantasy I would never entertain again.

Because I knew the risk. I knew what was coming, and I wasn't going to be a selfish ice pick and risk starting a war, or worse, just because I couldn't keep it in my pants.

That didn't keep me from fantasizing about it.

Only, Artica had added herself to the mix, making it so damn hard that I couldn't help palming my shaft.

Because *frost*, it'd been a long time since I'd indulged in pleasure. And even if I went out and found a willing selkie or Winter Fae to indulge me out there, it wouldn't be enough.

Prince Lark and Norden had consumed my thoughts.

And Artica now stood at the center of them, doing

wicked things in my mind that I should *not* be fantasizing about.

I groaned, my hand squeezing my shaft. I hated myself for allowing the fantasy to play out, because that was all it would ever be. That was all I would ever *let* it be.

But I couldn't stop, my veins burning with a need I had to sate. Even if it was just my hand doing the job.

I thought of Norden and Prince Lark showing Artica all the possibilities that the Winter Fae had to offer. Norden licking between her legs while Prince Lark took her mouth.

I observed from the shadows, enjoying the torment of observing without touching.

I'd join them soon.

Ignore the risk. Ignore the potential for doom.

Just revel in the moment of heat and lust.

Norden and Lark switched places, Artica moaning as she tasted herself on Norden's tongue.

Frost, I wanted to kiss them, too, to indulge in the flavor of her sweet arousal. She probably tasted like sweet berries and cream.

Or maybe coconut.

My hand tightened, my head falling back against the wall. Then I pictured myself kissing Norden, allowing the selkie to handle me the way his eyes always promised he would—with sensuality tinted with rough masculinity and the gracefulness of his kind.

Artica tasted just as sweet as I'd anticipated, her coconut taffy flavor an addiction that called to my soul.

It wasn't real.

But it certainly *felt* real.

I stroked myself harder as I felt her lips against my abdomen, envisioned Lark sliding inside her, the selkie going in from behind.

An onslaught of so many positions and images

destroying my ability to even consider how wrong this was to think about.

This was a courtship worthy of a fae like Artica.

She was perfect. I'd known for sure the moment I'd placed the snowflake pendant on her, but I'd suspected before that as well.

The pendant was a form of insurance—a magical artifact that displayed her compatibility with other fae. My compatibility with Lark and Norden suggested that they needed a Water Fae for their mate-circle. So I'd opted to try to find them the right one.

However, I refused to put her—or anyone else, for that matter—in the candidate position without knowing the true connections to the males courting her. Hence, the necklace. It served as a way to test the links to ensure whoever was put forth as a candidate was the right fae for the task.

My heart had damn well soared when I'd sensed her potential link to Norden. Because it meant I'd been right, that they were truly compatible.

The only one left to test was Lark, and I strongly suspected my heart would beat just as heavily after he met Artica.

A selfish part of me didn't want to give her to them.

No, that wasn't true. The selfish part of me wanted them to have her... *with me at their side.*

I swallowed, thinking about how the pendant had glittered against her pale skin. It would have turned black had Norden not been an ideal match. Snowflakes, she'd even made a secret wish for the selkie to say her name. While his flirtations had annoyed me, Artica had loved it.

I'd dampened my explanations to her, saying that Norden's advances were just a courtship.

But when Norden set his sights on someone, he didn't let it go. I knew from experience.

Which meant he'd likely win her over.

And if the prince was compatible with her, which I suspected he would be, then he would be even more insistent.

However, this was why I'd brought her here. I'd meant what I'd said about her application appealing to me, but it went deeper than that.

I knew she would be perfect for this realm. Her joy was palpable every time I came near her. Fae, her own dorm room was decorated for the Festivus despite it being several months away.

Her holiday persona made her a perfect fit for the internship.

And also made her the perfect candidate for Lark's mate-circle, too.

She maintained a conviction that I did not. A heart of gold. An obsession with love and romance. Lance had told me about how she'd helped him win over his human, Candela. The cupcake shop owner had a special affinity for North Pole magic, and if Lance recognized Artica's potential for belief that could make her a suitable princess of the Winter Fae, then I believed it.

Our people needed her. She would provide the alliance she had already so expertly deduced would help our realms unite, proving that she was the right fae for the task. She could mate Prince Lark and the selkie, and they could find another fae to safely complete the triad without my interference.

It was perfect, as long as I learned how to let go.

But oh… the image of what could be still played out in my mind.

With Royal Water Fae blood, I could match the

prince's power with my own. We would be able to give her so much pleasure that she would beg us to stop, and that was when we'd let Norden torment her, his sensual skills a match for any fae.

A tremble rolled over me as I worked myself harder, squeezing my eyes shut as I permitted just this small moment of weakness.

I pictured it all.

Artica as my mate.

Her legs spread for me.

Her lips saying my name.

The three of us worshipping her until she came.

Then taking her together. Lark between her legs. Norden at her back. Me in her mouth. Those luscious lips wrapped around my base, her throat working as she sucked me down like one of those candy canes.

Faeeee... I moaned, heat building inside me in a wave of intensity that overrode my power for a brief second of time, causing me to explode against the wall.

So powerful.

So passionate.

So... *right.*

Grief taunted the edges of my oblivion, threatening to dismantle my high. But I ignored it, continuing to believe, just for a brief moment more, that Artica and Norden and Lark were mine.

My mates.

My future.

My intended fate.

A beautiful destiny filled with promise and love and ardent heat.

A future that cannot be mine, I thought, my knees buckling beneath me.

My head thumped against the wall, defeat slumping

my shoulders as I vowed to undo the bond with Artica in the morning. I would show her around the palace, slowly unknit the connection throughout the day, and then I'd give her so many tasks that she wouldn't have time to see me until after the coronation.

I'd observe from a distance.

Protect from afar.

Norden was interested, and so was she.

They just needed fate to play her cards and the holiday magic to take hold.

While I hid in the shadows.

Because my being a part of their circle was a fantasy I could never allow to come to fruition.

ARTICA

S unlight flooded my senses, drawing me from my sleepy cocoon.

Mmm, these quilts were sooooo warm.

And the mattress resembled a fluffy cloud.

Stretching in the bed, I buried my face in the feathery pillow, the remnants of cozy, cheery dreams still at the edge of my subconscious but fading fast.

My first night at the North Pole had been a success.

Now, to survive my first full day here.

Kalt wanted to take me on a tour of the palace this morning.

So, uh, what time is it? With the constant sunshine, it was hard to guess.

I sat up, banishing the rest of sleep as I did, and checked the clock hanging above a chestnut dresser.

I was supposed to meet Kalt inside the cafeteria in ten minutes.

Rolling out of bed, I threw open my wardrobe and

noted my already unpacked clothes intermingled with several warmer outfits, courtesy of the Winter Fae Realm.

Gifts from the elves, perhaps?

A likely explanation, as I'd found a silk pajama set and fuzzy reindeer slippers waiting for me on top of my nightstand last night.

So what cute outfits will I discover in my closet? I wondered, flicking through the items.

Each piece was soft, either lined with faux fur or made with cotton. All of it was infused with a layer of Winter Fae magic that hummed pleasantly against my skin.

Don't mind if I do, I thought, pulling out a baby-blue knitted sweater that made me think of clouds. It was so lightweight, yet the magic woven through the fabric felt warm to the touch.

I removed my silk top and replaced it with the sweater. Then I swapped my bottoms for some skinny jeans and checked myself out in the mirror. The sweater was fitted, with a V-neck that revealed a bit of cleavage.

I smiled, running a hand over my white-blonde hair to pull the tangles out. I usually liked to braid the strands, but there wasn't time. Just like yesterday.

Oh well. It would have to do for now.

Although, if I still wanted to entertain Norden's advances, I needed to up my hair game. Something to consider more later.

Pulling on some socks and a pair of fur-lined boots, I rushed for the door, casting one last longing look back at my room. It was the perfect size, with a giant bed nestled up against a huge window that looked out over the ice sculpture garden.

Even now, I could see two arctic foxes playing, chasing each other around the carved figures.

If Kalt didn't keep me too busy, I'd have to find some

spare time to explore—maybe make a few more friends. Cute and furry ones like the foxes, preferably.

I left my room, hurried down the hall to the stairs, found the door that took me to the common areas of the palace, and then skipped toward the cafeteria at the other end. My feet just felt the urge to dance and prance, thanks to all the cheerful hums in the air.

The cafeteria was jam-packed with elves again, but this time there were a few Winter Fae, too. They were obvious by their taller forms, most of them possessing the traits of their original faedoms.

But a handful were tall and elf-like with white-blond hair and pointy ears. Those males, I assumed, were the born Winter Fae. Their creamy complexions resembled sun-kissed snow, and their eyes were all silver blue.

Very sexy elves, I decided, my lips curling. From what I read last night—because yes, I researched the whole hierarchy and mating thing via my in-room ice tablet before falling asleep—the mate-circles only produced male heirs. So there were no female Winter Fae Royals as a result. Just the females lucky enough to be picked by a mate-circle.

And the proof of that presented itself before me as the few blond Winter Fae males returned to tables seating two men and a female.

Real-life mate-circles, I mused, my lips ticking up. *Sign me up.*

Except maybe not that large, hulking...

I stopped in my tracks.

Huh. So *that* was what abominable snowmen looked like.

His head almost reached the ceiling, and he literally resembled a mountain of snow, with glowing eyes and icicle teeth.

He was definitely the least friendly creature in appearance that I'd seen thus far in the North Pole.

Note to self: do *not* fall into one of their traps.

"I see you've found a snowman," Kalt said behind me.

I whirled around, my eyes wide.

Fae, I'd already forgotten how gorgeous he was. His gaze held mine for a moment before flinching away.

I was probably making him uncomfortable again. But there was an odd sort of tingling between us. A static electricity I didn't quite understand. I'd felt it last night as well but had chalked it up to one too many drinks. Yet it remained now.

Interesting.

"They're, uh, bigger than I thought they'd be," I managed to reply, trying to keep the conversation on track before I asked something silly like, *Do you feel that hum between us? Maybe we should kiss or go dancing again. Then kiss. Definitely kiss.*

He inclined his head, his gaze on the snowman. "They look menacing, but they're literally made of snow and magic. Winter Fae magic, so nothing too nefarious." He glanced down at me again. "So, how did you sleep?"

"Like a baby," I admitted with a sigh. "Are all the rooms here that cozy?"

His lips twitched. "It's the aftereffects of North Pole magic. It's supposed to feel like waking up on Christmas morning. Every. Day."

"Like how we feel on Festivus?" I guessed, familiar with the Christmas traditions, thanks to Queen Claire.

"Exactly like that."

Last night—the singing, the dancing, the candy canes —came back to me. "Ah. Makes sense, then. Most of the Winter Fae traditions have been gifted to the humans."

"Hence the belief crystals. They're fueled by the belief of holiday magic in children. Every time they write to Santa or make a Christmas wish, a crystal is formed." He reached out to tuck a stray strand of hair behind my pointed ear. The light brush of his fingertips triggered a memory of last night, one of me blowing a snowy kiss in his face.

I'd wanted to do more.

To lean forward and take his mouth in a blistering passion.

Which wasn't anything new.

Yet the inclination to do it again right now without the fuel of alcohol or any true motivation behind it was a bit odd. Even for me.

Kalt and I were compatible, something I'd always known. However, the connection felt heavier now, more tangible, like we'd somehow linked.

But…

I frowned.

Is that a level-one bond I sense? Surely that was just wishful thinking. I would remember if we'd engaged in a commitment level, right?

They weren't permanent. But some could last up to a month before both parties mutually ended the temporary link.

Or enhanced it.

When—

"Shall we?" Kalt asked suddenly, jolting me from my thoughts. "I'm starved."

Right. Food.

"Sure," I said, my fingers moving to my snowflake pendant again.

Fae, he could feel it, too, couldn't he? So why wasn't he saying anything?

Unless it was all in my head. A likely possibility, considering my obsession with Kalt.

What if the effects of all that holiday cheer last night had weakened Kalt's inhibitions, thus allowing us to bond?

I chewed my lip. That would mean that I'd sort of tricked him into dating me. Or mystically enchanted him. Not that I had done it on purpose, but that would explain his lack of commentary.

Icicles.

My cheeks burned hot as we lined up to get our breakfast.

This was not how I wanted to start my internship—by forcing my boss to bond me while also becoming a candidate for the Winter Fae Prince.

Wait…

Would this impact my candidacy?

I nearly dropped the cinnamon roll I'd just grabbed.

Oh, fluff.

I needed a lot more cinnamon rolls and a mountain of hot chocolate before I continued pondering this problem.

And maybe a prayer or five to the Source that I didn't accidentally mate-bond with any other fae.

Sitting at a table, I stuffed a large bite of ooey-gooey cinnamon sugar into my mouth, and my eyes fluttered closed as I chewed. "All the food here is *so good.*"

Kalt cleared his throat but otherwise didn't comment. I peeked at him as he began eating some cranberry sauce and oatmeal cookies.

I watched him take a bite. "No coconut?"

He glowered at me. "No."

Talk about *frosty.* Norden's nickname was starting to make more sense to me now.

Of course, he might be pissed that I'd mate-bonded him.

Except it had to be mutual, right? The first level was all about shared interest. So... did that mean he actually wanted to mate me? Maybe it just took some alcohol to lower his inhibitions enough for the truth to come out.

Hmm. I much preferred that explanation. He was my boss and therefore couldn't be interested in another fae.

And his whole desire to save the world, too. He didn't want to be tied to anyone. But somewhere, deep down, he liked me enough to establish the first link.

Oh, yes, this was definitely a better outlook.

I shoved another cinnamon roll into my mouth, enjoying the flavor that much more. Sipping the hot chocolate, my insides melted at the rich, chocolatey goodness.

No wonder they only ate sweets here. It was what they *excelled* at making.

After our silent breakfast, Kalt led me out of the cafeteria and toward the back of the palace, where we crossed a gate into another building. This one wasn't quite as elaborate or tall, but still festive. And that gleeful note of happiness still hung heavily in the air.

Sigh.

"This is where all the magic happens," Kalt informed me as we entered the three-story building. "We live in the palace, as do many others, but the work is done here. Even the Winter Fae King and his elves like to have a work-life balance."

It was hard to imagine Kalt having a work-life balance. I suspected last night had been an exception based on making me feel welcome.

"What do you do in your free time?" I asked, genuinely curious since he'd been so intent to rush off last night even though it hadn't been *that* late. However, it had left me time to study up on the Winter Fae mating customs, so I wasn't complaining.

"My free time?" He glanced at me. "Why do you ask?"

"We ended the night kind of early yesterday." When he gave me a stricken look, I quickly added, "I mean, I wasn't bored. I found some naughty things to read," I said with a grin, hoping he'd like the joke.

"Naughty…" He turned positively white.

Oh, right, I'd said it wrong. "You know? Santa's list of names of who has been naughty or nice?" That was the joke, right? Queen Claire had mentioned it once. But maybe I had it wrong?

I swiped a hand over my face.

Yeah, I was making a fool of myself.

"Sorry, my attempt at a human Christmas joke. I suppose I still have a lot to learn. I actually just read about the Winter Fae mate-circles last night on the ice tablet in my room."

His face had taken on a reddish hue, making me frown. Was it the mate-circle talk making him…?

Oh.

Ooooooh.

Maybe *he* had gotten into something a little naughty last night. Not that I was jealous.

A lie. I was totally jealous.

"What *do* you do in your free time?" I waggled my eyebrows. "Perhaps you eat too many coconut taffies and go play with a particular selkie?"

"No," he said firmly.

"No?" I repeated. "Hmm. Then a certain prince, perhaps?"

The deepening hue of Kalt's cheeks told me I'd definitely struck a nerve of some kind. One that embarrassed him.

Because he's fantasized about it? I guessed.

Not because he'd actually gone through with it. Otherwise, he'd be mated to them and not level-one bonded to me, right?

"No," he stated again.

I grinned. I now had a new mission in life: to make Kalt stop thinking with his political brain and to actually consider what *he* wanted in this world. To maybe follow his heart, allow it to beat, and *enjoy* his existence.

Yes. A solid plan indeed.

ARTICA

K alt sighed. "Right. Enough of that. I need to show you around the workspace."

He took a step, then paused, sighing again.

"Um, I should warn you that Norden recently renamed all the departments around here. Part of Prince Lark's ascension is to make the palace his own, which includes handing over certain tasks to his mates. Or, in this case, *mate*."

Tasks like performing Interrealm Fae relations on behalf of the Elemental Fae and *the Winter Fae?* I wanted to ask. But I refrained, nodding instead. "All right. I can handle learning some department names."

Kalt glanced at me, his expression saying he didn't believe me. However, he turned again without a word and led me to a huge warehouse-sized area filled with echoes of hammering, buzzing, and high-pitched chatter.

"Oh!" I gasped, looking around at all the working elves with a couple of Winter Fae supervisors. "The toy room!"

"That's the appropriate name for it," Kalt said with a wince. "But it's now called the T&A."

I blinked at him. "T&A?"

He stared at me.

I stared back. "What am I missing?"

He cleared his throat and palmed the back of his neck. "Have you visited the Human Realm much?"

"Only on holiday with family," I admitted. "Oh, and I visited Lance recently at some springy place. Springy Falls? Spring Waters? I don't remember the name. But otherwise, Queen Claire has brought me up to speed on a lot of things."

"Including acronyms or slang?" he hedged.

"Uh, no, not really." I frowned. "Why? Is T&A something important to humans?"

One of the elves nearby chuckled.

And Kalt's face turned red again.

"What am I missing?" I repeated.

"Um, well, selkies are a form of Shifter Fae, right? They travel the Human Realm through the icy waters but often find themselves among humans in the chillier climates of the world. So they're well versed in mortal lingo. Hence, T&A. Also known as, uh, tits and ass, to most humans."

My eyes rounded, then I took in the toy shop before blinking back at him again. "I... I..."

"It's meant to be a crude joke, thanks to the lewd selkie in charge," Kalt went on. "But it actually stands for Toys and Arctic Center, just layered with sensual innuendo as the acronym."

I gaped at him.

Then a laugh bubbled from my throat. "I can't believe you just explained all that with a straight face." Well, and with an adorable little flush to his chiseled cheeks.

Which was twice now that I'd made him blush today. And something about that made my heart pitter-patter just a tad harder for him.

Because a flustered Kalt was an endearing Kalt.

"Trust me, the humor wears off after the hundredth time you've said it," he said, his full lips curling down. "Unless you're a selkie, then it's infinitely hilarious."

A giggle came from my right, and I turned my attention back to the elves fully engrossed in their work. A group sewed teddy bears, some painted small, buildable bricks, and others...

I narrowed my gaze. *Is that a dildo?*

An elf fumbled with a phallic instrument, his face almost as red as Kalt's had been. "Why do we have to make these?" he demanded while another elf rolled his eyes.

"It's not for the kids, Dec. It's for an adult human somewhere who still believes in magic. Or maybe a selkie. Or a mate-circle." He wiggled his brows suggestively. "Maybe even a fellow female elf."

Dec's lips twisted, some of the heat leaving his cheeks. "Hmm."

Kalt and I moved on, but the elf's words persisted in my mind. "What did he mean by 'still believes in magic'?" I asked.

"You know how you were able to see the palace after holding the crystal and filling it with your belief?"

I nodded, remembering the spectacular moment it had appeared at the top of the hill.

"Some creatures are more prone to belief in holiday magic than others," Kalt explained. "For example, human children. They could see everything here at the North Pole, whereas the adults would just see a frozen tundra. Because they've stopped believing in holiday enchantments."

"And the selkies can see it, too," I murmured.

"Most fae species can," he murmured. "Because we all know magic exists. But humans tend to write it off as superstition or fantasy. They can't see the Winter Fae elements because they don't *believe*."

"And belief is what powers Winter Fae kind."

"Yes." Kalt nodded, leading me to the back of the workshop. "They collect thousands of belief crystals and store them here." He opened a metal door and I peered inside.

"Fae," I breathed.

The room, plated with titanium, was stacked to the ceiling with shimmering crystals.

"What do they do with all of them?"

"Belief powers the crystals, which restores and powers Winter Fae magic. That's the whole point of delivering toys around the world. The belief of human children lights the crystals like a star. They make sure to include a bit of crystal in every toy. Here, I'll show you."

He closed the crystal room door and turned to the nearest elf, who was carefully inserting hair into the head of a doll.

"Mind if I borrow this?" he asked the elf.

She shook her head, handing the head over.

I stared at the half-bald head and shuddered. "Creepy."

Kalt ignored my comment. "See the eyes? They're made with a special glass the elves created with the crystals. The doll will be delivered to the child, belief in Santa Claus—the Winter Fae King—will heighten, and the crystal will transfer magic to the Winter Fae Source. And that's how Winter Fae have reliably held on to their magic for so long." He returned the doll head. "Any questions?"

I shook my head. "It's genius, really."

"It's certainly clever. Moving on."

We left the T&A—which I definitely wouldn't ever be able to say with a straight face now that I knew the naughtier definition of the acronym—and entered another workshop area.

The smell of warm sugar and the sparkle of tinsel drew me in. "And this place is…?"

Kalt's eye twitched. "The Baubles, Decorations, Sweets, and Magic Center."

"It smells delicious," I said.

But Kalt just stared at me again.

Which suggested I was missing yet another joke. I repeated the name in my head, my brow furrowing. "TBDSMC?" Was that another human term?

"If you remove the *T* and the *C*…"

"BDSM?" I asked.

He gave a single, curt nod.

My eyes rounded as I repeated it to myself. Because I knew that term from one of the books I'd read about human reproduction and their, uh, kinks. A lot of other fae were into similar activities but didn't necessarily refer to it by that acronym.

"You know what? I'm actually starting to like Norden," I decided out loud. "He has a fun sense of humor."

Kalt snorted. "As if you didn't like him before when he said your hair reminded him of sunlight under the waves."

Yeah, that had probably been the most romantic thing ever said to me, but I wasn't going to give Kalt the satisfaction of hearing me agree.

I ignored his jibe and moved forward, taking in the garlands, wreaths, ornaments, snow globes, and rows upon rows of candy—they took up an entire wall.

The elf behind the sweets counter waved me over, and I obliged.

"I've just made a new batch of salted caramel chocolates," he informed me, enthusiasm lighting his ruddy features. "Would you like to sample one?"

"Yes, please," I replied immediately. Because who could say no to something as faelicious as that?

A robust elf who stood as high as my waist hovered nearby, and as I reached for a delectable piece of candy, his hand shot out to grab one first.

The chocolatier slapped the big elf's hand away. "None for you, Jingle. You've already eaten half a pan this morning!"

Jingle huffed in reply and shuffled away with a dejected glower on his round face. Something told me he'd be back soon to try again.

And as I placed the chocolate against my tongue, I fully understood why.

Because *oh my Fae.* I groaned, the sound one I'd only ever made in the bedroom. When alone. And thinking about Kalt.

But this was as good as sex. Or how I imagined it would be. With Kalt, anyway. Not with the few fae I'd experimented with over the years. They definitely hadn't made me moan like this.

"Wow," I hummed, my eyes closing as I swallowed. "Wow, wow." I had no other words. No better way to describe it. Just praise and delight and faeliciousness! I opened my eyes, eager for another, and found the elf's face lit with pride.

"That good?" he asked.

"*Better.*" I reached for another, then paused. "May I?"

"Go ahead!"

I selected one last chocolate and moved away before my animal instincts took over and I ate the whole pan.

Jingle definitely had the right idea. I winked at him as we passed, and he smiled.

"Flirting with the elves is a dangerous pastime," Kalt muttered.

"Eating chocolate is flirting?" I asked, genuinely curious. Since apparently petting the hair of a selkie was the equivalent of exploring each other's *naughty* regions.

"No, but moaning and winking certainly are," he replied.

"Have you tried those salted caramel chocolates?" I asked.

"Yes. They're Norden's favorite."

I stopped walking. "You ate chocolates with Norden?"

"No. He sends them to me daily."

"Was that batch meant for you, then?" I wondered out loud, suddenly feeling a bit guilty that I'd interrupted whatever game he and Norden were playing.

"Those are going to the throne room with everything else, for the coronation," Kalt replied flatly. "The ones Norden gives me are from his personal stash."

There was a hint of something in his voice, arrogance maybe, or pleasure. But underlined with sorrow and annoyance. A mixture of emotion that he refused to release because of the expectations he had for his life.

I'd have to pry those out of him.

He wouldn't be a good soldier if he regretted not following his heart. He would become bitter and cruel, and that wouldn't benefit anyone, least of all himself.

Besides, how could anyone deny the joy of this realm? That had to feel like more of a punishment than a necessity.

"Tell me more about the coronation," I said, deciding it was a safe topic to explore. "Do they happen often?"

Often being a relative term, of course. Since fae tended to live for a long time, some even for eternity.

"Not exactly. Winter Fae Royals tend to reproduce when they believe it's time, just as the coronation is surrounded by belief as well. The Winter Fae King is in charge of determining when and how things transpire. And he decided Prince Lark's thirty-second birthday was the right day for the ascension."

I frowned. "Your tone indicates that you don't agree."

"Whether I do or not isn't relevant. It's just younger than most. I think the current Winter Fae King was closer to forty years old when he ascended. So some may feel this is a bit young, especially as Lark hasn't fully mated yet."

"And that puts his ascension at risk," I translated.

Kalt nodded. "The Winter Fae Source expects a balance, and if he's not ready…"

I swallowed. "That would be bad."

"Exactly."

"Yet his father believes in him, so he should be ready," I pressed, a hint of confidence flirting with my senses. I hadn't even met the Winter Fae Prince yet, but I somehow knew he was destined for this. "It'll be fine."

Kalt stared at me for a moment. "That's exactly the sort of belief he needs."

"Well, then it's a good thing I'm here," I joked, smiling. "How old is the current Winter Fae King?" I wasn't sure how long Winter Fae typically lived; I'd have to research that later.

"He's reigned for several centuries, so close to five hundred or so. Not that he looks it." Kalt shrugged. "But the Winter Fae King behaves as a conduit for the belief that powers the magic. Rather, he is the direct conduit from the Source. So youth is important, as is strength. Without it, the entire realm would be in danger."

I glanced around. "He must be pretty good at what he does because everything seems just fine."

"It is," he agreed. "And now it will be Prince Lark's job to ensure it stays that way." He started walking again, and I followed while considering that monumental task. It certainly sounded like a lot of responsibility.

"When is the coronation?" I asked.

"In a little over a week," he said, his eyes glinting with an excitement I didn't understand. "You'll be integral in ensuring it all runs like a well-oiled machine. It's why I needed you here immediately. And also why I wanted you to be a candidate."

A bundle of nerves formed in the pit of my stomach. "But I don't know the first thing about a Winter Fae coronation, or really what it means to be a candidate. Also, what if I didn't want to be a candidate?"

He glanced at me, his gaze dropping to the pendant at my breastbone before meeting my gaze again. "You just told me Prince Lark should be ready and everything will be fine. Your belief is so strong even without meeting him. You're exactly what this kingdom needs right now."

I frowned at him. "That doesn't answer my question, Kalt."

He stopped walking to face me again. "Can you honestly tell me the idea of being a candidate bothers you, Artica?"

"That's not the point. You made a decision on my behalf without even talking to me."

"And you told me last night that you were over that part of our arrangement," he returned.

"Well, I am," I said slowly. "I'm just…"

"Not really over it?" he suggested.

"No, I am," I repeated, feeling a bit more certain. "But

I don't understand how you could make that decision without knowing me."

"Who says I don't know you?" He stepped closer. "You're friends with Lance, who is practically a brother to me. I know all about you, Artica."

ARTICA

M y lips parted, my eyes widening. "All about me?" I squeaked. *Like, everything? My hopes? My dreams? My... crush?*

"Your dorm room was decorated for Festivus," he replied. "Which happened almost six months ago. Yet I imagine your room always looks like that."

"I mean, yes. I like decorations."

"And you have an affinity for ice that rivals my own."

I scoffed at that. "*No one* has an affinity as good as yours, Kalt."

"And you've already won over an army of elves with your holiday cheer," he continued, ignoring my response.

"Because of the enchanting candy canes," I pointed out. "That *you* made me eat."

"I didn't make you do anything, Artica," he replied, smiling. "You're a natural here, just as I knew you would be." He cocked his head. "Why do you think Lance dared you to apply?"

"Because he knew..." I trailed off, swallowing, as I'd

been about to say, *Because he knew I was in love with you.* "He, uh, knew I'd like it," I finished lamely instead.

Kalt's gaze sparkled. "Yeah? Is that what he told you?" His lips curled. "Then I'll let you keep believing that."

I frowned. "Was there another reason?"

"Ask him and find out," he suggested, turning to lead me to another area of the building.

Was he saying that because he knew the truth? That Lance had dared me because of my obsession with Prince Kalt? Or because there was something I didn't know?

I pondered the possibilities all the way to the next area, which Kalt informed me was named The Bell's Jingle Center.

This time, I knew to remove "The" and "Center" from the name, providing me with the acronym of *BJ*.

That one, I understood.

"You'll love this place," Kalt announced sarcastically.

My mind immediately went south, thinking about the invitation to explore a BJ with him.

At least until he added, "It's where we create new songs… and rehash others a million times."

He opened the door, and a wave of music assaulted my eardrums. "Just because I don't enjoy singing doesn't mean I don't like music!" I shouted.

We stepped deeper inside the room, which had a stage at the center and enchanted snow falling from the ceiling.

A cute number was being performed in the middle with a row of elves dressed in traditional elf attire decorated in bells and finished with green tights. They kicked their feet into the air, spun each other around, and ended with every one of them posing differently.

I clapped heartily. These guys knew entertainment!

"Kalt!" one of the elves—a ruddy-faced male with a white beard—called. "Who's the beauty?"

"This is Artica, my intern," Kalt said as we approached the stage. "Just giving her a tour."

"Delightful! Do you enjoy holiday music, my dear?"

I nodded enthusiastically. "Yes, and you perform so well."

"Ah," he replied, kicking his feet and looking down bashfully. "I *have* been head choir elf for two centuries. Most of the music you've heard was likely written by me."

My lips parted. "It's an honor to meet a master at his craft."

"Okay, okay," Kalt cut in. "We're all *very* impressed."

Apparently, I was flirting again. At least according to his standards.

But why did he care? Because of our partial bond? Or something else?

"Which is your favorite?" the choir elf asked, ignoring Kalt entirely.

Kalt responded by scowling and collapsing into one of the plush chairs.

"Um…" Most of the music I knew was from my world, so probably not something he'd be familiar with, as I suspected his commentary about writing songs revolved more around human holiday tunes than those of the various faedoms.

But I'd heard some mortal music from Queen Claire.

Most of them were sweet and charming, but one of them always made me giggle. So I decided to go with that one now. "'I Caught Mommy Kissing Santa Claus,'" I said, hoping that was the right title.

Kalt burst into laughter behind me. "I think she means 'I *Saw* Mommy Kissing Santa Claus.'"

"Oh." My nose scrunched. "Yes, well, I did mean that one. It's fun and cheerful."

A statement that only made Kalt laugh harder. Which

told me he wasn't laughing at my mistake so much as my choice. At least he wasn't poking fun at me.

The choir elf grinned broadly. "Not one I've written, but an annual favorite!" he exclaimed without judgment.

I liked this choir elf.

"We'll perform it for you," he said excitedly.

"Oh, no, you don't have to—"

"We'd be *delighted*," he interjected.

I glanced back at Kalt for permission. He shrugged. "Might as well."

I happily settled into the seat next to him as the elves on the stage rearranged themselves, grins plastered on their faces.

Did they ever grow tired of smiling? Probably not. And it was rather infectious.

The choir elf held his arms in the air, poised to direct. Then, with a nod to the band, they began.

An elf ran to the front of the stage and shouted the opening dialogue, which sent me into a fit of giggles.

Kalt raised his brows in amusement. "You know 'Santa Claus' was just 'Daddy' all dressed up, right?"

"Tell that to Queen Claire," I whispered, eager for a personal performance. "This is one of *her* favorite songs."

He chuckled and leaned back in the seat. "I'll have to tell Cyrus to dress up as Santa Claus, then."

"From the images I've seen, Sol might be more appropriate, if you give him a pillow for a belly." Because the Earth Fae was brawny and tall, but solid muscle.

Kalt smirked. "The Winter Fae King would be offended by that depiction."

"The Winter Fae are the ones who spread that image around," I replied. "Right?"

He nodded. "To keep themselves better hidden."

"Then he won't be offended at all," I said, confident.

We fell silent as the elves picked up their pace, singing and dancing all over the stage. They even threw each other around cheerleader-style, flying in the air and landing deftly on their feet.

It was truly delightful to witness.

Magical, too.

When the same elf at the start ran forward to deliver the final dialogue, I burst into laughter. Corny, yes, but I loved it.

Standing, I clapped until my hands hurt. The elves all bowed and smiled, and Kalt grabbed my arm, tugging me away. "Thanks for the show!" he called. "We'll be on our way."

"But I don't want to leave yet."

He tapped his wrist. "Other things to do today, Artica."

With a pout, I turned and waved at the elves, who waved back and then started another song.

"Funny," Kalt said as the door closed behind us and the music was cut off. "That song was actually inspired by Lark's mother and father."

My eyes widened. "What? Is that why you found my choice so humorous?"

He nodded with mirth dancing in his expression. "It drives Lark crazy whenever he hears it. I can't wait to tell him it's your favorite."

I laughed. "You wouldn't!"

His hand was still wrapped around my upper arm. His gaze dropped to mine as he smiled.

Then he bent and swept warm lips over my cheek.

I stood stock-still, staring at him, my insides turning to goo. "What was that for?"

"Luck. You're going to need it." He released my arm and walked away, leaving my heart spinning.

Kalt. Just. Kissed. Me.

Lightly touching the spot where his lips had met my cheek, I followed him, bewildered.

The next item of business was lunch.

As we feasted on carrot cake and lemon tarts, I reviewed everything I'd learned so far while trying not to dwell on the electrified sensation of Kalt's lips on my skin.

It was a lot.

But somehow made easier by Norden's sensual naming conventions.

I hadn't seen him yet today, which was disappointing, so I asked about him instead.

Kalt nibbled on a lemon tart. "The selkies often frequent the Arctic lands, which is why they're considered allies of the Winter Fae. But Norden's mating sort of makes him the bridge between the species, solidifying their alliance."

"Sounds familiar," I said.

Kalt ignored me.

But if the alliance was strengthened between the selkies and the Winter Fae through the simple mate-bond, couldn't the same be said about the Winter Fae and Elemental Fae?

"Can you tell me about Prince Lark? Is he as fun-loving as Norden?"

Kalt laughed, the sound hearty and bringing tears to his eyes.

I frowned, not sure why he found this so humorous.

"Prince Lark is Norden's opposite. He's a broody royal who takes his tasks around here more seriously than anyone I've ever met."

"Yet he let Norden name all his departments with underlying sexual connotations?"

Kalt shrugged. "Norden tries to make Lark loosen up.

And Lark allows it to an extent. He has a real soft spot for that selkie."

I can see why, I thought. Norden was the definition of *charm* and *seduction*.

We finished lunch, and Kalt escorted me back to my room for the afternoon. "Why?" I groaned. "I thought you said there was more to do today."

"Oh, there is." He opened my bedroom door, and I inhaled a sharp breath at the desk in the center of the room laden with books and thick documents. "Apologies that this couldn't be loaded onto your ice tablet, but some knowledge is better absorbed the old-fashioned way."

"Um, yeah," I breathed, gaping at the library he'd left on my desk.

"You need to familiarize yourself with holiday magic, Winter Fae customs, and general coronation preparation. It's a big deal around here, so the more information you arm yourself with, the better." He chuckled at my shock. "Close your jaw, Artica."

I clacked my teeth together. "But… but there's so much. You want me to read all of that *today*?"

"Pace yourself. You have a week until I return for the coronation." He gently pressed his palm against the small of my back to nudge me into my room.

A week… until he returns?

"Wait. Where are you going?" Why was he leaving me here by myself? I wasn't ready for that. And… and I thought we would be doing this… together.

"I need to head over to Greenland to check on the Interrealm Fae Academy that Queen Claire has commissioned," he said. "And there are a few other Interrealm Fae relations that need my attention as well."

Except a muscle in his jaw ticked as if something was

upsetting him. I almost asked about it, but he wasn't done speaking.

"Typically, the coronation is only attended by Winter Fae and Arctic supernaturals, but Queen Claire thought this might be a good opportunity to bring some other fae into the mix as a good-faith step for the Winter Fae integration."

"And you're only inviting them now?" I asked, stunned.

He shook his head. "No. Just smoothing over some concerns. Thankfully, Lark is all for the diversity at his coronation, but there are other fae who are, well, hesitant." He nodded at my desk. "You take care of your side of things, and I'll take care of mine."

"Okay," I said slowly. "Um, what about the meeting with Prince Lark?"

"Norden will arrange it."

"And... I'll attend alone?" I asked, my heart hammering in my chest.

"You already believe in him," Kalt replied, his lips tilting up into a weak smile. "You'll be fine."

I blinked at him. "You're trusting me, the clumsy new intern, to meet Prince Lark... *alone?*" I couldn't help repeating that. I mean, was he nuts?

"You'll be fine," he said again. "Trust me." He reached for my arm, giving it a reassuring squeeze as his gaze fell to the snowflake pendant glittering against my skin. He stared at it for a moment as if expecting it to change. "If you need me, just wish for me and I'll be here for you."

I wasn't sure what to make of that, so I nodded.

Seemingly satisfied, he backed out of the room and shut the door.

Staring at the empty space he'd just occupied, I rubbed my arm, missing his touch already.

Well, if I only had a week, I probably should start

reading. Because there were a heck of a lot of books on my desk. And I really did want to be prepared for this coronation.

I tentatively approached the desk.

Snowflakes. These books were thick. *When did Kalt have these delivered, anyway?* Probably by an elf.

Sighing, I resigned myself to my task, shuffling through the books and finding a wrapped present among the items. A sugar crystal glittered like ice inside of it, the candy almost too beautiful to eat.

Smiling, I set it to the side.

I'd admire it for now and enjoy the treat later.

Thank you, Kalt, I thought, smiling. *Maybe I can enjoy you when you return, too.*

NORDEN

"So, did you manage to undo your mating link?" I asked as Kalt exited the palace gates.

I'd been following him and Artica around all morning, causally observing their tour and sensing his magic running all over her curvy little figure.

That moan she'd released while enjoying my favorite treat had almost lured me out of the shadows. I'd wanted to feel that sound against my cock.

But I could be patient.

For now.

Kalt froze, the hairs along his neck standing on end as he found me leaning against the icy posts of the exterior gates. "I thought I felt you earlier."

"Oh?" I pushed off the pole behind me. "You *sensed* my presence, did you?"

"Not like that."

"*Exactly* like that," I corrected. "Because you're part of our triad."

"Stop, Norden. I'm not in the mood."

"My sweet, frosty darling, you're never in the mood," I murmured, sauntering toward him. "That's part of the problem. You refuse to indulge in the festivities of this place. Including the absolute joy Prince Lark and I could show you between the sheets."

Kalt sighed, the sound filled with pain and longing and calling to my selkie soul to soothe him. Because he was mine to placate. Mine to indulge. Mine to make feel better than life itself.

Yet he denied me at every turn.

Prince Lark, too.

And I was over this show of self-inflicted torment.

"You're conflicted on your beliefs," I told him. "That's why you couldn't break that bond with her. Part of you wants to sacrifice yourself for the greater good, while your soul knows your heart's true desire. You're meant to be here, Kalt. With us. With *her*."

His teeth ground together. "I mean it, Norden. I'm not in the mood for this today."

"Because you failed to break a bond that your soul wants more than air itself," I replied, unbothered by the icy glint in his alluring gaze.

He could punch me, hurt me, do whatever he needed to do. I'd allow it for him. Be the one to carry his bruises if that was what he required to free his heart and soul.

"You don't know anything about Elemental Fae bonds," he told me. "Or how hard it can be to break a mating connection when the other party fancies herself in love." He sounded frustrated, which only made me smile.

"So our mate is stubborn," I said, amused. "Good. Prince Lark will like that."

"She's not *our* mate."

"Well, no, not yet. She's only yours. But we'll share soon."

He muttered a few unflattering words, most of them human in nature. "I'm not joining your triad."

"I think you fail to understand that you're already part of it," I told him. "You're just struggling to believe in your destiny, is all. Which is fine. Lark is patient. But it sounds like our Artica is not patient at all, and that delights me to no end. Do you think she would invite me into her bed right now? Show me how far that stubbornness goes?"

Kalt stepped forward, his gaze radiating violence. "Give her space, Norden. She's still learning."

"If you're so concerned about her *learning*, then why are you leaving?"

"How do you know I'm leaving?" he countered. "And how do you even know about the bond?"

"We're connected through magic," I told him. "I can sense everything about you, especially when it relates to sensual energy. And I know you're leaving because you don't know what else to do, since our mate is proving to be *stubborn*, as you say."

He pinched the bridge of his nose, releasing a sigh I felt all the way to my soul.

I could go easy on him.

I could offer to let him flee, to run and hide from his heart, but then I wouldn't be the right mate for him. He needed the coaxing, the pushing, the blunt *truth*.

Lark gave him room to breathe.

I did not.

Because Kalt needed to know that I believed in him, in us, in this triad and our future. There was more than enough belief inside me to carry into him, to bolster our connection, if he would only open himself to it.

I stepped forward, our chests touching as I gripped the back of his nape.

He didn't move, didn't even breathe, his gaze finding

and holding mine in a secret battle of wills. "You belong here, Kalt. With us."

"I don't."

"You do," I stressed, my grip tightening. "And Artica belongs here, too."

He continued to stare deep into my eyes, his soul begging me to push him just a little further, to make him understand, to *feel*.

"Watch her for me," he whispered. "Protect her while I'm gone. I'll be back in a week."

I frowned. "Kalt—"

He misted out of my grasp, disappearing into thin air via his mystical water abilities.

I growled, irritated by his slippery move.

There had to be chains somewhere that could hold a Water Fae in place. I'd have to find them and use them on him. Tie him to a bed, suck him off until he finally caved to the sensual embrace of our triad.

Maybe I'd enlist Artica's help as well.

Surely she'd enjoy morphing his version of torture into something more pleasurable.

Sighing, I wandered back into the palace, heading for Lark first. He would have felt Kalt leave, but he might not know about the bond between him and Artica yet. So I'd tell him and ask him when he'd like to meet her. Hopefully soon.

Then I'd go *watch* Artica for Kalt.

A task I would very much enjoy indeed.

Maybe I'd coax her to dream...

ARTICA

I woke up with a start, a spike of pain shooting down my neck at my awkward sleeping position.

At some point, I'd fallen asleep while reading at the desk.

And then I'd dreamt of Kalt, which wasn't surprising. But I'd chained him to a bed and tortured him with my tongue until the sexy selkie told me it was okay to let him come.

I'd swallowed with a moan.

Only to be jolted awake by this rude agony at my nape.

"Ugh," I complained, forcing my body to uncurl and sit upright. I'd skipped dinner last night, too caught up in all the texts. But the sugary confection had been a nice delight.

I was hungry now, though.

What time is it? I wondered, glancing at the windows automatically, only to realize it was still just as sunny as whenever I'd fallen into the erotic dreamland. However, there was a note sitting on the windowsill, one that hadn't been there before.

I frowned at it, then stood up to retrieve it.

My name was etched onto the exterior in a perfect cursive script. More words in the same penmanship waited for me inside.

Prince Lark wants to meet you after breakfast. Don't be late. — N.

I glanced at the clock and cursed. It was definitely after breakfast time, which meant that I was late for my meeting with the Winter Fae Prince.

Good thing I'd showered last night.

"Blizzard," I muttered, finger-combing my wavy strands—which would so not impress the selkie—grabbed a cute long-sleeved blue dress from the closet, and paired it with a fuzzy set of boots that went all the way up to my knees.

Glancing in the mirror, I decided it would have to do and took off into the hallway.

Only to pause upon realizing that I had no idea *where* to meet the prince.

This is why you shouldn't have left me here alone, I thought at Kalt. *I'm already screwing up, and I haven't even met the prince yet!*

"Icicles!" I cursed as I combed my fingers through my hair again and hurried down the stairs toward the common areas of the palace.

Scanning the grand halls, I searched for anyone who could help me.

"Excuse me!" I shouted at a miniature elf who scampered with a pile of toys in his grip. "I just... oh!"

He tripped when I startled him, and the toys scattered all over the ornate gold-and-silver rug. The little elf groaned and began picking them up. "Freaking fae always causin' a mess," he grumbled.

Wincing, I helped him collect the trinkets from the rug, placing a broken one underneath the pile with the hope that he wouldn't notice.

He glared at me.

"I, um. Which way do I go to see the prince? Prince Lark, I mean. I'm, uh, supposed to meet him." *Very eloquent, Artica.*

I again cursed Kalt for leaving me *alone* to meet the future King of the Winter Fae.

The miniature elf looked like he wanted to slit my throat. "You could try the palace throne room."

Right. Palace.

"Sure…" I ventured, glancing back down the halls to where Kalt had shown me around. I really should have paid better attention. "I mean, the palace, yeah. I just… aren't we in the palace?"

"You're very observant," the elf deadpanned.

I blinked at him. "Okay, well, um, where is the throne room?"

"Try the center of the palace," he suggested. "Look for the big chair, otherwise known as a throne. You know what that is, right?" He glanced at a chair along the wall. "Like that, but much bigger. Grander. Probably has Prince Lark sitting on it, too."

I nervously chuckled as I backed away. "Yeah! Got it, thanks!" *Middle of the palace. Cool.*

Except… that was the cafeteria.

But this must be some sort of guest wing.

Right. Okay.

I wandered toward the working area Kalt had shown me yesterday, then up and around, searching for the "center" of the grounds, and finally found a giant crystal dome glittering with light.

That, I thought. *That has to be it.*

It was sparkling in the sunlight, beckoning me forward.

I practically ran for it, then froze as a pair of gingerbread sentries stepped into my path near the front doors.

I couldn't really tell if they were looking at me or not because their eyes were made of candy.

"Um, I'm here to see the prince," I said weakly.

One thumped his staff and the door opened. "He's waiting."

Tucking my chin to my chest, I murmured my thanks and hurried inside.

The inside of the palace took my breath away, but I didn't have time to appreciate the snowflake chandeliers or candy cane walls with gumdrops. I rushed straight through the various gingerbread men guarding doors until I reached the center of the palace—which really felt more like the end since it was soooo long.

A gingerbread man opened a final massive door, and I ran full speed inside.

Then froze as I spotted the Winter Fae sitting on the massive throne inside. His athletic thighs were parted, the male leaning forward with one arm resting on his knee as he spoke to an elf beside him.

Then his gaze lifted to mine.

And I forgot how to breathe.

He wore a silver tux, the fabric practically molded to his muscular form, and had long, flowing blond hair that resembled waves of white gold around his wide shoulders.

And his face.

Oh. My. Fae.

His face was the most gorgeous display of masculinity

and grace that I'd ever seen. And that included Norden and Kalt.

This fae was like a bigger, badder version of Kalt. Tall and corded with predatory muscle that lurked beneath silk fabric, he commanded attention and obedience.

The power that emanated from him made me swallow the thick lump in my throat.

The sentries announced me, and Norden burst into the room a moment later, grinning at me. "Ah, finally. I do love a fashionably late entrance, don't you, my prince?"

Prince Lark ignored Norden as he continued to stare at me. He leaned forward a bit more, then beckoned me to come closer. "Let me get a better look at you, Water Fae. Norden tells me you're to be a... *candidate*."

No formalities.

No hellos.

Just an *I want to see you.*

Would he ask me to strip next?

Would I say no?

Because I really doubted I could. Not with his mint-green eyes taking my measure in a sensual manner that lit my soul on fire.

I tried to move forward, to follow his command, but the hungry glimmer in Prince Lark's gaze held me captive.

Norden seemed like good fun, but the prince? Yeah. He was as terrifying as he was sexy.

The selkie must have taken it upon himself to assist me, because he strode up to my side and pressed a palm to the small of my back, not being shy about gliding his hand up to curl a lock of my hair around his finger. He grinned at me. "There's nothing to be nervous about, Artica. You're safe with us."

Somehow I doubted his definition of *safe* matched my own.

Approaching the throne, I decided that if I was going to be playing this game, then I was going to make my terms clear.

And since we were obviously avoiding formalities, I would jump straight to the point.

"I'm not sure how you do things in the North Pole"— not exactly true since I'd spent most of yesterday and the night before reading all about it. However, they didn't need to know that—"but in my realm, mate-bonds are mutually decided after a courtship period."

I glanced at Norden, my skin heating at his proximity. His damp hair suggested he'd just finished with a swim, the strands shimmering with salty chocolate that fell around his shoulders in waves.

I wanted to touch him again.

But… but not until I made myself heard here.

I cleared my throat. "So, I'm not opposed to exploring this *candidacy*, but I just want to make my intentions known. I'm here as Kalt's intern, and my priority is to Interrealm Fae relations. However, I'll… I'm okay with, uh, *this.*"

Way to end on a confident note, Artica. Really well done.

But Norden had tightened his grip on my curl, giving it a little tug that inspired heat to pool between my legs.

So. I'd been a bit distracted by my desire to remain standing instead of ending up in a pool of need on the floor.

How did one tug evoke such a strong sensation? I marveled, glancing at the mischievous selkie.

Norden smiled, and I nearly fainted at the sight of it.

I made the mistake of shifting my focus to the prince, hoping his terrifying presence would set me straight.

But no.

He'd tilted his head, his own lips curling a little at the edges as amusement shimmered in his gaze.

I am going to melt into a puddle of Artica goo. It's just my fate. I should accept it now and kneel and let it all happen. Yep.

"Hmm," Prince Lark hummed, the deep tenor of his voice reverberating across my skin. "I can see why the baubles chose you. All business, yet with a flavor of festivity that I can almost taste on my tongue."

Norden brightened. "Is that a yes, then?"

"A yes to… what?" I asked. "The candidacy?"

"No." Prince Lark leaned back in his throne, confusing me greatly. "It's a *yes* to keeping you."

Uh, excuse me?

"Um, no," I said without hesitation, sending Norden's delight into shock. "I agree to be courted, but you can't just *keep* me. I'm not an ornament for a tree or a stocking for your fireplace." Two items Queen Claire had educated me about for the human holidays. "My name is Artica and I'm a fae with feelings, and I make my own decisions, thank you very much."

There. That was much more eloquent than before.

Yet the Winter Fae Prince's resulting smile appeared more indulgent than anything else. "It's adorable that you Water Fae think you have a choice."

Shaking off Norden's hand that had still been twirling in my hair, I felt the anger in my chest rise. I'd been questioning Kalt about his resistance to joining the prince's triad, but if *this* was what he was like, I was starting to understand his hesitation.

"We *do* have a choice, you… you *overgrown elf*." Norden choked, and Lark's mint-green eyes flashed with interest. "Elemental Fae have four levels of bonding, all of which require *mutual consent*. Maybe that's a new term for you, what with being a prince and all, but you should look it up. Because I only agree to be courted, and so far, you're not impressing me."

His eyebrows lifted. "I'm a future king."

"Is that supposed to sway me?" I deadpanned, folding my arms. "I worked for Queen Claire. I've been surrounded by royalty for years. Next attribute, please. Because so far, I have arrogant, possessive, and rude, which are not points in your favor."

His lips parted. "You call me rude? Yet you're the one in *my* throne room throwing insults at *me*. As a visiting emissary, I might add."

"As a candidate you claim to want to keep," I corrected him, entirely unamused and unimpressed by His Royal Majesty's approach. "I'm not interested in the position."

A complete lie. A romantic part of me was absolutely interested. But not if he was going to treat me like property.

His green eyes narrowed. "Don't be stubborn like Kalt."

"He's not being stubborn. He's probably just refusing to be your toy," I said. "As am I."

"I don't want to make you a toy, sweetheart. I want to make you my queen," he replied. "And I will."

"Keep telling yourself that," I muttered, not willing to be wooed by a fancy title.

"The harder you make me work, the more I'll want you."

"Then be prepared to work really hard," I told him. "Because I'm very much not interested right now."

His lips curled. "You're absolutely perfect."

"The feeling isn't mutual," I said, choosing my words on purpose.

"It will be," he promised.

"If you say so."

Norden sighed. "It's going to be a long week."

I arched a brow. "You think he's going to convince me

to like him in a week?" I laughed without humor. "That's not going to happen." I looked back at *His Highness*. "Now, if you'll excuse me, I have a lot of important reading to do."

With that, I spun on my heel and marched out of the room.

I was probably the worst Interrealm Fae intern to have ever existed, but at that moment, I really didn't care.

Prince Lark could eat a dirty block of ice.

It didn't matter that my Elemental soul felt the instant compatibility with him. He was a rude ice pick. And I did not want to be mated to an arrogant snowflake.

This had to be the real reason Kalt had refused them.

Or perhaps it was the reason that had made it easier for him to deny them.

Regardless, I fully understood the situation now. And I had no interest in being a candidate. So I'd focus on my internship instead.

LARK

Artica's hair reminded me of a snowdrift as it cascaded over her shoulders to the middle of her back. So pretty and light, the kind of texture that begged to be stroked.

I understood now why Norden had not only selected her but also indulged in a hair exchange.

"She's delightful," I murmured, my heart soaring with an excitement I'd very much missed over these last few weeks. "Shall we invite her to dinner?"

Norden stared at me. "I'm pretty sure she'd rather pelt you with a dozen snowballs, *Your Highness*."

I frowned. He only called me that when I struck a nerve, which was a hard feat to accomplish with Norden, as he usually could care less about my moody behavior. "Why are you displeased with me?"

"Because you just made the same mistake with her as you did with Kalt," he bit back, the anger uncharacteristic for my selkie mate.

I glanced around the room, noting the grimaces coming from my elves. "Leave us," I commanded.

They were quick to disappear as though relieved to be out of my presence.

Which meant I was about to hear an earful from my mate.

"The Elemental Fae are all about mutual consent," Norden said as the door closed behind the final elf. "And you just told Artica we're keeping her."

"Because you told me you wanted to keep her just yesterday," I reminded him. "And I was agreeing."

"Yes, I said that to you, but not to *her*."

"I fail to understand the difference." Weren't relationships founded on honesty?

"We have to woo her, Lark. We can't just demand she join us without giving her a reason to kneel." He stepped toward me, his hands in the pockets of his pants— something he very rarely wore in my presence but obviously felt inclined to do so today. Probably because we were in the throne room about to meet our future queen.

"I'm a king. That should be reason enough to kneel," I pointed out. "It worked on you."

He smiled. "Because I've known you most of my life and knew from a young age that we were destined to be together. Artica just met you for the first time, and you didn't so much as greet her properly before stating you were keeping her. That's not how her kind work. They need romance. They need seduction. They need to know that they are *loved*."

My lips curled down once more. "I barely know her. I can't love her yet."

"And that's precisely why she just rejected you, my prince." He pitched his voice low, his sensuality caressing each word. "She needs time to accept you, to accept *us*, just like Kalt."

"But I could feel the belief pouring off of her. She practically radiates joy and holiday cheer. How could she deny our triad?"

"Well, for one, it's not complete yet," he reminded me gently. "And from what I've seen, her heart very much belongs to Kalt right now. So that's holding her back. Secondly, she's not from your kingdom. She has her own expectations when it comes to mating. You're going to have to prove yourself worthy of her."

"To win the belief in her heart," I translated, sighing. Something I had known in theory, but the reality of claiming a mate from one of the other faedoms was proving more challenging than I'd anticipated.

However, given the history between my parents, I should have at least expected it.

The belief from Artica was there. I felt it as true as my own heartbeat.

Yet, my selkie had a point. His kind was well versed in seduction and courtship. Two items I'd so far been failing at quite miserably.

"Precisely," he murmured in response to my statement.

However, his confirmation rang true with my thoughts as well.

Norden climbed the stairs to where I sat at the top, not stopping until his legs touched mine. Then he leaned forward, his palms grasping the arms of my throne as he met my gaze straight on.

"We have to seduce her, my prince. Make her feel worthy of a queenship. Ensure she understands how thoroughly we'll worship at her feet. Show her what it means to be a Winter Fae Queen."

"I don't even know where to start," I admitted. "I've only just met her."

Which made it insane that I felt this need to claim her, but my soul had sensed the pull toward her almost immediately.

Whether she realized it or not, I had been searching for her for two years. A complete triad made it easier to locate the female, but I'd come of age around my thirtieth birthday. And I'd been seeking all of my mates ever since.

Norden had been easy.

Kalt, not so much.

And it seemed Artica would be just as difficult.

However, she was meant to be mine. To be *ours*. Kalt had proved that by finding her. And Norden had confirmed it when he'd picked her.

Which meant my triad was finally here.

I just had to find a way to convince them all to believe in me, to believe in the power our mate-circle could achieve.

And I'd apparently screwed up my introduction to our future queen.

"Leave it with me," Norden murmured. "Wooing is what we selkies do best."

"I want to be involved," I said, catching his wrist. "She needs to know I want her, too. And not as property." The words tasted bitter on my tongue. "I didn't mean to imply that." They were soft, vulnerable words. Ones I would probably only whisper to him, my confidant.

A king shouldn't make mistakes.

However, owning those mistakes was what made a royal a true leader, something I'd learned early on in my upbringing.

It's not the mistakes you make, but how you fix them, my father had once said. *And how you grow from them, too.*

"I know you didn't, my prince," Norden replied, his silky tone wrapping around me in a soothing embrace. "You were just excited to finally meet our future."

"She's perfect," I told him. I barely knew her, and yet, I could sense the truth of that statement all the way to my soul. She was cheerful, at least until I'd pissed her off. But then fierce, the way a queen should be, and passionate about her beliefs.

That last part was what had sealed the deal.

She would be our queen.

"Tell me what to do, Norden. Tell me how to fix this."

He smiled. "Let's start by sending her some more selkie candy…"

NORDEN

I'd given Artica two days of space while I'd kept an eye on her from the shadows. An easy feat, considering she'd rarely left her room other than to eat and to take the occasional stroll outside.

She'd appeared determined each time I'd seen her. But she'd barely smiled. And I very much disliked that. Her cheer and happiness were what had drawn me to her immediately.

I wanted my queen to smile.

Did she miss Kalt? Was that what had darkened her joyful aura?

Or was she upset about Lark?

Maybe even about me?

I should have stepped forward and said something the other day. But I'd been too shocked by her outright denial and strong statements.

Then Lark had worsened it with his amusement.

He wasn't an asshole. Not intentionally, anyway.

After the failed meeting, he'd sent an apology note with

a box of selkie candies, just like I'd recommended. Artica hadn't thrown either item away, something we'd both taken as a good sign.

So Lark had followed it up with a bouquet of ice lilies for her bedroom the next morning.

A peek in Artica's window had shown them to be sitting on her desk beside her books.

Another good sign.

He'd sent her dinner that evening, a plate filled with our favorite foods, and a mug of spritemead—something we knew Elemental Fae enjoyed, thanks to Kalt.

She'd eaten all of it, including the piece of selkie candy I'd added to the tray.

This morning, Lark had sent her a dress with a card saying the snowflake design reminded him of her affinity for water.

She'd worn it, and the boots I'd sent with the dress, to breakfast.

But she still hadn't appeared all that joyful, eating her food and returning to her room almost immediately to continue reading all the books Kalt had given her.

"We should try inviting her out tonight," I decided out loud, having spent the last few minutes pacing Lark's bedroom. "Take her to see the penguins, perhaps?"

The prince lifted his gaze from his coronation papers, his brow furrowing. "Are you going to eat one?"

I snorted. "Selkies don't eat penguins."

"Then what purpose would it serve? It won't prove our strength as a triad."

"Not all things in life are about power and strength, my prince," I reminded him gently. "This is about romance. And penguins mate for life. What better way to demonstrate our intentions than to introduce her to the tiny beings who understand fate at first sight?"

He considered me for a moment, then nodded. "This is a sound idea."

"Of course it is. I thought of it." I smiled. "Now, we should prepare a basket for a picnic, too."

"We should make her hot chocolate," Lark suggested. "From my personal stash."

His personal assistant, Holly, lifted her head at that, her eyes rounding.

Because Lark agreeing to give someone a taste of the hot chocolate from his personal stash was unheard of. He didn't even let me touch his hot chocolate.

Well, unless he wanted me to lick it off his skin.

Then, yes, he gave me a taste. Followed by his own version of whipped cream.

I cleared my throat. "Uh, yes, I think Artica would love that."

He nodded. "And maybe we can have something brought in from her kingdom. Some sort of dish she might be missing, perhaps. I imagine all the sweets are a bit much for one from another realm."

"I'll ask Kalt for advice." It would give me a reason to check up on him.

Lark smiled. "Yes. Please do. Invite him as well."

"I will." It wouldn't work, but persistence was key. "I'll send Artica appropriate clothes with a note to request her presence this evening. Unless you'd like to write it yourself?"

"Why don't we each write one, so she knows we both intend to be there. It should be obvious, but I'd like to not make the same mistake twice, and ensure she understands our intent this time," he said, proving that a prince really could learn how to woo when prompted.

"Excellent idea," I murmured.

Holly handed Lark a pen and paper, her lips curling up

into a sweet smile. "Tell her you miss her, my prince. Or say you want the opportunity to watch the sun playing in her hair."

He grinned. "I'll think of my own words, but thank you, Holly."

Her eyes sparkled, the elf clearly enthused by the notion of us courting our intended queen.

Well, it was a sentiment we shared.

As I very much wanted to impress Artica.

I just had to find the right thing to say, then I'd call Kalt for dinner advice.

ARTICA

I stared at the two notes on my desk, my lips twisting to the side. I had exactly five minutes left to decide what I wanted to do.

Dearest Artica,

Will you do us the honor of joining us on an outside adventure this evening? Norden loves to watch the penguins play, and he knows the perfect spot to observe them. We can show you their natural habitat and discuss your courtship.

Because you were right.

I handled our introduction poorly and would like a chance to make it up to you. If you'll allow it, then please meet us by the palace entrance at six o'clock.

Sincerely,
Prince Lark

The Winter Fae Royal seal was beneath it—a pair of candy canes crossed over a snowflake. And the other note was much shorter and to the point.

Sunshine,

Please come out and play. I promise to feed you well.

Yours,
N.

He'd paired the letter with a salted caramel brownie—a delicious variant of the chocolate candy—and a box of clothes.

Clothes that I'd already donned.

A pink turtleneck and a blue skirt that flared out around my knees.

Navy tights.

Ankle boots.

And a matching snow hat with a fluffy ball on top.

It was an adorable outfit that fit me perfectly. Just like this morning's dress.

I nibbled my lower lip.

What would it hurt to go? I was the Interrealm Fae intern. It wouldn't be kind of me to refuse them.

And they had asked nicely.

Norden had also promised to feed me, and I was tired of eating alone.

So…

I shrugged.

Prince Lark had certainly come off as an arrogant snowflake, but his apology the other day had been appreciated. I'd also liked the candies he'd sent with it. As well as his letter this afternoon.

And Norden, well, I wouldn't mind seeing him again. He'd been rather nice during our first meeting. I didn't want to hold his mating choice against him.

Assuming he'd even had a say in the decision.

Maybe Prince Lark had "kept" him, too.

I'd have to ask Norden about it later.

With a final glance in the mirror, I headed out of my room, down the hall to the stairs, and out the side door of the palace. I'd only been through the front gates once before, so they would be easier to find from the outside as a result.

Fortunately, it wasn't difficult.

Particularly as a handsome Winter Fae Prince and a sexy selkie waited just in front of them.

Several elves stood around them, chittering away. One was particularly loud, asking if Prince Lark could do something about the arctic foxes stealing his cherry canes.

"They're everywhere, Your Highness. I need an enchantment that will keep them off my canes."

"Would you be willing to plant two gardens?" Prince Lark asked, his mint-green gaze finding mine briefly and smiling upon seeing me. But rather than greet me, he returned his focus to the stocky elf at his side.

"Two gardens, my prince?" he repeated.

Prince Lark nodded. "Yes, one that I could enchant for you and one to continue feeding the arctic foxes."

The elf's brow furrowed. "If that's what you desire, then yes."

"I want everyone fed," Prince Lark replied. "So I think this would be a fair offering. I'll protect your canes so long as the foxes still have a few to munch on as well."

The elf considered it for a moment, then nodded. "All right, my prince. I will start working on a second garden tomorrow."

"And I'll be by to help you enchant it soon after," he promised.

"Thank you, my prince." The elf bowed low.

"You're welcome, Eski," he replied.

Norden slid up to my side during the exchange, his fingers playing with the end of my braid—something I'd decided on today, as I was missing the Water Fae back home. Braids were very common among my kind of Elemental Fae. No real reason why—we just enjoyed the wavy texture after releasing the long strands of hair afterward.

Besides, the braid also looked good with my new hat.

"This is very lovely," Norden murmured, his fingers teasing the braid where it met my spine. "As are you, Sunshine."

My lips curled. "Thank you."

"No, no. Thank you for coming," he whispered against my ear as Prince Lark excused himself from the other elves. They all glanced at me with keen interest before chittering among themselves and wandering off with enchanting grins decorating their faces.

"Hello, Artica," Prince Lark greeted formally, giving me a little bow. "It's a pleasure to see you again."

Is it? I nearly asked. But I decided to play nice. I was an intern for fae relations, after all. Being rude would definitely confirm my status as the worst intern ever.

So I smiled instead. "Hello, Prince Lark." I gave a little curtsy, something I would have done the other day had he not treated me like an object to be claimed. "That was very nice of you to think about the arctic foxes."

He blinked, his brow furrowing. "It was?"

"Yes. You made sure they maintained their food source."

"Well, of course. This was their land first. We have to

coexist with them, not take it from them," he replied, his words wise and honorable and pulling a genuine grin from my lips.

Because I rather liked the way he'd said that.

"Elemental Fae feel very strongly about equality in our realm," I informed him. "We treat all life with equal respect."

His white-blond hair flirted with his broad shoulders as he dipped his chin in a nod. "Yes, it's my understanding that your kind isn't a fan of human cuisine because it's heavy on animal meat."

My nose crinkled. "It's not my favorite, no." So I really hoped that wasn't on the menu for tonight. The sweets I could handle. But some of the human specialties? No.

"It's not my favorite either," he confided softly, his expression almost sheepish. "Sometimes I'm forced to eat it when someone brings it as a gift, but I much prefer our version of sweet confections and pies and—"

"Hot chocolate," Norden interjected, his arm brushing mine as he finally released my braid. "Which will become cold if we don't enjoy it soon, my prince."

"Yes, right," Lark replied, not at all irritated at the interruption. Instead, he flashed his mate a thankful grin and turned to retrieve two large hiking backpacks from the snow. Norden wandered over to take one from his hands, slinging it over his shoulder as though it weighed nothing.

It was then that I realized they were both dressed in casual attire of sweaters, jeans, and boots. Lark's sweater was a silvery white that matched his hair, while Norden wore a black turtleneck that complemented the sun-kissed tones of his skin.

I rather liked the look on both of them, the winter vibe sexy and accenting their musculatures.

Of course, Norden naked was absolutely preferred.

But that would probably distract me far too much on this outing, so I was thankful for his clothing choice.

He winked at me, making me wonder if he could read my mind. Or maybe my mouth had gaped open again.

Either way, I swallowed and gave him a tentative smile. "So, um, where are we going?" Lark's note had mentioned penguins—an animal I'd yet to see outside my window.

Although, I had spotted some from a distance decorating the ice when I'd first arrived. I was curious as to what they looked like up close.

"Not too far," Norden promised. "But if you get tired, we can carry you."

I frowned. "I don't tire easily, and my body is literally built for this element."

His lips curled. "That sounds like a blatant invitation, Sunshine. One I will happily explore after we eat."

My cheeks heated. "That's not—"

"It's about half a mile up the shore," Lark said softly, his green eyes glittering with amusement. "The penguins tend to stay away from the fae and the elves."

"But not the selkies," Norden commented, looking pointedly at Lark. "Because we don't eat them."

I gasped. "Winter Fae and elves eat penguins?!"

Lark sighed. "No. We don't. He's teasing me for something I said earlier."

"He thought I intended to eat one to impress you," Norden replied as he led the way out of the gate.

"That would not impress me," I informed them both as I followed him. "I would… I would…"

"Scream?" Norden supplied.

"Among other things," I muttered.

"The only place I intend to make you scream is in the bedroom, Sunshine." He flashed me a sensual grin. "And I promise they will only be screams of delight."

My skin prickled with warmth, his teasing more blatant than anything I'd ever experienced before in my life. Elemental Fae could be very direct, but Norden played on a level very few fae could ever aspire to reach. Sensuality practically poured off him, wrapping around me and urging me to invite him back to my room so he could demonstrate his promise.

But my feet fortunately listened to reason, carrying me forward rather than backward.

His brown eyes crinkled at the sides, knowledge shining in their chocolate depths.

He knew his prowess.

And he wasn't afraid to use it.

Kalt had been right—when selkies courted their mates, they were aggressive. Just not in a physical sense so much as a sexual one. And not by forcing it either.

No, they were masters at seduction.

"I haven't seen many selkies around the palace," I said, swallowing. "Are they common here?"

"Yes. But most choose to live near the water on ice rather than on land. It's why Lark keeps a pool for me in his suite, so I can swim whenever I want." He flashed the prince a loving glance.

Lark smiled in return. "He thanks me by walking around naked all day. Can't say I'm sorry for my gift."

My skin warmed at the thought of these two in bed.

Something that very clearly happened often by the looks they were passing back and forth.

Talk about erotic, I thought, my heart skipping a beat. *These two have to be dynamite in bed.*

And they want me to join them.

I shivered, the notion appealing to me more and more with each passing step.

Except for the whole ownership thing.

But Lark was definitely showing a much more charming side of himself today. His arrogance seemed to have taken a back seat to his nurturing side, something he'd demonstrated with his elf and the protective way he walked alongside me now.

Perhaps the selkie had talked some sense into him, which only confirmed why a triad was important, and being a part of it would help Prince Lark grow in all the right ways.

I certainly found myself wanting to help Prince Lark *grow*, too. Just maybe not in the same way. Or in an additional manner, anyway.

Shaking my head, I tried to rid myself of the sensual thoughts and instead focused on my footing as the ground jutted with lumps of ice.

The prince kept his hands loose at his sides as though ready to grab me on a second's notice. Maybe because we were walking so close to the icy edge of the water.

"Does your skin naturally acclimate to the weather here?" I asked, curious as to how he shielded himself from the climate. I hadn't read up on that part of Winter Fae culture yet.

"My magic protects me," he replied, his tone soft yet somehow authoritative. The voice of a king. "Similar to how yours is protecting you."

"You can sense that?" I asked, surprised.

"Your elemental gift calls to me." His minty irises met mine before fixing once more on the path ahead. "Just like Kalt's speaks to me, too."

"Is that normal?" I wondered out loud. "Do you sense the gifts of all Water Fae?"

He shook his head. "No. I met King Cyrus once, and his gift didn't appeal to me at all, yet he's supposedly the most powerful Water Fae."

"Not 'supposedly,' he *is* the most powerful of my kind."

"Well, he didn't call to me. Not like you and Kalt do."

He lifted a shoulder. "It's part of our mating link and why I know our destinies are intertwined."

That certainly sounded a bit better than his whole *you don't have a choice; you're mine* talk from the other day. However, both statements held the same meaning. One was just a lot more romantic than the other.

We wandered in silence a bit more, only pausing as a pair of seals broke the surface to bark at Norden.

He waved in response, his lips pulling upward.

"Friends of yours?" I guessed.

"Brothers," he replied. "They're giving me shit for wearing clothes."

I laughed. "They don't like clothes?"

"Selkies prefer skin or fur, nothing else," he confirmed. "But I thought you might be more comfortable if I wore appropriate attire for our date."

"He's lying. I made him wear clothes," Lark said.

Norden just grinned unapologetically back at us.

"You're wearing clothes to the coronation, too," Lark added.

Norden's grin grew into a challenging smile. "Only if Artica agrees to wear a tiara."

"A tiara?" I repeated, my lips parting. "Why would—"

A splashing sound cut me off, drawing my attention to an adorable little penguin in a tuxedo.

Not a literal tuxedo.

He just appeared to be wearing one with his black coat and white accents.

"Oh my Fae, it's adorable," I cooed, freezing midstep as he shook the water off his coat.

Norden grinned. "That one is a flirt. I should have known he'd be the first to greet you. I call him Tux."

"Well, hello, Tux," I said, squatting down to see him. "I'm Artica. It's a pleasure to meet you."

The penguin cocked its head a little, then waddled toward me to bump me with his beak. I giggled, floored by his attention. "I had no idea penguins were so friendly." I'd never met one before, so I really hadn't known what to expect. But the two arctic foxes I'd seen earlier hadn't been all that inclined to let me pet them this morning after breakfast.

"They're usually not," Lark replied, joining me in my squatting position. "But the water here is enchanted. And it's the one place on Earth they are absolutely safe from humans because no one knows they exist."

"That's why the selkies all hang out here, too," Norden added. "Humans can be cruel to water creatures."

"They're not known for being kind to their elements either," I murmured, smiling as the penguin butted me again. I gave his head a little scratch, and he released a soft clicking sound in response. "But what do you mean the water is enchanted?"

"The natural climate is too cold for water to form," Lark explained, his gaze shifting to a second penguin waddling over. This one was a bit more plump and moving slower. "So humans have no idea that these penguins live up here. They think they're all in the Southern Hemisphere."

"Applies to a lot of seals, too," Norden replied as another pair of penguins approached him. "No, I did not bring you fish today. But I'll help you catch a few later."

The penguins made a strange sort of calling sound back at him, one I'd never heard before. Sort of like a bird's caw but mixed with a vibrating undertone. Unique and beautiful. I wanted to hear it again.

"We protect a lot of species up here." Lark spoke as he

petted the plumper penguin. "So this water is melted by magic and stretches all the way through the Arctic Circle to the Arctic Ocean. But it's enchanted, so all humans see is ice."

"The marine animals can see through the veil," Norden added. "It's how selkies first discovered the Winter Fae."

Lark nodded. "That happened several centuries ago. The selkies have been our allies ever since."

"That's amazing," I whispered, awed by all this information. None of it had been in the texts Kalt had given me.

"If you want to see something truly amazing, then you should follow me up over that snow mound." Norden waggled his brows, then continued in that general direction.

The view of his ass was certainly amazing.

But I suspected that wasn't what he had in mind.

Not entirely, anyway.

So I bid adieu to my new penguin friends and trailed after the selkie.

And when I saw what waited for us on the other side, my jaw dropped.

ARTICA

P enguins.
Everywhere.

All different shapes and sizes, suggesting there was a variety of species that lived here. Some were only a foot tall. Others were closer to knee height.

A group of them waddled up to Norden like he was an old friend or a fellow penguin.

He sat on the ground, his pack beside him, and let the smaller creatures climb all over him. Lark joined him, both males grinning as the penguins chattered away, making those vibrating clucking sounds that I couldn't really define.

Then they looked at me and beckoned me with their eyes.

I joined them easily, loving the way the animals burrowed into our sides and snuggled with us like we were their own personal ice blocks.

"This is probably one of the best moments of my life," I admitted on a laugh as a penguin tugged on my braid.

"These things are adorable!" And Prince Lark's kind protected them, giving them a place to escape and thrive.

Wow, I'd misjudged him entirely.

Well, maybe not entirely.

But there was so much to understand about the Winter Fae and how they interacted with other species. It was no wonder Queen Claire had reached out to them for an alliance. They were caring in nature and beautiful fae beings.

I lay back in the frosty snow, giggling again as a smaller penguin climbed onto my stomach to sit, treating me like some sort of ice bench. Snowflakes stirred in the air between us, created by my magic, only to be swept up in a swirl of wind that danced around the beautiful creature.

My lips parted, startled by the mystical energy.

Then I realized it had come from Prince Lark.

He smiled at me, then used his gift to swirl the snowflakes around several other penguins, caressing their cheeks and beaks along the way.

The enchantment reached all the way to the water, where my snowflake dissolved to join the enchanted stream.

"Beautiful," I breathed.

"Yes," Lark agreed, his gaze on me as he said it.

Norden nudged him. "Hot chocolate."

The prince startled, then quickly grabbed his bag. "It should still be all right. I can use some energy to reheat it if needed."

Norden waggled his brows at me in expectation.

I'd tried the hot chocolate already around here and could admit it was delicious, but Norden's expression suggested there might be more to it than a bit of melted chocolate in milk.

Prince Lark produced a large canister, a bag of candy,

some sort of brown stick, a bunch of fluffy white clouds, and a silver can and then dug around before pulling out three mugs. "Oh," he said, taking out some red-and-white-striped candies. "In case you wanted peppermint in yours."

Norden opened his own pack to pull out a blanket that Lark moved everything onto, including himself. He patted the space next to him for me to join.

I reluctantly sat up again to crawl over to him. A penguin followed, climbing into my lap to watch Prince Lark work. Norden remained on the ice, something I suspected was a preference, as his blanket could easily fit him and another.

"So the trick is to heat the milk first." Lark opened the canister. "Usually over a fire, which I did prior to packing it. But it could use a little boost." He placed his palm over the top, stirring another hint of that delicious energy in the air. After a moment, he nodded, showing me the simmering liquid.

"Chocolate goes in next, but not just any chocolate." He started explaining the ingredients his elves used for his special batch, which included a hint of caramel and butterscotch mingled in with the dark cocoa flakes and other items.

The fluffy clouds, which he called *marshmallows*, were added next. But not all of them. Just enough to melt into the liquid.

His silver canister contained another sort of chocolate mix, this one in powder form. "I blend the spices in myself," he told me proudly.

Norden stretched out beside us on his side, his warm gaze on the canister as Prince Lark started adding more of his special ingredients to it. "He's never shown me any of this before."

I frowned. "He hasn't?"

"No, I haven't," Lark admitted. "It's one of my personal hobbies. Similar to how Norden feels about his hair."

"He's hoping this will convince me to let him pet me," Norden said, waggling his brows suggestively.

"You don't let him touch your hair?"

"Not normally," Norden replied as a penguin started waddling up his long leg to find a spot to nestle in near his hip. "Selkies are very particular about their hair."

"And Winter Fae are private about their favorite treats," Lark added, showing me the brown stick. "Cinnamon. But you don't just put it in; you stir it for exactly twenty stirs before discarding it. Want to do the honors?"

My lips parted. "M-me?" He'd just told me the importance of this drink, and he wanted me to help? What if I fluffed it up? Ruined his *favorite treat.* I swallowed. "Um…"

"I'll help," he offered, holding out his palm toward me. "We can count together."

"O-oh, okay," I stammered.

He wanted to hold my hand.

Yeah, I could… I could allow that.

I moved closer to him and set my palm against his. Electricity hummed between us as our magic mingled across our skin, sending a tremble up my arm.

He felt warm.

Comfortable.

Like a cozy blanket on a chilly day.

I wanted to snuggle into him but focused on the task instead as he slid the cinnamon stick into my grip. He wrapped my fingers around it, securing my grasp, then folded his own hand around mine.

"All right, we want to enter slowly," he said, his voice lower than before and sending a tingle down my spine.

Because that phrase could be taken so many different ways.

Not now, sex-starved self. I need to focus.

But the rumble of his voice as he murmured, "Yes, just like that," did not help cool my libido. It warmed it up that much more.

I swallowed, forcing myself to concentrate on the hot chocolate.

Lark began to count as he moved my fingers in a clockwise motion.

"Nice and slow," he said as we completed our second round.

By the number five, I'd forgotten what numbers meant.

All I could do was feel his magic seeping in through my pores and stroking my soul with a fire I had never experienced before.

And he was barely touching me. Just my hand and the occasional arm brush since we sat close together.

I'm in so much trouble.

How did Kalt deny this triad? The chemistry was absolutely there. Yeah, I didn't know him yet. However, my soul seemed to understand him on an instinctual level. Like I could trust him without thought or provocation.

This male would never hurt me.

Even if he had threatened to *keep* me.

He'd said he wanted me to be his queen. What exactly did that mean to him?

"Twenty," he whispered, drawing me from my thoughts. "Very good, Artica." He guided my hand upward and caught the stick with a towel in his opposite palm.

I had no idea where the towel had come from.

I didn't really care.

I was too disappointed that he'd just released my hand.

"Now we pour the drinks and add another layer of marshmallows to the top," Lark informed me. "Unless you want some peppermint, too?"

The aroma of sensual notes hit my nose, making me shake my head. "I would like to try it without first." Because it smelled delicious on its own.

"A good choice," Lark replied, expertly pouring the contents into three steaming mugs.

He topped them with more of those cloud puffs before blowing on each one. Magic stirred in the air again, suggesting he'd just blessed it with some sort of Winter Fae enchantment. Then he handed me the first mug.

His minty green eyes held a note of intrigue, as though he were testing me somehow with this hot chocolate. Or maybe he was testing himself.

Regardless, one inhale of the contents had my mouth watering for a taste. So I very carefully took a sip.

A groan followed, my taste buds cheering at the amazing flavors that burst along my tongue. "Oh my Fae," I breathed, taking more into my mouth. "This is so good!"

It was far better than the hot chocolate at the cafeteria.

It was like... like oblivion in a mug.

Lark's expression lit with delight, a hint of relief in his eyes saying I'd passed whatever test he'd had in place. Norden sat up and joined us on the blanket, his brown irises glittering as Lark passed him one of the remaining cups.

"Thank you," Norden whispered to him reverently.

Lark cupped his cheek for a moment, winking, then took his own mug.

It was an exchange I didn't fully understand. Maybe Lark didn't allow Norden to try his hot chocolate often?

He'd said it was a private treat. Which meant he was giving me a gift of himself through this liquid delight.

Given how flavorful it was, I could see why he kept this to himself. It was the most delicious beverage I'd ever had the pleasure of drinking.

Lark started drinking last, his expression content as we all enjoyed our hot chocolate in amicable silence.

So many unspoken words seemed to float through the air.

An apology from Lark. Mild forgiveness from me. Sensual intrigue from Norden.

If this was their idea of courtship, then I absolutely approved. Because this mug of faeliciousness was positively divine.

I finished it far too quickly, the marshmallows all melting in my mouth on the way down with the steaming liquid.

"That was amazing," I said. "Thank you for the experience."

Lark dipped his chin, his eyes twinkling. "Thank you for allowing it."

Norden smiled, his hot cocoa already gone as well. He'd remained on the blanket but kept one hand planted on the ice beyond it as though he needed that chilly touch to remain grounded. "Dinner should be arriving soon."

"Arriving?" I repeated.

"Hmm," he hummed noncommittally. "Would you like to ice-skate in the interim? Or meet more penguins?"

My interest was immediately piqued. "Ice skating?" I repeated. That'd been one of my favorite activities back home, before the Academy. We had a rink right down the street from my house that never melted, thanks to the Water Fae magic.

"I think that's a yes," Lark murmured as he began returning all the hot chocolate items to his bag.

"There's a place just over that snow mound." Norden gestured to it with a tilt of his head. "Solid sheet of smooth ice, perfect for a few rounds on skates. Want to give it a whirl?"

I perked way up. "Yes, please!" *Except...* I frowned. "But I don't have skates." And I doubted he'd brought any that would fit my feet.

"Good thing you have a wishing charm," Norden murmured, glancing at the snowflake necklace dangling against my sweater.

My fingers grazed the edges. "Oh, yes. You know what this is?"

"I know *exactly* what it is," Norden confirmed. "Which means you can wish yourself a pair of ice skates, and maybe a set for us, too." He looked at Lark. "He didn't want to put anything sharp in the bags."

"Safety first," the prince replied without remorse.

"Indeed." Norden glanced at me, his chocolate brow lifting to his hairline. "So, Sunshine? What'll it be?"

I grinned. I didn't even need to think this through. Because obviously we were going ice skating. "Three pairs of skates coming right up."

ARTICA

Prince Lark and Norden were naturals on the ice.

Not surprising given their heritage.

But they both seemed equally enamored with my ability to skate circles around them. I did a few twirls and jumps, showing off my former figure-skating talents, adding just a hint of water magic along the way.

My affinity for ice made me graceful in a way I couldn't replicate on normal ground. I danced across the frozen space, zigzagging and jumping and grooving to my own tune.

When suddenly a presence prickled the back of my neck.

A pair of eyes I wasn't expecting to feel.

Kalt.

He stood at the edge of the ice wearing a blue button-down shirt that hugged his torso, the top button undone to reveal his masculine throat. Gray slacks decorated his legs. And his feet donned a pair of expensive-looking black shoes.

Not exactly winter appropriate.

However, he maintained an insulation layer, just like I did, that protected his skin.

I nearly tripped over my ice skates at the unexpected sight of him.

Norden caught me by the hips, pulling me gracefully upright in a move that appeared practiced but was entirely coincidental.

"I've got you," he whispered against my ear, spinning me around to face him instead of Kalt. I swallowed, a shiver that had nothing to do with the cold skittering down my spine.

"Thank you," I breathed, my fingers clutching his forearms as he continued to skate us in a circle.

"He brought dinner," Norden explained softly, gently guiding me toward where the Water Fae Prince stood.

Lark had already exited the ice, his skates having been swapped with his boots.

A sight that suggested Kalt had been standing there for at least a few minutes while I'd danced around the ice.

I wasn't sure if that pleased me or not.

He would have grown up seeing Water Fae on ice, making my ability nothing special. Although, I had won several awards for my gracefulness while growing up. So maybe I could skate better than most.

What I could do on ice, I was punished for on land with clumsiness. Which meant it all balanced out in the end.

Norden gave my hips a squeeze. "Ready to eat, Sunshine?"

The nickname warmed my heart a little, his use of it all evening something I could definitely become accustomed to hearing.

"Yeah, I'm hungry," I admitted, my stomach clenching in affirmation.

Norden smiled. "For food, or…?"

I blinked, his handsome face seeming to invite me to respond in any way I desired. If I said for him, he'd probably take me on the ice. Maybe even while skating.

Kalt cleared his throat, telling me we were close enough for him to hear the conversation. I glanced at him and nearly slipped again.

He brought dinner.

After saying he would be gone for a week.

But he was here now.

With food.

Norden's lips brushed my cheek, drawing me back to the sexy selkie. "You skate beautifully, Sunshine," he told me softly. "Like a star dancing across the moonlit sky."

My skin heated with the compliment. "Thank you."

"He's right. Your affinity for ice just makes you that much more alluring to watch." Lark held out a hand for me, inviting me into the snow. I stepped into it with his help, then Norden knelt beside me to begin undoing my skates.

I almost told him I could do it myself, but Lark's hands went to my hips to help me stay upright, and my brain forgot how to make words flow to my mouth.

His minty irises captivated me, holding me hostage beneath his alluring stare.

It struck me again just how beautiful this fae was, his handsome features fit for a king. But there was a kindness to him that I'd failed to notice in the throne room.

"I like you better out here," I whispered, not really thinking about what I was saying. "You're… nicer."

He chuckled, the sound breaking the spell a bit and causing my lips to part.

"Oh, I mean… I didn't mean… well, I did mean, but I… oh, fudgesicles." I'd completely botched that up, and right in front of my *boss*, too.

Yep. Worst intern ever.

"The throne room reminds me of my upcoming ascension," Lark replied, his touch burning right through my leggings to the magic caressing my skin.

I could feel him tasting my enchantment with his Winter Fae essence, brushing the magical quality of my insulation and marveling at the mechanics of it.

Such a strange sensation.

But a welcome one.

"What I mean is, the throne room makes me feel… impatient," he finally added. "And I regretfully took that impatience out on you." His grasp tightened as Norden freed my foot from one of the skates and slid it into my ankle boot.

"Most Winter Fae Princes don't even attempt an ascension without their triad in place. Yet my father believes it's my time, so I have no choice but to try. Which is making me eager to claim what my soul knows is mine."

"How do you know it's yours?" I wondered out loud. "All the research I've done states that Winter Fae mate-circles usually have several female candidates."

"True, but not my familial line. My father knew his mates immediately, just as my grandfather did." His grasp tightened again as Norden removed my other skate.

My stance wavered for a hairsbreadth of a second, only to be righted by Lark's firm hold. I realized then that he would never let me fall. It was written plain as day in his features.

This male hardly knew me but very much considered me to be his to protect.

"Our family acts as a conduit for the Winter Fae

Source," he went on. "Which means we're very in tune with the needs and wants of our souls. And that makes it easier for us to know our fates."

"Oh," I whispered, unsure of what to say to that.

Fortunately, he wasn't done.

"I know who my mates are meant to be. But a key part to all of this is belief. Just because I know something doesn't mean you"—his gaze flicked to the side, landing on Kalt—"or *you*," he said before returning his gaze to mine, "believe it."

Well, that was certainly a better explanation than the one he'd given me in the throne room. He'd pretty much ridiculed Water Fae for thinking they had a choice. Which, to him, we didn't, because his soul told him we belonged to him.

"But enough of that, let's go eat," he said, smiling. "I'm looking forward to trying whatever Kalt brought for us."

Norden appeared at my side, his skates already swapped for his boots. "Me, too." He held all three pairs of our skates by the laces and led the way back to the blanket.

Where several paper bags waited for us.

Bags Kalt must have misted in from somewhere.

I glanced at him. "Hi."

His lips quirked up, his dimples flashing. "Having fun?"

"They have *penguins*," I told him. "So yes. Very much having fun."

He chuckled and shook his head. "You're easy to impress."

"Penguins, Kalt," I repeated. That did not make me easy to impress. "*Penguins* are impressive."

Several of them surrounded our blanket as though to prove my point. They didn't try to touch our food, instead lounging around and taking cues from Norden. He clearly had some sort of bond with the creatures.

"How many species are there?" I wondered aloud, noticing all the variants in colors and sizes.

"Several," he replied, shrugging as he stretched out beside the blanket again on the ice. "The North Pole welcomes all types of arctic creatures. But some of these guys are from as far as Australia. They migrate from all over the world, the magic of this place calling to them."

Kalt set to work handing everyone plates and silverware while Norden started talking about the other types of wildlife that existed out here.

Polar bears were the ones that interested me most. "Can I meet one?"

Norden's lips twisted. "They're not very nice."

"He says that because one tried to eat him as a seal pup," Lark supplied, amusement coloring his tone.

"Hence, they're not very nice," Norden repeated, scowling.

Lark shrugged. "He responded to me just fine."

"Because you waved your magic fingers at him. Pretty much everyone submits when you do that." Norden glanced at Kalt. "Well, almost everyone."

Kalt ignored him.

Lark merely smiled. "Some are easier to tame than others."

Norden snorted. "If you think I'm tamed, then you've clearly not been paying attention."

"I'd never dream of taming you, Nor," Lark murmured, the nickname one I hadn't heard him use yet in my presence.

Nor sounded sweet.

And the way Norden's cheeks blossomed with color told me he liked it, too.

I almost asked if I should call him that as well, when a familiar scent made my nose twitch. I finally focused on just what Kalt had removed from the bags, and my lips parted. "*Dragon steak?*"

"With salad patties and some shrooms as a side," Kalt replied. "Oh, and spritemead. Because we can't indulge in Elemental Fae cuisine without it." He pulled out two jugs of it and four glasses.

"You brought me Elemental Fae food?" Actual tears tickled my eyes. "I thought you said we shouldn't eat it here."

"It was their idea," Kalt told me, gesturing to Lark and Norden. "They wanted to try some of our specialties. I enlisted some help from Vox on the matter. The dragon steaks are from him."

My lips curled at the mention of Queen Claire's mate. Vox was an Air Fae with a penchant for cooking.

"He also told me something about troll fat," Kalt continued, his brow furrowing. "I'm… not sure… I want to try it."

"What about troll fat?" I asked.

"That it's like bacon?" Kalt sounded unsure.

Lark gagged.

Norden snorted.

"Not a fan of troll fat?" Kalt guessed.

"Not a fan of pig meat," Lark corrected.

"*Pigs?*" I repeated, mortified. "Vox likes to eat pigs?!"

"No, apparently Queen Claire loves bacon, so he makes her troll fat instead." Kalt sounded as disgusted by it as I felt.

"I don't want to try that."

"Good. Because I don't either," Kalt admitted, wincing. Then he slid a dragon steak onto my plate, along with a healthy dose of salad patty and shrooms.

I about melted at the sight of some of my favorite dishes from home.

The spritemead came next.

Followed by healthy silence as we all dug into our meals.

ARTICA

Norden and Lark surprised me by trying everything without judgment, even commenting on the dragon steak being pretty good. Although, Norden appeared pretty perplexed by the notion of eating a dragon since he was friends with a few Dragon Fae.

"You've met a Dragon Fae?" I asked, shocked. "Aren't they rare?"

"Very," he confirmed. "But I've met two. They were wandering the Human Realm, searching for potential mates."

My eyes rounded. "Human mates?"

He shrugged. "There are no female Dragon Fae. So, similar to Winter Fae, they tend to mate with other species. The bond makes a human immortal, after all. Therefore, it works for them."

"Huh," I mused, intrigued as I ate another bite.

"Dragon steaks don't actually come from dragons," Kalt explained as I munched on my salad patty. "It's a type of plant in our realm with a meat-like texture. Similar to the shrooms."

"Orc burgers are real, though," I said. "They're a type of beast that like to attack Elemental Fae. Rather than burn their bodies, we eat them. But we only kill the ones that try to hurt us." Which was the majority of orcs. They were vile, mindless beasts who didn't really think beyond murderous rage.

"Orc burgers," Norden repeated, frowning. "Not sure I'd want to try that."

"They're good when smoked," Kalt told him with a shrug. "But the fish you've caught and baked for me are better."

Norden's whole face lit up. "So you did eat my gifts."

Kalt lifted a shoulder. "I'm an Elemental Fae. We don't let resources go to waste."

"Hmm, is that all?" Norden appeared entirely undeterred by Kalt's nonchalant response. "Lark likes my fish, too."

The prince nodded in agreement as he finished the last morsel on his plate. Then he washed it down with a healthy swig of spritemead. "So tell me more about the Hell Fae issue." His focus went to Kalt. "What's Typhos done now?"

"It's not what he's done; it's what he's planning to do," Kalt replied, his expression darkening. "He's exchanging deals for females. And no one knows when he intends to collect or what he plans to do with them."

"I see." Lark scratched the smooth line of his jaw. "Is he still planning to attend my coronation?"

"He told me he's sending Prince Melek in his place," Kalt replied. "But in my experience, Typhos, whom most know as Lucifer, never lets Melek go too far without his presence nearby. He's very protective of his mate."

Lark nodded. "So we should expect them both."

"Yes. And the Midnight Fae Queen has said she will be attending with all her mates as well," Kalt went on, making my lips curl.

I liked Queen Aflora. I'd met her once when she'd visited Queen Claire at Elemental Fae Academy. She was very sweet. It would be nice to see her again.

Kalt and Lark continued discussing the various attendees, with Kalt giving Lark a full report on each, making me wonder if it had been Prince Lark or Queen Claire who had given Kalt the task of following up with all the Interrealm Fae attendees.

Norden slid over to me, taking my empty plate to set on top of his. "Can I brush your hair?" he asked softly, not wanting to intrude on the political discussion happening beside us. "I want to see how wavy it is from your braid."

I almost giggled. *This male and his hair fetish...* "Can I brush yours, too?"

He nodded eagerly. "Yes. I would like that very much." And the manner in which he said the words told me he wasn't lying.

He turned toward his pack, but Lark was already handing him a brush, having heard our conversation. "I want to brush your hair later, too," he told him as he released the handle into Norden's palm.

The selkie froze for a moment, then nodded slowly. "Okay."

"Okay," Lark repeated before returning to his conversation with Kalt.

"Do you not let him brush your hair?" I guessed in a low whisper.

"Not usually, no. But he let me have his hot chocolate today, which was a very intimate gift. So I will return the favor tonight." He handed me the brush. "Hold that, please. And don't let it touch the snow. It's a family heirloom." Then he settled behind me on the blanket, this time not touching the ice at all.

I studied the golden handle and fine bristles as he began unbraiding my hair. His fingers worked quickly, but without tugging or pulling, his deft touch a welcome experience against my scalp.

When he finished, he reached around me to take the brush again and began drawing it through my hair. So gently and easily, starting at the bottom and working his way up, the grooming technique clearly one he'd perfected throughout his life.

"Do all selkies cherish their hair?" I asked.

He hummed in confirmation before adding, "Our hair contains the magic of our seal pelts. We have to care for each strand to guarantee our shifter magic remains."

"So when someone else touches your hair...?" I trailed off, uncertain of how to finish that sentence, yet oddly understanding it at the same time.

"Our magic mingles with the essence of the other being," he finished for me. "Which is why we only let our mates or potential mates feel our hair. It's a sort of courting for my kind. A way to test our magical compatibility."

"But you don't let Lark brush your hair?" I pressed, confused. "He's your mate, right?"

"I'm part of his triad," he responded slowly. "I care for him. He's mine, and I allow him to touch my hair in moderation. But I crave a female mate, too. And my female is the one I want to bond with via the magic of my pelt. Similar to how Prince Lark didn't share his hot chocolate with me until sharing it with you."

That was... *heavy.*

Like, a lot of information.

Details I wasn't sure I was ready to hear.

Because this selkie had pretty much just said that he'd allowed me to play with his magic upon first meeting because he knew I was his female.

"Do selkies have fated mates?" I wondered out loud, my voice a bit hoarse.

"No, but my magic is tied to Winter Fae magic now. The most powerful Winter Fae magic of all, actually, with Prince Lark being the future king. So I'm very aware of my soul, just as he is, which is how I knew who you were the moment you arrived in this realm."

He leaned forward to press a kiss to my hair, the brush stilling near my spine.

"You don't have to be afraid," he added in a low whisper, his lips skimming my ear. "We won't pressure you, Artica. I'm only trying to answer your questions honestly, as Lark says that's the key to a positive relationship."

The prince snorted nearby, telling me he and Kalt had overheard every word. But they continued their political discussion, giving us the illusion of privacy once more.

"Let's switch positions," I said, my voice possessing a subtle squeak at the end. Because that had definitely been a potential innuendo, something Norden's eyes told me he heard as he shifted around to sit in front of me.

But rather than comment, he merely handed me the brush and pulled all his luscious brown hair over to his back for me to comb through.

I used my fingers first, noting that the silky texture was exactly the same as before, and sighed at the shimmering quality of his hair.

Now that I knew more about his kind, I could feel the subtle vibration of energy tickling my fingertips. It called to my Water Fae instincts, inviting me out to play. But I would never freeze his beautiful hair. Maybe I would stroke it with some cool water or create a brush of ice bristles to comb through his hair.

However, I used the item in my hand instead, drawing it along his mane and sighing at the beautiful cascade of chocolate brown strands.

Absolutely stunning.

I took my time, just as he had, enjoying the moment and allowing the magic to trickle through my veins.

This could be my life, I realized. *Surrounded by these three men, indulging in enchanting experiences such as this, for the rest of my existence.*

Except Kalt refused to accept this fate.

I could feel his resistance now, the weight of it heavy in the air as he kept everything strictly business with Prince Lark.

A hint of disappointment followed, the source of it the Winter Fae Prince. Because he needed Kalt to believe in the triad, to believe in *him*.

What would happen if Prince Lark didn't have our belief by the coronation?

It was a week away now.

The timeline shrinking with every missed second.

And Kalt was standing to leave now. We'd finished our meal, and he claimed he had to return to his tasks.

The expressions on Norden's and Lark's faces told me they knew he was lying. Or maybe I picked that up from the distrustful air around us.

Something about this was very wrong.

Why didn't Kalt believe in them? I understood that he didn't want any ties that might hold him back from his dreams, but maybe he needed to consider a new dream.

A dream where he lived happily as a Winter Fae Prince, mated to the Winter Fae King. Leading the joy and festivities of the world.

Indulging in passion and happiness.

Smiling every day.

There were ways to be a hero beyond being a badass fae.

Sometimes the strongest fae of all won their plights by giving a little heart to the matter. But his icy gaze told me he wasn't considering any of that now. He didn't even hug me goodbye.

Just said, "I hope you enjoyed the meal," and misted off with the paper bags in his hands.

I sighed, slumping back into Norden. He'd moved behind me again, his fingers back in my hair. But his brush had been carefully stowed in one of the backpacks on the ground.

"He'll come around," Norden promised me.

I shook my head. "I'm not so sure. He's set on a life path underlined in loneliness."

Prince Lark stared at the space Kalt had just occupied, his lips flattening into a grim line. "We should head back. I need to meet with Holly again on the seating arrangements now that even more fae are expected to attend the coronation."

A darker note invaded his tone, reminding me of the prince I'd met the other day. The arrogant ice pick who'd treated me like an object.

Rather than comment, I stood, saying with my body that I would obey him in this mood even though my heart longed to stay for just a few more minutes, to fall back into the happy existence we'd created here.

I took a step, aiming to move onto the ice, but found my foot caught in the blanket. The world began to tilt, but Lark caught me with a strong arm around my waist, yanking me backward until my shoulder blades met his chest.

I froze, the embrace shooting warm sparks through my veins to every nerve ending. He felt *good* against me. All hard, masculine lines. Strength personified. An alpha in his prime.

"You all right?" he asked against my ear, that dark tone disappearing beneath the concern in his voice.

I swallowed, nodding. "Yeah. I'm much more graceful on ice than I am on other surfaces."

He chuckled. "Most fae are the opposite."

"Most fae don't have an affinity for water," I murmured.

"True," he agreed, his hands sliding to my hips as he picked me up to place me deftly on the ice. I immediately felt more stable against my element.

"Thank you," I whispered. "Thank you for today. Thank you for the gifts. Thank you for respecting the courtship."

He seemed to freeze behind me, then ever so slowly, he turned me to face him.

"I never meant to disrespect the courtship," he told me seriously. "I would never purposely jeopardize something so special, Artica. It's my duty to protect and honor you as my intended queen." He reached up to tuck a stray strand of my hair behind my ear. "I'm sorry for acting to the contrary. I won't make that mistake again."

Oh Fae, I wanted to kiss him.

He looked so contrite, so *sad*.

No Winter Fae being should ever be that conflicted or hurt or disappointed in himself.

Maybe it was partly a result of Kalt's abrupt departure. Or maybe the prince felt he was failing at every turn. But I couldn't let him go on in this manner. He had to know that I believed in him enough to feel certain he would make this right, that he'd already taken several strides in the right direction tonight.

I might not be ready to become his queen or his mate yet.

But I sensed the potential.

And I *believed* that we just might be destined for each other after all.

So I went to my toes and pressed a kiss to his full lips.

A bold move, one I had never done before in my life. However, this prince needed to know that he had my support. And if he kept going in this direction, I just might give him my heart, too.

His palm slid up my spine to my nape, his fingers curling around my neck as he returned my embrace. His opposite arm encircled my waist, holding me flush against him, his warmth a welcome sensation that melted all my inhibitions.

I slid my tongue into his mouth, engaging him in a much deeper kiss than I'd originally intended. But he felt so right. So perfect. So *mine*.

A startling realization.

A spark of beautiful hope.

He really is meant to be mine, my Water Fae spirit whispered as I easily engaged him not just on the first level of bonding but on the second as well.

It was so unexpected, taking the breath right out of my lungs.

My pulse raced, my veins lighting with a fire that I couldn't seem to control. I grabbed his muscular shoulders, needing more, my tiptoes beginning to burn from standing on them for too long.

I started to slip, but his arm held me with ease, his mouth claiming mine with a ferocity I felt all the way to my soul.

It was intense, beautiful, all-consuming passion.

And exactly what I'd dreamt about at night.

Maybe it was Lark I'd desired all along.

No, it was definitely Kalt.

But now it was Lark, too.

Norden as well.

Oh Fae, I was in trouble now.

Prince Lark's gaze held a note of wonder and adoration as he finally pulled away, his handsome face alight with desire. "You mated me."

"On the second level," I whispered, my cheeks burning. "I... I didn't mean to..."

"I'm not upset by it," he replied, smiling.

"H-how does bonding work for Winter Fae?" I stammered, kicking myself for not researching that enough. I'd read all about mate-circles and how the fae were from all over the faedoms, but I hadn't actually found information on how the mating process worked other than that it was founded in belief.

"We don't have levels," he murmured, his palm shifting from the back of my neck to my cheek. "We just... *believe*."

I frowned. "Then what happens if someone stops believing?"

He considered that for a moment and shrugged. "I don't know. I've never seen that happen."

"Because it would never happen," Norden chimed in, the heat of his body suddenly a strong presence at my back as he joined us. "My belief in our circle is resolute. It's why Kalt considers me aggressive. That's not a selkie trait. We're sensual, yes. We follow our hearts. But it's my unerring belief in what we mean to each other that drives my actions."

He pressed a kiss to my pulse, unleashing a shudder through my body.

"But I think this is enough courting for one night," he continued. "You've been given a lot of information to ponder. So we will escort you back to your room now and leave you with your books."

"Unless you want to come back to my room…" Prince Lark trailed off, his gaze on the selkie behind me. "Right, you need to study. Another night, then."

I glanced over my shoulder, trying to catch whatever expression Norden had given him. But all I found was a secret little smile.

As much as I wanted to take Prince Lark up on his potential offer, Norden was probably right. I had a lot more books to read before next week.

And I really needed a minute to think all this through.

Just two days ago, I'd been adamant that Prince Lark would have to grovel for a year before I'd forgive him for that stunt in his throne room.

Yet one evening in his presence and I'd mate-bonded him on the second level.

Kalt would have felt that since we were bonded as well.

Fortunately, Elemental Fae could take more than one mate, or my soul would be in some serious trouble right now.

Clearing my throat, I nodded. "Yes, I should go back to my reading."

"Maybe one of us can meet you for breakfast tomorrow?" Norden suggested. "In the cafeteria?"

"I would like that," I admitted, my heart warming at the thought of having someone to share a meal with in the morning. "Just let me know what time."

"Or I could come get you," he offered. "That way you won't sleep in."

My lips twitched. "That might be wise, actually."

"Yes, that's Norden. Very wise," Prince Lark said,

smiling. He kissed me on the cheek before releasing me and picking up one of the packs from the ground.

Apparently, Norden had been busy cleaning up everything while Lark and I had shared our, uh, bonding moment.

The selkie grabbed the second pack, then bent down to say goodbye to his penguin friends. "I'll be back in an hour for some fishing," he promised them.

"Do they understand you?" I wondered out loud.

"Not my statements, just my intentions," he answered, straightening. "You'll come to learn that my actions always speak louder than my words."

He winked and led the way again, making me ponder his comment all the way back to my room.

His actions truly did say a lot about his intentions.

Because his actions were underscored by obvious belief.

He'd allowed me to comb his hair tonight—a clear act of trust, one that confirmed he truly expected me to become his mate.

As did Lark.

So what about Kalt?

KALT

F*ae fire*, I muttered, pacing back and forth outside of the Elemental Fae Academy gates.

I'd meant to mist to the Chancellor Home that Queen Claire had built a few years ago, but I'd ended up here because my instincts were rioting at me to go back to the Winter Fae Realm.

I'd just left Artica with Norden and Lark.

And while I trusted them immensely, a heartfelt part of me yearned to go back to them, to see where the night took them.

But I also didn't want to know.

Except I could feel it in my chest.

Artica had just initiated another mating bond.

My teeth ground together in frustration, my soul torn somewhere between relief and agony.

She's mine, it kept saying.

No. She's. Not, was my mind's response.

What the fae is wrong with me? I marveled, pacing once

more. Norden had torn me up a bit with his advances, making me regret having to say no on more than one occasion.

But this was ripping me apart.

The notion of Artica being with Norden and Lark *without me* was... Well, it sucked. It more than sucked. It hurt almost as bad as the former death fields in the Spirit Kingdom.

Because that was where my soul had run off to.

It felt shredded and destroyed.

A sensation I had not expected to experience. Yes, Artica and I were compatible on many levels. I found her attractive and intelligent and so delightfully cheerful that my heart ached just thinking about her.

But I didn't love her.

No, I *couldn't* love her.

There, that was better. I wasn't allowed to feel that way.

Of course, my soul clearly didn't agree since it continued to drag around inside me, making me *walk* the rest of the way to the Chancellor Home up on the hill because my ability to mist no longer worked.

Fudge.

That had better control itself soon, or I'd have to use a portal.

A very idea that made me shudder. Because ugh. Not being able to mist made me feel weak.

But so did sensing Artica mate another male.

By the time I reached Queen Claire's door, I was in probably the worst mood of my life.

So, naturally, my cousin, Cyrus, was the one to greet me. "Well, you look like shit."

"Thanks, cous," I muttered, pushing past him with all

the bags Vox had given me. We'd eaten all the food, but the dishes were his.

"Nice to see you, too," Cyrus drawled at my back. "What frost pick found its way up your ass?"

"A certain Water Fae beauty who doesn't realize her singing voice is heavenly," I replied without missing a beat.

Cyrus misted to the kitchen, blocking my entry. "Artica?"

I glared at him. "Move."

"Not until you tell me what's frozen your balls." He leaned against the door frame and folded his arms, his body roughly the same size as mine and thereby making it impossible for me to just shove him out of my way. "Out with it. That Winter Fae Prince still trying to claim you?"

I ground my teeth together. "You know he is."

He nodded. "Future kings tend to go after what they want. Isn't that right, little queen?"

"Stop harassing your cousin, Cyrus," Queen Claire replied from behind me. "He's trying to return Vox's dishes."

"He can mist them into the kitchen, then." Cyrus arched a white brow that met his light blond hairline. "Right?"

I really wanted to punch him. "My misting abilities seem to have shorted from using them too much today."

He grunted. "Is that your excuse for your rioting soul?"

"You can sense that?"

"I'm your cousin and your king. Of course I can fucking sense it," he returned, finally moving out of my way. But he didn't leave me alone.

No. He followed me into the kitchen.

And continued to pester me about my *fractured soul*.

"Maybe if you tried, I don't know, embracing the idea

of mating with Prince Lark and Norden, you would feel more complete," he offered. "Or, you could try indulging in the first level bond I sense between you and Artica."

"I really don't appreciate your insight into my dating life," I grumbled.

"Cyrus isn't known for minding his own business," Exos said as he entered the room with an empty glass. "Of course, I don't need to tell you that, Kalt. You're fully aware of my brother's antics."

"More like annoying habits," a third voice said as Titus joined him. The auburn-haired Fire Fae went straight for the fridge, picking out some sort of red juice that he proceeded to drink directly from the carton.

Which earned him a hiss as Vox appeared in the kitchen entryway. "Titus! Use a glass!"

Titus ignored him, instead taking a seat at the table and clutching the carton as though it were his firstborn child.

And speaking of children, Sol, Claire's Earth Fae mate, entered last with a toddler sitting high on his broad shoulders. "Kalt," he greeted.

"Sol," I returned, my gaze lifting to the beautiful boy on his shoulder. "Hello, Ciro."

The boy mumbled something unintelligible back.

"He says hi, too," Sol translated for me.

Claire gazed up at them both fondly before leaning into the giant Earth Fae's side.

"Tell Uncle Kalt that he should go back to the Winter Fae Kingdom and let Prince Lark claim him," Cyrus cooed, reaching up to brush a kiss of snow across his son's cheek with his thumb.

"He's technically not an uncle," Vox pointed out conversationally. "More like a second cousin, I think?"

"Good enough to be an uncle," Cyrus murmured. "Because he's a smart Water Fae Prince, just like you, Ciro. Except I think you would absolutely follow your heart and soul, wouldn't you? Yes, you would."

I wasn't sure what concerned me more—that my cousin was speaking about me in a baby voice or that he was speaking to his son about my love life like it was some sort of platform for future relationship advice.

"Leave Kalt alone, Cyrus," Queen Claire said, pressing a palm to his abdomen and pushing him toward the counter behind him.

"Technically, it's my duty to *not* leave him alone. Both as his king and his reigning family member," Cyrus pointed out. "In fact, I could demand he indulge Prince Lark, and take all the guesswork out of it entirely."

"But you're not going to do that because you don't want to upset your mate," Queen Claire told him sternly.

Cyrus narrowed his gaze. "You know how I feel about challenges, little queen."

"This isn't one you want to take me up on," she countered.

"Hey!" Titus said suddenly, drawing our attention to the table. "I was drinking that."

"No, you were defiling it," Vox snapped, the carton of juice swirling around at the top of the room on a wave of air.

Flames danced along Titus's fingertips as he stood. "Return it, or I'm going to burn your ass. And not in the way you like."

"Right, that's my cue to go," I said slowly, setting everything down on the counter beside Cyrus. "Thanks for the dishes, Vox. They loved the dragon steak."

I started to wiggle my way out of the very small kitchen —which was normally quite large in size but had shrunk due to all five of Claire's mates having joined us in said space—but Cyrus caught me by the arm.

"I'll walk you out," he said, his tone losing the teasing edge and holding a note of seriousness that told me it wasn't a request but a command.

Sighing, I nodded.

Because what else could I say?

He didn't speak until we were outside, his hand having left my arm to give me at least a few inches of space. But the stern expression in his features suggested that was the end of his leash.

"Why won't you accept Prince Lark's offer?" Cyrus asked. "I can feel your compatibility. So I know it's not for a lack of interest. Is it because you want Artica for yourself?"

"What? No." At his persistent stare, I repeated, "*No.* I would never demand that of her, not when she's clearly compatible with Prince Lark and Norden, too." I ran my fingers through my hair, blowing out a breath. "It's... it's complicated."

Cyrus glanced back at the house, his lips curling down. "Is it the notion of a mate-circle that concerns you?"

"Yes. No." I shook my head. "Not in the way you think."

"So sharing doesn't bother you?"

"Does it bother *you*?" I countered, finding the question absurd. "Mate-circles are the epitome of true love. Lark and Norden love each other. They'll love Artica just as much, once they truly get to know her."

"Are you concerned they won't love you, too?"

"No, I'm concerned that they will love me, too," I muttered back at him. "I don't want the obligatory ties of a relationship, other lives to worry about beyond my own."

"But don't you see that the whole purpose to life is to

love?" Cyrus asked. "Love is what makes us want to rise in the morning, what gives us reason to exist. Without it, who are we?"

I stared at him. "Love is a burden that comes with responsibility and potential failure."

He snorted. "Failure is part of the relationship process, cous. And trust me when I say, make-up sex? Yeah, totally worth the failure or mistake that led to it."

"Not when the failure may lead to the death of your loved one," I snapped.

His expression sobered. "Kalt…"

"Prince Lark's ascension is tied to belief, Cyrus. What if I don't believe enough? What if my concerns about what could go wrong end up becoming a reality?" I swallowed, my throat constricting with the words I'd not wanted to say yet felt compelled to make him understand. "I don't think I could live with myself if that happened."

Cyrus fell silent for a moment, a rarity for him, which meant he was processing my statements. "Why don't you believe in him?"

"I do believe in him," I admitted. "I… I just worry that it's not enough."

"You won't know until you try," he replied after a beat. "And if you give up entirely, before you even give it a shot, then your belief was never worthy of him or his mate-circle."

My heart gave a pang at his words, my soul rioting inside me at the wrongness of them.

Because that wasn't true.

My belief was worthy.

Except… I was terrified to accept it.

"Our destinies are not always what we think they're meant to be," he continued. "I never foresaw this situation of sharing a mate with my own half brother. Sure, we have our kinks, but this life… it's more than I could ever have asked for, better than a dream. I don't know what I did to deserve it, but I thank the Source every day for making it my reality."

He stepped forward, his hand clapping me on the shoulder.

"Your soul understands your fate better than your mind ever will," he added. "Don't ignore your instincts. And please don't disregard your heart. It's the conduit for our soul and what makes life worth living."

Cyrus pulled me into a hug, one I returned because I hadn't realized how much I'd needed one until I felt his strength around me.

"I'm going to support you no matter what you decide, Kalt. I hope you know that." He kissed me on the head before releasing me. "We're family. No matter what."

I nodded, my throat tightening as my vision blurred just slightly. "Thank you," I managed to choke out.

He nodded in return. "Is there somewhere you'd like me to mist you?" he offered.

I considered it but shook my head. "No. I need to embrace the consequences of my actions right now."

He dipped his chin. "There's the royal fae that I know. Let me know when you fix it."

"I will," I told him, swallowing thickly. "See you next week."

He smiled. "Can't wait."

And just like that, my teasing cousin had replaced the Water Fae King.

Next week would be either a moment to cherish and remember for a lifetime…

Or a complete and utter clusterfuck.

I prayed for the former and feared the latter.

While walking slowly toward the Academy to find the dreaded portal room.

Frost, it's going to be cold. Because something told me my insulation ability was about to falter, too.

NORDEN

I'd met Artica for breakfast every morning while Lark had seen to his coronation duties. He'd joined us on two separate evenings, enjoying a stroll outside for one and another picnic with the penguins for the other.

But he'd given Artica space each time, wanting her to make the first move again.

It was important to our triad's foundation that she follow her heart and choose to believe in our future.

I could feel that belief growing stronger each day.

But Kalt's missing presence had certainly placed a dark shadow over us all.

The coronation was in twelve hours, and he still hadn't returned. He'd been in touch with Lark a few times regarding political matters. But there was an overarching sense of dread pulsating throughout our mate-circle.

And it was doing strange things to all of us.

Like during our outing with the penguins last night, Artica's insulation technique had temporarily failed.

Oh, and the other day during breakfast, she'd

accidentally shot an icicle across the cafeteria into one of the lemon tarts at the buffet. She'd just been pointing toward it, showing me where she'd found her lemon bar, and... proceeded to shoot an ice dagger at it.

Several of the elves had clapped in uproarious applause, while she'd gaped at the destruction in distinct mortification.

I'd told Lark about the incident.

And he'd witnessed the one last night.

Then this morning, I'd found her in her room covered in a snowdrift.

While sound asleep.

Which was precisely why I now stood sentry at her door to ensure that didn't happen again tonight.

Because something strange was definitely going on, and I suspected it had something to do with Kalt and his continued disappearance.

Lark had asked him to mist back for a meeting, but the Water Fae had insisted on conducting it via a video chat on their ice tablets instead.

"He may just be hiding from the intensity forming between us all," Lark had said afterward. "But I suspect there's something else going on. Something feels wrong, and not just because of his denial."

I'd nodded in agreement.

"Keep a close eye on Artica," he'd added after that. "She may be experiencing side effects of Kalt's... waning belief."

It had been the next morning that the icicle incident had happened, confirming his suspicions.

But the snowdrift was what really concerned me.

"You won't be doing that again, Sunshine," I said as I relaxed against her door.

I considered knocking, but I didn't want to interrupt her studies.

So, instead, I braced my back again—

"Oof," I breathed as the wood behind me moved.

"Are you planning to just hang out in the hallway or come inside?" Artica asked above me.

She was wearing a cute pair of silky shorts and a matching tank top. Reindeer slippers covered her dainty feet.

I relaxed on the floor, perfectly content to stare up at her from this angle. Those shorts lived up to their name, barely reaching the middle of her thighs. And they were baggy as well, providing a tantalizing glimpse of the lace beneath.

"I think I'll stay right here, if you don't mind," I said. "It's quite a view."

She frowned down at me, then realized what I meant and blushed furiously. "Oh, you slippery selkie!"

"Slippery is absolutely something I enjoy, yes," I admitted, grinning as she ran backward a few steps.

I casually rolled to my stomach, then deftly pushed up off the ground and stood to follow her.

"Shall I demonstrate for you, Sunshine?" I asked, kicking the door closed behind me with a booted heel. "Show you just what I can do with my tongue?" I glanced at the empty wrapper on her desk. "Or have your dreams provided enough of a demonstration?"

"Dreams?" she squeaked.

"Yes, dreams." I picked up the wrapper and set it in the bin, then searched for another selkie candy on her desk. I'd been sending them to her daily, the little white crystal delights layered in sugar and pleasant thoughts that typically led to some wild dreams.

Her eyes narrowed. "What's in those candies?"

"Tell me about your dreams, and I'll tell you what's in the selkie candy," I countered.

"You've been drugging me?"

I laughed. "No, Sunshine. Just courting you via candy."

"Candy that induces erotic dreams?"

"Candy that shows you what you want," I told her, meaning it. "The selkie candy heightens sensation and expectation, showing you what you want and allowing you to experience it in your dreams."

Which was how I knew exactly what impact the candy would have on her.

But that was neither here nor there.

Artica's mind created the fantasy. I just helped urge it along with a few sweets.

Her lips parted. "D-dream candy?"

"Mmm," I hummed. "Another name for it, actually. Others also call it *aspiration fuel*, but it's made with a hint of selkie magic. Hence, the appropriate term is actually *selkie candy*."

"Magic from the hair?"

"Just the essence of it," I explained. "A selkie will allow a candymaker to pet him while creating it, which is why it's a rare candy. Not many selkies agree to the process."

She frowned. "So someone petted you while making these?"

"No, Sunshine. You're the only one allowed to pet me," I promised her. "I don't know which selkie assisted in these, honestly. I just placed an order and have been sending them to you all week."

I flopped onto her bed, the size perfect for a party of four. Long, too. Which would make for some delicious treats indeed.

She nibbled her lower lip. "So the candy is why I keep dreaming of…"

"Sex?" I offered, causing her brow to furrow. "Me devouring you between your legs? Kalt fucking you to oblivion? Lark taking your ass?" I flipped onto my side, propping my head up on my hand. "Please share, Sunshine. I'm dying to know."

Her red cheeks were utterly adorable. "I can't decide if I love you or hate you right now."

"Oh, it's most definitely the former," I promised her. "And you would love me even more if you let me make some of those dreams come true."

"Given how hot and bothered I've been all week, you almost owe me that much," she muttered under her breath.

I sat up, happy to indulge in that little grumble. "Allow me to make it up to you, my sweet. I'll devour you just like you've devoured those candies."

She flashed me a look. "I should not have invited you into my room."

"But you did."

"Because you were sitting in the hallway."

"How did you know that, by the way?" I asked, genuinely curious. "Did you sense me?"

"I could smell you," she replied.

My brow furrowed. "*Smell* me?" I nearly lifted my arm to check my odor.

But her cheeks blossomed into that delectable shade of red again. "Like sea salt and nutmeg. The kiss of the ocean. A cologne that is very you."

Oh, now that I liked. "Tell me more."

She sighed. "You're incorrigible."

"I'm in love," I corrected her. "Well, on my way to it, anyway. You are my heart, Sunshine. Your wish is my command."

She gaped at me. "You're professing love to me now?"

"Are you really all that surprised?"

"We've known each other a week!"

"Almost ten days, actually," I corrected her, thinking about our last week of breakfasts and the initial day we'd met. "And my soul knows what he wants, something I've been up front about since the moment I met you."

She blinked. "Well, that's true."

"I don't lie. I don't hide. And I absolutely do not cheat." I sat up on the bed and scooted back to rest against the headboard. "I also won't pressure you, Artica. I may tease, but I understand the word *no* loud and clear."

"I'm not saying *no*," she hedged.

"I'm aware of that, just making sure you know that I do understand and value consent." I smiled. "And I would love to hear more about your fantasies. I mean, dreams."

She blew out a long breath, then shook her head on a laugh. "Only you, Norden. Only you."

My lips curled down. "You only fantasize about me?" That couldn't be right. She'd level-bonded Kalt and Lark via her Elemental Fae soul. She had to be thinking of them, too.

"No, I mean only you could provoke me to actually want to admit my dreams out loud," she said, sliding onto the bed beside me. "But you know what I think I'd like more?"

I cocked my head, my selkie heart pounding a little harder in my chest. "Tell me and I'll indulge you in any way you desire. Unless you want me to leave. Then I may be rather disappointed."

She smiled. "I don't want you to leave, Norden." She crept a little closer. "I… I would like you to stay instead."

"I'll stay as long as you want me to," I promised her. *And then afterward for the night in the hall because I'm not letting you suffocate in a snowdrift.*

It was probably tied to the nightmare I'd experienced last night. I'd been swimming, as I often did in my dreams, when I'd felt a disturbing presence. So I'd followed it, only to find a lock of Artica's sunlit hair floating ominously in the icy water.

I'd woken with a start, then hurried to her room.

To find her in the snowdrift.

I'd played it off like I'd come over early for breakfast, but the nightmare was what had made me arrive when I had.

And I couldn't shake that ominous feeling clouding our mate-circle.

Artica must have sensed it as well because she appeared relieved that I'd agreed to stay. She leaned forward a little more, her snowflake pendant glittering brightly against her skin.

Kalt probably thought I didn't know the importance of her necklace, but I'd studied the various faedoms and their magics for years. So I'd recognized the enchantment encircling her pendant.

The glimmering pendant meant her soul was compatible with mine, and not only that.

She *wanted* me.

The snowflake revealed a mate's intentions. If her heart had been dark toward mine, it would have shown up by now.

Same with Lark and Kalt.

She desired all three of us, her heart pure and true.

She was our destined queen; of that I had no doubt. Which was probably why Lark had entrusted me with her safety. He knew I understood her importance, and what was more, he believed in her place at our side, too.

Kalt remained our only problem.

One I intended to solve as soon as he returned.

Because I was done with this game of chase.

He needed to accept our triad, accept Artica, and support our intended king.

Artica's palm met my cheek, her gaze searching. "You're thinking very hard about something. Is it tomorrow's coronation?"

I nodded since it was technically tied to that.

"Do you need to be with Lark?"

"No, he's with his dad right now," I told her. "Reviewing the last-minute details. He'll call if he needs me."

"Call?" she repeated.

I pressed my palm to her heart. "Yes, *call*."

"He can do that?"

"It's like a tug of need," I replied, not removing my hand. "I can sense him inside, just as I can sense you and Kalt. If someone were in pain or needing me, I would know." Which was how I knew something was very wrong with Kalt.

And from her expression, she felt it, too. Or at least, she sensed something ominous, just like me and Lark.

Because she was closer to joining our triad than she could even understand.

There was no ceremony or soul-bonding like her Elemental Fae heritage.

Our connection was based on an understanding and acceptance of rightness between our spirits. All driven by that famous word around here—*belief*.

Her gaze went to my mouth before slowly reaching my eyes again. "You feel warm."

I smiled. "Because I'm content to be with you."

"I'm content to be with you, too," she whispered.

"Content enough to tell me about your dreams?" I asked, waggling my brows.

She shook her head. "No." My heart started to sink, but she leaned a little closer, my palm slipping down to her breast. She didn't pull away, instead inching toward me until her lips nearly touched mine. "But I'm content enough to share them with you." Her mouth caressed mine, her peppermint breath a seductive kiss that I longed to taste. "I'm content enough to *show* them to you, too."

I groaned, her invitation one I could never deny. "Show me," I breathed. "Tell me what to do, Artica."

Because I would do whatever she asked.

So long as she never stopped touching me.

She straddled my thighs, bringing her delicious heat close to my now throbbing cock. "Kiss me, Norden."

Who was I to say no to such a precious request from my sunshine?

My Artica.

My future queen.

ARTICA

Norden tasted like salted caramel cookies.

Addicting. Salty yet sweet. And oh-so faelicious.

I wanted to devour him. To kiss him for eternity. To lose myself in his embrace for the rest of my days.

Because *wow*, Norden could kiss.

He took his time, his tongue gently teasing mine, learning my preferences and intensifying the sensations by introducing me to his own methods.

My toes curled, my legs tensing against his thighs as his palm curled around the back of my neck.

He wore jeans and a sweater again, the attire seeming to be his favorite when not playing in the icy water. I ran my fingers along the dark cotton fabric covering his chest, loving the way his natural heat bled through the fabric.

A slight purr emanated from him, or maybe it was a subtle growl. I wasn't sure, but it told me that he approved of my *petting* him.

I ran my fingers through his hair next, careful not to tangle the silky strands.

Then I drew my touch down to his shoulders, back to his pecs, and followed the corded muscle of his torso to the hem of his shirt near his hips.

"In my dreams, you're shirtless," I whispered.

"Only shirtless?"

"At first," I clarified, tugging the sweater upward to reveal his rippled abdomen.

He lifted his arms, making it easier for me to tug the fabric up and over his head.

I focused on fixing his hair first, my fingers automatically combing the strands and ensuring they framed his muscular shoulders.

His lips quirked upward, telling me I'd done the right thing.

Then his sinful gaze dared me to do more.

I kissed him again, this time leading with my tongue and loving how he met me stroke for stroke. He was giving me control, letting me play and push as far as I desired.

He'd meant what he'd said about consent.

And that just made me burn that much more for him.

My Elemental Fae bond snapped into place, putting us on the same level as me and Lark. But I barely felt it, too consumed by the heat pulsating through my veins.

I'd been dreaming of Kalt, Lark, and Norden all week. And while those selkie candies might be partially to blame, I doubted they were the entire reason.

Because I'd been dreaming of Kalt for years.

Norden and Lark were new, but this connection to them was undeniable.

I felt them inside me, burrowing deeper each day.

Maybe it was the holiday cheer. Maybe it was this happy atmosphere. Maybe it was just my soul finally finding males worthy of my heart.

Regardless, I chose to embrace it.

Because that was who I chose to be. A believer. A risk-taker. A *dreamer*.

I pulled my tank top over my head, needing to feel Norden's warm skin against mine.

He was so smooth and soft, just like his hair. It made me wonder if that applied to all parts of his body.

I wanted to kiss every inch of him. Explore him with my tongue. Trace every muscular detail.

My lips whispered across his on my way to his neck, nibbling and licking the masculine cords down to his broad shoulder. So athletic and firm. So sleek and perfect.

He didn't grab me or pet me or make a single move, instead allowing me to lead at my own pace.

The perfect selkie.

My beautiful Norden.

I thanked him with my eyes, holding his gaze as I slid off his lap to continue my exploration.

His muscles clenched, demonstrating his restraint.

I could see the need radiating in the chocolate pools of his irises.

"You look like you're ready to eat me, Sunshine," he murmured. "And I have to tell you, I'm very all right with that."

I smiled against his abdomen. "You taste like sea salt and chocolate." I had no idea how that was even possible, but it didn't make it any less true.

"It's a combination of the sea enchantment and my bar soap," he replied, his knuckles brushing my cheek. "The elves make a myriad of products. I'm sure you've tried a few in your shower."

"I like the cherry shampoo," I admitted. "And the coconut." *Because it reminds me of Kalt.*

"Mmm, cherries. I wonder if that's what you taste like between your thighs." Norden's accented tones were pitched low, vibrating along my skin and somehow managing to stroke me in the place he'd just mentioned.

I nibbled the button of his jeans, my legs squeezing together as I fought the urge to let him have his way with me.

"What do you taste like between your thighs?" I asked him, my fingers joining my mouth to pop open his pants. I drew the zipper down with my teeth, only to realize he was bare beneath the fabric. No boxers. Just one hundred percent man.

"Open your mouth and find out," he dared me.

My lips curled. "That's part of the fantasy."

His irises melted into dark chocolate rings, his sensuality thickening the air. "It's part of my fantasy, too."

I arched a brow. "Have you also been eating selkie candy?"

"Every night since you arrived," he replied, his accented voice stroking me deep inside, urging me to fulfill both our desires at once.

But I focused on my initial plan first, my tongue parting the seam of his pants to trace his long, thick shaft all the way up to the head. A hint of precum waited for me, giving me a heady introduction to his sweet and salty flavor. "Like salted caramel," I whispered.

He grinned. "There are benefits to some of the candies."

I tilted my head. "Is that why you prefer the salted chocolate cookies?"

He tapped me on the nose and wiggled his brows. "You're learning."

"Hmm, I've been eating a lot of those." I followed my admission with another long lick.

"Perfect," he hummed, his fingers gliding back into my

hair to gently fist the strands. "I very much hope this fantasy includes you coming on my tongue."

"It does," I promised in a whisper, my lips near the tip of his cock. "But only after you come down my throat." I sealed my mouth around him as I used my hands to tug his pants away from his hips.

He groaned, his grasp tightening just enough to tell me he approved. Then he growled as I released him to finish removing his jeans.

At some point, he'd kicked off his boots. Maybe when he'd lain down. I really wasn't sure, nor did I care. I was just happy to finish the job by removing his socks and leaving him very naked on my bed.

"I can see why Lark prefers you in this state." Something I'd inferred from the commentary about the ice bath in their suite.

Norden smiled. "You flatter me wonderfully, Sunshine. Thank you."

"It's well-earned flattery," I promised him, crawling back up to kiss his arousal.

But this time he caught my hair and tugged me all the way up, his gaze burning with unveiled passion. "I should be worshipping you."

"This was supposed to be my fantasy."

"And your fantasy is you exploring my body to your heart's content?" He sounded rather pleased by that. "Well, my fantasy is quite the opposite, Sunshine. It involves me fucking you with my tongue until you pass out from screaming so hard."

I shivered. "O-oh." That was definitely, um... "Okay. Yes. I think. I mean, yes, please." It came out a bit rushed and convoluted, but no one had ever spoken to me so crudely and directly before.

I... I rather liked it.

He grinned as though he could tell I appreciated the blunt honesty.

Then he kissed me hard, his mouth telling me that what he'd shown me before was merely a soft introduction.

This was his true self, the sensual shifter who knew exactly how to destroy a woman with a few strokes of his tongue. And his resulting smile said he would enjoy it, too.

He rolled me to my back, his lips leaving mine to travel down my neck to my breasts.

And oh my Fae, no male had *ever* been this thorough in licking and nipping every inch of my chest.

He didn't go straight for the nipples like every other male I knew. No, he kissed me everywhere *except* the stiff peak, ensuring I was practically weeping and begging before he finally took that aching part of me between his lips.

I moaned, my fingers sliding into his hair as I held him against me, making sure he sucked the tender area to completion.

Then he went to the other mound, repeating everything and taking my sensitive tip between his teeth.

"*Norden.*" I nearly came from that alone, my legs shaking with a need I'd never experienced outside of my dreams.

The pure, unadulterated sex warming the air between us nearly suffocated me, leaving me shaking and begging for so much more.

My shorts disappeared.

Followed by my lace—something he removed with his teeth, dragging it inch by inch down my thighs before carefully setting them on the pillow beside me. He was reverent about it, as though he didn't want to risk destroying the fabric.

"I like them," he explained, noting the question in my

eyes. "I shall buy you many pairs to match, but in different colors."

These had been a dark blue that matched my eyes. "What color will you buy first?"

"Pink," he replied immediately. "To match your pretty, wet flesh."

Oh Fae... My skin was on fire, his words and accent doing something wicked to me inside.

And those eyes.

Sweet frost, they were the most alluring eyes I'd ever seen.

Chocolate brown swirls of lust and devious promises. He sat back on his haunches, surveying me, contemplating his next move, or maybe just admiring the view.

I went to my elbows, wanting to return the favor, because all the sun-kissed skin and sinewy muscles were worthy of my deep appreciation.

He was beautiful.

Over six feet of solid man, but with an underlying softness of a being who cared about his appearance. He took care of his skin and hair, and it showed.

Oh, did it show.

"I have a confession to make," he whispered, his gaze still caressing my curves. "I have experienced several different fantasies about you, Artica. And I don't know which one I want to bring to life first."

My lips curled. "I know how that feels. I've had several about you... and Kalt... and Lark."

"Always together?" he asked, canting his head a little.

I swallowed. "Sometimes one at a time." It came out in a whisper. "But it usually ends... with all of us."

"Do you want me to invite them now?" It was an honest question, his expression brimming with curiosity.

"Kalt won't come," I confessed, my heart stuttering at

the admission. "And, um, I like it being just you. For now." The notion of all three at once intimidated me. While Norden... he was sweet and soft and caring.

And he clearly knew how to please a fae.

"Are you sure?" he asked, his hands on my ankles as he gently pulled my legs apart to reveal my intimate flesh to his gaze. "Lark would join us willingly, if you need both of us."

"All I need and want right now is you," I promised him, my voice low and ending on a moan.

Because the way he was looking at me... it made me feel so alive. So complete. So *in need*. "Please, Norden," I breathed. "I want to feel—"

I bowed off the bed as his tongue met my damp folds, his touch and precision absolute. He wasted no time in showing me just what he could do with his mouth and his hands, his palms gliding up my thighs to my hips.

He sucked, licked, nipped, and *penetrated... ohhh...* I very much enjoyed every bit, but that... *that* was... "More," I begged. "More of..." I nearly screamed as he slid two fingers inside me, stroking a place so deep and complete that I forgot how to move.

Stars erupted in my eyes.

I wasn't even coming, but I was so close.

I felt as though I were flying in the clouds, the oxygen thin, my chest beating a chaotic rhythm born of fear and exhilaration.

He kissed my clit, then circled it with his tongue before sucking it deep into his mouth.

"Norden..." I wasn't going to last, his expert touch undoing me faster than I could even pleasure myself. "Oh, oh Fae... Oh..."

Every part of me shook, my stomach clenching with an almost painful sensation.

Then his teeth gently skimmed my sensitive flesh as he hooked his fingers upward, shooting me into the sun, where I exploded into a thousand Artica pieces.

Like, broke.

Utterly fractured.

Because there was no coming back from this.

Nor did I have any intent to ever resurface again.

This was true oblivion, filled with warmth and happiness and the most amazing pleasure known to fae kind.

When I finally drifted down from the clouds, I found Norden staring down at me with a look of male pride. "You come beautifully, Sunshine. And you taste divine. Shall we begin again?"

I palmed his cheek, pulling him down to kiss him, wanting to experience the flavor on his lips.

Salted caramel chocolate, I marveled, grinning against his mouth. *With a hint of coconut and sugary spice.*

This place truly was magical.

In the spirit of wanting to experience everything in kind, I whispered the words I needed him to hear. "Make love to me, Norden."

We could wait. We could see if this bond was truly meant to be. We could prolong the courtship and continue dating.

Or we could enjoy the obvious chemistry between us.

And flourish in the warmth blossoming in our souls.

He kissed me again, his hips aligning with mine to draw his thick arousal through my weeping heat. "Are you sure?" he whispered.

"Yes," I promised. *Unless...* "Do we need protection?" It wasn't something Elemental Fae needed; our males controlled procreation.

But I didn't know anything about selkies.

"I won't be able to impregnate you," he murmured. "Not until the triad is fully established and with Prince Lark's blessing."

"He has to approve it?" I asked, my legs wrapping around his hips as he rubbed intimately against me, ensuring my wetness coated him from head to base.

"He has to bless it," he confirmed. "And typically, in his position, he will want the first heir."

"Oh," I whispered. As he was the future king, that made sense. "Then we don't need protection." Because illness wasn't really a concern for a fae.

"No, we do not." He drew back a little, his head near my entrance.

"But do we… need his permission?" It was a weird question to voice, but Prince Lark was the future king. And Norden was his mate. So…

"To play?" Norden asked, a smile in his voice. "No. We'll never need his permission. Besides, he'll feel every part of this via our triad bond."

I swallowed. "*Every* part?"

"Well, the warm bits," he murmured, his lips brushing mine. "My heart beating for yours. My body indulging in the carnality of the moment. My resulting pleasure of hearing you scream."

A tingling sensation grew inside me with each statement, the notion of Prince Lark feeling our embrace a rather erotic twist of fate. "Oh," I breathed.

Norden smiled, his nose brushing mine. "Tell me again that you're sure, Sunshine."

I tightened my legs around his waist, my hands finding his cheeks. I stared deep into his eyes, ensuring he understood how I felt. "I'm sure, Norden."

Because I wanted to feel him.

To embrace him.

To embrace *this*.

He kissed me, his lips whispering words of a sweet benediction against mine as he slowly slid into me, his impressive length filling me to completion.

He wasn't wide so much as long, and slightly angled at the end to perfectly caress my sensitive spot inside.

His tongue stroked mine, his hand going to my hip while the opposite cupped my cheek. And then he began to move slowly, reminding me of a low tide shallowly caressing the shore.

Rhythmic.

Experimental.

Indulgent.

He was learning again, discovering my preferences and mingling them with his own.

When I clenched or moaned, he did it again.

When I inhaled sharply, he slowed.

When I raked my fingernails down his back, he smiled and eagerly struck me deep again.

Within minutes, we had our pace, his body taking mine with a knowledge that surpassed lifetimes. Like we were always meant to be here, dancing just like this, intimately connected and indulging in explosive passion.

Our souls rejoiced.

Our hearts beat as one.

The third level of the Elemental Fae bond snapped into place.

And I knew he would officially be mine forever.

There was no going back now, and in the moment, I couldn't bring myself to care. I just wanted *this*, him, our moment, our time in the sun together.

I could feel it streaming through the windows, illuminating our bodies as we mated. Our pace increased, turning into a frenzy of pants and harsh breaths, his mouth whispering words of encouragement against mine.

He wouldn't come until I did.

He wouldn't stop until I screamed his name.

I wrapped my arms around his neck, my legs still squeezing his hips and lifting my lower body in time with his thrusts.

"Harder."

"More."

"Faster."

"Oh Fae…"

The words were tumbling out of my mouth without recourse, my mind fracturing as he drove me back into that world of intense sensation, causing me to tumble headfirst into an oblivion only our souls would ever know together.

I felt him convulse, his pleasure pouring into me in a hot wave that branded my insides, claiming me as his in the same way my soul had already claimed him.

Forever bound.

Forever mated.

And as I drifted off to sleep in his arms, I realized I wouldn't have it any other way. This selkie might be new to me personally, but my soul knew his.

We were destined to be together. Right here. Right now.

My heart warmed, belief and hope mingling inside my veins.

Tomorrow is going to be a good day.

KALT

Today is going to blow frost nuts.

I'd barely slept last night, what with Artica bonding Norden and sending ice shards right through my heart.

Not literally.

But she might as well have.

I'd just fallen asleep when I'd felt their bond click into place. Then it'd deepened to a point that had told me what they'd done.

Because there was really only one way to achieve a third-level bonding as an Elemental Fae.

Via sex.

With seriously deep feelings.

It took most Elemental Fae months to achieve that sort of comfort and status with each other. But Artica was no normal Elemental Fae. She let her heart guide every decision. She lived in the moment. She was a being of cheer and delight.

And, admittedly, Norden was pretty easy to love.

Mate-bonding to him should make it easier for me to break this level-one connection with Artica.

Except it felt stronger than ever. Unbreakable, even. Like somehow Artica's resolve had only grown, making it that much harder for me to dismantle our link.

I blew out a breath, my insides churning with a mixture of ice and heat.

Artica and Norden were just down the hall.

They had no idea I'd returned last night, no idea that I'd been attempting to sleep just a few doors away from them.

Not that it mattered. I would have been able to sense their activities from realms away. They were both under my skin, ingrained in my heart, and I had no idea how to fix it.

Worse, the coronation was only mere hours away now.

Which meant I needed to check in with Artica to ensure she was ready for today. I'd leave the task in Norden's hands, but it really was my responsibility.

Just as I shouldn't have left this week.

Well, no, that wasn't true. I had to leave. But I should have taken her with me. She was my intern, after all. It was literally my job to teach her and prepare her for a role in Interrealm Fae relations.

Something that was even more pressing now, what with her bonding the selkie last night.

Prince Lark would be next.

Then whomever he recruited as third for the triad.

My stomach soured at the notion. I could easily accept her being with Lark and Norden. Fae, I'd spent all week imagining it while playing in the shower.

But Artica with another male? The very notion of it turned my insides, making me feel sick.

My head fell to my hands as I groaned. This was

precisely why I'd left, to try to rid myself of these possessive instincts, to give her a chance to grow with Norden and Lark without my involvement.

Yet, I'd felt every experience last night.

And Lark had kept me updated every time we'd spoken.

Not to mention Norden's lewd messages all damn week. He'd described several scenarios he intended to fulfill upon my return.

Which was usually what led me into the shower.

Frosting selkie.

He knew what he was doing. He very clearly—

A knock sounded on my door, the heavy reverberation familiar and sending an icicle down my spine. I knew exactly why he was here and what he would want.

But my answer remained unchanged.

Swallowing, I pushed off my bed to answer the door.

Prince Lark stood on the other side with a garment bag and a box in his hand. "Welcome home," he told me, pushing through the threshold without an invitation. "Your suit is in here, as is Artica's gown. When you're done getting ready, please ensure she receives her dress. And tell Norden that his tux is in our suite."

He turned without another word, exiting the way he'd come.

"That's it?" I called after him, stunned.

He paused at the door and turned. "Were you expecting a speech?"

I frowned, then cleared my throat. "Sort of." It came out as a grumble.

"Would you like a speech?"

"No."

He shrugged. "Then I'll see you in a few hours."

I gaped at the doorway, which was now empty since

he'd walked away. I ran into the hall after him. "My answer is still no, Lark."

He paused and glanced at me over his shoulder. "Who says the offer still stands, Water Fae?" He arched a brow, leaving me speechless. "See that my future queen is ready. After today, she'll no longer be your concern."

And with that, he left.

My jaw practically hit the ground. *Did he just… reject me? After all these months of stating I'm his and that it would only be a matter of time before I accept my place in his triad?*

I took an unsteady step back into my room, my heart skipping a beat in my chest.

"Who says the offer still stands, Water Fae?"

Did something else happen last night? Did he realize I wasn't meant to be with them because of Artica mate-bonding Norden?

I swallowed.

This was exactly what I'd needed him to realize.

So… so why does it hurt? Why does it feel wrong?

Like he'd just punched a hole right through my fucking heart, leaving me here to pick up the pieces.

Alone.

Just as I'd desired. Just as I'd said I'd wanted.

How much worse would this hurt if I'd bonded them, only to lose one of them to death?

My father went through that shortly after my birth. I didn't witness it, but I saw how sad and lonely he was over the years.

Was this how he'd felt?

No, it had to be worse. Because they were actually bonded. I wasn't fully bonded to any of them, only partially connected to Artica. And that would fade, as would this ache in my heart.

I'm doing the right thing, I told myself, standing straighter. *It's good that Prince Lark has finally accepted my decision.*

Nodding, I closed my door and focused on the garment bag and box.

Today, I would support him as a friend, not a lover. I'd break this initial link with Artica, leaving her in their capable hands. And I'd... I'd talk to Cyrus and Queen Claire about my next steps.

Because staying here and watching Lark, Norden, and Artica seek a mate-bond with someone else... would kill me.

Of course, it was what I deserved. So knowing Cyrus, he'd make me remain as a punishment. Or maybe he'd let me go.

He had a heart buried somewhere in that frosty chest of his.

I'd appeal to it and beg him to set me free of this torment.

Then I'd live my life... *alone.*

Clearing my throat, I focused on the task of preparing for the day. One more day in the happiest place on Earth. One more day of witnessing the life I could never have.

I can do this, I told myself. *I have to.*

Shoving the details away to mourn later, I worked on showering—this time, without fantasizing about Artica or *her* mates.

Then I donned the suit that Prince Lark had brought for me. It was a navy blue fabric that fit me perfectly, as did the pale blue button-down shirt beneath. I couldn't find a tie in the bag, so I left the top button undone and styled my hair around my shoulders.

As an emissary and a Water Fae Prince, I really should wear a crown, but the only item in the box was a tiara, which he'd clearly had made for Artica.

My lips curled as I ran my fingers over the fine edges.

This was going to be stunning on her.

I almost looked forward to delivering it, along with the gown.

At least until I actually reached her door and realized Norden was still inside.

Because I could hear him groaning.

My throat worked, my heart beating extra fast in my chest. I had no idea what she was doing to him, but he was clearly enjoying it.

"Swallow for me, Sunshine," I heard him say, making it *very* obvious what was happening inside.

A vivid image of her lips wrapped around his cock slammed into my mind, nearly forcing me to my knees on a wave of need so fierce that I couldn't breathe.

And then the door opened.

"Would you like to join us for breakfast, Frosty?" Norden asked casually, his chocolate hair damp from a recent shower, and a pair of blue flannel pajama pants sitting low on his hips. "Artica was just enjoying her first fruit cupcake of the morning."

My eyes narrowed.

That slippery selkie…

His gaze fell to my groin. "Hmm," he hummed. "Unless you're looking for another kind of breakfast?"

He stepped backward, allowing me to see Artica sitting on the bed with her hair wrapped up in a towel. She was wearing a pink robe that flirted with her thighs, and she had a bit of frosting on her nose from the strawberry cupcake in her hand. Her eyes brightened upon seeing me, her happiness infectious.

"Kalt!" She set her cupcake down and ran for me, throwing her arms around my middle and making the problem in my pants that much worse.

Because she felt amazing against me.

So curvy and perfect.

So happy and filled with joy.

"Careful, Sunshine," Norden purred. "You're going to make a mess of his suit." His brown eyes glimmered knowingly at me before he drew his finger across her nose to steal the bit of frosting. "Want some?" he asked, holding it to me first.

I glared at him.

He shrugged, unperturbed, and made a show of licking his finger clean. I could only imagine where else that'd been this morning.

Which *also* worsened my pants problem.

Because Fae, I was hard.

I should have fantasized in the shower. Scratched this unending itch. Fucked my hand until I could no longer think.

"Kalt?" Artica asked, slowly releasing me to meet my gaze. A hint of concern lurked in her features.

Because I'd gone as rigid as an ice sculpture.

And not just in my trousers.

I'd also not returned her embrace, something I actually did have an excuse for since I had a garment bag in one hand and a box in the other. "I, uh, have your gown for today." I held it up lamely.

"Oh," she replied, her brow furrowing. "Right. Thanks." She took the items from me to place them on the bed, her eyes no longer meeting mine. She kept her gaze averted as she waited awkwardly for whatever I'd say next.

Frost, I'd screwed this up.

Norden's resulting glare said he agreed.

But rather than scold me, he flashed a bright smile at Artica. "Let's see what Lark finally decided on."

"Finally decided on?" Artica repeated.

Norden nodded. "He had five different gowns made and couldn't figure out which one he wanted you to wear."

She blinked at him. "*Five?*"

"You're our Crystal Princess, Sunshine. He wants you to shine."

"But it's his coronation day. He's the one who needs to shine," she pointed out.

"Yes, with you playing a key part in it all." He brushed his knuckles against her cheek, the gesture so intimate that my heart ached.

"What part am I playing?" She sounded uncertain.

His touch moved to the back of her neck, where he curled his palm around her nape in a protective manner. "You'll be placing the crown on his head at the beginning of today's ceremonies."

"*What?*" She gaped at him, then at me, then at him. "Ohhhh, no. No. No. No. That's a disaster waiting to happen."

"It's a beautiful moment of respect filled with belief," Norden corrected her. "And it's the unique role always taken on by the future queen of our kind."

"Except we're not fully bonded yet," she reminded him. "I'm not the queen yet."

"No, you're the *future* queen," he said patiently. "Not all mate-circles are formed prior to the coronation. But you placing the crown on his head is a symbolic gesture meant to demonstrate your faith in him as a ruler, which is very important to the future success of our king."

"Shouldn't you do it as his actual mate?" she pressed.

"I have my own roles to play. Plural because the third member of his triad has yet to be firmly established." He cast me a glower at that before turning his gaze to her. "So I have to play double duty today. And you will be the

Crystal Princess in today's ceremonies. Which I know you've read about, Artica. So this can't be news to you."

She shivered, her eyes rounding. "I… I…"

"You're going to be perfect," he promised her, his forearm flexing as he tightened his grip. "All you have to do is go retrieve the crown from elves in the T&A and deliver it to Prince Lark on his throne. It's a ceremonial walk framed by patient elves and gingerbread men and said to be one of the most beautiful parts of the coronation. Hence, your exquisite gown and"—he used his free hand to gesture to the box holding the tiara—"this."

"Norden…"

"Shh," he hushed, pressing his lips to hers. "It's going to be all right, Artica. We'll be with you every step of the way."

"No, you won't," she replied, her hands going to her hips. "That Crystal Princess walk thing is all on me. *Alone*."

He grinned. "Well, I'll be watching you every step of the way. Undressing you with my eyes, thinking about how you taste between your thighs, and wondering what wicked delights we'll engage in *after* the ceremonies. Or during, if you like. I'm flexible."

She narrowed her gaze at him. "This is serious, Norden."

"Who says I'm not serious? I will absolutely fuck you on the throne, if that's your wish," he offered in that infamously sultry tone of his.

"Give us a minute," I interjected, knowing what she needed.

Norden arched a brow at me.

"Prince Lark said to tell you that your tux is in your suite. Why don't you go get ready while I talk to Artica?" I phrased it as a suggestion but told him with a look that it wasn't a request. It was a demand. Because she needed my brand of confidence right now.

"All right," he murmured, kissing Artica on the cheek. "I'll be back to escort you to the T&A in a bit." His gaze roamed over her. "A very accurate acronym, by the way. One I cannot wait to see come to life in that beautiful gown."

"Norden." I couldn't help the impatience in my tone. His sensual comments were not helping.

He sighed. "Always so frosty, Frosty." He kissed Artica once more, whispered something in her ear, and then winked at me on his way out.

I didn't even want to know what he'd said to her.

Particularly as it had turned her cheeks bright pink.

The door closed behind me, leaving Artica and me alone.

She still wouldn't look at me, her gaze on the open garment bag. It displayed a stunning ice-blue gown glittering with blue diamonds. A dress fit for a queen. Made just for her.

"Artica," I began.

"No, it's fine. I'm fine. I'll… I'll figure this out." She gave me a weak smile, my glamorous jewel appearing a little less bright. "You don't have to lecture me on the importance of today, Prince Kalt. I already know. And I'll do my best to make sure everything I do is right, to ensure I don't start a war between our kingdoms or anything improper."

I frowned at her. "That's not what I was going to say."

"But it's what you're thinking," she told me, looking at me now with hard sapphire eyes. "This is the position you wanted for me, right? To become the queen and help marry our kingdoms together?"

"It's a position I hoped for, yes. But I would never—"

"Well, you got your wish," she said, a humorless laugh falling from her lips as she touched the charm at her throat. "Guess I don't need this anymore." She flicked the clasp off her necklace, letting it fall to her palm. "Here. You can give it to someone else who needs it more."

She held it out for me to take, but I didn't move.

"What the fae is wrong with you?" I demanded. "Put that back on. It was a gift."

"A gift?" she repeated. "No, Prince Kalt. It wasn't. None of this was a gift. It was you playing with fate. Which worked out in the end." This time her smile was sad. "I don't begrudge you. This is the sort of happily-ever-after that most fae dream about. I can't fault you for making that a reality."

"Then why are you so sad?" I asked, my heart breaking at the sight of tears gathering in her eyes. "Did Norden do something? Did he say something?" I moved toward her, only for her to step back, keeping the distance between us. "Artica—"

"Norden said all the right things," she told me. "He's charming and beautiful and very much a part of me now. Prince Lark will be soon, too."

"Is it the ceremony? Are you nervous?" I wanted to understand her dimming light, to fix whatever had been broken inside her.

"Of course I'm nervous," she snapped, the tone one I'd never heard from her. "I've spent the last ten days reading everything I can because my mentor abandoned me. Fortunately, Norden and Lark have helped answer some of my questions. But I had no idea I would be part of the ceremony today. However, I suspect you knew."

"I knew the details, yes. But I wasn't sure if you'd be involved or not. There can be several Crystal Princess candidates. And when that happens, they all perform the ceremony together."

Which was admittedly rare, as most mate-circles were formed prior to the coronation. But I hadn't expected all this to move so quickly.

Of course, I should have known that Artica would follow her heart. She possessed a soul so purely innocent that she would never hesitate to listen to her instincts.

Unlike me.

I could never make up my mind, never choose my desires over fate.

"You're going to be amazing today," I told her, hopeful that all she needed was a little confidence. "You're perfect for this role, Artica. You're sweet. You're jovial. You know how to follow your heart and embrace the holiday spirit. And your affinity for ice only makes you that much more special here."

"Perfect for the role of Winter Fae Queen, but never good enough for you," she said sadly, her lips twitching, but not to smile. Her gaze left mine again, and something about it felt final. Like I would never be permitted to look upon her again.

Which was when I felt the fracture—not in her, but in my own soul.

As she released me from our mating bond.

Her tight hold founded on hope and belief and pure love had just... dissolved.

"Artica," I breathed, my chest suddenly empty as though she'd taken my heart with her.

"It's all right, Prince Kalt," she said, a formal note to her tone. "I know you never meant to mate me. Knowing me, I probably just wished for it."

She let the snowflake charm fall to the floor, the

glittering pendant the only sign between us that her heart still craved mine. But she was releasing me.

Out of love, I realized, my insides melting beneath the understanding of her sacrifice. She was giving me my freedom at the expense of her own joy. Of her own happiness. Of her own *heart*.

"I need to prepare myself," she continued, her shoulders straightening. "So, if you'll excuse me, I should be ready in about twenty minutes."

"Artica..." I wasn't sure what to say, my mind seeming to stutter to a halt, a sensation that was made worse as she finally looked at me again without an ounce of feeling in her gaze.

"There's nothing left for us to discuss," she said, her tone flat. "I know my purpose and understand my duty. I won't let you down, Prince Kalt."

She turned away from me as she finished speaking, her focus on the gown and tiara.

I stared at her for a long moment, my fingers tingling with the need to touch her.

But she'd made her decision.

She... she rejected our link.

And with that act, she'd just broken my heart.

ARTICA

The door whispered to a closed position behind me, confirming Kalt's departure.

I stared at the gorgeous gown and tiara, the two items that resembled my future. My purpose in life.

Yet I'd never felt so conflicted.

Part of me rejoiced, my connection to Norden thriving inside my soul.

And part of me wept, my realization that Kalt had never wanted to be mine a literal stab to the heart.

He hadn't even embraced me. Over a week apart, and he couldn't even try to hug me? He'd been so stiff. So unyielding.

Which was when I'd realized he'd been trying to pull away.

Not physically, but spiritually.

He doesn't want me.

He's never wanted me.

A fact he'd made more than clear when he'd selected

me to be his replacement candidate for the Winter Fae mate-circle.

It was never about him joining and also potentially mating me as well.

It was about giving Prince Lark another ice elemental.

I glanced at the wish charm on the ground.

He'd claimed that was to help me when I needed it. A wishing pendant to fulfill whatever I desired. *Within reason.*

It would never give me Kalt's heart.

How foolish I'd been to ever think I'd had a chance with him.

We were compatible, but fae needed more than that to mate.

He'd chosen his lonely fate over his potential connections. There was nothing left for me to do other than respect his decision.

And move on.

Sunshine? Norden whispered into my mind, using our freshly established mating bond.

Sometimes mates could start hearing each other around the second level and talking around the third, but it was guaranteed by the fourth. The fact that we could speak freely now was indicative of our intense compatibility.

Are you all right? he asked tentatively.

You felt that, didn't you? I thought back at him.

Yes.

I swallowed. *He doesn't want me, Norden. He doesn't want us.*

I know, Sunshine. I know.

A tear escaped my eye and I wiped it away. *I need to get ready.*

I'll be back soon to hug you.

I would like that, I admitted, another tear finding my cheek. I froze it with my water magic and flicked it off. *No more of that.*

No more of what?

Sorry, talking to myself, I muttered.

Hmm, I'm going to enjoy this link.

You already did this morning, I reminded him, thinking back on how I'd accidentally woken him with my dream.

That he quickly turned into a reality with his mouth.

I look forward to an eternity of mornings with you, Sunshine. His words touched my heart, helping to melt away some of the frozen edges. *Prince Lark says he's looking forward to it as well.*

I'd been in the middle of loosening my robe and paused. *He… he's not mad, is he?* Norden had made it sound like we could play freely last night, but now I wondered if Lark was jealous or upset that we'd bonded without him.

Norden's chuckle tickled my thoughts. *Oh, he's not mad. He's turned on as hell, though.*

My cheeks heated. *Turned on?*

Yeah, he's pissed he has to go meet with his father. Otherwise, he'd be in my ass right now. Norden sounded delighted. I wasn't sure if it was Prince Lark's torment or the potential sex that amused him. Perhaps both.

He released another chuckle, causing my lips to curl. *Can you keep talking to me?* I asked, needing to hear his cheerful tones.

Oh, always, he replied. *Now that I have this link, I'll never leave you alone. I mean, think of all the naughty things I can whisper to you, even from afar.*

I finished untying my robe. *Well, I am putting on the pink underwear you made me wish for earlier,* I told him, finding the lacy panties from the dresser. *They're really soft and silky.*

Mmm, tell me more. I could almost picture him lounging on a bed, head propped on his elbow, free hand, er, not so free below.

I'm naked and bending over to slip one foot in, and now the other… Oh, yes, these are softer than I thought, Norden. They're sliding right up my legs all the way to my candy center.

He chuckled. *Candy center?*

Do you have a better term?

Pussy? Cunt? Sweet haven? Norden's favorite snack? He kept going while I laughed, his brand of humor exactly what I needed to help me find the remainder of my joy inside. *Lark's future pound house. He goes hard, by the way. But he might be softer with you. We'll see. Oh, it could also be called a sausage slider, or a—*

A sausage slider? I repeated, the gown in my hands now. *You think* that *is better than "candy center"?*

Hmm, a decent point well made, he said. *Candy cane shoot?*

Another laugh burst out of me. *Is your cock a candy cane now?*

Ohhh, say cock *again, please. I very much enjoyed that particular term in your mind.*

Maybe I should give you some nicknames, I replied instead. *Lollipop. Popsicle. Oh, no, wait. Creamsicle.*

You going to swallow all my cream for me, Sunshine?

My legs clenched. *Fae, you really can turn anything dirty, can't you?*

I really can. It's a natural talent of mine.

I finally pulled on the gown, but the lace-up back gave me pause. *Frost.*

I think it's too soon for me to be making Frosty innuendos, he replied solemnly.

No, I just realized my dress laces up the back. I bit my lip and glanced at the door. *I'm going to have to ask Prince Kalt for help.*

Prince Kalt, is it? He sounded a bit sad by that.

It's his title. I should call him by it. I considered the door again and instead slipped out of the dress to focus on my hair first. That way I would be completely ready apart from my shoes by the time I had to face him again.

Assuming he was even still there.

He seemed to have a penchant for disappearing.

Blowing out a breath, I tossed the towel off my head and used my water ability to suck the moisture from my strands of hair. Not too much, just enough to create a dry texture. Then I combed it out and added a little more water back in, freezing a few curls in place around my face.

There, I thought, returning to the case to pick up the tiara. It glittered like ice, the glass-like quality delicate and beautiful.

What happened to my play-by-play? Norden asked, a hint of a pout in his tone.

I'm working on my hair.

Then you should absolutely be detailing every moment to me, he replied.

Giggling, I went through my process with him in my head as I centered the tiara and froze it in place with a little magic.

No snowdrifts, all right? It's not in season this year, he told me.

I snorted, the unladylike sound thankfully not traversing mentally through our link. *With my luck, I would end up with icicles for curls.* My magic had been acting a bit weird all week. I suspected it had something to do with Kalt, and now that I realized he'd been dreading our bond, I could understand why.

Perhaps that was the only positive that had come from letting him go—my powers would return to normal.

Sighing, I went back to the dress. *I'm going to ask Prince Kalt to help me.*

Yes, do, he encouraged.

It won't fix anything, Norden, I warned him as I pulled on my dress. *What's done is done. Once a fae bond is broken, it cannot be fixed.*

Well, technically, at the first level, it was possible.

However, the two Elemental Fae had to really want to give it another shot for the bond to reignite.

It was the second stage that would be irrevocably broken if fractured.

And if an Elemental Fae tried to break the third level? Well, that would be bad for all parties involved. It was the equivalent of a marriage with the fourth level being the soul-binding ceremony.

Clearing my throat, I ignored Norden's sigh in my head and pulled the dress back up. Then I walked to the door with my head held high and opened it. An amazing feat, really, considering I was holding my dress up with one dignified hand.

Kalt stood opposite, his spine erecting instantly upon seeing me on the threshold. "Artica—"

"I'm not ready yet," I interrupted. "But I need some help. The ribbons at the back lace up and, well, I can't lace them. So…"

Rather than say anything else, I just turned around to show him my back.

To which he didn't respond or move.

My jaw ticked.

This was ridiculous. He wanted me in this position; he could at least assist me in being properly dressed for it.

Oh, but he couldn't help me all week with my studies. He'd left me to do it on my own.

So of course he expected me to do it again now.

I should have known better than to even—

His fingertip brushed my spine, sending a chill through my entire being. It felt wrong. It felt right. It *hurt*. It made my heart sing.

I closed my eyes, my throat suddenly thick with too many emotions for me to speak.

He didn't comment or say a word, just allowed his touch to glide down to the base and back up to the space between my shoulder blades where the initial row of lace met my skin.

Kalt grabbed both ends, pulled them tight, and began the process of threading the lace through the hoops all the way down my back.

It was a corset top that flattered my curves, giving me a decent amount of cleavage. Admittedly, the snowflake pendant would look lovely there. But I refused to wear it.

The "gift" felt tainted. Cruel. Like it held some sort of dark secret I would never understand.

Just like Kalt.

I'd never understand him, either.

He worked in silence, the air thick between us. When he finally reached the bottom, I released my death grip on the front and opened my eyes, only to sigh at how beautiful the ice-blue fabric looked against my skin.

I feel like a porcelain doll, I thought at Norden.

"You look like a queen," my selkie replied out loud, startling me.

I looked sharply to my left and found him waiting in an all-white tux that popped beautifully with his sun-kissed coloring. "I didn't realize you were back." I'd sensed him nearby but assumed that was just our bond thriving with joy.

He smiled. "I was admiring the view."

Kalt cleared his throat and took a step back, his work done.

"Thank you, Prince Kalt," I said, needing to say something to show my gratitude. Although, it fell a bit flat, my tone sounding brittle to my ears.

He didn't reply, just as silent as before.

But Norden's infectious grin distracted me from the

frost pick digging into my heart. "You're stunning, Artica," he praised.

I faced him and curtsied. "You look pretty good yourself, selkie."

He chuckled. "I look amazing."

"And so modest, too," I teased.

"Always," he replied. "Now, where are your shoes?"

"Oh!" I'd almost forgotten that I needed them. Between Norden's appraisal and Kalt's brooding silence, I was a bit lost in my emotional cloud.

I started forward, but Norden caught my wrist. "Ah, ah. Stay right here. I will grab them."

I frowned after him, then risked a glance at Kalt to see if he understood.

Which was a mistake.

Because he was staring at me with a look of wonder on his face, his icy gaze filled with so much emotion that it made my heart hurt.

That was the look I'd longed to see on him for so many years, the look that said he finally *saw* me. But it was too late now. And I suspected he didn't even really mean it. He just wanted to help me feel more confident about my task, ensure I didn't screw this up.

Because today wasn't just important for our relations with Winter Fae kind. It was a demonstration for all the visiting realms.

A demonstration of unity and grace and *inclusiveness*.

The commingling of the races, even for something as innocent as a coronation, would never have been permitted with the old way of thinking.

The Winter Fae were better than all the other realms for so many reasons, namely their ability to accept differences. Typically, when two fae of different faedoms mated, an abomination could be created—a being of power that was to be feared.

As the future Winter Fae Queen, I would inevitably abandon my Source and embrace a new one, which was the only accepted practice of mating outside our own races —similar to the Fortune Fae who abandoned their Source completely.

That wasn't necessarily new for the Winter Fae, but having guests attending from all the different realms was absolutely a change.

Because today's coronation served as the first official Interrealm Fae event since the signing of the Interrealm Fae Treaty—an agreement between the faedoms that Queen Claire had organized via a series of votes.

There would be abominations present today— abominations who would be accepted and allowed to mingle.

And there would be the possibility for unmated fae to meet potential mates during arguably the happiest and most romantic occasion of this realm. This alone was unheard of among fae kind, a brand-new development in our relations among the faedoms.

Because times were changing.

Queen Claire, a powerful Halfling, had saved the Elemental Fae from extinction.

Aflora, the Earth Fae Queen and now the Midnight Fae Queen, had mated into Midnight Fae lines, managing to convince the Dark Source and the Earth Source to work together.

Both queens were considered abominations who had made the Interrealm Fae efforts possible. And they weren't even really born of separate fae lines, just became extremely powerful via their mate-circles. But they used their powers for good, not evil, establishing a new precedent for all of fae kind.

Until their reigns, abominations had been so frowned upon, the faedoms secluding themselves in an effort to avoid creating any crossing links, that fae had lost touch with each other. We'd lost touch with our true purpose in life.

To live.

Kalt cleared his throat. "You really are stunning, Artica."

I forced a smile, his words ones I'd only ever heard in my dreams. How I wished they were true now. Heartfelt. Filled with the emotion I craved. But I knew better now. "Thank you, Prince Kalt," I said, repeating my statement from earlier and returning my focus to Norden.

His brown irises were twinkling with delight as he approached me with a pair of silver heels. "Lark had the elves enchant these not to hurt your feet," he said as he knelt in front of me. "May I do the honors?"

Just like before, his contagious energy pulled me out of my saddened state, making me grin. "I'm starting to think you have a foot fetish in addition to the hair fetish."

"I have many fetishes, Sunshine," he confided, winking up at me.

Then he took hold of my ankle and slid my foot into the shoe. His deft fingers buckled it easily.

"Use my shoulder to balance," he murmured as he reached for the other ankle.

"My shoulder makes more sense," Kalt interjected.

I frowned but agreed because of the height differential, so I gingerly placed my hand on his shoulder to balance while Norden worked on my other foot. As soon as he released me, I removed my hand, then wiggled my fingers to dispel the residual tingle in them.

Norden stood, the heels only making me eye level with his mouth. Which I suspected he'd done on purpose.

I glanced up into his eyes to find him smiling down at me. "You're going to be the most beautiful queen this kingdom has ever seen," he told me. "I cannot wait to announce you."

"Announce me?" I repeated.

"My role," he reminded me, making me realize I'd forgotten all about today's coronation activities despite reading through the rituals over a dozen times.

"Right. At T&A."

He chuckled. "Almost as fun as hearing *cock* roll off your tongue." He frowned then. "Actually, I haven't heard it yet from your mouth. Care to indulge me?"

Kalt cleared his throat again, reminding us of his presence. "We should go."

"Spoilsport," Norden accused.

Kalt just looked at him, then he glanced at me. "I'll escort you to the *toy shop*. Norden will meet us inside."

Norden sighed loudly. "Double spoilsport." With a shake of his head, he brushed a kiss against my cheek. "See you soon, queen of mine. I'll be the one in white waiting for you at the altar."

My lips parted, the rest of the ceremony suddenly revealing inside my mind. "Oh Fae…" *I'm totally going to frost this up.*

LARK

"**Y**ou are not walking Artica down the aisle," I said flatly. "Kalt will do it."

"No, he won't," Cyrus insisted, the Water Fae King just as arrogant as I remembered. "Artica broke her mate-bond with him. I just felt it. Which means he isn't the right fae for this task. As his cousin, and the Water Fae King, I will handle this part of the ceremony."

A ceremony Cyrus only knew about because I had been foolish enough to inform him of how today would work.

I had thought it was a form of friendship, a way to solidify the partnership between the Winter Fae Kingdom and the Elemental Fae Kingdom. I was about to mate two Water Fae, after all. Best to keep their king aware and involved.

But this was not the plan.

"I need Kalt to do this," I stressed. "He's part of my triad, and it's the only way to include him in the festivities. Otherwise, he'll be forced to watch."

"Which is exactly what you should do," Cyrus replied.

I folded my arms and considered the Water Fae King. He was roughly my height, a little more slender, but still muscular, with short white-blond hair and eyes that reminded me of Kalt's. I could definitely see the resemblance between them. Not to mention their shared interest in politics and strategy.

"Tell me why," I said, curious to hear his thought process.

The Water Fae King smiled. "He needs to see the life he's giving up in exchange for his path of loneliness. He thinks that avoiding mate-bonds will ensure his heart never aches, but I can sense his pain via the Water Source right now. Artica's rejection has unnerved him."

"So now you want me to hurt him more by removing him from the ceremony?" I asked, not enjoying this logic at all. It wasn't the Winter Fae way. We believed in love and embracing life. This sounded like a punishment.

"No, I want you to grant his wish of solitude so he can realize it's not what he really wants," Cyrus replied. "Sometimes one has to witness the triumphs of others to realize what life is truly about. Show him what it means to live, make him crave it, and inspire him to believe that it's what he deserves to experience."

"By shoving him to the side, I'm essentially telling him he doesn't deserve it," I pointed out.

"By giving him the *option* to stand down, you're telling him that you are agreeing to his wishes, whatever they may be."

I frowned. "You told me that you're walking her down the aisle, not giving him an option."

"Because I will be," he replied, a note of exasperation in his tone. "I know what my cousin will choose if offered the option, which is why I'm telling you that I'll be walking her down the aisle. But you're missing the point—by giving him the gift of a choice, you're saying you respect his decision. Then you'll demonstrate what he's missing through today's ceremonies, so he realizes the error of his choice."

"And if he doesn't realize the error?" I pressed. "Do I just let him go?"

Cyrus's expression turned sad, his chin dipping into a nod. "Yes, you do."

"I can't do that."

"You can," he countered. "Because if he still doesn't agree to join your triad after the beauty of today? Then he's not worthy of you or Artica."

His words sent ice cubes down my spine, his regal stance and tone befitting his station. But it was the wisdom radiating from him that called to the strategist inside me.

Because he was right.

If Kalt rejected us after today, after everything he felt and experienced, he truly wasn't worthy of us.

My queen deserved more.

Norden deserved more.

And if Kalt wasn't willing to give them what they both deserved?

Then he wasn't meant for our triad.

My soul ached at the thought, the Winter Fae Source vibrating with a cord of belief that wrapped itself around my heart so roughly that I gasped.

This wasn't just about testing Kalt.

It was about believing in him to make the right choice, to choose *us*, to be with his triad.

But I couldn't force his choice.

I merely had to believe that he would come to terms with his fate and accept it.

"All right," I finally said. "Give him the option."

Cyrus nodded. "Don't be surprised when he tells me to walk her down the aisle. And don't give up hope. Seeing is believing, right?" He grinned at his play on words, the popular phrase one the humans spouted frequently.

"You've studied more than you admitted," I accused him.

"Of course I did," he replied with a laugh. "This is my mate's dream, a union between the realms. I read every damn book I could find about your kind."

"Yet you came to me and asked me to explain the ceremony."

He shrugged. "I didn't say I wasn't familiar with it."

"But why ask?"

"Interrealm Fae bonding," he replied, clapping me on the shoulder. "Again, it's all about making my mate happy."

"And it has nothing to do with your cousin's happiness?"

He grinned. "Well, Kalt being happy would make Claire happy, so…"

"I see." I returned his grin. "Life is all about Queen Claire."

"And it's an amazing life indeed," he murmured, his gaze sliding to where his queen stood across the throne room with their other mates. "Kalt deserves to experience love, even if he doesn't believe it himself."

"We'll make him happy," I vowed.

"I know, or I wouldn't be helping." Cyrus returned his gaze to mine. "But he's vulnerable right now. Having a mate-bond broken, even at the first level, can hurt. And he's more devastated than he even realizes."

I nodded. "I can sense his pain. Artica's, too." It'd taken serious restraint not to go to her, but Norden had promised me he would handle it.

And from what I could sense in the forming bonds of my mate-circle, he'd given her some balance. But she was still hurting, a sensation I really didn't want for her ever, and especially not today. Not when she would be experiencing the Winter Fae Source for the first time.

However, I knew she could handle it.

She'd proved this week to be the perfect fae for our kingdom. She'd studied hard yet found moments of enjoyment. She'd embraced the magic of my kind. She'd indulged in all the various foods, never once denying a single sample. She'd laughed and smiled and pranced around the halls.

And she'd mated Norden last night.

That had confirmed everything I needed to know.

Time was irrelevant.

Because our souls all knew where we belonged.

Right here. Together. Today.

For this Winter Fae Coronation.

ARTICA

M y eyes narrowed. "You want me to walk with *King Cyrus* into the toy shop?" I couldn't believe my pointy ears. "After everything you've orchestrated here, *that* is your final send-off?"

I'd moved from the sad stage of grieving to the furious stage of grieving.

Because *this* was unacceptable.

"Well, your father would have been a good alternate choice, but he hasn't answered Cyrus's summons."

My eyebrows lifted. "King Cyrus reached out to my parents?" Somehow, that made this all worse. The Academy would have sent them a notice about my internship placement, but in all the faesanity of the last ten days, I'd failed to reach out to them even once.

Of course, they were on summer holiday at the moment.

So they wouldn't be easily reached, anyway.

"He tried, but with the lack of communication

technology in our realm, it's hard to locate them directly," Kalt replied.

"They're on summer holiday," I muttered. "They might not even be in the realm." They often traveled to other faedoms or the Human Realm for vacation. So it was hard to say. I would have been with them, but I'd wanted an Interrealm Fae internship instead.

And look where that had landed me—right smack in the middle of the Winter Fae Realm, preparing to walk down the aisle with King Cyrus.

I shivered. Despite last night's excitement, I rather preferred finding my parents right about now.

He sighed. "Artica, you realize it's an honor for the Water Fae King to escort you, right? Think about the fae relations and what this symbolizes? It shows the Elemental Fae approve of this joining." Kalt appeared ready to break, but I didn't care. I wanted to introduce a snowball to his overly handsome face.

"An honor," I deadpanned. "Awesome. Well, it was nice working for you, Prince Kalt. Enjoy the rest of your day." I started to walk away, then stopped and spun around to face him. "You know what? You should just leave. It's not like you want to be here anyway." I resumed my stomp toward the workshop.

"*Artica*," he snapped, sending a chill down my spine.

Because yeah, I probably shouldn't be speaking to royalty like that.

I swallowed and glanced back at him. "Sorry. I shouldn't have said that. You've worked really hard to bring us all to this point, and I'm sure you want to see the result of all that effort." I curtsied low and stood. "Thank you for your service to our kingdom, Prince Kalt."

There. That was much more professional and semi-sweet.

I turned again, only to have my wrist caught in his grip. "*Stop*," he hissed against my ear. "Just. *Stop*."

A few of the elves outside paused to look at us. They'd been in the middle of streaming the final lights along the walkway I would be gracing soon as part of the ceremony.

"Everything all right?" a cool voice asked from my left.

My heart skipped a beat at the sight of King Cyrus approaching us in a suit very similar to Kalt's—all navy blue with a light-blue shirt beneath. No tie. "Everything is perfect, my king," I lied, trying to curtsy but finding my wrist still trapped in Kalt's grip.

"Hmm," King Cyrus hummed, his gaze going to my arm and then to the man behind me. "Kalt? Having second thoughts?"

"No," he replied, releasing me immediately.

"Pity," King Cyrus said. "Well, you may want to find a place to watch inside. It's starting to fill up." He moved to my side. "I'll take her from here."

I was partly thankful for the save and partly terrified to be left alone with one of the most powerful Elemental Fae of my existence.

King Cyrus's intimidating presence made me feel a bit weak in the knees. But at least I wouldn't have to start this off on my own.

"Of course," Kalt replied, bowing. "You'll be amazing, Artica."

I nearly snorted at him. Because wow, what a *kind* thing to say.

But he was already walking away, not even caring what I had to say in response.

My shoulders started to cave inward, my heart sinking even lower than before. Because he'd just left me here to be escorted by King Cyrus.

It was an honor; I couldn't deny that.

Yet somehow it felt like an even bigger rejection than his lack of a hug earlier.

"Let's fix that tiara," King Cyrus said suddenly, stepping in front of me to nudge my chin up with his knuckles. His icy eyes crinkled at the sides as he stared down at me. "There, that is so much better."

I blinked at him, then realized he was straightening my spine for me and telling me to hold my head high. "Sorry, I..." I wasn't sure how to finish that. *I'm sorry. I'm in love with your cousin, and he doesn't like me, so I've turned into a pouting princess.*

I frowned.

That is not who I am, I reminded myself.

Then I glanced around at the elves, noted their cheery dispositions and the light shimmer of snow in the air.

This *is who I am*, I thought. *A Water Fae in the middle of a winter wonderland. This is a dream come true. I need to embrace it, not pout about it.*

King Cyrus smiled as though he could read my mind. "Yes, much better indeed." He released my chin but didn't step out of my personal space. "Prince Lark is ready in the throne room, awaiting his crown. Which I'm told you will be delivering to him personally."

I swallowed. "I, uh, yeah. As the Crystal Princess of today's ceremony."

"As his intended queen," he replied. "And I could not think of a better candidate than you, Artica."

I gaped at him. "You can't?" *Not even Kalt? Your own cousin? A Water Fae you actually know?*

"My little queen has told me a lot about your festive spirit. You helped her decorate her office last year, and the Chancellor Home."

My lips started to curl. "That was fun."

"If you say so," he replied, his own mouth curving at

the edges. "Your infectious joy is just what this kingdom needs. You'll make a fine Winter Fae Queen."

"I'd listen to him," a higher-pitched voice said. "He's not the type to placate or tell false truths."

"No, I am most definitely not," he replied, his expression softening as he faced Queen Claire.

I curtsied low, my cheeks filling with warmth at being in their regal presence. Yes, I'd interned for her for a little over a year. But they were two of the strongest elementals in Elemental Fae history.

They'd even defeated the *plague*.

"You look beautiful," Queen Claire praised.

"Why, thank you, little queen," King Cyrus replied, brushing his knuckles down his suit jacket. "My mate selected this for me."

"Yes, Vox has amazing taste," she deadpanned. "And I was speaking to Artica."

King Cyrus pressed a palm to his chest. "You wound me, my love."

Queen Claire rolled her blue eyes. "Doubtful." She looked at me, her expression brightening. "You remind me of a snowflake, only so much prettier."

I smiled. "Thank you, my queen." I took in her regal gown of gold and silver. "You look amazing." I noted her braid and the crown on her head, smiling. "And you've perfected your hair."

"Oh, this?" She pretended to fluff up her crown. "Just an old trick I learned from one of my favorite interns."

"Favorite, huh?" I repeated.

"You know it's true," she told me. "Which is why I know Cyrus is going to treat you with great care as he walks you down that aisle to the toy room."

"I would never think to do anything else," King Cyrus vowed, bowing to his mate. Then he caught her hand and brought it to his lips. "You really are stunning, little queen." Her cheeks turned pink at his praise.

"I'm still not giving you another son yet."

He sighed. "I know. We need better games."

"Do not start that again," Queen Claire immediately snapped.

King Cyrus merely chuckled. "You enjoyed them, little queen."

She cleared her throat, her cheeks now a bright red. "Have fun today, Artica. You've earned it."

"Thank you," I said, smiling as she quickly walked back to the Spirit Fae King, who had been waiting for her a few steps away. He shot a grin at King Cyrus as he wrapped his arm around Queen Claire to escort her to wherever they intended to observe today's festivities. Likely the throne room, as that was where the real magic would take place.

"She says she doesn't want another baby yet," King Cyrus informed me conversationally. "But we know she's been dreaming about one."

"Are you giving her selkie candy?" I wondered out loud.

King Cyrus frowned. "Selkie candy?"

"They inspire you to dream about your fantasies," I explained. "Norden's been, uh, giving them to me."

The Water Fae King chuckled. "I've only met Norden in passing, but I dare say we may need to become better friends."

"He doesn't bless the candy, or rather, he isn't part of the process. He just orders them."

King Cyrus stared at me. "What?"

"It's how the selkie candy is made," I said slowly, thinking that was why he wanted to be better friends. But now I understood that he'd meant something else entirely

—that he liked the sound of Norden's style of, er, *seduction.* I cleared my throat. "Never mind."

Sunshine? Norden's concerned voice popped into my head. *Everything all right out there?*

I'm fine. Just making a fool out of myself in front of the Water Fae King.

Ah, yes, Prince Lark mentioned he would be walking you inside. I'm sure he adores you.

More like he adores you, I replied.

Everyone adores me, he hummed in return. *I'm very lovable.*

I smiled. *Yes, you are.*

"Artica?" King Cyrus asked, drawing me back to him.

Because he still stood in front of me.

And I was grinning like a loon now.

Wow. I really could not make this any worse. "Sorry, Norden is in my head," I explained.

He smiled then. "Ah, new mate-bonding." He leaned forward, his icy gaze far friendlier than I'd ever seen it. "Can I let you in on a little secret?"

"Um, sure?" I cleared my throat. "I mean, yes, please."

"Hearing your mate in your head will always make you smile," he confided softly. "Claire's voice will always be the first and last sound I crave inside my mind. And I suspect your mates will mean the same to you soon."

He offered his arm. "Now, I think it's time for us to begin."

I glanced around at all the silent elves, their gazes expectant.

Then the sound of a bell chimed, bringing huge grins to all their cheery faces. I found my own lips curving in kind.

This felt right.

Mostly, anyway.

But as I gazed at King Cyrus, I realized I wouldn't have this any other way.

Because he at least *believed*. I could sense it in his aura, a strange sort of tingling energy I'd never known existed. Yet it hummed along his presence, calling to my soul in a manner I didn't fully understand.

However, I trusted the process.

And slipped my arm through his.

"I'm ready," I announced. The words were confident and bolstered from deep inside. The Winter Fae Source was calling to us all, stirring electricity and cheer across the kingdom.

"Oh," King Cyrus murmured, releasing me. "I nearly forgot." He pulled out a box from his pocket and held it out for me. "This is for you. From Prince Lark."

It was a little red package similar to the one Kalt had given me before he'd first brought me here.

I opened it hesitantly, afraid of what I would find inside.

A note waited for me beneath the paper.

Dearest Artica,

This necklace might be from Kalt, but some of the magic in the snowflake is from me. And I would be honored if you continued to wear it.

Remember, we exist here because of our beliefs.

Everything happens for a reason…

Yours,

Lark

. . .

I stared at the snowflake pendant. The same one I'd left in my room. Norden must have retrieved it when he'd gone in to find my shoes.

Sneaky selkie, I thought at him.

Who, me? he hummed back at me. *Sultry, definitely. Sneaky, only when it benefits me.*

The snowflake necklace? I prompted.

A benefit, I'm sure, he returned.

I sighed and shook my head. *I don't want to wear it. I don't like what it represents.*

The pendant glitters when you're near your intended mates, Sunshine. And it burns brightly around Kalt, something he needs to see one more time.

The pendant glitters around my intended mates? I asked, startled by that information.

Kalt bespelled it to ensure you weren't coaxed into something that wasn't right, Norden replied. *He thinks we don't know, but Lark added his own brand of magic to the necklace, too.*

What did he add?

You'll have to ask him, Norden murmured. *But please wear it. We need to remind Kalt where he belongs.*

I sighed. *But he doesn't want us.*

He does; he just has to believe, Norden whispered back to me.

I considered that for a moment, my eyes automatically scanning all the smiling elves and gingerbread sentries.

All these beings existed because of the belief in this realm.

Prince Lark still believed in Kalt.

Norden did, too.

What kind of queen would I be if I chose not to believe in him? *The kind that broke our mate-bond,* I thought, grimacing.

But just because I'd broken it didn't mean we couldn't *fix* it.

However, for that, Kalt needed to believe.

So I'd give him this boost since Lark and Norden had requested it.

I'd show him that I still had a glimmer of hope.

But it was on him to accept it and make the next move.

"There," King Cyrus said, grinning as I donned the necklace again. He took the box from me and pocketed it once more, then extended his arm. "*Now* we can begin."

KALT

The hum of magic in the air caused all the hairs along my arms to dance. I could almost taste the holiday spirit on my tongue, the fresh surge of cinnamon and spices a tangible essence in the atmosphere.

Almost as though someone had lit a bunch of incense.

Norden stood at the door to the workshop, his back straight as he somehow managed to hold a serious expression—something I'd really never seen on him before —while everyone else in the room grinned with expectation.

Their future queen was coming.

On the arm of the Water Fae King.

My stomach twisted, my soul screaming at me for taking the cowardly way out. But when Lark had offered me the option, I'd immediately told him Cyrus was the more appropriate Water Fae for the job.

From an Interrealm Fae relations standpoint, he made the most sense.

Because I wasn't Lark's mate.

Not really, anyway.

While the pull was certainly there, I'd far from acted like a good triad member. I didn't deserve the honor of standing beside Artica and walking her down the aisle to greet the elves.

Because I pushed her away. I pushed them all away. And for what?

I really only had myself to blame for all of this. It'd been easy to accept this fate when I felt as though it were for a good cause.

But Artica's expression earlier—the way some of her joy had literally died when she'd severed our link—had opened my eyes to a new world of pain.

A world of pain that *I* had caused.

Not just for myself—something I could have accepted —but for her, too.

When she'd kept calling me *Prince Kalt* and acting as though we were nothing more than colleagues, I'd nearly snapped. Because she knew damn well that she meant more to me than that.

Except.

She *didn't* know that, because I'd run away from her rather than embrace our bond.

A bond she'd severed.

Because she no longer believed in me.

A self-fulfilling prophecy, I thought numbly. I didn't believe in myself, either. That was the whole problem. I didn't trust my own belief to be good enough for the triad, good enough for *her*.

And I'd proved it through all my actions, pushing her away to the point where she'd rejected me.

However, it wasn't just me she'd rejected, but part of her own heart. *That* was the part I hadn't seen coming, the part I hadn't factored into any of this—how my denial would impact those I was destined to love.

I thought by pushing them away that I would be protecting us from eventual heartache. But that wasn't the case at all; I was merely escalating that heartache and ensuring it came to fruition.

My cousin's words echoed in my mind about love being the key to life, how his mate-circle gave him purpose.

Without that purpose, who am I? I wondered. *An emissary hoping to bring the realms together? But for what cause? What drives me to follow that fate?*

Not love.

Not my triad.

No, it'd been the concept of running away from my mates while giving myself a false purpose to hide behind. And it'd all been done as a way to ensure I never experienced pain like I had this morning when Artica had rejected our bond.

Which meant I'd tortured us all for nothing.

And now, they might never forgive me.

I shivered as a bit of ice drizzled down my spine, the origin seeming to come from outside. Probably from Cyrus. My eyes narrowed as I took control of the element and melted it.

Only, another ice cube appeared, this one touching my hand.

I glanced at it, frowning. *What are you playing at?* I thought at my cousin, quickly turning the element to steam.

"Hey!" an elf shouted from across the room, startling me. "Who threw that?"

I blinked. *What in the fae's frozen realm?*

The elf had a fresh kiss of snow against his cheek, his black eyes searching for the perpetrator.

"Hush," Norden told him. "The coronation has started." Something that was evidenced by the hymn being sung outside the doors by the elves lining the street. It meant Artica had begun the walk toward the workshop and would soon be inside.

Another elf screeched, causing me to glance his way in confusion. He also had a bit of snow on his chin.

And another ice cube formed against my palm.

I quickly melted it, then searched for the cause of water disrupting the coronation. Cyrus might mess around with me, but he certainly wouldn't risk an Interrealm Fae disaster by starting a snowball fight in the Winter Fae toy room.

More elves jumped as snow pelted them unexpectedly, the source coming from outside.

From Artica.

My lips curled down. *Why…?*

A knock sounded, Norden's gaze meeting mine before he cleared his throat. He appeared rather nervous, given the disruption in the room, but as everyone fell quiet, he nodded.

"May I present Artica of Elemental Fae Water Kingdom, Price Lark's intended queen." He bowed, his speech short and sweet, just as it was destined to be, and opened the door to grant her entry.

She stepped through the threshold, resembling a goddess in that stunning dress.

But my eyes were immediately drawn to her throat and the beautiful crystal snowflake dangling from the chain near her breasts.

My heart fucking stopped.

She's wearing my charm.

She'd taken it off in front of me, tried to return it, and yet wore it now during this incredibly important moment.

Because she hasn't given up hope.

My lips parted, my heart quickening in my chest. I should be there beside her, escorting her, helping her through this ceremony, and ensuring she felt safe.

Yet I'd left her in the hands of another.

The Water Fae King, who bent to whisper something in Norden's ear.

Something *I* should be whispering.

It was all part of the tradition, a secret exchange of words no one would ever hear except the two men conversing by the door.

The two men meant to be the second and third part of the future king's triad.

Except Cyrus wasn't the right fae. He already had a mate-circle.

And he only stood there now because I'd allowed it. I'd *chosen* it.

Snowflakes, I fluffed this up, I thought, furious with myself.

Only to be distracted by yet another drizzle of ice against my hand. *What in the fae are you doing, Artica?* I melted the crystal once more, but two elves shrieked along the outskirts of the room.

Artica and Cyrus froze, as did Norden.

Then a giant snowball flew through the air and hit the wall right beside Artica. Her eyes widened.

This isn't good. Not good at all.

"What the fuck is wrong with you?" Norden demanded, some of his regal dominance coming out to play. He rarely displayed it, choosing to follow the friendly selkie route instead of the entitled prince route.

However, having that snowball land so close to his mate had clearly triggered the latter side of him to appear.

Because as Lark's mate, he was technically considered a Winter Fae Prince.

Which gave him royal jurisdiction to delve out punishment as needed.

The room fell silent once more, the selkie's eyes narrowing a bit. Then he glanced at a very startled Artica. "Are you all right, Sunshine?"

Cyrus glanced at me in the crowd, the knowledge in his gaze telling me he'd also discovered the cause for the spontaneous water and didn't understand it.

Artica nodded. "I'm fine." She sounded confident, but I suspected that, inside, she was very *not* fine. Her lips curled up into a delighted smile for the room, hiding any nerves she might be possessing. "A little snow doesn't scare me."

A few of the elves giggled.

Norden grinned as well. "Well, that's good, considering we're surrounded by hundreds of miles of it." He cocked his head, some of his tenderhearted energy returning to his features. "Now, where were we?"

"You were about to introduce my escort," she told him, playing along beautifully.

"Ah, yes, Cyrus, the Water Fae King from the Elemental Fae Realm," Norden said, loud enough for the entire room to hear. "It's an honor to have you and your queen with us today."

"We're honored to be here," Cyrus replied. "It's not every day a Water Fae joins the Winter Fae Court."

Norden's gaze met mine briefly before he said, "No, definitely not every day."

My teeth ground together. *Yeah, yeah, point taken, selkie.*

More ice grazed my knuckles, warning me that another snowball might appear. But a flare of power from Cyrus crossed my senses first, suggesting he'd caught it before it could form.

His gaze met mine again. *What the fuck is going on?* he seemed to be asking.

The fae if I know, I told him with a responding glance.

The formalities continued as Norden asked Artica a series of festive, related questions, such as her favorite treat, her favorite color of wrapping paper, what toy she would pick for a baby selkie, and lastly, how she promised to uphold the holiday cheer of this realm.

"By believing," she replied beautifully, her words piercing my heart and eliciting sighs from the crowd.

"Well," Norden murmured, glancing around. "I think she's a perfect Crystal Princess for Prince Lark's triad." His gaze briefly met mine, the words *and you* whispering unspoken between us. "Of course, I'm biased as one of his mates." He returned his focus to the elves. "It's you all who have to agree. Is Princess Artica worthy of carrying the future king's crown?"

Another layer of ice lanced my skin, making me jump.

Cyrus's power immediately followed, melting a snowball in midair over the room.

My lips parted as three more followed, all of them dissipating in an instant beneath his power.

But something was seriously wrong.

And Artica seemed completely unaware of her elemental affinity stirring up all these random snowballs.

A chorus of positives echoed around us as the elves all agreed in unison that Artica was fit to carry the crown. Not that I'd doubted her, but if she didn't stop trying to attack them all with snowballs, we were going to have a serious problem.

Her eyes smiled as she took in the elves, her lips curling at the edges. "I am most honored and humbled by your acceptance," she told them all, her words fit for a queen.

She curtsied low, showing the elves that she respected

them just as much as royalty—a custom in this kingdom of mutual affection—and slowly rose to begin her final steps toward the toymaker in charge of the crown.

Cyrus didn't accompany her for this part, his chaperoning responsibilities complete.

Which was a very good thing because more snowballs were whistling around in her wake. He melted them all, a bead of sweat populating his brow. It was taking serious energy to control the water before it formed, and despite being the closest fae to the Water Source, he would exhaust himself eventually.

The elf handed Artica a box containing the crown, explaining that it had already been blessed with belief by all those in the room. She thanked him with another curtsy, then took the wrapped box from his hands. "I will see that all those in the throne room bless this as well," she vowed, her role even more important from this point forward.

Because that crown contained the ascension powers.

And if anyone infused a hint of disbelief into that crown, the coronation could go terribly wrong.

Which was precisely why I hadn't touched it yet.

Because I wasn't sure how I felt.

I believed in Prince Lark. I believed in his path. But I hadn't believed in his chosen triad. I hadn't believed in myself.

But watching Artica now, seeing Norden embrace her as she met him by the doorway, I realized just how wrong I'd been.

Because I should be up there with them.

Not Cyrus.

He glanced at me a final time, his gaze knowing as he stepped out of the room with Norden and Artica at his side. He would now finish the escort to the throne room.

The doors closed with a finality, my heart leaving the room with Artica and Norden.

I started toward them, wishing to follow, only to be struck upside the head with a snowball the size of my fist.

Several other elves shouted in dismay as snow began falling from the ceiling in large fluffy balls.

Cyrus had clearly released his hold on the water, likely keeping his focus on Artica's journey to the throne room.

Which left only me with the ability to clean this up.

But it was too much.

And the water didn't feel right.

It *sparkled*.

I glanced down at a drop near my feet, frowning at the colorful texture of the snow.

A mixture of ice and confetti.

Two sources blending as one.

My gaze shot to the door. *Oh Fae… Artica's in serious trouble.*

I started to run after her, only to be slammed with yet another fist-sized sphere of fluff.

"Snowball fight!" one of the elves yelled, clearly taken by the idea of playing in the fresh snow.

Several others began to join, the little creatures losing their minds to the festive cheer blossoming inside the closed toy room.

Too much cheer, I realized.

They were getting drunk on it.

Leaving them to their merriment, I escaped into the hallway and took off after Artica. But a pair of gingerbread men stepped into my path. "No disruptions," they told me at the same time—a very eerie echo that I never wanted to hear again.

I ground my teeth together. "I'm the Elemental Fae Emissary. I'm needed in the throne room."

"Prince Lark says you are not to interrupt," they repeated in unison again.

My eyebrows rose. "Well, as a member of his triad, I disagree," I snapped. "Now *move*."

They glanced at each other with those googly candy eyes.

Yeah, fluff this, I thought, misting to the courtyard outside the main palace.

Then I blinked.

That'd been the first time I'd been able to mist in over a week.

I nearly froze beneath a mixture of confused excitement.

Was it because I'd begun to accept my purpose? Or because I already had?

Oh, it didn't matter right now. I had to reach Artica or Norden, to tell them what was happening in the toy room.

But there were too many elves lining the walkway, their beautiful songs gracing the air as gentle snowflakes fell.

Jumping into the middle of this would cause a scene.

The throne room, I decided. Artica would have to walk that present around to each person in the room.

I'd catch her there and warn her.

Because something told me that snowball fight in the toy room was just the beginning.

ARTICA

I felt bubbly and light, like I'd enjoyed a little too much spritemead.

A giggle teased my throat, my enjoyment of holding so much cheer in my hands infectious.

Norden remained beside me as I walked, telling me that while it wasn't exactly the tradition, he knew Prince Lark wouldn't mind.

And the elves appeared to love it.

Or maybe it was King Cyrus that intrigued them.

Because he'd come along, too.

Oh, it was a great display of Interrealm Fae relations. Queen Claire would be so proud.

"How are you feeling?" King Cyrus asked me as we neared the palace.

"Hmm?" I hummed, glancing at him. "Oh, I feel full of life!" Like I wanted to dance and spin and sigh, all at the same time.

King Cyrus's gaze went from me to Norden. "Is this normal?"

"For Artica? Or for this realm?" Norden asked.

"Both," he replied.

Norden shrugged. "She's a very joyful fae. It's why she's our intended queen."

"I see." King Cyrus didn't sound very sure, but I didn't worry about it. He'd always been rather serious, hence his intimidation. Seriously hot, though. Something all the Water Fae spoke about. Which made Queen Claire a very lucky fae indeed.

But I felt lucky, too.

Because I had a sexy selkie.

And a Winter Fae Prince.

They would feed me all the selkie candy, salted caramel cookies, and hot chocolate I would ever desire.

So faelicious and perfect, I all but sighed.

"Artica," King Cyrus murmured. "Perhaps we should take a break before entering the throne room?"

"A break?" I repeated, laughing. "Oh, no, I don't need a break. This is amazinggg." Yes, I sounded a bit drunk, but who wouldn't? This was the most alive that I'd ever felt!

Norden flashed me a charming smile that reached his bedroom eyes and led me through the main doors of the palace.

More elves waited inside, their songs echoing off the walls and filling me with such happiness that I felt oh-so high on joy alone.

Cinnamon spiced the air, making me inhale greedily.

Such beauty.

Such excitement.

Such blissful harmony.

Part of me wanted to skip toward the doors, but I held myself back. The package in my hand was precious and needed to be handled with care.

Two gingerbread sentries met us at the door. They tapped their staffs three times in unison before declaring, "Artica, Future Queen of Winter Fae Kingdom, has arrived!"

A roar of excitement went up inside, making my lips curl.

This queen thing was really quite fun.

Why had I been so nervous before?

I almost giggled at my ineptitude. *Obviously,* I was destined for this.

Norden blew me a kiss before taking King Cyrus by the arm to pull him away. The Water Fae King seemed dubious, his mouth voicing a complaint I didn't quite hear.

Then the doors opened and I entered.

Like last time, my eyes immediately went to the sexy fae on the throne.

And also like last time, I paused to take in his startling beauty.

Because sigh. Prince Lark really was dream-worthy in every way.

He smiled, his eyes crinkling as he beckoned me forward while everyone else watched. The ceremony standards stated that I couldn't give him the gift yet, but I could greet him.

So I did by sauntering up to the throne and curtsying low while holding the present.

This was the part I'd been concerned about.

But my legs worked like they did on the ice, allowing me to present myself gracefully as I rose to my full height once more.

Yesss, I didn't fall on my ass!

Norden laughed in my head. *Well done, Sunshine. Although, I wouldn't have minded playing your knight in tux armor.*

I smiled. *Maybe I'll fall for you later.*

Oh, please do, he murmured back to me. *Preferably to your knees.*

My cheeks warmed. *Stop. I need to focus.*

May I suggest looking at Lark's face, then, instead of his, uh, Christmas package?

And it wasn't the present in my hands that he meant.

I cleared my throat, my eyes darting up to meet the amusement in Prince Lark's minty green gaze.

Holy Fae, what has gotten into me? I wondered. I really did feel drunk. On magic perhaps?

"Hello, dear intended," Prince Lark greeted me. "Is that gift for me?"

"It is, my prince," I replied, somehow remembering my script. "But you can't have it yet."

He pouted. "Why not?'

"It's not been blessed with enough belief." *Where are these words even coming from? Oh, right, dayssss of reading.* "But don't worry, there are believers all over this room who are willing to bless this gift. Isn't that right?" I glanced at the crowd on cue and smiled as they all cheered with Christmas delight. Even the foreign fae, visiting from realms far away, smiled and joined in.

The holiday cheer was absolutely infectious indeed.

"May I greet them, Your Highness?" I asked, my lips seeming to move without my permission. Which was probably for the best because I felt a bit tongue-tied in my brain at the moment.

"Yes, yes, of course," he replied. "But only for a kiss."

Ohhh, naughty Prince Lark. That's not in the script!

Best to give him what he wants, Sunshine, Norden murmured.

I smiled. *Don't have to tell me twice.* Because Prince Lark looked positively faelicious in that all-white tux, just like

Norden. Only Prince Lark's hair resembled silvery snow against his shoulders, calling to my Water Fae soul.

I carefully set the package down, not wanting to risk it touching him too soon, and felt an immediate hum of energy grace my arms as I stood upright.

That's odd, I thought.

But Prince Lark beckoned me forward with his gaze, and I wasn't about to disappoint him.

Wandering all the way up to the throne, I leaned forward to kiss him.

However, that wasn't what he had in mind.

He grabbed my hips, pulled me into his lap, and planted an all-consuming kiss on my mouth.

The Winter Fae in the room went wild, cheering loudly as he bestowed his affection upon me. I even heard a few whistles, which I thought might be from the visiting fae.

They were probably in for the show of their lives here.

I giggled and shook my head. "You're incorrigible," I whispered, my words for him alone.

"Norden is incorrigible," he corrected me. "I'm merely demanding."

"Hmm," I hummed, agreeing with him. "May I go bless your package now?"

"You realize that sentence carries a double meaning, right?" His gaze twinkled, his happiness a beacon that called to my spirit.

"I'll bless that package later," I said against his ear. "Assuming you earn it."

His *package* began to stiffen beneath me. "Go before I call this whole thing off and take you up on that right now."

I laughed and squirmed off his lap, making sure my curves hit him in all the right ways.

I mean, he was the one who'd put me there. Why not torture him a little?

You vixen, Norden accused. *I think I just fell in love with you.*

You didn't love me before? I teased him, aware that we'd really only just met.

Oh, I was well on my way, Sunshine. But that little act just solidified it all for me. Feel free to take my heart with you wherever you go.

I smiled at him as I bent to retrieve the package. Another hum trailed up my arms, causing all the hairs to stand on end, and another shot of giddiness swept through me. *This is so much fun.*

That's what this realm is all about, Norden told me.

I sighed, unable to even remember what had made me sad earlier today. Whatever it had been clearly paled in comparison to everything happening here.

A circle formed as fae joined each other to help bless the gift with their belief. Not everyone participated, many of the visiting fae uncertain of how this all worked. I assured them that it was fine, that I had enough belief for us all.

And it was true.

This whole experience was like a dream, a fairy tale I'd never even known I needed.

Filled with sweet confections, enchanting energy, and so much life.

Oh, yes, I want to stay here forever, I decided just as I reached a familiar face. I squealed as Juniper gaped at me from beside a Fortune Fae. "What are you doing here?" I asked, excited to see a fellow Water Fae.

"My Fortune Fae mentor invited me to attend, and I thought I might get to see you." Her bluish green eyes rounded. "But I definitely didn't expect *this*."

I giggled. "Yeah. It's been... an experience."

"I'll say." She placed her hand on the present, her eyes still round. "Wow, Artica. This is…"

"Amazing?" I whispered.

"Yeah," she breathed. "Definitely that."

Another zap sailed up my arm, making me flinch.

Juniper released the gift as though she'd felt the same.

This belief magic really was no joke.

"I'll find you later," I promised her, continuing on to the Fortune Fae at her side, who shook his head.

"I best not touch that, Princess," the male said, grinning with his eerie gaze.

One eye was a silvery color with fractures through the iris, whereas his other was a bright green that reminded me of evergreen trees.

He held up his hands. "Unless you wish for a vision?"

Hmm, no, I decided. *My future ends in a happy ending.*

Mmm, I do love a happy ending, Sunshine, Norden supplied in my thoughts. *In fact, I very much look forward to giving you one tonight.*

Giggling, I sighed. *Both* of my mates were incorrigible.

The Fortune Fae gave me a funny look, and I realized I was grinning like an idiot again, thanks to Norden infiltrating my mind.

The male at his side with long, dangerous fangs and sliced irises lifted his lips in distaste. "No visions, Rache. The last thing I want is to be called into the Collegium to write out a ten-page prophecy involving elves and gingerbread men."

Rache pouted.

The male with him appeared to be the most bored fae in the room.

Nope, scratch that, the Midnight Fae beside him was definitely the most bored in the room. His silver-blue gaze seemed to see right through me. "Your Sources are mingling," he said conversationally. "It's giving me a headache."

I frowned. "What?"

"Kai," a sweet voice interjected, drawing my attention to the petite Earth Fae Royal at his side.

My lips parted. "*Aflora*."

She smiled, her cerulean gaze swirling with power.

"*Queen* Aflora," the male beside her corrected.

She elbowed him in response. "Aflora is fine," she said, glancing up at him before looking at me with a kind expression. "Besides, it seems Artica is about to become a queen herself."

"If she can wrangle her Source problem," the male muttered.

Aflora sighed. "Don't listen to him. He's not a fan of being friendly, and this cheerful atmosphere is playing at his nerves."

Another male snorted. "It's playing at *all* our nerves." This one had green eyes and stood at the same height as the other, but his voice was much deeper.

"We'll have to catch up when you're done," Aflora said, ignoring the dark-haired male.

"Yes, don't mind Zeph and Zakkai. They're not nearly as well versed in Interrealm Fae relations as we are," a third male said, this one with burnt gold irises and auburn hair edged with ash.

"Yes, not all of us were born as Midnight Fae Princes," the dark-haired one drawled.

"Both of you, quiet," Aflora said, looking back and forth between the men I assumed were her mates. There was a fourth one as well, but he remained silent, his expression underlined in quiet amusement. "I'm sorry, Artica. We'll catch up soon."

"Yes, I would like that very much, *Queen* Aflora," I said, looking pointedly at the male with long white hair.

His lips curled with gratitude, and I felt a weird sort of tendril snake up my arm.

Odd.

None of them touched the present, which didn't surprise me. Their heritage as Midnight Fae made them rather dark.

Moving on, I found Queen Claire and her mates. King Cyrus again asked how I was feeling, and I again told him I was fine. Strange male, always concerned, apparently. Although, I couldn't remember him ever asking me that before.

Regardless, I kept going until I reached Norden, who stood with several selkies.

Given their similar appearances, I guessed that these were his brothers. "My brother Yule wanted to meet you," Norden told me.

"He did?" I brightened, pleased that each of the males touched the gift without question. I'd just been through several who weren't interested, but most were visiting fae.

"I did," he replied. "I recently made friends with an Elemental Fae in the human world, so you could say your kind intrigue me."

"Oh?"

"Yeah, fine fellow. That husky shifter mate of his, though, is extremely rude," he said, frowning.

I laughed. Because I understood the sentiment, given my history with Shifter Fae.

Except… "Did you say husky shifter?"

"Yep. And rude," he repeated.

"Was the Elemental Fae you met named Lance?"

His pale blue eyes brightened. "Yes. Fire elemental."

I smiled. "He's one of my friends, actually. How's he doing?"

Yule tilted his head, causing his long silver mane to cascade like a waterfall to one side. "He seems to be doing well. He's madly in love with his human, too. Happy and all."

I laughed. "Really? Lance is usually pretty grumpy, so that's great to hear."

He grinned. "I suspect he was infected by the human's affinity for Christmas cheer. Similar to you, Princess. Our magic looks good on your kind."

"Thank you," Norden interjected, smiling as he held the present hostage in his hands. "I worked very hard last night."

I shook my head at him but couldn't help returning the grin. "Give me back the package."

"Nope, there's one more fae who needs to bless it," he said, turning pointedly toward Kalt, who appeared to be the last one in the line.

My lips parted, surprised to find him standing beside the throne.

But it appeared he'd just been speaking with Lark while I'd circled the room.

Both of them narrowed their gazes at me, making me frown. *What did I do?* I asked Norden slowly.

Nothing that I'm aware of, he answered with a similar tone of voice. "Everything all right, my prince?" His voice was quiet, meant for the four of us alone as we gathered around the throne.

But before he could answer, a trumpet sounded, and the gingerbread men announced the final part of the ceremony.

Because Prince Lark being surrounded by his mate-circle was the cue for it to begin.

Music broke out through the room, making my heart sing with joy as I tried futilely to concentrate on whatever Lark, Norden, and Kalt were saying.

I just couldn't hear them over the beautiful song, each melodic stroke touching my heart.

Kalt took the gift, handing it to me while saying something.

I jolted, the magic inside stronger than ever.

It made me feel lighter than air, happier than life itself, like I could float the heavens on a cloud of fairy dust alone.

"May I present," the gingerbread shouted, "the reigning King and Queen of the Winter Fae Kingdom."

Oh Fae... I'd forgotten about this part with Lark's parents.

I had to meet them.

And crown their son.

While high as a Christmas Day kite.

Well, what better way to meet the family than while embracing holiday cheer? I thought happily, sighing as his parents entered with their full mate-circle around them.

Three males. One female.

My future.

As Winter Fae Queen.

I accept, I thought dreamily. *Oh, I definitely do accept.*

LARK

O f all the times for Kalt to do exactly what I needed, it had to be right now, at this very precise moment, causing us to enter the next stage of the coronation.

The symbology of him standing by my throne, talking to me as Norden and Artica arrived, was not lost on anyone in the room.

My mate-circle had united.

But for all the wrong reasons.

Artica executed a perfect curtsy, utterly unaware of the problem mounting within her. She was drunk on Winter Fae magic.

Which carried the beautiful impact of allowing her to present a flawless performance as the ascending Winter Fae Queen in front of all our peers.

And the dangerous side effect of potential death.

Because she was far too close to the Winter Fae Source for a not fully bonded mate.

I had no idea what had caused this, but I could feel the

power radiating around her, embracing her soul in a dance meant for a male Winter Fae Royal heir.

She didn't know how to handle it.

That wasn't to say she *couldn't* handle it, just that she had no training for this. And she was also an Elemental Fae, which meant she was still anchored to the Water Source.

Hence the snowball fight in the toy shop—an event Kalt had detailed to me at length while Artica had wandered the room.

I'd watched her carefully, noting the strands of wintry magic flowing around her, growing with each step.

She radiated *belief*.

And she possessed more cheer than the entire kingdom put together.

I should have noticed it when she kissed me, but I'd been so lost in the moment, in the perfection of her appearance, that I hadn't focused on the enchantments swirling inside her.

She'd executed her part in this ascension so beautifully that I'd almost wept at the sight.

I had no doubt she would have done just as well without the holiday boost, which only made her that much more amazing in my eyes.

But now I was worried about her, and I had no way of moving this along or pulling her to the side.

The presentation of my father's mate-circle had begun.

They were each introduced by name and their formal title, my father being the Winter Fae King and my mother being the Winter Fae Queen. Their mates were Winter Fae Princes of the Highest Order. A designation only given to the males of a mate-circle. Other Winter Fae Royals took on titles of Princes of the First Order, Second Order, et cetera.

It was all about the presentation of the royal court, labeling the families in order of succession all the way down to the dukedoms. Very similar to the royalty structure in several mortal countries—something they'd unknowingly inherited from the Winter Fae culture.

Our customs had been trickling down into human affairs throughout the ages.

As had the customs of several other faedoms.

A consequence of sharing access to the Human Realm, I supposed.

When the final Winter Fae Royal family had been announced and introduced, the package ceremony began again. But this time, Kalt and Norden assisted Artica with the challenge. It was customary for the mate-circle to work together when established prior to the coronation, and on the surface, it appeared my mate-circle had been decided.

Except Kalt hadn't actually joined us.

He was only helping now out of fear for Artica's safety.

However, the symbology of the moment made him very much mine. Which was something we would discuss at length later because I suspected he still intended to fight his place in our circle.

My parents were the last to bless the gift, their smiles filled with pride and intrigue as they met Artica for the first time. They were immediately enamored with her, as I'd suspected they would be. She redefined the meaning of *cheerful*.

Which was a trait I very much adored.

Except, right now, it was bolstered by far too much holiday magic.

Norden and Kalt hadn't allowed her to touch the box at all while making rounds with the Winter Fae Royals, but it hadn't seemed to help. If anything, she was somehow emanating even more power.

I swallowed as they approached, my heart in my throat. Because I honestly didn't know what was going to happen next.

The ceremony called for Artica to open the box and present me with the crown. Then place it on my head.

Which meant she had to touch the gift again.

And the magic inside.

Magic that acted as a direct conduit to the Winter Fae Source.

Her dark blue eyes met mine, the irises glistening like sapphire orbs. I spread my legs for her to stand between them, her hands finding my shoulders as she bent to kiss me in front of the entire court.

It wasn't part of the ceremony.

But I'd stolen a kiss from her earlier, and she appeared to be repaying the favor. "This is so much fun," she whispered against my mouth.

"I'm glad you're enjoying yourself," I told her honestly, my palm cupping her cheek. Magic hummed between us, the electric currents zipping through my veins and going straight to my heart.

I wasn't sure she could handle the crown at all in this state. It just might send her over the edge, but there was no other way to do this. If Norden or Lark opened the package, it would demonstrate a preference for them over the future Winter Fae Queen. And while I intended to worship my mates equally, Artica was considered the gem of the mate-circle. She was the heart that glued us all together, while my power protected us.

However, she appeared to be both at the moment—heart *and* soul.

Artica stood, flashing a grin at the crowd, her appearance and understanding of the ceremony absolutely flawless, as though the Winter Fae Source led her through the steps on autopilot.

Maybe it did.

Maybe that was what aided her in knowing exactly what to do.

She'd studied, yes. But this went beyond reading books and memorizing statements.

This was a spirit enchanted by the Source itself.

A female embracing her new life as Winter Fae Queen.

Norden's eyes caught mine, concern radiating in his depths. He could sense it now, the overindulgence of cheer inside her. Or Kalt might have told him. I suspected the former only because of his mental link, which meant her mind was showing signs of holiday insanity.

"And now, for the crowning of our intended king!" my father roared, garnering applause from everyone in the room.

Artica beamed, her hands taking the present from Norden and sending a shudder through her form. It was as though she was *absorbing* the magic, but I didn't know how that was even possible.

Norden and Kalt closed in on either side of her, their bodies instantly on alert as they attempted to protect her from falling or any other side effect that might arise. The action placed them against my knees as she still stood between my splayed thighs.

I leaned forward, the gesture likely appearing eager to the crowd. However, it was more so I could try to help siphon some of the energy from her.

It didn't work.

The Winter Fae Source was going directly into her, the power increasing as she untied the bow and lifted the lid to display the ice crown inside.

"Oh, it's beautiful," she breathed. She set the present

on my lap, positioning it between us to allow herself to grasp the crown with both hands.

More tendrils of Winter Fae enchantments swirled between us, pouring out of the box into my skin.

But it wasn't enough.

She'd already absorbed too much—a feat that should have been impossible for a non-Winter Fae.

She wasn't even my mate yet.

What in the fae is happening?

I caught her hips as she swayed, the reaction probably being viewed as her responding to the power in my lap. Which served as a euphemism to the crowd that garnered us a round of snickers and applause.

I was too focused on her to comment or react, my heart thudding rapidly in my chest as her hands disappeared into the box to retrieve the crown.

She jolted, her lips parting as a wave of intensity splintered between us, crackling with an icy fervor that went straight to our souls.

The crown shattered in the box in the next moment, drawing a gasp from her mouth as her eyes rolled into the back of her head.

Kalt and Norden wrapped their arms around her— another show of my triad coming together—while I held her upright with my hands on her hips.

But the deed was done.

The Winter Fae Source had entered her heart, body, and soul, taking control and turning her irises into a delicate light blue. She blinked down at me, confusion written into her features.

Almost like she'd just woken from a dream.

"Oh," she whispered, her focus falling to the ice in the box.

Kalt's essence blossomed between us, causing the

shattered pieces to dance and mold back into the shape of an ice crown. "Put it on his head," he told Artica under his breath. "Do it right now."

It wouldn't fix a damn thing. The Winter Fae Source had gone into our Winter Fae Queen.

However, it would allow us to continue the ceremonial expectations and momentarily hide the issue. As my intended mate, the power would be seen as radiating from my mate-circle, not just her. And everyone would assume it was *my* essence they felt.

"Yes, put it on my head," I agreed, my voice barely audible and meant only for my mates to hear.

There were several Shifter Fae in the crowd that could pick up on our conversation, but they would merely assume we were coaching her through the ceremony.

Artica's hands shook as she complied, her skin as pale as snow.

But she powered through, lifting Kalt's ice crown to my head and carefully placing it on top of my hair.

Her knees buckled in the next minute, something Norden and Kalt allowed, following her down to the ground as they knelt to show their respect and pride. It wasn't a mandatory element of the ceremony but spoke of their trust and faith in me as a king.

Something that would have made me smile with pride any other day.

But not today.

Which probably made me look arrogant to those in the room, yet it didn't stop them from applauding and cheering.

Artica shivered, causing Norden to glance up at me with a panicked expression.

Whatever he was hearing in her head… it wasn't good.

I set the package aside and stood, raising my arms to

thank the crowd. It was customary for the new Water Fae King to deliver a speech, and while I had one prepared, I couldn't remember the words now.

"I'm breaking tradition," I told them all. "You'll hear my speech at tonight's Coronation Feast."

A few of the Winter Fae Royals glanced at each other in surprise.

"Our new Winter Fae Queen performed so admirably that I want to share my first words as king with her and our mates in private." I did my best to add innuendo to that statement, aware that the power exchange typically created an influx of desire in the freshly bonded mate-circle.

The responding grins and knowing looks told me I'd succeeded. Even my father and mother smiled at each other, likely recalling their own ascension.

A subject I definitely did not want to think about.

However, I'd prefer that to my wilting queen.

Her eyes were barely open, her body held upright by Norden and Kalt alone.

I bent to scoop her into my arms, aware that it would look like I was about to carry my prize to my chambers and didn't give a damn what anyone thought of it.

The stolen kisses during our ceremony certainly would aid in this temporary explanation of my absence.

Cheers erupted in the throne room, the attendees thrilled with this presentation of events. Or maybe it was the holiday spirit wafting off my queen that seduced them all.

Regardless, I plastered an overly joyous smile on my face and made my way through the crowd with Kalt's crown on my head.

He'd woven some sort of magic into it, securing the piece to my hair with ice.

I'd thank him later for the save.

Both he and Norden followed close behind me, yet again demonstrating the unity of my mate-circle.

It would leave Kalt with no choice now, something he would likely despise me for. However, I'd happily accept his hatred if it meant saving Artica.

Not that I had any clue how to save her.

This was all so unprecedented and new, and each passing second made my heart thump louder and louder in my ears.

By the time we reached the grand hall, it felt as though hours had passed. And we still had more attendees to greet.

Gingerbread sentries and guards.

Elves.

Selkies.

A clan of polar bear Shifter Fae—a group I suspected Artica would have loved to properly meet, but she'd fallen asleep against my chest by that point.

No one seemed to notice, too taken with the beauty in my arms and the power radiating around me—*from her*—to comment.

Holly met us by the entrance to my private wing, her eyes bright with excitement. "Congratulations, my king." She bowed low. "Would you like some refreshments and snacks brought to your suite?"

I almost said no, that I wanted to be alone.

However, I suspected Artica could use the energy.

So I agreed and left Norden to order for us.

Kalt followed me down the hall, the silence a welcome change from all the chanting and singing behind us.

He said nothing, his mind probably racing like mine.

Norden caught up to us near the double-door entry to my suite, likely having run down the hall at a dead sprint.

He immediately took Artica from my arms as we entered, rushing her to the bed, his hands roaming all over her.

They were more closely bonded at this point, giving him priority and the ability to sense her.

"Can you hear her thoughts at all?" I asked, my throat dry.

He shook his head. "Her last coherent thought was, *Happy Festivus*. And then she started singing something about icicles."

"*Icicle Bells*," Kalt murmured. "A popular carol for Water Fae."

I glanced at him. "Do you have any idea what's going on?"

The door to my chambers crashed open before Kalt could answer, the Water Fae King entering with a stoic-looking Midnight Fae at his side. "We need to talk."

KALT

"I realize you're both kings in your own realms, but in this kingdom, *I* am reigning monarch, and it is considered quite rude to barge in without knocking," Lark seethed, taking a protective stance in front of the bed.

"Cyrus can feel the Water Source reacting to whatever is happening inside Artica," I interjected before my cousin could lose his temper or snap back a retort.

And I definitely didn't want to risk upsetting the terrifying Midnight Fae beside him. I didn't know Zakkai well, but his entire mate-circle gave me chills.

"The Water Source is… Well, it's protesting." I wasn't sure how else to explain it. But I felt it, which meant Cyrus *really* felt it.

"It's doing more than that," Zakkai said flatly. "Her soul is trapped between two competing Sources, and neither is willing to release her."

"We think it's a result of your mate-bonds," Cyrus added. "It's perfectly acceptable for a Water Fae to join a Winter Fae triad and accept the Winter Fae Source. But that's not what happened here. Artica bonded two Winter Fae, creating a disturbance between the Sources."

"An imbalance," Zakkai corrected. "She's siphoning Winter Fae magic through her bonds, causing the Water Source to react possessively in return. In summary, the Sources are fighting over her soul, and today's little coronation delivered the winning hand to the Winter Source."

"How do you know all that?" Norden asked.

The Midnight Fae glanced at him, his silver-blue irises radiating power. "I'm the Source Architect."

"A Quandary Blood with immense power," Lark translated without missing a beat, obviously aware of the Midnight Fae Source and the bloodlines that maintained it. "Perhaps even more powerful than the Midnight Fae Queen herself."

Zakkai lifted a shoulder, his long white strands of hair wavy as though he'd run his fingers through his mane repeatedly today. "As she's my mate, the distinction is moot."

"What happens if the Winter Source wins?" I asked slowly, thinking about what Zakkai had just revealed. "You said it was dealt a winning hand. But what does that mean for Artica?"

I could guess. However, I didn't want to. I wanted him to tell us exactly what he expected to happen here, to lay out the stakes and ensure we were all on the same page.

"She won't survive," Zakkai replied. "Not in her current state. Or rather, not in *your* current state."

I blinked at him. "Meaning?"

He stared at me. "Your elemental bond link is shattered." His gaze went to Lark and Norden. "The Elemental Fae bonds she's started establishing with the two of you are also incomplete." He focused on Lark. "And your mate-circle is weak at best. It's missing strong bonds, suggesting you haven't fully developed it yet."

Because of me, I thought. *Because I refused the triad.*

And the irony was, I'd refused because I feared I wouldn't be good enough for Lark to ascend. That I wouldn't believe in myself enough for him to properly embrace the Winter Fae Source.

Yet it was Artica who suffered.

Artica who might not survive... because of my choice.

"In summary, it seems that the Winter Fae Source started siphoning magic into Artica through your initial bond," Cyrus said, his focus on Lark. "Something that was heightened last night when she third-level mated Norden. And has been made exponentially worse today by having a Source conduit placed in her hands."

"So the little power outbursts this week were all linked to this?" Norden guessed.

"What power outbursts?" I interjected, frowning.

"She shot an icicle across the cafeteria when pointing at a lemon bar," Lark stated flatly. "And her water insulation failed the other night."

"Don't forget the snowdrift," Norden muttered. "She almost suffocated herself with it."

I gaped at them. "Why didn't you tell me any of this?"

"When would I have done that?" Lark demanded. "While you were hiding in Greenland, pretending to be on an Interrealm Fae assignment?" He scoffed and shook his head, dismissing me for Cyrus. "What about the snowballs in the workshop?"

"She seemed entirely oblivious to it," Cyrus commented.

"Of course she was," Zakkai replied. "She was enthralled by the Source conduit. Her soul has been lost between two power beacons all week, and one of them had finally found a way to truly call to her."

"Because her other link to the Water Source wasn't here." Norden glared at me, the accusation clear in his statement.

Had I been here, I might have noticed or sensed all these changes in Artica.

And I might have been able to stop this problem before it worsened to this point.

My jaw ticked, my fists clenching at my sides.

Not only had I left Artica when she'd needed me most, but I'd also abandoned Lark and Norden, *and* I'd possibly just assisted in the death of the new Winter Fae Queen.

It was almost laughable how much I'd feared negatively impacting Lark's coronation before.

Because I'd made it even worse than I could ever have imagined.

My gaze drifted to Artica on the bed. She was so beautiful in that gown. So princess-like and perfect. However, the pale color of her cheeks and the light sheen of sweat on her forehead betrayed her condition.

She's fighting for her life.

Because of me.

Because of my decisions.

Because of my fears.

That made me the worst kind of mate. Entirely unworthy of a sweet being like Artica. Because I'd well and truly failed her.

"All right. We know the problem. Now how do we fix it?" Lark demanded.

Norden moved to the bed to run his fingers through Artica's hair, his concern palpable.

I wanted to touch her, too. Hold her. Make things

right. But I had no idea how. Was it even possible? Would she ever forgive me for putting her in this situation?

Lark hadn't known what a bond would do. Norden hadn't either.

However, I, as her Water Fae mate, should have known. I should have protected her. Should have fucking *been* here for her.

"*Kalt*," Cyrus snapped, making me jump.

Frost had begun creeping up my arms from my fists, my emotions taking control of my element and allowing it to show. I immediately dissolved the ice crystals, my focus falling to my cousin. "How do we fix it?" I echoed Lark. "What can I do?"

"You can start by accepting your triad," Cyrus told me. "Then the three of you will need to mate Artica." He paused, meeting each of our gazes head-on. "You'll need to engage in the fourth-level soul bond. As a Water Fae."

"*What*?" Lark gaped at him. "That... that would mean..."

"Joining the Sources as a mate-circle and providing balance to each other," Zakkai deadpanned. "We do it for Aflora every day."

"As Artica isn't the queen of her element or even a royal, it should be easier for the four of you to manage," Cyrus added. "And as luck would have it, I *am* the Water Fae King. Therefore, I can assist with the ceremony."

"Assuming Artica even accepts it," I said, frowning. "She *broke* our bond."

"Because she thinks you don't want her," Norden told me, his brown eyes flashing darker than I'd ever seen. "She broke your bond to let you go because she refuses to force you into a situation you don't want to be part of."

I flinched.

"She thinks you only mated her because you were

drunk on holiday spirits from the bar," he continued. "Or that's what I picked up in her thoughts, anyway."

"Norden and I know you belong with us," Lark said, his minty eyes flashing. "But Artica doubts it. Artica doubts *you* because *you* doubt yourself. Which means we can't form this triad until you get over whatever this issue is and either embrace us or risk losing everything."

"And starting a war," Zakkai supplied helpfully. "Because I doubt the Winter Fae are going to take kindly to their Source imploding inside their new queen because the Water Source wouldn't play nice."

"Is there really nothing you can do as the Source Architect?" Cyrus asked, his fear palpable.

Which meant he didn't believe in me making this choice either.

And why would he?

I'd told him for months that I didn't want to be part of this triad. I'd told Artica the same. Norden and Lark, too.

I thought today would prove that they didn't need me.

Instead, it had demonstrated how much I truly was needed... and how epically I'd failed them.

"She's still alive." Zakkai folded his arms. "Why do you think that is?"

"But can you do something to redistribute the power?" Cyrus stressed. "To pull it out of her and push it back into Lark?"

"What do you think I've been doing for the last hour?" Zakkai asked him. "She only managed to finish the ceremony because of my influence. But the Sources will not stop fighting over her soul. She has too many incomplete bonds. If her mates don't want to fix her and this, then nature will take its course."

"So you—"

"We need to finish the triad," I said, interrupting my cousin.

Debating what the Source Architect could and couldn't do was irrelevant at this point. He'd already stated he was the reason Artica hadn't already been ripped apart by the Sources.

And I *really* didn't want to find out how long his goodwill lasted.

Nature would take its course.

But it would be the *right* course.

By fixing my mistake and accepting my fate. Disbelief tossed us all into this mess. So I'd just have to use belief to pull us all back out.

I'd been afraid of the pain tied to loving another and had inevitably broken my heart via my own foolish means.

I would *never* make that mistake again.

"We will complete the triad," I reiterated. "Then we'll begin the Water Fae ceremony."

Artica and I were bonded as of this morning, and first-level bonds could be created again if both souls were compatible enough. And ours certainly were.

I'd known that for years, which was how I'd known the Winter Fae magic in the bauble would select her.

She was perfect for Lark and Norden.

Because she'd always been perfect for me.

I faced Lark and Norden, my stance resolute. "I'm ready. Tell me what I need to do." *Tell me how to fix this and save Artica's soul.*

ARTICA

F*loating*, I mused lazily. *I'm floating on a cloud of confetti mingled with ice.*

A giggle caught in my throat.

Part of me understood that something was very wrong here. But the festive atmosphere kept pulling me into a dizzy circle of colorful mist.

Or was it frost?

It kept changing, dancing between icy landscapes and candy cane fields.

So much color.

Followed by white snow.

Another giggle tried to escape me, the lunacy of my situation making me feel drunk on life.

Fa la la, I hummed dizzily. *La la.* I frowned. *How many more las and fas? Oh, snowflakes. I'll have to start again.*

But the words melted into a tune about icicles and cherry blossoms. No. *Sugar* blossoms. *What is a sugar blossom?*

I tried to shake my head to clear it, to focus on the very

real danger of my predicament, but another whirl sent me tumbling down into a snowdrift.

Except I couldn't feel it.

Because it's not real.

The cold certainly felt real. I shivered, my soul weeping inside me. I felt so broken and alone. So lost and confused. Torn in half. Stretched in two directions I couldn't define.

What is happening to me?

Ice slid down my spine, my heart freezing in my chest as I forgot how to breathe.

The world began to sway, my legs no longer floating but sinking.

Down. Down. Down.

Oh, this cannot be good.

I clawed at the air, trying to swim back into the clouds, only to pause as warm male tones surrounded me. *Familiar. Intense. Mine.*

I began to drift, allowing the current to carry me toward my anticipated haven. Except a sheet of ice blocked my path, firmly separating me from my males.

My males, I repeated to myself on a giggle. *Sigh.*

Norden and Lark had looked so handsome in their silvery white tuxedos. And Lark with his crown, he'd...

I frowned. *Hold on...*

He'd resembled a king with that crown. But it hadn't been right. The crown—

My eyes flew open, a gasp caught in my lungs.

White surrounded me. A world blanketed in pure snow without any of the holiday delight. It was all ice and cold and chillingly quiet.

The crown shattered, I remembered. *I... I broke the crown.*

But I didn't know how I'd done that or what had led to it. Only that I'd felt so alive and filled with more joy than I could contain. I'd wanted to burst from the inside, allow the entire world to feel my festive cheer.

"It's all about belief," a deep voice said from behind the ice sheet. The words vibrated against my ears, echoing all around me in my frozen prison. "Norden and I already know you belong with us. It's on you to truly believe it now."

"I'm not sure I do anymore," a sensual tone replied.

Norden. My heart attempted to beat, to sing to my selkie mate. But my insides resembled the wall standing between us—solid and cold and refusing to move.

"I don't think he's worthy of Artica," Norden continued. "Or of us."

"Norden." That was from Lark, the one whom I'd heard speaking first. His commanding tone sang to my soul, his powerful essence one I craved now more than ever.

I need you, I thought. *I need you to thaw the ice and warm me back up with your innate cheer.*

So different from when we'd first met.

So much more impactful now.

So *right*.

"What? Maybe Artica had the right idea with breaking the bond. He failed all of us, and now look where we are." Norden's angry tone did little to dispel the underlying sultry quality of his voice. But hearing him like this hurt my heart.

Norden? I tried again.

No response.

Because of this frozen wall.

I tried to raise my fist to it, to beat it down, but my limbs resembled icicles at my sides. My water magic refused to insulate my skin, leaving me susceptible to the outdoor elements.

"She's as cold as ice," someone said. Kalt, maybe? "We don't have time for doubt right now."

Norden snorted. "Well, that's rich coming from you."

"Look, I'm sorry, all right?"

"A bit late for that," Norden muttered.

"What the fae do you want me to say?" Kalt demanded. "Do you want an explanation for my hesitation? A speech about how I was worried my disbelief might impact the whole circle?"

The pain in Kalt's voice pierced my frigid heart. I wasn't sure why I heard him so acutely, or what was really happening, but I could feel his agony as though it were my own.

"I've always expected to be alone," he continued. "I... The triad took me by surprise, as did my intense reaction to it. And the dreams. I know you're responsible for some of those, but..."

I desperately wanted to see his expression. To hug him. To tell him everything would be all right.

But the icy walls were morphing around me, boxing me in under some sort of armored igloo. *Is that my magic?* I marveled, sensing it weaving into the ice. *Building me a protective house? Why do I need it?*

Fortunately, the barrier allowed for some unexpected warmth, causing my limbs to thaw.

"I didn't want to accept my fate." Kalt's voice reverberated around me again, suggesting I'd missed some of what had been said. "But Artica breaking our bond this morning felt so incredibly wrong. I haven't felt okay since."

"That's normal," someone else commented.

"It's not, though. I've had first-level bonds before. They've never hurt to break. They've felt *good* to break. And I tried to break this with Artica before I left, but I couldn't. I thought it was because of her crush on me or her belief in us being soul mates, that maybe she was just anchored a bit more than anyone else I'd met. But it wasn't that at all."

His comments echoed now off the icy barriers, bouncing to my ears in an odd sort of vibration.

"*I* couldn't break the mate-bond, because deep down, my soul knew she was the one. However, I destroyed her belief in me as her intended mate. Which allowed her to break it. And doing so told me how wrong it was."

"Then why didn't you tell her that?" Norden asked him, his tone still radiating fury. "Why didn't you try to fix it?"

"She wouldn't give me a chance!" Kalt replied, exasperated. "And I wasn't sure what to say."

"Yet now you're certain that you can handle this?" Norden didn't sound like he believed him at all, the doubt in his tone so uncharacteristic from the male I'd begun to know.

Is this even real? I wondered. *Or is this a dream?*

At some point, I'd made a bed for myself on the ice. Or maybe I'd fallen without realizing it.

Regardless, I curled into a ball on my chilly slab and craved more warmth. Craved Norden and his heat. Lark and his strength. Even Kalt and his affinity for ice. He would be able to melt this igloo, wouldn't he?

But I didn't want to force him to help me.

Hopefully, this is just a dream.

"I'm not certain that I can handle anything." Kalt sounded exasperated. "But I'm certain that I have to try, that I have to give in to this connection between us. I've felt it from the beginning. To you, to Lark. I've denied it because I felt that you could do better than me. Just like I ran from Artica because I wanted her to be with someone more capable of belief."

"Why do you doubt your belief?" Lark asked quietly. "Your magic shines here, Kalt. It always has."

This is such a strange dream, I thought sleepily, yawning. *I must not have eaten enough selkie candies today.*

My stomach clenched at the thought, hunger striking me deep within.

What did I eat today? I wondered, frowning. *What happened after I crowned Lark?*

Wait, the crown...

I pictured it shattering, the magic depleted.

Where had it gone?

"Belief is a unique sensation," Lark went on. "It comes from the heart and soul, not our minds. It's what provides influence to thought. Belief tells us what to see, how to feel, and how to react. You can't force it. But you can misinterpret it."

His voice is just as pretty as his face. A funny thought that made me giggle. Or, more accurately, *gurgle.* Because my lungs were frozen again.

I really want to wake up. Soon, please.

Magic brushed my body once more, my affinity for water attempting to insulate me again. It hummed and fizzled, weaker than I'd ever felt it.

What's happening? I repeated to myself. *Am I dying?*

"You've known from the first day we met that your destiny brought you here for a reason. I watched you embrace our magic, thrive on it, *enjoy* it. What's held you back is your own determination to be someone you think you need to be, not the man you're destined to be." Lark's voice held a touch of warmth that I craved to feel against my skin.

Silence fell, the chill of it an unwelcome kiss to my senses.

I wanted to weep. To scream. To call out for help. But

my lips were frozen shut, my eyes forever lost to the whiteness around me.

"This is how you fix it." Lark's murmur stirred me from the icy fog in my mind. "By accepting the connection and realizing that the belief was always there and that you just had to embrace it."

"I've always felt it," Kalt admitted, his voice low. "I... I just felt you both deserved better."

"Something you attempted to prove today," Norden pointed out, a note of something other than anger in his tone. A sense of intrigue, maybe. Whatever it was, it enhanced his usual sensuality, causing a tingling sensation to blossom in my heart and spread through my veins.

I sighed, relieved by the flash of warmth.

"You berated me on purpose," Kalt muttered.

"Had to make sure you really meant it," Norden replied, sending another bolt of heat through my veins. "I won't accept you running away again, Kalt. I won't accept your doubt. And I absolutely will not accept you hurting our Artica ever again. Do you understand me?"

"Sort of hard not to with you grabbing my neck like that," Kalt grumbled back at him.

"That's not a response, Frosty."

"I understand, selkie." Kalt sounded a tad flustered, something I really wished I could see. "But you're getting ahead of yourself. I still need to earn Artica's forgiveness and make that vow to her personally."

"Do you think she'll forgive you?" Lark asked softly.

I frowned. *What am I forgiving Kalt for?* It wasn't his fault that we'd bonded initially. He'd been drunk. I'd let him go. What more was there to forgive? He could live his life now. Be whoever he felt he was meant to be.

My frown deepened. *What am I really dreaming about? What are they doing? Why am I still covered in all this ice?*

I longed to move, to see them, to understand what was happening. Their warmth radiated through my veins, the hum of electricity a welcome sensation through my body. *Does that mean I'm going to wake up soon?*

Because sigh. I really wanted to see again. To breathe. To sit by a warm fire and enjoy some sweets. *Mmm.*

"I won't be giving her a choice," Kalt said, breaking through the delightful fantasy in my mind. "She might have lost her faith in me as a mate. But I believe that connection is still there. And I believe she's going to give me another chance."

"You're going to do a lot of groveling," Norden pointed out. "Some worshipping between the thighs, perhaps."

"That sounds like more of a treat than a punishment."

"I can make it a punishment," Norden offered. "Delay your gratification in exchange for hers."

Someone cleared a throat, the sound not belonging to any of the three men. "I'm here for the bonding ceremony aspect, not the festivities that follow."

Oh Fae… That was King Cyrus's voice.

And what did he mean by 'bonding ceremony'?

"To do this, I have to remove my influence," a fifth voice declared, the owner of it familiar and yet not. Someone I'd met recently. Perhaps in the throne room?

Where the crown shattered, I recalled all over again. *What happened—*

Ice speared my chest, drawing a sharp, silent scream from my lips. *Fae!*

ARTICA

The walls around me began to melt, the sun bright and hot overhead, blinding my vision in another sea of white as the frost surrounding me turned to damp tears of agony at being overpowered by the external force.

This no longer felt like a dream.

It felt like a nightmare.

An agony-induced, harsh frenzy of a nightmare.

So much pain. So much heat. So much *joy*.

To the point that it hurt to breathe. I couldn't see beyond the brightness, the cold having left me entirely.

I felt hot. Too hot. Like an Elemental Fae embracing the Fire Source for the first time and having no idea how to control the flame.

Except it wasn't elemental at all.

It was another Source entirely.

The Winter Source.

And it… it was consuming me.

Drowning me in an ocean of foreign magic and demanding I accept all of it into my heart at once.

291

"You're killing her!" someone shouted.

"No, I've been saving her from death. Now it's your job to pull her back," another snapped. "You have the power, Water Fae. Draw her to your plane and let your king guide the ceremony."

I whirled around, confused by the voices and the sensations ripping through me.

The twirling increased, round and round, making me dizzy to the point of losing consciousness for a split second in time.

Then I landed on another ice slab, the precious material eliciting a cry of relief from my overheated lungs. I pressed my cheek to the texture, forever thankful for the coolness and familiarity of the power.

Artica, a deep voice rumbled through my mind.

I blinked, realizing it had come from the ice.

No, not ice.

Man.

I lifted my gaze—an action that required serious effort for my exhausted form—and found a pair of icy blue irises looking down at me.

Kalt, I whispered.

His palm found my cheek, the frigid touch drawing tears of relief from my eyes. His thumb wiped them away as he gently pulled me up his body as though I weighed nothing.

Wait, no.

It wasn't him.

Someone else's palms.

Followed by a blanket of snow against my back that felt soooo good and welcome that I sighed.

Lips caressed my neck, the icy tingles calming the heat along my skin in the best way.

And all the while, Kalt held my gaze.

Something stirred behind him. A glimmer of light in the otherwise sheet of white.

I squinted, unable to make it out until another chilly palm found my thigh to draw my leg over Kalt to the male behind him.

Lark.

Those minty green eyes held more power than my heart could handle, causing it to thud blissfully in my chest.

I tried to reach for him, very much preferring this dream to all my others, but my arms refused to move.

A whimper left my lips, the need to touch Lark and allow him to absorb some of the magic inside me a stark need that clawed at my insides.

Shh, Kalt hushed, drawing my gaze back to his.

I wasn't sure why he'd entered my dream.

Well, I knew why.

He was *always* in my dreams.

But I'd finally let him go. So why come to me now? Why embrace us here?

Was it my heart's way of saying goodbye? By creating one final false memory to last a lifetime?

This isn't a dream, Artica, he told me. *We're near the Water Source.*

I frowned, but he used his thumb on my chin to draw my gaze to the blistering light near our heads.

I used my blood connection through Cyrus to bring us all here, but we don't have much time. We need to begin the ceremony before it's too late.

As a Water Fae Royal, he would be permitted to almost touch the Source if the head of his familial line allowed it. So this made sense in a way. But it felt too fantastical to be real.

It's real, he breathed, clearly hearing my doubts.

Something I didn't understand. *We're not bonded.*

Not as Water Fae, no, he replied. *But we're going to fix that.*

I already fixed it, I told him. *I let you go.*

Yes, and in doing so, you helped open my eyes to my true purpose. His gaze was sad as he stared down at me. *You* are *enough for me, Artica. You're more than enough. In fact, you're too good for me.*

My lips curled down. *I don't understand.*

You said you weren't good enough for me earlier, he whispered, his thumb stirring snow crystals across my skin. *But that's not true. You're the perfect Winter Fae Queen, and you're too perfect for me. I doubted my worth, not yours. I doubted my belief, never yours. And I doubted my own strengths, not yours.*

I swallowed. Now I knew this was a dream because he was saying all the right things.

I will never forgive myself for shattering your belief in me, Artica. And I'm going to spend the rest of my life trying to be worthy of your faith. Once more.

He pressed his lips to mine, sending a tingle of magic across my skin and into my veins. My heart beat in response, my soul seeming to perk up at the embrace.

I could feel the mate-bond humming between us, daring me to engage it.

Frowning, I pushed it away. Even if this was a dream, I didn't want to risk trapping him again.

He sighed. *Artica, I know I hurt you. I'm sorry. I was too caught up in who I thought I* should *be, not understanding that who I am right now is what matters most. I've already achieved my destiny. It just felt too good to be true, like it was a misstep I'd accidentally taken on my intended journey. A beautiful chance I wasn't actually worthy of experiencing.*

Lips met my pulse again, the snowy essence behind me humming along my skin as a hint of magic brushed my shoulder.

Norden.

His hair resembled silk, his body strong and sure along my back as he sandwiched me in against Kalt's chest.

With Lark looking on over Kalt's shoulder.

Just the three of us in a sea of white, being chaperoned by the Water Source above.

A true fantasy.

A dream.

A reality, Kalt assured me. *We completed the triad, Artica. It's why I can sense you. But we need to engage the Water Fae bonds.*

I frowned. *That doesn't make any sense.*

You initially bonded us all as a Water Fae, with Norden being on the third level. If you don't complete it, the Sources will continue to fight over your soul.

I stared at him, searching his gaze for something I didn't understand. *Fight over my soul?* Was that why I kept feeling hot and cold? *The intense heat battling the icy walls...*

The Water Source is trying to hold on to you, while the Winter Source is attempting to force you into the ascension because of your link to Lark. Your third-level bond to Norden pushed it along, then the conduit finalized it.

The crown, I translated.

Yes.

It shattered, I whispered for the thousandth time.

Yes, he confirmed. *And the magic went into you and your bond to Lark. It's killing you, Artica.*

So you completed the triad, I said slowly.

We did.

Because... the Sources are fighting over my soul. Not a question, but a statement. One that pierced my heart.

Yes, he said. *And now we need to complete the elemental mating to anchor you between the Sources.*

I swallowed. *Or my soul will be ripped apart.*

Yes. He sounded relieved.

But I wasn't relieved at all.

You're doing this to save me. Not because he wanted it. Not because he wanted me. He just didn't want the Sources to kill me.

A noble decision and one I could respect.

Because that would lead to inevitable war.

But it would also tie Kalt to me for eternity, something I knew he didn't really want.

Artica, he said, his palm pressing harder into my skin. *No, that's not true. I* do *want this. I want you. I want Lark and Norden, too. I always have.*

I wasn't sure I appreciated this development of him hearing my thoughts. Was it because he'd taken us to the Water Source? Making him the strongest of all in this plane? He was a Water Fae Prince. A royal. A being of immense elemental power.

It made sense that he could see through me and hear all my thoughts and concerns.

But I couldn't hear his.

I couldn't feel his true intentions.

And all his actions told me this was to save the kingdoms, to ensure our kind didn't go to war as a result of what I'd done.

No, Kalt said sharply into my mind. *This is not your fault, Artica. This is* my *fault. My disbelief led to all this, not yours. I doubted my worth. I doubted my fate. I doubted us. And that is why we're here now. You did everything right. You followed your heart and soul. I ignored mine.*

I don't want our kingdoms to go to war, I thought back to him. *Is there another way to fix this? One that doesn't force you to give up your soul for eternity?*

You're not hearing me. Kalt's palm went to the back of my neck, his icy irises swirling with intensity. *Not being with you would be giving up my soul for eternity, Artica. Not being part of this mate-circle would be me giving up my soul for eternity. Turning my back on our fate would be me giving up my soul for eternity. It was what I was prepared to do because I thought I wasn't worthy.*

His grip around my nape tightened.

But I was wrong, Artica.

He nuzzled my nose, the chilly kiss going straight to my heart.

This *is my path and chosen eternity.*

His lips brushed mine.

You *are my chosen mate.*

His tongue slid into my mouth, breathing wintry life into my being and showering me in snowy bliss.

I choose you. I choose this. Choose us.

He deepened our kiss with each statement, his power flooding my veins as he urged me to feel him, to *see* him.

My heart hurt from beating so fast, my soul perpetually frozen inside and uncertain of our next move.

Your snowflake charm is glittering brightly, he told me. *I know you know what that means, Artica. I know you can sense how right we all are together. And I know you believe in our future together.*

Norden's lips caressed my neck, his tongue gliding along the column of my throat and stirring goose bumps in its wake.

Lark's palm skated up my thigh as well, the skin-on-skin touch a welcome caress. I wasn't sure when I'd lost my gown. I wasn't sure that I cared either.

Not with Kalt's tongue in my mouth and his chilly skin pressed along the length of mine.

I've avoided my dreams for so long, lost in a world of ambition and set on a path of loneliness, that I couldn't see the gorgeous gift standing right before me, Kalt said softly. *You're the future I want to wake up to every day, Artica.*

My skin tingled, their collective touch shooting sparks all over my body.

Kalt kissed me again, his tongue captivating mine.

Your joy is infectious, he whispered. *Your heart is pure. Your beauty is unworldly. And your soul is so full of life and love.*

I moaned, his kiss providing the oxygen I hadn't realized I needed.

A palm met my side, then slipped between me and Kalt to rest against my abdomen. *Norden,* I recognized, his hand a block of ice against my overheated skin.

You're the queen I never knew I needed and will never be able to live without, Kalt continued. *My life would be meaningless without you. Without Lark and Norden, too. I would be lonely and desolate and alone. And while I deserve that after everything I've done, I'm going to spend eternity ensuring I deserve more.*

Kalt's mouth left mine, his eyes locking on my own.

I'm going to spend eternity ensuring I deserve you, he told me. *If you'll have me, Artica, I vow to be yours forever. To worship you. To love you. To prove to you every day that we're meant to be and that I believe in our fate.*

I swallowed, my heart beating too fast in my chest.

Mate me, Artica, he murmured. *Mate us all.*

KALT

I held my breath, waiting for Artica to respond.

The three of us were lying on the ice bed inside Lark's suite, near the edge of the indoor pool. Norden had called it a bathtub, but it took up over half of the enormous bedroom, extending all the way to the en-suite bathroom.

We had stripped off our clothes first, including Artica's, in an effort to bring her body temperature down. She'd immediately calmed upon feeling the icy slab beneath, then sighed when I'd wrapped her in my water magic.

Cyrus had told me to hold her, then Norden had slid in behind her with Lark lounging at my back.

They were supporting me while I attempted to anchor her.

It was taking an absurd amount of power to keep her near the Water Source, something Cyrus helped with by allowing me to use the Source's plane to communicate with Artica via our souls.

I was both aware and not aware of my surroundings. I

knew we were lying down. I knew where Lark and Norden were positioned. But my mind was entirely focused on Artica and the Water Source above us.

I could see her glowing in the light, her blonde hair almost as white as snow. But it was her deep blue eyes that held me captive as I waited for her answer.

She thought I was doing this to avoid a war, a sense I'd picked up on through the Winter Fae part of our link. They weren't so much words that I heard as they were feelings. Like I could sense the intentions of her heart.

She didn't want to trap me.

Yet felt she would be doing exactly that by forcing the bond.

It was Lark who said out loud what the problem was, that her belief in my intentions was wavering. And Norden who confirmed it since he could read her mind.

"Kiss her again," Norden told me now. "It helps anchor her."

I didn't hesitate, doing exactly what he told me to do, my mouth taking hers in the spirit realm as I gently pressed my lips to hers on the ice platform in Lark's suite.

It was a bizarre sensation, our bodies connecting while our souls danced on a plane of existence few others had ever experienced. Bringing Lark and Norden with me had taken serious power, something they both aided me in via our Winter Fae bond.

None of this should be possible.

Or rather, none of this was *allowed*.

But with Cyrus's blessing, we made it work.

I suspected Zakkai helped, too. Not that he would admit it. However, there was a reason he hadn't left yet. A reason he just refused to voice out loud.

Artica sighed, both on the spirit plane and physically,

her body seeming to relax against mine. *You are just as good at kissing as I've always dreamed. Maybe even better.*

Wait until you really kiss me to decide, I whispered, nuzzling her cheek on my way to her ear. *I can't wait to taste you in all ways, Artica.*

Norden hummed in approval, causing her eyes to blink open again. Not the ones attached to her body, but the ones giving life to her soul. She tried to see him, but her spirit was too weak to allow much movement. Which was why we'd moved her on our own, why we'd joined her here instead of coaxing her back to her corporeal form.

It was all up to the Water Source now.

And Artica's willingness to bond.

"Ask her again," Lark said.

He and Norden appeared unable to talk to her in this plane, probably because they weren't Elemental Fae. Fortunately, Norden's bond still allowed him to hear her. For some reason, she couldn't hear him, though.

Artica, I whispered. *You know Elemental Fae require consent. And I know these are not the most ideal of circumstances. But I want this. I want you. And Norden and Lark do, too.*

I found her hand and pulled it to my heart, both physically and spiritually.

Do you feel my links to them? Do you feel the belief that ties us all together? You're the core of that, Artica. The one we all revolve around. Not the Winter Fae King, but the queen we're destined to cherish for the rest of time.

She shivered, her eyes falling closed again. *A mate-circle. Yes.*

To save us all from war.

No, I replied immediately. *To be together as one. To love and respect each other. To share the Sources of power and be the most powerful mate-circle the Winter Fae have ever seen. To spread cheer and happiness through all the realms. And to show the fae that we can unite, we can thrive, and that love truly does conquer all.*

But you don't love me, she whispered.

I sighed. *Artica, I want the chance to love you. I want the chance to grow with you. I want the chance to be good enough for you.*

I palmed her cheek again.

You shattered my heart when you broke our link. It was a sensation unlike any I've ever experienced. And I want to piece it back together—for you, I stressed. *Please, Artica. Please let me love you. Let us love you.*

Her snowy eyelashes parted to reveal her pretty blue irises. She stared deep into my eyes, allowing me to see the hurt inside her, to sense the distrust and the pain she harbored within.

And the resolve that iced over the top. The realization that there was no other choice.

That while she could give up her own soul for my freedom, she couldn't allow her decision to drive the realms toward war.

Lark sighed, clearly sensing the same in her aura.

Norden then warily confirmed the words out loud, telling us her thoughts.

She would agree because she had to. And she would regret forcing me into this bond.

"She thinks it's her own obsession with you that brought us all to this point, that had she just realized before that you would never love her, she could have let you go before this began. And she regrets taking the dare for the internship," Norden concluded, his irritation palpable.

I understood.

Because now she was being unreasonable.

But I'd driven her to that point. So I would yank her back from it.

"Will it be enough to finalize the Water Fae bonds?"

Lark asked, the question seeming to be for someone else in the room. "Or will the mate-circle need to truly be complete to balance the Sources?"

I ground my teeth together. The Winter Fae mate-circle required belief, and Artica clearly didn't have it in her right now.

Because of me and my stubborn actions.

I'd driven her away, and now the joyous heart of our circle no longer believed in our destiny.

"There's only one way to find out," Zakkai replied. "It should grant you enough time to temporarily balance her soul. However, the Winter Source will continue to fight until you either establish a permanent balance or remove the contention from the Water Source."

In other words, we either figured out our mate-circle…

Or we still forfeited Artica's life.

But if we could return her to her corporeal state, even temporarily, then I could convince her of my intentions.

A mate-bond would also give her access to my mind.

Which she could use to process my words and actions.

"It'll be enough," I promised Lark and Norden. "Once she's linked, she'll feel our belief."

"And the mate-circle will settle itself," Norden said.

"Yes," I agreed.

He nodded against her head. "Do it."

Lark squeezed Artica's thigh, which rested over my own, his lips pressing into my neck. "Lead the way, Water Prince."

ARTICA

K alt said all the right things.

But something held me back.

I couldn't define it, couldn't say why I didn't fully believe him, other than that this situation seemed so far out of the realm of repair that I knew there was no other alternative.

Any good fae in this situation would do what was right to save the realms.

And Kalt was one of the best fae I'd ever known.

It was why I'd always loved him. A love that now felt tainted because it was the reason he currently had no choice.

Or maybe he did.

But I couldn't know that until we finished this bond.

Which was a shame because then I'd have access to his heart and mind and I'd learn the truth that I already suspected—he was sacrificing his happiness for the sake of the realms.

I'd be miserable with him.

Well, not entirely.

Because Lark and Norden would help heal my ache. And I'd help heal theirs, too.

I know you don't believe me, Kalt whispered into my mind. *But that's okay, Artica. Because I'm going to prove it to you as soon as we're done.*

I didn't reply because I didn't trust myself to speak.

I also didn't trust myself not to *hope* for more.

Because I wanted to believe him. I wanted his words to be true more than anything else in the faedoms. But I refused to allow myself to wish for a happily-ever-after that might never come to fruition.

Cyrus is ready to begin, Kalt told me as a new presence joined us near the Source. *This is rather unconventional with you being unconscious.*

I frowned. I hadn't really considered why we were here and speaking in spirit rather than in person.

Mostly because I'd been convinced that this was all a really weird dream up until a few minutes ago.

And honestly, I still wasn't entirely sure.

But the Water Source felt very real, as did my soul. *Why am I unconscious?*

Because your spirit is too weak to power your body, he told me, sounding sad. *The bonds will fix it. We'll give you our strength to heal.*

I swallowed. *And marry our souls together for eternity.*

As far as I'm concerned, that's an added benefit, he said, his lips whispering across mine again. *Norden and Lark feel the same.*

They're not concerned about being linked to the Water Source?

They're more concerned about losing you, Artica, he replied. *We'll figure this out together, as a mate-circle.*

His words warmed my heart.

But not enough to inspire hope.

Okay, maybe a little enough to inspire hope.

However, I ignored that flicker. Or tried to, anyway.

Cyrus is starting, Kalt told me, his words accompanied by a wave of magic that prickled my senses. So chillingly beautiful and full of mystic energy.

My soul sighed, bowing to the greatness of the Source and the king who wielded the power.

This was a true blessing to be mated formally by the Water Fae King. Few fae would ever be gifted such an experience.

And yet, I was only feeling it in my spirit, not hearing the formal words or chants he evoked to begin the process.

But it didn't matter. I'd dreamt of this union all my life, thinking about what it would be like when Kalt and I finally said our vows.

Now we would.

For all the wrong reasons.

Which saddened my heart until I felt Norden's lips against my throat, reminding me that I wasn't alone. That he and Lark were here, too.

My intended mates.

A selkie and a Winter Fae King.

A total dream come true.

Thank you, I thought at him, disappointed when I couldn't hear his response.

He says not to thank him, Kalt told me. *But if you're interested in thanking him later, he has an activity in mind.*

I frowned. *You can hear Norden?*

Not mentally. He's aware of what we're doing and can read your mind. And now Cyrus isn't amused by his interruption.

My lips almost curled. *Leave it to Norden to interrupt a king.*

He has a lot of practice with Lark, Kalt told me. Then he cleared his throat. *We're almost to the vows. Cyrus is hurrying because he can feel the Winter Source trying to intrude.*

A blast of heat touched my heart as he spoke, confirming his words. Kalt pressed his palm to my chest, immediately soothing the ache with an icy caress.

We will mate first, he told me. *Followed by Norden and then Lark.*

I swallowed. This was either going to make things a lot worse or—

Have faith, he whispered. *I know I don't deserve it, but have at least a little faith.*

A dangerous request.

Please, Artica. His nose nuzzled mine. *Listen to your soul. It'll guide you.*

I thought of last night with Norden, how I'd allowed my spirit to take hold and just went with the moment.

Why couldn't I do the same with Kalt?

He'd wounded my heart. But he hadn't been the one to end our bond. I'd done that. Maybe I owed it to him to try again, to give him the benefit of the doubt.

Hadn't I been the one to vow to make him live for himself? To try to convince him to join Norden and Lark's triad?

Why had I stopped? Because he'd hurt my feelings? Because he'd refused my hug?

Why had I let him win so easily? Why hadn't I fought harder?

I'd wanted him for as long as I could remember. I even applied to this internship *for* him. Sure, it'd also been a dare. But at the end of the day, he was why I'd really wanted the position.

Because I'd wanted him.

I *still* wanted him.

I wanted Kalt. I wanted Lark. I wanted Norden.

And by some happenstance of fate, they were all mine.

Why was I mourning my life like something terrible had happened? This negative approach wasn't me. I didn't do sadness. I didn't do brooding.

I lived and enjoyed every minute as though it were my last.

Why should this be any different?

Another spire of heat entered my chest, followed immediately by Kalt's cooling palm. *We need to say the vow now, Artica. I'll tell you the—*

I, Artica, accept the power that binds me to Kalt, born of Water, I said, not needing him to tell me what to say at all.

I already knew each and every beautiful word.

And I opened up my soul as the benediction fell from my mind.

To cherish and respect through all of the eras and time that may fall before us, until our souls do us part, I continued softly.

The words were mostly the same for all Water Fae, with a few personal bits. Assuming the fae involved wanted to deviate a little from the traditional words.

I was one of those fae.

Because this was the part I'd always dreamt of saying —the three attributes I'd gift to Kalt as my intended mate.

I give unto him my joyful touch, my love of pure snow, my warm admiration, and accept his in return.

The rest was just semantics, a vow spoken to my mate's soul beneath the grace of the Water Source.

My element is now his just as his is now mine, to the fae heavens may we never part. And I shall never forsake him for another, my water forever belonging to him and... I trailed off. The words, *to him alone,* stuck on my tongue.

Those were the final words of the pledge.

But my water wouldn't just be for him.

Because we had Norden and Lark, too.

And to our mate-circle, I finished instead.

Silence fell, Kalt's icy gaze swirling with emotion.

My throat started to swell, my own eyes frosting over with tears.

Because this would cement us together forever.

And if he rejected me now, I—

I, Kalt, Water Fae Prince, accept the power that binds me to Artica, Queen of the Winter Fae Realm. To cherish and respect, through all of the eras and time that may fall before us, until our souls do us part. I give unto her my heartfelt devotion, my icy vow of truth, my snowy serenity, and accept hers in return.

The frost in my eyes melted into real tears, his words a caress to my soul I'd never anticipated.

Because he'd gifted me parts of himself that surpassed the normal pledge.

He'd put thought into those words.

Making the rest a whisper on the wind.

My element is now hers just as hers is now mine, to the fae heavens may we never part. And I shall never forsake her for another, my water forever belonging to her and to our mate-circle.

His lips captured mine, a spark of electricity igniting in the air as our souls mated before the Water Source, cementing our spirits as one.

But we weren't done.

The ceremony continued with Norden spinning me to face him, his chocolate gaze holding mine as Kalt took over the role of kissing my neck, his mind opening to mine with each passing second.

I could feel his intent now, sense his real purpose for being here, and the acceptance in his heart that this was his true destiny. That he'd been fighting it for all the wrong reasons instead of embracing his fate.

Say your vow to Norden, Kalt whispered. *He should be able to speak his back to you once you've said it.*

It was hard to focus with Kalt's mind warming mine, his body pressed up against my back, his lips on my neck, and Norden's mouth curling into that seductive grin that said he was next. That he would soon join my spirit, too.

Oh Fae...

That's not the vow, Kalt hummed back at me, his teeth skimming my ear.

My whole body burned for him now, my soul wanting to finalize our bond in the most spiritual of ways.

But Norden's gaze held mine, the promise lining his lips one I could almost taste.

I, Artica, accept the power that binds me to Norden. To cherish and respect, through all of the eras and time that may fall before us, until our souls do us part. I give unto him my playful side, my adoration for ice, my good hair days, and accept his in return. My element is now his just as his is now mine, to the fae heavens may we never part. And I shall never forsake him for another, my water forever belonging to him and to our mate-circle.

Norden grinned, his lips whispering over mine as his voice began to hum in my mind. *I, Norden, Sexiest Selkie Alive—*

He paused, sighing heavily and pulling away, making me frown.

Only formal titles are allowed, Kalt explained. *Cyrus is chastising him.*

Do I need to go again?

No, Norden will fix it.

I, Norden, he said again, *the Winter Fae Prince of the Highest Order, accept the power that binds me to Artica, Queen of the Winter Fae Realm. To cherish and respect, through all of the eras and time that may fall before us, until our souls do us part. I give unto her my sexual prowess, my eager co...* He cleared his throat. *Uh, my eager creamsicle, my warm worship, and accept hers in return. My selkie heart is now hers just as her element is now mine, to the fae heavens may we never part. And I shall never forsake her for another, my silky pelt forever belonging to her and to her alone.*

I couldn't help but laugh at his clever alterations. Only Norden...

Cyrus is furious with me, Norden said. *Kiss me so I don't have to listen to his chastisement.*

I pressed my lips to his, accepting his vow and feeling our fourth-level bond flow into place. Clearly, the Water Source didn't mind his crude take on the vows.

Fae loved sex, after all.

We were all about embracing life.

And what better way to do that than to be honest about our intentions?

This is why you're meant to be mine, Norden hummed, his delight at being in my head again rivaling my own. *You understand me.*

I also like you, I told him.

Well, that's good. Because we're stuck together forever now.

I can think of a lot worse fates, I admitted, thinking about the Sources fighting over my body.

His touch turned serious, his tongue sliding into my mouth as he kissed me so hard I couldn't breathe. *Never scare me like this again. Ever.*

I'll try not to, I whispered.

Good. Now mate Lark so we can fuck, he said.

Kalt laughed behind me, clearly able to hear that. Or maybe he'd spoken it out loud.

I could only imagine King Cyrus's face right now.

The bodies around me moved with Lark and Norden swapping places and Kalt remaining at my back as the Water Fae anchor.

Lark's expression was far more serious than Norden's, his minty gaze holding a touch of reservation.

He's just worried about what the Sources are going to do once we finish the mating, Kalt told me. *He's not having second thoughts.*

I didn't think he was, but I thanked Kalt for explaining Lark's concern.

The Winter Fae King cupped my cheek, his lips whispering over mine. I returned his kiss, his power calling to my soul on a level that sobered the moment.

Because I needed him. His touch was an addiction to my senses, my soul immediately rejoicing at his nearness and craving more.

But his palm slid to my throat, pushing me back just a bit.

The vows, Kalt reminded me.

Right.

I, Artica, accept the power that binds me to Lark, Winter Fae King. To cherish and respect, through all of the eras and time that may fall before us, until our souls do us part. I give unto him my... I paused to think, evaluating him and what gifts I would bestow on him.

I give unto him my heartfelt festivity, my wintry abilities, my cheerful disposition, and accept his in return. My element is now his just as his is now mine, to the fae heavens may we never part. And I shall never forsake him for another, my water forever belonging to him and to our mate-circle.

Lark smiled, his lips brushing mine again as his grip tightened just enough to hold my eagerness at bay.

Because Fae, he tasted divine.

Like Festivus holiday miracles and faeliciously sweet confections.

I, Lark, Winter Fae King, accept the power that binds me to Artica, Queen of the Winter Fae Realm. To cherish and respect, through all the eras and time that may fall before us, until our souls do us part. I give unto her my holiday heart, my winter pride, and my unerring belief that we're meant to be together, and accept hers in return. My Winter throne is now hers just as hers is now mine, to the fae heavens may we never part. And I shall never forsake her for another, my Winter Fae heart forever belonging to her and to our mate-circle.

He kissed me as magic unleashed around us, whirling in an inferno of heat and ice. I wrapped my arms around his neck, thankful for the use of my limbs, as Kalt and Norden clung to my back.

A cascade of emotion and sensation clawed at my skin, at my heart, my soul, my very being, to the center of my core, stirring an explosion that left me shaking.

Shouts rang out through the air.

A few curses followed.

And my vision went black as night.

But warmth continued to surround me, flourishing through my veins, anchoring me to my mates, and giving me an outlet for all the power mounting inside me.

I screamed, the sound endless and silent as my heart shattered into a thousand pieces.

Only to be immediately glued back together by my mates.

Not real. Not real. Not real, I chanted to myself.

But Fae, it felt real. It scorched my insides, sending me into a whirlpool of ice where I forgot how to breathe.

Fingers in my hair pulled me back up, air infusing my lungs as the water rippled around me again to drag me under.

Give me more, Lark said into my mind, his voice a command I couldn't say no to.

I just had no idea what he meant.

Then his lips found mine and another eruption poured out of me, the intensity stealing my breath.

He continued to kiss me, his body flush with mine as he pulled me into his lap. I straddled him, unable to see, but I could feel him. I felt his warmth, his familiarity, his *strength*.

I clung to him as he devoured me, his mouth a lifeline I hadn't known I needed.

He held me close, his powerful body dominating mine and providing me with renewed life.

I ran my fingers through his damp hair, noting the icy texture of the strands, and kissed him again as my legs tightened around his waist.

He was hard.

Hot.

Passionate.

Take me, I begged.

No, he replied, his palm on the back of my nape. *Not like this.*

I didn't understand his refusal, my body pulsating with need as another explosion left my mouth on a scream that he swallowed with his tongue.

Faeeeee. I shivered, my muscles so tired, my legs starting to shake.

I was torn between sleep and wanting to ride him, the most convoluted conundrum of my existence. But the former started to win, my arms losing their grip around him as he continued to kiss me.

Tenderly now.

Softly.

Adoringly.

I sighed, his tongue a gentle caress in my mouth that lulled me into my dreams.

Which were filled with snowy hills and twinkling lights.

And a king smiling at me from a throne of glittering ice.

My king.

My Lark.
With two princes at his back.
My princes.
My Norden and Kalt.
My mate-circle.
My Water Fae mates.

NORDEN

"I need to go address the Winter Fae," Lark said as he ran his fingers through Artica's hair. She was settling now, her skin regaining that beautiful pinkish tone once more.

Kalt had his arms wrapped around her in the bed, both of them naked beneath the sheets with her back pressed to his chest. "I'll stay with her," he said softly. "There are still some things for us to discuss when she wakes."

Lark nodded. "Yes. Her belief is almost there, but not quite."

"It'll be resolute by the time I finish," he vowed.

"I know," Lark replied, his belief in Kalt as strong as my own.

We were all in each other's heads now—a new development that I rather enjoyed. Kalt suspected it was a result of the Water Fae bonds we now shared with Artica. Because this didn't typically happen for Winter Fae mates.

But there was nothing typical about our mate-circle.

"I'll go with you," I told Lark, rolling off the bed. I'd been lounging near Artica's legs, just running my palm up and down her thigh. The need to touch her was riding me hard, and not necessarily in a sexual manner. I just needed to feel her skin, to know she was alive and coming back to us.

Lark ran his fingers through her hair one more time, sighing as he followed me off the bed. He'd been lounging on his side, facing her, his cock hard and decidedly unsatisfied after his little playtime with her in the water.

Well, *playtime* might be a bit of a frivolous term.

More like a *power battle* whereby he'd absorbed as much holiday magic from her as she'd allowed, helping to anchor her on this plane of existence and satisfy the two warring Sources.

We were nowhere near done with this yet, something Zakkai had ensured we understood before taking his leave.

He was no longer involving himself, allowing our mate-circle to handle the redistribution of power.

Cyrus, however, was still very much involved as the Water Fae King. He'd been irritated, telling us to fix it quickly, before going to see his mate and to check on their little faeling. I suspected they would not be at tonight's Coronation Feast.

Which was a good result with all things considered. Because Lark and I would not be staying long. Not with Artica still recovering in the bed.

She needed our touch.

Which required her to be more awake.

But while she slept, we would handle the politics of the evening and then indulge her body and soul for however long she required to properly heal.

Lark donned his royal white tuxedo. I put mine on as well, refraining from muttering all my usual complaints about formal attire. When forced to wear clothes, I much preferred jeans and a sweater.

Alas, today's events had numbed me from my usual sarcasm.

I'd done my best to keep things light during the mating ceremony, as I'd wanted to distract Artica from the mounting concern in our mate-circle.

Snow had started to fall throughout the room, which would have been sweet, except the flakes had been as large as fists. They'd been feathery soft, but morphing quickly.

At one point, it'd turned into colorful confetti as the Winter Source took over by infusing holiday cheer.

That was when we'd really started to worry.

Because Artica's skin had turned even whiter and her breathing had started to shallow.

Her mind had fortunately remained with us, coherent each step of the way.

And I'd done my part by making her smile.

I'd also pushed Kalt even when my belief in him had never faded. But I'd sensed he'd needed that extra kick in the ass.

Lark pressed his lips to my cheek. "Ready, Nor?"

I nodded, my gaze falling to Artica. "Let's make it quick." Because I wanted to return to our queen as soon as possible.

"I don't think you've ever said those words to me before," Lark murmured.

"And I don't think you've ever attempted to make a joke to distract me before either," I replied, smiling as I turned toward him. "Thank you, my *king*." I kissed his mouth rather than his cheek, my tongue gliding along his lower lip in blatant invitation.

He wrapped his palm around the back of my head to

deepen the embrace, not only accepting my invitation but also *owning* it.

I groaned, his mouth wicked and dominant and giving me exactly what I needed—a distraction.

He was also thanking me for agreeing to attend with him. I could sense his need, not just sexually but also emotionally. He was worried about Artica, concerned that he hadn't taken enough out of her to provide a temporary balance. Until we finalized this mate-circle, we were all at risk, especially her.

We're going to be fine, I promised him, feeding him my belief with my mind and tongue. *She's perfect for us and she knows it. Kalt will fix it.*

I know, he sighed back at me. *I'm more disappointed that we may miss it.*

So we'll hurry, I reiterated. *And we'll join them as soon as we can.*

All Lark had to do was make a speech, thank the Winter Fae, and then apologize for needing to tend to our queen. Mate-circles were known for requiring a lot of *bonding* in their first few months. The Winter Fae—no, *all* the fae—would understand this need.

He pressed his forehead to mine, his eyes drifting closed for a private, intimate moment. Lark never showed weakness around anyone other than me. It'd been like that all our lives, since we'd met as children.

Our parents had always known we would end up mating. It was just an obvious bond we'd created when chasing elves around the Winter Fae playground and building ice forts in the snow.

The emotions had grown as we'd aged, lending toward experimentation and eventual sensual intimacy.

He'd been my first.

As I'd been his.

We had sometimes entertained others, either together or on our own, but no one had ever compared.

Until Kalt.

And now Artica.

Lark's need to taste them both, to properly initiate them into his bed, was a palpable presence in the air. But he redefined the meaning of *patient*. He would wait until they were ready.

My polar opposite.

Because I'd had no problem trying to seduce Kalt these last few months.

And when Artica had told me to make love to her, I couldn't refuse her. Lark hadn't been jealous at all, just turned on and waiting for me when I'd returned.

Only, we'd had the coronation festivities to think about, which meant he'd survived a very long day of prolonged gratification.

Which explained the hardness in his pants right now.

I pressed against him, allowing him to feel my own as I caught his lower lip between my teeth and nibbled. *If Kalt doesn't offer to suck you off later, I will.*

You'll be doing more than that, Lark vowed.

I smiled. *Promise?*

He growled, making me purr in delight. I loved a worked-up Lark. He always performed admirably in bed, but when he reached this level of need, he was an absolute beast.

Just make sure you use us before you touch Artica, I told him. *I can handle you. I'm sure Kalt can, too. But Artica needs soft and sweet.* At least for our first group activity.

Lark nodded. *I know.* He kissed me again, then released me and met Kalt's burning gaze on the bed. "We'll be back in thirty minutes."

The Water Fae swallowed, his pupils dilated with

interest. "We'll be waiting." Three words underlined with promise.

I winked at him. "You look good in our bed, Water Prince."

"I'd look better with you behind me, selkie," he returned without missing a beat.

"Ohh, he's learning," I murmured, pleased with the flirtatious banter. "Let's try to make it twenty-five minutes, my king. I believe Kalt just gave me permission to fuck him in the ass."

Lark smirked. "We'll see."

I sighed. "Always the alpha."

"It'll never change," he replied.

"I know." And I didn't mind one bit. "See you soon, Water Prince."

Kalt's lips were near Artica's temple as he replied, "Looking forward to it."

Lark led the way, leaving the ice crown behind. He didn't want to risk anyone sensing the missing magic within it. He also wasn't sure if it would maintain its structure without Kalt around to keep it frozen.

If the Winter Fae asked, he'd say he left it in the room for safekeeping with our queen.

I walked a step behind him as he moved down the hall, only for him to freeze part of the way and meet my gaze directly. "I want you beside me, Nor. Not behind me. Not in front of me. But next to me."

I arched a brow. "Not in front of you? Because I'm rather certain that's one of your favorite positions, my king."

His lips curled. "When naked, absolutely. When clothed, you're to be next to me. Always."

I made a show of moving forward to press my shoulder to his, which left him facing the opposite direction since he hadn't rotated around as I'd moved. "This could be a fun experiment, too."

"With the addition of the others, I do agree," he murmured, his lips brushing my shoulder as he spun to face the same direction as me. Then he grabbed my hand, something he'd not really done before, and twined our fingers together.

I gave his palm a thankful squeeze, which he returned in the next beat. *Please don't leave my side, Nor.*

Never, I vowed.

He nodded, then continued forward.

I could feel his nerves ratcheting up with each step, his concern for Artica mingling with his uncertainty over tonight's feast.

It was customary for the whole mate-circle to attend.

Breaking customs raised questions.

Questions he knew his father would be asking directly after Lark's speech—a revised coronation speech that he was still trying to formulate in his mind.

I gave his hand another squeeze, reminding him that he wasn't alone.

Thank you for coming with me, he whispered.

I wouldn't miss it for the world, I replied.

I suspect if Artica was awake and sucking your cock, you'd absolutely miss this.

My lips twitched. *You would want to miss it, too.* And I meant that in regard to Artica sucking him off, or him watching her with me. Either activity would prove distracting indeed.

Have I told you today that I love you, Nor?

You might have mentioned it this morning, I whispered back. *But I've not heard it via our new mental bond yet.*

He paused at the door to the grand hall, his eyes finding mine. *I love you, Nor.*

I love you, too, Your Majesty.

He leaned forward to brush a sweet kiss against my mouth. *Twenty-eight minutes.*

Twenty-seven, I corrected. *So you'd better make this a fast speech.*

It'll be quick and efficient, he promised me. *And hopefully Artica will be awake for our return.*

Oh, I'm hoping she'll be more than just awake, I told him. *I want to hear her screaming with pleasure down this hallway.*

Kalt will make it happen.

He will, I agreed. *And then we'll make it happen again.*

And again, he echoed as he opened the door.

And again, I repeated, walking through the threshold with him. *Twenty-six minutes now.*

Then we'd better walk quickly, he said.

Indeed.

ARTICA

On the first day of mating, my true loves gave to me…

I frowned, the low hum of music echoing in my mind.

An orgasm in a jacuzzi.

My brow furrowed. *What?*

And on the second day of mating, my true loves gave to me…

Two exceptional blow jobs,

And an orgasm in a jacuzzi.

My eyes opened, the room around me foreign yet warmly familiar.

And on the third day of mating—

I get it, another voice responded, both of which were inside my mind.

You asked why I suggested twelve days. Now you know.

A sigh followed. *Where are the voices coming from?*

Sunshine! See, I knew my song would wake her up.

You're derailing my focus, Nor.

Sorry. Keep her entertained for us, Frosty, he murmured.

"I will," a third voice replied, the lips near my ear.

I jolted, then groaned as a wave of agony splintered through my being. *Fae*, it felt as though I'd just swum five miles against the tide. I lifted a shaky hand to my head, muttering, "*Frost.*"

Norden continued to hum in my head, the music surprisingly soothing.

Stop, Lark said.

But I didn't finish my twelve days.

You have my permission to demonstrate them instead, Lark replied. *Just. Stop. Singing.*

"Why are they in my head?" I asked on a moan, wincing from the raspy quality of my voice.

"It's the mate-circle mingling with the Water Fae bonds." Kalt spoke softly into my ear, his body warm against mine.

I vaguely recalled craving his ice before.

Now I wanted his heat.

Because I was so *cold*.

My skin resembled ice, my movements stiff as a result. "What happened?" I breathed.

Kalt gently took hold of my wrist to lower my hand away from my head. Then he replaced my touch with his own, his thumb massaging circles into my temple.

I groaned, the sensation positively divine.

"How much do you remember?" he asked after a minute. "Do you remember mating us all?"

I swallowed, starting to shake my head, only to realize that made me feel worse.

A negative response also wasn't entirely true.

"The Water Source," I began. "I… I remember saying vows in spirit form."

To stop our realms from going to war, my mind added. *Because the Sources are battling inside me.*

My hand went to my chest. *Frost.*

325

"We're balancing you," Kalt said, his hand leaving my head as he shifted away from me.

I started shivering, but he moved me to my back and immediately snuggled into my side, propping himself on his elbow to stare down at me as his palm curved around my cheek.

"That's why you can hear Norden humming his erotic rendition of 'The Twelve Days of Christmas' in your head." His lips twitched. "Lark just announced to everyone that we will be hosting a Mate-Circle Celebration Feast to properly introduce his royal circle. And Norden added that it would be in twelve days."

I blinked. "A Mate-Circle Celebration Feast?"

"They're at the Coronation Feast right now, which customarily requires the new Winter Fae King to formally introduce all his mates. But we couldn't attend, something he's playing off as us being too busy consummating our bonds. And Norden promised we would be ready to meet everyone in twelve days."

"Twelve days," I repeated, apparently incapable of coming up with my own words right now.

"Yes, like the song." His lips twitched again. "And that led to the singing, which he's ensured we all hear because he's amused."

"And I'm hearing it because we're all... mated." I didn't phrase it as a question but as an uncertain statement.

It wasn't a dream.

I just mated three males.

One of whom is Kalt.

Fae... My eyes widened. "You accepted the triad."

"I did," he replied, his expression holding far more joy than I could ever have anticipated. "And I've never felt so relieved in my life."

I stared at him. "Really?"

He nodded. "I've been running from fate for too long, Artica." His thumb drew a line across my cheekbone. "And it took you rejecting me for me to realize what a fool I'd been."

I frowned—an expression I seemed to be making a lot right now. "I rejected you?"

"Our bond. You broke it."

"Because that's what you wanted."

"It's what I thought I needed," I clarified. "But it wasn't what I wanted. Not at all. That's why I couldn't break it before. I thought it was you holding me back, and you were in a way, just not the way I thought you were."

"I…" I trailed off, uncertain of what to say. A hazy memory of his words earlier hummed at the back of my mind, all the statements he'd made about the future and how he'd misunderstood his hopes and dreams. How it was me and Lark and Norden that he truly wanted all along.

How he wanted to wake up to me every day.

How he would prove himself to me until I believed in him again.

How he intended to taste me, to really kiss me, and make me know his true feelings through our bonding.

His mind was wide open to me now. His soul, too. And he didn't hesitate in showing me everything, allowing me to *feel* his own feelings and emotions, his previous uncertainties and renewed sense of self-purpose.

His belief washed over me, warming every inch of my soul.

His heart beat for mine.

His spirit danced along the edges of the Water Source, inviting me out to play, to embrace him, to *love* him, and to be loved in return.

"You've always been the perfect Water Fae for me," he

whispered, his icy gaze holding so much adoration that my heart physically hurt. "I'm sorry it took me so long to accept it. It wasn't for a lack of noticing, Artica. I always noticed you. It's the real reason I chose your application. I knew you completed it on a dare, but I didn't care. You were right for this position because you've always been right for me."

I swallowed. "Kalt…" I still didn't know what to say. This felt too good to be true. Too perfect to be real. Too intense to be happening to me.

Like a dream come to life in the form of a Water Fae Prince in a glamorous bed framed by a mural of the sea. I didn't need to ask to know where we were. I could smell the familiar hints of salted caramel in the air, strengthened by wintry ocean, nutmeg, and faelicious masculinity.

Lark's suite.

We're in the Winter Fae King's bed.

Because he's my mate, too.

Kalt's lips curled. "We all can hear you right now, Artica."

On some level I knew that, our mate-circle seeming to communicate all at once. But I could sense in my mind where I could shift the connection to be one mate at a time. I suspected they could do the same.

As evidenced by Norden's and Lark's sudden silence.

"Can you still hear them?" I wondered out loud.

"No, I suspect they're giving us a moment of privacy," he replied. "They'll be back soon, though."

"But it's the Coronation Feast. Shouldn't we be joining them?" Not that I really could. My voice still had a weird rasp to it, and my limbs felt shaky at best. I wasn't even sure if I could stand.

"No, we'll be formally announced and introduced

during the Mate-Circle Celebration Feast that Lark just announced."

"Oh, right." He'd mentioned that. "In twelve days."

His lips twitched. "Yes. Well, I think technically thirteen, as Norden appears to have plans for each of the twelve days until that point."

"Knowing him, it really is in twelve days, and he intends for us to do something at the feast," I replied.

Kalt chuckled. "Yes, likely accurate. And it'll probably be something from me. He's intent on making me grovel."

I studied him. "And you're okay with that?" *You're okay with us?* was my real question.

"I'm very okay with it." His expression turned serious, his gaze holding mine. "I'm more than okay with it. I'm the luckiest fae in the realms."

Some would probably argue that *I* was the luckiest fae in the realms, given I'd just mated three of the sexiest males in existence. But I didn't interrupt him with the clarification.

"I'm sorry for letting you down, Artica. I'm sorry for not realizing I was hurting us all with my actions, not just myself." His forehead touched mine, sending another splash of warmth across my skin.

I sighed, the comforting touch soothing the ache inside my skull and leaving me that much more at ease.

"And most important of all," he continued softly, "I'm sorry for not being there for you when you needed me most. I vow to never fail you again. I will spend the rest of my existence living every moment to the fullest with you, in whatever capacity you'll have me as part of your world."

He fell silent, waiting for me to speak.

But I didn't have anything I wanted to say.

Because sometimes emotions weren't meant for words, they were meant for something so much more.

I pressed my lips to his, tasting him for what felt like the first time. It was a tentative brush of a kiss, one that scattered goose bumps down my arms.

I hadn't realized I was naked until now.

Or that he, too, was without clothes.

The Artica of yesterday would have ogled him unashamedly.

The Artica of today didn't want to rush the exploration.

I wanted to savor the moment. Enjoy this. Indulge in every single second of bliss.

Energy hummed between us, our spirits hungry for the physical connection between our bodies. Elemental Fae typically worked through the bonds separately, taking each step one by one.

Yet Kalt and I had surpassed them all.

Without ever once being truly intimate outside of our minds.

I ran my tongue along his lower lip, sighing at the subtle traces of coconut on his mouth. It matched his scent, telling me he would taste the same.

I wasn't wrong.

Coconut mingled with peppermint on my tongue as I deepened our kiss.

His fingers slid back into my hair, holding me to him while allowing me to dictate our pace. But I sensed his need for control throbbing inside, his desire to devour me riding him hard.

His ability to hold himself back floored me, his determination a strength I couldn't help but admire.

It was how he'd managed to deny his triad for so long. How he'd accomplished pushing me away. How he'd been able to stay away from us all for over a week.

However, it'd taken a piece of his soul to do it.

A broken, fractured part of him wounded by the forced separation and inevitable heartache that had followed.

I really had hurt him when I'd freed him from our bond. I could sense it now deep inside, that ache caused by my perceived rejection.

Pressing my palm to his chest, I tried to heal him now, to show him through touch that I was here, that I'd accepted him again, that we were forever bound.

But he needed more.

He craved my forgiveness, my acceptance, my *belief*.

Our kiss deepened again, our tongues mating as I slid my touch up to his neck. So masculine and beautiful. So hard and muscular. I wanted more, to push him to his back and straddle him.

But my limbs wouldn't allow it.

I feel so weak, I whispered to him.

You need to physically bond with your mates, he replied. *Our souls are connected, but our bodies are not. And you just underwent an extreme power struggle between the Sources. They're demanding balance through our mate-circle.*

Which isn't fully established, I realized, sensing the frayed edges of our mating. *Why?*

Because it's new. He slid his thigh between mine. *We haven't proved our mutual belief in each other yet.*

How do we do that? I breathed, arching beneath him as a jolt of electricity radiated from my core.

He grinned against my mouth. *You know how we do that, Artica. We* mate.

I shivered, my palms going to his shoulders and then down his arms as he rolled on top of me.

Now both his thighs were between mine.

Placing his *icicle* right against my core.

He chuckled, likely hearing the euphemism in my

mind. "Norden tells me you say *cock* beautifully," he murmured. "Say it for me now."

"Creamsicle has such a nicer ring to it," I replied, arching into him again and shuddering as the head of his *creamsicle* hit my clit. *Faeee…*

"Hmm," he hummed. "That makes me thirsty, darling little flurry." He kissed along my jaw to my neck, his endearment going straight to my heart.

Flurry, like snow.

My own personal flurry of emotions mingled with wintry elements and sweet confections, he murmured back to me. *Sweet confections I long to taste on my tongue.*

I shivered as ice trailed down my chest, followed by his tongue, the chilly kiss immediately soothed by his hot mouth. It was an alluring sensation that only a skilled Water Fae could create, and Kalt executed it beautifully.

His touch skimmed my nipples, causing them to bead painfully until his lips eased the ache away. I moaned, my legs attempting to tighten against his, but he kept them spread as he tortured me with his power and his mouth.

I couldn't fight him, my limbs too weak to force what I desired.

Except I felt strength throbbing through my veins with each lick and nip of his mouth, his power seeming to taunt mine to the surface in a much-needed exercise of insulation.

You're making me exercise.

No, I'm playing with my Water Fae mate, he corrected. *Maybe you can try this on my cock later.*

My stomach clenched at the thought. *Yes.*

He grinned, his touch moving south as the ice skated along my hip bones, down along the crease at the top of my inner thigh.

I groaned, his mouth doing wicked things to my flesh

and driving me toward the brink of no return. Yet he hadn't even touched my dampness yet. Hadn't even kissed my mound. He was just teasing that sensitive space along my thighs. "Kalt…"

"I've dreamt of this," he whispered back to me, his nose skimming the place I desired him to lick. He inhaled, causing my legs to tighten once more as my insides blossomed with renewed flames, chasing away the ice in my veins.

"I've fantasized about it, too," he continued. "In the shower. In my bed. Countless times while I was away, Artica. All I've wanted this week is this moment, right here, right now. This intimate kiss that only you can provide." His icy gaze met mine, allowing me to see his stark need, his mind open and granting me access to the longing he felt down to his very soul.

Then his tongue gently slid along my seam, stirring more heat than I could possibly imagine between my thighs.

This has to be a dream, I marveled, the sensation stealing my breath.

A dream come true, he whispered back, increasing the pressure against my intimate center. *You taste divine, little flurry. Like sweet cream.*

Fae….

Kalt, he corrected. *Your Water Fae Prince.*

I nearly cried out, the intensity of his tongue combining with the emotions and one of my most precious fantasies coming true all blending to leave me breathless and shaking beneath his mouth.

And then he found my clit, causing the tumultuous insanity inside me to brew into a maelstrom of sensation that culminated in a euphoric explosion.

Fae… I was already coming.

My body so primed and ready after *years* of fantasizing that he barely needed to touch me to send me over that rapturous edge.

Or maybe it was the freshly created bonds.

Or the thoughts in his mind.

Or the emotions in his heart.

It didn't matter. I was lost to the sensations, my vision blinking in and out of realistic existence, as quivers overwhelmed my limbs and sent me falling into a stunning oblivion that stole the air from my lungs.

"So damn sweet, little flurry," he praised. "I could lick you all night."

Oh, I would like that.

But there was something I wanted more.

No, something we *needed* more.

I nearly asked him, but another ripple of pleasure shot down my spine, stealing my ability to process or think aloud.

Time escaped me.

Sensation my only purpose in life.

And then Kalt's mouth met mine, his body gliding over me with renewed promise, his tongue offering me the lifeline that taught me how to breathe again.

Strength overwhelmed me, allowing me to wrap my legs around his lower body, welcoming him inside me without so much as a thought.

He groaned as he slid all the way to the hilt. I hadn't been able to acquaint myself with his size, but he seemed to fit me perfectly. Not too long, not too thick, just right.

Each pump of his hips against mine seemed to empower my limbs even more, allowing me to fully embrace him and thrust upward to meet him.

His tongue stroked mine, feeding me the sweetness of

my previous orgasm and taunting me with hints of coconut divinity.

I wrapped my arms around his neck, holding him tightly, devouring every kiss as his body married mine.

It was better than anything I'd ever dreamed.

Because it was real.

Prince Kalt had not only noticed me, but he'd also *mated* me. And now he was inside me, kissing me, and filling me with so much adoration and need that my heart nearly burst with sensation.

I've always noticed you, he whispered. *It just took me a while to realize why I noticed you.*

His lips caressed mine, his pace slowing as he cupped my cheek and pulled back a little to stare down at me. "You're stunning, Artica. I would have to be blind not to see you. And even then, your heart would have drawn me in because you are just as beautiful on the inside as you are on the outside."

Tears gathered in my eyes, his words made that much more powerful by the echo of truth in his mind.

Because he meant every statement.

He kissed me again, this time softer, as though ensuring I felt every whispered word against my tongue. He wanted me to know his intentions, to hear his vow to love me, honor me, and cherish me for the rest of time.

His love might not rival my own for him yet.

But one day it would.

We would both grow together, our hearts beating as one, living and learning for eternity.

And I was okay with that.

Because I believed in his intentions.

I believed in us.

He deepened our kiss, his cock pulsating inside me with a need that matched my own. His body began to move again, this time with purpose, as he slid a hand between us to tease my clit. I jolted beneath him, his touch reigniting the fire in my lower belly.

His opposite hand went to my hip, tilting me upward into a position that allowed him to hit me impossibly deep.

I shook, the sensation touching my very soul.

"Again," I begged against his mouth.

He slammed into me, his thumb stroking my nub, his mind utterly open to mine. All of it at once created a cacophony of sensation that sent me shooting to the stars on another wave of pleasure that flooded my veins with pure ecstasy.

"Artica," he groaned, his cock throbbing as he came undone inside me.

Heat.

Bliss.

Brilliant light.

Our souls rejoiced, the bond thriving with life and expectation. I felt renewed. Reborn. Full of so much energy and excitement that I immediately begged him for more.

Power thrummed through my veins.

Power that I needed to expel.

Kalt groaned as some of it rippled through our bond. My name fell from his lips, part plea, part sigh. His palm went to my throat, his mouth capturing mine as he accepted another hit of power.

A growl emanated from his chest as I thrust my hips up again, needing more. Needing him. Needing further relief.

Because the power kept building, mounting inside my abdomen, whirling with intensity, and begging for an outlet.

No, it demanded one.

I whined, the energy too much, my veins throbbing with the heat and abundance of unexpected magic.

The Sources, I realized on a pant. *They're… they're…*

I screamed as another explosion left my body, this one not nearly as orgasmic or blissful as the eruptions Kalt had inspired.

He groaned as the power went into him as well, our Water Fae souls being overtaken by Winter Fae magic.

Lark! Kalt shouted via our bonds.

If he responded, I didn't hear it, the power rolling through me so violently that I lost sight of the room, my ears buzzing with static electricity.

I'd craved energy, wanting to feel more alive.

And the Sources had granted me that wish.

But this was too much. My soul wept beneath the onslaught, begging for an outlet as more power pushed from me to Kalt.

He didn't release me, his cock still throbbing inside me, but I felt his pain. It was too much. We needed our other mates.

We needed *King Lark*.

Several Minutes Earlier

"If you don't stop singing, I'm going to shove you up against that wall and make day six of your little song come true," I told Norden under my breath.

"Promise?" he asked, positively high off the mating lust warming our bonds.

Artica and Kalt had definitely made up, stirring an excited energy beneath my skin that begged me to run back to my suite and join them.

But Norden had suggested we give them an extra ten minutes of privacy to allow their bond to fully form.

I'd begrudgingly agreed, aware of how much Artica needed—

A jolt to my heart made me stumble midstep, causing my father to glance up from the table beside my mother. I'd been on my way to tell him we needed to meet later, but the glimmer in his gaze told me he already knew that.

And he'd felt the disturbance that had just tugged on my soul.

Norden pressed his palm to my back. "Everything all right?" Then he jumped as though the same spike pierced his chest. "*Fuuudge.*" He rubbed his pec, his brow furrowing. "What in the fae was that?"

"We need to go," I said, meeting my father's gaze. He gave me a little nod, telling me he understood. As the former king, he would have sensed the same disturbance in the Source that I did.

And given the speech I'd just finished delivering about the newly formed Mate-Circle Celebration Feast, he likely knew something was going on with my mates.

Namely, Artica.

Another spike through the bonds had me practically skipping from the room, which raised a knowing applause in my wake.

At least fae were easily amused.

Otherwise, they might have been offended by my abrupt departure.

Once in the hall, I took off at a run with Norden right beside me—the selkie true to his word about never leaving my side again.

The gingerbread sentries jumped out of our way upon seeing us, allowing me to bolt directly through the door to my private wing.

We went right by the trays Holly had delivered earlier, reminding me that I'd requested food that none of us had touched—something to rectify once we solved the problem waiting for us in the suite.

Norden reached the handle first, twisting it as I pushed, the two of us spilling into the room at the same time.

To find Kalt and Artica vibrating with unrestrained power on the bed.

"Lark," Kalt breathed, his icy gaze glowing with far too much energy. He was trying to anchor Artica through the bond, but it was too much for him to imbibe.

I didn't think.

I acted by joining them on the bed.

Then I grabbed Kalt by the neck and kissed him hard, sucking the power out of him through my touch alone. He sighed in immediate relief, while Artica groaned beneath him.

Norden was already stripping, joining the two of them on the bed and pulling Artica out from under Kalt to kiss her.

She moaned, her arms encircling his neck as she pulled him on top of her. "Fuck me, Norden," she begged, the crude words ones I'd never heard cross her lips. "*Please.*"

Do it, I told him, hearing his momentary reservation about her lust-drunk state. *She needs the physical contact to ground her.*

Her scream in the next second told me he'd complied, giving her what she needed while I continued to calm Kalt's energy sources down with my tongue. He curled into me, something I doubted he would normally have done, but the power radiating off his skin had melted away his ice and driven him to a point of near combustion.

He eventually calmed, his arms sliding around my neck as he returned my kiss with a blossoming intrigue.

My lips curled. *Finally see what you've been missing, hmm?*

He responded by loosening my belt and unbuttoning my pants.

Not my shirt.

Not even my jacket.

Just went straight to my groin.

You and Norden have a lot in common, I told him as he tugged down the zipper.

I hadn't put on anything beneath, giving him access to my aching cock.

He wrapped his palm around me, stroking roughly as he learned my length and girth. It felt fucking phenomenal after all these months of waiting. All these months of *yearning*.

Coupled with the events of last night, as I'd felt Norden release himself inside our queen.

Then the long-awaited connection today with my mates, delaying my gratification that much more.

And now hearing Norden fuck Artica beside us.

Fae, all of it only made me that much harder. *I'm not going to last,* I warned Kalt, my body too primed for a genuine round of foreplay.

The power in the room. The lust. The perfection of scents. Artica's blissful moans. Norden's sensual grunts. Kalt's expert grip and knowing tongue.

It was all too much.

Kalt pushed me to my back, his lips leaving mine as he slid down my body to take me into his mouth.

"*Sleigh bells,*" I hissed, the intimate sensation of his tongue against my shaft going straight to my tightening balls.

He took me deep, adding a little touch of ice with his tongue that stirred a mixture of pleasure and pain against my skin.

That little trick prolonged the torment.

Something I both enjoyed and hated.

Because I'd waited all damn day for a release and he was fucking taunting me. "*Kalt.*"

He hummed, liking the way I'd growled his name. Liking the way I tasted. Enjoying the way my touch grounded the power flooding his veins.

I felt it all.

Every thought. Every blissful emotion. Every dark desire.

He'd never been with a male. Yet he was doing a fine job of sucking me off now.

Because he was leaning on Norden's expertise—the selkie was feeding him information, telling him exactly what to do with his tongue while he drove Artica to oblivion beside us.

I reached for her hand, needing that connection, and found her palm waiting for mine. We locked our fingers together, creating a torrent of power that stirred in the air between us.

And then we were kissing.

I wasn't sure how it happened, then realized Norden had nudged Artica's head closer to mine. We formed the top of a triangle on the bed with both our backs against the mattress and our heads angled toward each other.

While Kalt continued to devour me with his mouth.

And Norden now licking Artica between her thighs.

It was fucking heaven, the orgasmic connection throbbing through my veins as I continued to hold her hand.

My opposite palm went to Kalt's head, not to direct him, just to hold him. Because he was driving me insane with his tongue.

And Artica's kiss… it was perfection redefined.

She was lost to the bliss, the power having taken over her mind, body, and soul, driving us all into this rapturous state of existence.

I welcomed each pulse of power from within her, absorbing it deep into my veins and spirit.

Her whines turned to moans.

Her shudders of pain turned to quivers of pleasure.

And her mind quieted into a swirl of blissful oblivion.

I felt her orgasm in her tongue, the vibration of her pleasure pushing me to follow her into that wonderous world of ecstasy.

Kalt groaned, swallowing each drop as Norden hummed in approval between Artica's legs.

It was one of the most intensely erotic moments of my life.

And as Artica's eyes opened to reveal blue orbs darkened with amorous intent, I knew this was just the beginning.

You were right, I whispered to Norden. *We're going to need at least twelve days.*

Then we'd better move this to the jacuzzi, he murmured, referring, of course, to his pool in the corner. *Because on the first night of mating, my true loves gave to me...*

An orgasm in a jacuzzi, Artica finished for him.

Norden chuckled. *Merry orgasms for all, and for all, a pleasurable night.*

NORDEN

A rtica practically glowed, her hair resembling sunlight even in sleep.

"Twelve Days of Orgasms"—a song I was absolutely going to have the elves pen as my first assignment as a Winter Fae Prince—had exhausted us all.

Except for maybe Lark, who had been undeniably controlled throughout our mating frenzy. He'd spent more time pleasuring us than pleasing himself, his focus having been on regulating the power structure within our bond.

Something that would have likely been smoother had he actually fucked Artica.

But he'd been taking his time, learning her likes and dislikes, finding the right way to pleasure her with his mouth and tongue first, while leaving his own orgasms to me and Kalt.

Are you worried she won't enjoy your brand of fucking? I asked as we rested in his bed with Kalt and Artica between us. He had Artica spooned back against his chest while I ran my fingers through Kalt's hair. It was soft and pretty, reminding me of frost—which was why he would be keeping his pet name.

I want to make it perfect, he confided.

Twelve Days of Orgasms wasn't perfect enough? I wondered at him, my lips curling into a taunting grin. *Because I thought it was pretty snowalicious myself.*

He smiled. *It was a reasonable start to a lifetime of pleasure.*

Reasonable? I snorted. *Do I need to come over there and suck you off again, Your Majesty?*

His gaze twinkled. *I would never deny your mouth on my cock, Nor. But Kalt and Artica are finally sleeping, and I don't want to disturb them.*

I know how to be quiet.

But we both know you won't be, he countered, seeing right through me as he always did.

Well. Doesn't mean I don't know how to be quiet, I pointed out.

He kissed the back of Artica's head, his gaze holding mine. *I'll be all right. She's almost ready for me.*

She's more than ready for you. She hadn't outright begged him, but she'd certainly attempted to seduce him a few times with her alluring curves and delectable mouth.

But he'd always distracted her with an orgasm or by letting her watch Kalt suck him off—something she had *very* much appreciated. As had I.

The Water Fae Prince had one hell of a tongue on him, blowing all my expectations out of the icy water. Literally.

Because he'd been the one to give me my orgasm on the first day of mating.

In the jacuzzi.

I very much wanted a repeat, but there were so many other positions to try and ways to play.

Artica had let me take her ass—something that had almost enticed Lark to fuck her last night.

But the Winter Fae King had held back. *Again.* Proving his resistance to be the strongest of all of us.

You just want her to climb you like a tree, I decided.

His lips curled. *I would not be opposed.*

Then fuck her already.

Patience, he murmured. *Delayed gratification has its rewards.*

Or are you worried about what it'll do with the Sources? I asked him seriously, truly trying to understand his hesitation.

But he shook his head. *No, I already told you that I just want it to be perfect.*

I narrowed my gaze. *What are you planning to do? Fill the suite with ice flowers?*

You'll find out tonight, he replied. *After the Mate-Circle Celebration Feast.*

My interest was piqued. *Are you planning a surprise?*

He merely smiled.

I want to help.

He shook his head. *This is for you all. Just be patient, Nor. You'll thank me later for it.*

Artica stretched then, her full lips parting on a moan that went straight to my groin. Kalt immediately stirred in response, his palm automatically finding her breast before he'd even fully woken up.

Lark arched a light brow at me.

I didn't say or do anything this time, I promise. But influencing our Water Fae mates was absolutely something I would do and had done all week.

However, this time I'd been too interested in Lark's thought process to think about feeding the two Water Fae more selkie candy before they went to dream.

Artica arched again, causing Lark to wince, his cock lodged against her delectable ass. I waggled my brows.

You sure you can wait until tonight, my king? She's super tight. Even tighter than Kalt. Something we both now knew from experience.

Lark growled. *Stop it, selkie.*

Artica moaned in response, writhing as she lifted her leg over Kalt's hips.

I kissed his neck, urging him to wake up faster.

He was already hard. I could practically smell his arousal. A little nibble to his pulse made him groan. *I'm exhausted*, he muttered into my mind.

Artica's hot cunt is waiting for you to fuck it, I said back, purposefully using crude words to stir him from his slumber.

He practically jolted against me.

Then Artica lunged at him, another wave of power rippling from her through our bonds.

I groaned, the heat a welcome sensation in my veins.

Kalt's hips moved, his body automatically engaging Artica's as he slid home in a single thrust. Our queen was always ready, her body primed from the endless fuck fest of the last twelve days.

Maybe I'd been wrong about the timeline.

Maybe we needed to stay in bed for another twelve days and go the full twenty-four.

Imagine the lyrics I could create with twelve more days of playing? I thought at Lark, earning me a growl in return.

I am not postponing our mate-circle introductions. You're all mine, and I want the entire kingdom to know it.

Is that why you invited all the faedoms back? I asked him. *For only our kingdom to know it? Or the entire faedom?*

His minty eyes met mine. *I want your mouth on my cock now, Nor.*

That's not an answer, my king.

No, it's a demand.

I smiled. *I thought we were delaying our gratification until later?*

We are, he replied, reaching across Kalt and Artica for my hair. He didn't grab it; he just ran his fingers through it. *But I very much want your mouth. Please.*

Hmm, begging. I rather approved. *Let's take care of our Water Fae first. Then I'll indulge you in the shower.*

He smiled, his lips pressing against Artica's hair as he continued to fondle mine. *I want all the faedoms to know,* he admitted to me softly. *That's why I invited them to stay.*

His assistant, Holly, had handled the abundance of accommodations, assisted by several of the other elves. They'd been thrilled by the announcement of visitors being allowed to stay in the realm until the Mate-Circle Celebration Feast.

And as nothing had been urgently brought to our attention, I assumed everything had gone smoothly— which marked a new age of Interrealm Fae relations.

Lark continued to kiss Artica's neck while I reached around to thumb her clit. Kalt's mouth worshipped hers as he fucked her into oblivion with powerful thrusts that made me achingly hard. Because each shift of his hips caused his firm ass to brush my groin, and fuck, that Water Fae had a very nice backside.

Artica cried out with a convulsion that rocked the bed, power seeping from her into all three of us as she came down from her energized high. Kalt groaned out his own release, spilling himself inside her before turning to indulge me in a kiss that went straight to my dick.

I pulled him out of her and nudged him to his back while Lark did the same to Artica, and we both went down to lick the sex off their skin and thighs.

It was a mutual act of adoration and worship, meant to demonstrate the power and bond of our mate-circle.

However, it was interrupted by a light tapping on the door only a few minutes after we'd begun.

Kalt groaned as I removed my mouth from the tip of his cock. "I'll get it," I said, not wanting to take Lark away from his breakfast between Artica's thighs.

I didn't bother with pants.

Anyone knocking on Lark's doors knew what was happening in here.

And they were very likely familiar with my naked form.

I twisted the handle to find a blushing Holly on the other side, making me curse myself for jinxing our fun. I should never have thought about how they had all left us undisturbed apart from the daily delivery of food and water.

Holly curtsied. "Prince Norden."

"Hi, Holly," I said on a sigh as I leaned against the door frame. She started to speak, but I held up a hand. "Hold on. If we're going to do this, then I want to guess. Did the Hell Fae end up staying?"

She bit her lip and nodded.

"Are they causing problems?" Because they were the obvious bet here. The Hell Fae King had shown up to the Coronation Feast after missing the actual coronation. It had shocked the fae out of me and Lark, but there hadn't been enough time for us to introduce ourselves properly.

She shook her head. "The king and prince have been wandering the Human Realm and merely staying here in the evenings."

My eyebrows rose. *Well, that's an interesting development.* I'd revisit that fun fact later. "Okay, then is it a Shifter Fae?" My selkie brethren knew how to behave around here, but some of those wolf clans were positively uproarious.

"Prince Norden, it would be more prudent if I just told

you," she said, biting her lip again. "Queen Artica would very much want to know this."

That straightened my spine, dismantling all my previous humor. "What is it?" I asked, far more serious now and a tad concerned.

"Um, well, her parents have arrived," she said. "And they want to see her."

Lark joined me at the door, obviously having heard every word. He had a robe cinched around his waist, his modesty taking over. "They'll need to wait until the Mate-Circle Celebration Feast, Holly. If they ask why, just say she is otherwise indisposed with her mates. We'll deal with any hard feelings later."

"Of course, my king," she said, curtsying low. She stood and started to leave before pausing and glancing back at us. "Um, would you like some lunch, Your Highnesses?"

"Yes, that would be lovely. Thank you, Holly," Lark replied, as elegant as ever.

She curtsied again, then skipped off down the hall.

I glanced at him and then at Artica on the bed. She was sitting up with wide eyes and an expression that was far more alert than it had been the last few days. "Did... did I just hear her right? My parents are here?"

"They are," Lark told her, walking back toward the bed as I closed the door. "But we have a few hours before we'll greet them."

She shivered, her gaze skating over all three of us. "That's... that's good... because I'm not sure what to say about any of this yet."

"I have a song that could help you," I offered.

Her lips twisted. "I... I think I just need..." Her cheeks reddened, making me grin.

"Yeah, Sunshine? What do you need?"

"A few more explosions," she whispered.

"They're called orgasms," I said conversationally, joining her on the bed and pushing her down with my palm. "Here, I'll spell it for you with my tongue. Against your clit."

Then I'd sing my song to her all over again.

And demonstrate each act along the way.

We're so going to be late for this feast, Kalt murmured.

Fashionably late, I corrected him. *Now kiss our queen while I make her come.*

Fae, I loved my life.

Licking our queen until she screamed?

Mmm, yes, please.

ARTICA

This all started with me being late to Interrealm Fae Internship Day.

So it only seemed fitting that I was late to my own Mate-Circle Celebration Feast.

Except this came with the added embarrassment of my parents being the first to see me after days of playing with my new mates. And since they surprised us in the hallway, they received the full dose of my frazzled state.

Hot cheeks. Swollen lips. A libido that apparently would not die. And two Sources battling over my soul.

No big deal.

Totally fine.

But yeah, I definitely would have preferred Professor Elway's angry glare right now over my mother's wide blue eyes.

This is going to be fun.

"Artica!" she exclaimed, grabbing my shoulders as she took in my gown and tiara—an outfit similar to what I'd worn on Coronation Day, only this dress was silvery white to match my mates' tuxedos.

And beneath it was a pair of unsteady legs, thanks to Kalt's and Norden's attentions only minutes ago.

"Mother," I said, smiling meekly at her and my father.

This was definitely not the family reunion I'd anticipated.

What's going on? Lark asked from wherever he'd run off to.

He'd disappeared more than once over the last few days—I assumed to see to Winter Fae Realm business. But I was disappointed when he'd left before us tonight. I had thought we would all enter the ballroom together for the announcement.

Hopefully, he would meet us there.

And maybe he would explain why he hadn't truly touched me yet.

It certainly wasn't from a lack of me trying. But I wondered if it was a result of the warring Sources. Maybe he couldn't truly touch me yet? Or maybe he worried about what it would do?

Regardless, I wished he would just tell me.

Because part of me kept feeling like I'd done something wrong.

Artica's parents are here, Norden told him when I didn't immediately reply.

They are supposed to be inside the ballroom, Lark replied flatly. *With my parents.*

Just give them a moment, Norden murmured. *They're obviously worried about their daughter.*

Lark snorted. *They gave up their right to be concerned when they ran off on holiday without leaving a method of contact behind.*

That's fairly typical for Elemental Fae, Kalt informed him.

I cleared my throat because it was hard to focus with all the males chatting *in my head.*

"I'm, um, sorry you only just found out about all of this," I said lamely, waving to Norden and Kalt.

Since Lark is missing. I made sure to keep that thought to myself rather than broadcast it to the whole circle—a trick I was slowly beginning to learn.

"Sorry?" my mother repeated. "Dear, don't be *sorry.* Not for this!"

"I suppose it was a shock," my father admitted, earning a glower from my mother. "Especially since we only found out yesterday. That's not a lot of time to process."

"Just yesterday?" I asked, frowning. "I was told that King Cyrus attempted to reach you before the coronation."

"Oh, he did but we were out of range," my father said gravely, giving my mother a grin. "We were summering in the Human Realm, and as you know, Elemental Fae towers don't really exist there."

"Right," my mother added. "We didn't receive the message until we returned yesterday, and we came straight here."

"Which was a bit funny, considering we'd just been in this realm, only we were staying at the West Coast Regional Alpha of the Fortune Fae's summer retreat in Los Angeles. So even the Fortune Fae phones wouldn't have been able to reach us there."

"Oh, uh, that sounds like it was an experience," I hedged. "So, um, about the cor—"

"It was *quite* the experience," my mother said, clapping her hands excitedly and cutting me off. "Did you know that the Alpha owns a fleet of the finest sailboats? We went all the way down to the territory the humans call the Baja Peninsula on one."

Kalt slipped his fingers through mine, giving my hand a squeeze. While I'd inherited my sense of joy from my parents, I'd fortunately avoided their penchant for blabbing like sea lions.

Clearing my throat, I attempted again to speak, only for my father to say, "Beautiful reefs down that way. Your mother wanted to bring back some coral for the Water Fae King's stepmother as a royal present." He grinned. "She does love the sea organism for which she's named."

He pulled a piece of gorgeous pink coral from his pocket. I noted it still thrived with life, protected in a layer of water magic gifted by my parents.

Kalt smiled. "Aunt Coral will love it."

My father blinked, glancing at Kalt for what appeared to be the first time. He'd been so caught up in seeing me and telling me about their adventures that he hadn't even seemed to notice the men standing behind me.

Or the approaching Winter Fae King at their back.

A Winter Fae King who wore a scowl that kept me from speaking. "You must be Artica's parents," he said, causing them to stiffen and glance his way. "My parents are waiting for you in the ballroom. My assistant, Holly, will escort you to them."

He stepped out of the way to allow a small elf to give a little wave. "Hello," she greeted with a smile. "If you'll follow me."

"B-but we haven't been properly introduced yet," my father sputtered.

"No, you were too busy going on about your vacation," Lark replied without missing a beat. "Perhaps you'll allow your daughter to do some of the talking when we see you again in the ballroom."

Now that's certainly one way to make an impression on the in-

laws, Norden drawled, his fingers finding a strand of my hair and giving it a gentle tug.

You suggested Artica sing a song about orgasms to explain her absence these last twelve days, Lark reminded him. *You think that would be more impressive?*

I seem to recall you lecturing me recently about the importance of honesty in a relationship. I was merely suggesting our Artica be honest about her activities of late.

Lark snorted.

I'm sure they would have been more impressed by that than your blatant dismissal, Norden added as Lark passed my father without a second glance to stand right before me, thereby blocking my parents' view of me.

I'm a king. I'm impressive by nature.

I swallowed at the steel glint in his minty green gaze as he evaluated me slowly, taking in my tiara all the way down to my silver heels.

Besides, he continued, his palm cupping my cheek as he glanced over my head at the selkie behind me. *They haven't impressed me, what with prattling on about their own lives instead of acknowledging their own daughter's coronation. She's a queen now. And she will be treated as such.*

They're just excited, I explained lamely.

"Well, I guess we'll see you soon," my mother said, her voice far more deflated than before.

Sighing, I stepped around Lark—royalty or not, I couldn't just dismiss my parents like this.

I pulled my mother into another hug. "Sorry, we're trying to follow formalities," I whispered. Not that anything had been established yet with this being the first Mate-Circle Celebration Feast. But I had to say something.

"No, he's right. We were being rude," she said as she released me. "I look forward to meeting your mates. And… and I'm proud of you, Artica."

"We're both proud of you, sweetheart," my dad echoed, his gaze unsure as he glanced over my shoulder.

Because Lark was looming behind me.

And I suspected he had a very regal expression on his face.

"She's a stunning Winter Fae Queen," he said, his hands finding my hips. "We're very lucky to have her."

That's much better, Norden praised.

He wasn't wrong. My parents immediately beamed.

"I can see you're in good hands." Some of the cheer had returned to my father's voice. "Fine hands indeed."

My mother smiled. "Just a few weeks ago, you were talking about this internship. I would never have expected... I mean... It's..."

"A fairy tale?" I offered, smiling meekly again.

"Not a fairy tale," Kalt said, moving to my side to find my hand again. I wasn't sure when I'd released him. Maybe when I'd gone to hug my mom?

Norden went to my opposite side. "No, it's a dream come true."

"Yes," Kalt agreed. "But it's a dream Artica made a reality because of her joy, which I can see she's inherited from both of you."

Aww, he is totally showing you up, Lark, Norden said.

As I've already stated, I don't need to make a good impression. I'm a king.

"Prince Kalt," my mom said, her tone suggesting she'd been trying to place his name and just realized his identity. Her gaze widened, her lips parting in appreciation.

Because, yeah, Kalt induced that sort of reaction for everyone in his path. And he was even more deadly in his pristine tux with his arctic-white hair all soft and tousled to his shoulders. Not to mention those ice-blue eyes.

"Lovely to meet you," he said softly.

"Oceania and Muriel," I supplied, giving their names.

Lark sighed. *I guess we're making introductions, then.*

Sorry, I whispered, grimacing.

His lips brushed my temple. *Never apologize, my queen. I will always respect your choice.*

Lark politely introduced himself and Norden, explaining the customs of the Winter Fae mate-circle, then again asked my parents to please follow Holly to the palace ballroom. They agreed with a bit more contentment this time, saying again how proud they were of me before disappearing with Lark's assistant.

He still had a hold of my hips, spinning me in his arms as soon as the door at the end of the hall closed.

"Artica, you steal my breath away," he whispered, his minty irises holding that serious glint again. "I'm sorry I wasn't here to say that the moment you stepped out of my room. I was handling a last-minute guest issue with Holly."

"Guest issue?" Kalt repeated, once again next to me with Norden on my opposite side.

"Just a minor altercation between two errant Shifter Fae."

I narrowed my gaze. "Wolves?"

"Mmm," he hummed, confirming what I already knew.

"They're animals and feral and *mean*," I told him seriously.

His lips quirked upward. "Are they?"

"They tease fae who can't shift," I informed him. "And they bite."

"I feel there is a story here that I very much want to know," he murmured, smiling. "But we really need to go. The guests have been waiting for over an hour, something they're tolerating only because I didn't release any sort of schedule. But I'm sure they are growing hungry."

"Exactly how are we being introduced?" Norden asked.

"The old-fashioned way—via the gingerbread men."

Norden frowned. "How boring."

"Do you have a better idea?" Lark asked him.

And it was the sort of question he probably should never have asked.

Because Norden's eyes immediately lit up. "Yes, actually. I do."

ARTICA

A penguin parade.

My heart soared at the sight of all those waddling feet marching through the ballroom ahead of us with Norden as their guide.

"Sorry for the delay!" he broadcast to the room. "This took a little more coordination than we anticipated."

A clever way to explain our tardiness.

But in reality, he'd managed to orchestrate this in fifteen minutes.

After telling Lark he had an idea, he'd wandered off. Then told us via the mental mate-circle link to meet him by the palace ballroom doors.

Where the penguins had already begun their entrance.

The fae and elves inside were all beaming at the display.

A few other males appeared to be helping Norden with the organization. I recognized one of them as Yule and guessed the others might be selkies, too.

When I asked via our mate bonds, Lark pressed his

palm to my spine and placed his lips near my ear to tell me all their names.

"Wow, Norden has a lot of brothers," I whispered.

"Seven is customary for selkies," he replied, making my eyes widen.

"Customary?"

He smiled. "Some of them are twins."

"Twins?" I squeaked. "Will Norden want...?" I couldn't finish the question. Because *seven* selkies? I... I wasn't sure my body was up for that. *Can I even have a selkie baby?*

"Our children will all be of mixed magic," Lark replied, still speaking against my ear.

No one but Kalt noticed because all the attendees were too busy watching the waddling wonders move around the ballroom.

"So no selkies?" I felt sort of sad about that. I didn't want seven. But one or two might be nice.

"A selkie with water and winter magic," Lark corrected softly. "Definitely possible."

I looked at him. "When you allow it, right?"

He frowned. "No, my queen. When *you* allow it."

"Norden said you control reproduction," I said slowly. "That you have to bless it." Was he wrong? Because if he was, then—

"My power blesses the creation, yes. But I would never use it without your consent. It's *your* decision when and how we procreate." He smiled. "I will just be your magical form of birth control until we are all ready for that step."

"Magical birth control," I repeated, my lips twisting upward to match his smile. "Sounds like magic sperm."

Is that why he hasn't really touched me yet? Because he doesn't want to until I'm ready for an heir? The private thought caused my smile to falter, something he noticed because his brow furrowed.

"What's wrong?" he asked.

I shook my head. "Nothing. Just thinking about having seven selkies." My heart clenched at the lie.

And his expression told me he sensed it, too. "Artica—"

"Ladies and gentlemen!" a male called to the attendees in the room. "May I present the new Royal Winter Fae Mate-Circle!"

Uproarious applause met his announcement, making my cheeks heat. *Who is that?* I wondered, not recognizing the tall, dark-haired male. While his physical appearance placed him in his thirties, the ancient air around him suggested he was much older.

Norden's paternal grandfather, Berg, Lark replied, his eyes grinning at the sight. *This is a great honor. Norden's family rarely comes onto shore. I've met his grandfather only once, but never his grandmother.*

What about his parents? I asked.

Lark cleared his throat. *His parents are no longer with us.*

Oh. I hadn't realized... *I... I'm so sorry to hear that.* It made me realize how much I still had to learn about my mates.

They perished outside of our protective wards, either from polar bears or humans, we're not sure, he added as Norden faced us with a dazzling smile.

Don't be sad for me, Sunshine, he murmured. *And don't worry about my longevity. Selkies aren't entirely immortal, but as a Winter Fae Prince, I might as well be.*

I hadn't realized we'd been speaking in our mate-circle. The whole channel thing in my head was confusing. Private thoughts required me to block them all out— something I'd learned. But shifting between single mate channels and our group hive mind was still a work in progress.

Something that was made more difficult with emotion.

Hence, I'd accidentally spoken to all my mates when Lark's explanation had made me sad.

Norden wandered over to us, his palm finding my cheek as he pressed his lips to mine.

Applause followed, along with his grandfather making formal introductions of our names and titles and ending with a comment about us being unable to stop touching each other.

Norden chuckled. "Can you blame me?"

"No, son, I cannot," his grandfather replied as he wrapped his arm around a petite female near his side. *Your grandmother?* I guessed.

Yes. Grandmother Ester, he confirmed. *And she very much wants to meet you all. As do my brothers.*

Have you met his brothers? I asked Lark.

Only Yule, he replied.

The penguins waddled from the room under the careful supervision of Norden's brothers. Then Lark addressed everyone with a quick speech, thanking them all for joining us for the first Mate-Circle Celebration Feast.

"You may have noticed that we like sweets around here," he continued, stirring a few laughs from the crowd. "But we are working on our Interrealm Fae relations. So I've requested that a few delicacies be brought in from all the faedoms. I hope you enjoy tonight's feast, but first, let us indulge in a round of holiday spirits. Cheers!"

An army of gingerbread men ascended, holding trays of flutes and various candies.

Everyone responded with a resounding "Cheers!" and the celebration officially began.

We met with Lark's parents first, sharing kisses on the

cheeks and pleasantries. Then we continued our parade around the huge ballroom.

Kalt and Norden walked a step ahead of us, their arms linked, while Lark kept his palm against my back.

We greeted all the guests as a circle, thanking them for being here and accepting their well-wishes.

Well, most of them, anyway.

"Your Sources are still not fully appeased," Zakkai informed us after Lark thanked him for his help after the coronation.

I'd learned of his involvement in our bonding through my mates and voiced my gratitude for him saving my life.

He nodded stiffly before looking straight at Lark and returning to his previous statement. "I suggest you finish fixing this Source problem soon, King Lark. We're leaving tomorrow."

Aflora sighed, shaking her head, clearly not pleased with her mate's less-than-pleasant commentary.

"We will," Lark promised him before steering us away from the Midnight Fae and toward the next group. I wanted to ask what Zakkai meant, but I suspected that I already knew.

My links to Kalt and Norden were solid.

And while I felt bonded to Lark, there was definitely something missing.

Intimacy.

"King Lucifer," Lark said, drawing me immediately out of my thoughts.

Hell Fae King.

"I hear you've been enjoying the Human Realm," Lark continued.

"Have you?" King Lucifer replied, sounding bored. "Fascinating." A word that did not match his tone.

"We've been enjoying the human advancements in

technology," a male with striking features said from beside him. His multicolored eyes seemed to glimmer beneath the lights as he smiled. "We are also enjoying your festive cheer."

"We are?" the Hell Fae King asked, arching a dark brow.

"We are," his companion confirmed.

"Hmm." He lifted his dark eyes up to the mistletoe over their heads. "Yes, I suppose we are." He grabbed the other male by the back of the neck and kissed him with a passion that reminded me of Norden.

When they finally pulled away, Lark finished making introductions, providing me with the name of the striking male—Prince Melek.

The two Hell Fae certainly seem hot *for each other,* I joked, earning a chuckle from Norden and Kalt.

All fae are capable of joy, Lark replied, seemingly pleased by the display as we started toward the overly long table set up on one side of the palace ballroom.

It was a massive space meant for entertaining, the size rivaling the cafeteria. Except everything in here was much more formal with candlelit chandeliers and gold curtain accents.

I expected more holiday grandiosity, I admitted.

Did you? Lark glanced at me, his lips twitching. *Your wish is my command, my queen.*

He waved his hand, using his new access to water magic to create glittering snowflakes in the air, followed by a display of tinsel and dancing water pixies.

A beautiful demonstration of our combining powers that drew a collection of "oohs" and "aahs" from the crowd. If they didn't know about the mingling Sources in our mate-circle, they certainly did now.

Not to be outdone, Norden formed a group of tiny

seals out of the moisture in the air, then sent them off to chase the pixies around the room.

Several of the guests giggled with delight. Others gaped at us with wide eyes.

"Show-off," Kalt said as he rolled his eyes, but the smile touching his lips suggested he approved.

In any other era, we would have been an abomination-circle. But here, we were accepted. I could feel it in the air, the joy and the anticipation inspired by our mating.

We were bringing about a new era of life.

Introducing a new way to exist.

And proving that the combination of power could be used for good instead of evil.

A group of Elemental Fae stood close to the end of the table, the crowd including Kalt's father. I recognized him immediately with his long, flowing white hair and dimpled smile. But the grin didn't quite reach his eyes the way Kalt's did.

He'd missed the coronation ceremony because Kalt hadn't invited him, something he apologized for as soon as he saw him. I already knew Kalt had lost his mother as a boy, so I wasn't expecting to see her, but I whispered about her loss to Norden and Lark so that they would know not to ask.

Except Norden surprised me by saying he was already aware.

As was Lark.

It served as a reminder of the months the three of them had shared together before I'd arrived. I wasn't jealous, but I very much wanted to make up for lost time.

Something I probably needed to tell Lark when I asked him about his hesitation later.

Kalt captured my attention as he embraced his dad,

the sadness in his father's gaze providing yet another insight into Kalt's hesitation to take on the mate-circle.

He'd witnessed that loss for years, had seen what the broken link had done to his father, and hadn't wanted that for himself.

Yet he'd experienced a dose of that pain when I'd pushed him away.

By the time the introductions were finished, all I wanted to do was wrap Kalt up in a hug and tell him how much I loved him.

But he beat me to it, pulling me into his arms and kissing me with a passion that elicited yet more applause from the room.

This feels like a mating ceremony, I breathed into his mind.

Good, he whispered back at me. *Because we're mates.*

I smiled. *Yes. We are. You're mine. Officially and irrevocably mine.*

He chuckled. *You sound quite pleased about that.*

I am.

Can I let you in on a secret? he whispered, catching my gaze. "I'm pleased, too." He leaned forward to kiss me again, only for a voice laden with power to interrupt us.

"I'm pleased as well," the Water Fae King interjected.

"Cyrus," Queen Claire hissed.

"What?" he asked with false innocence. "I'm very pleased Kalt finally followed his rightful path. Am I not allowed to voice it?"

Kalt slid his arm around my waist as we faced his cousin. "Yes, you were right. I was wrong. On this, I'm rather pleased, so I'll concede to your victory," Kalt said as Norden and Lark stepped up behind us. Lark's hands went to my hips, his heat a welcome caress against my skin that inspired power to hum through my veins.

Power that he immediately absorbed as though he

knew I was about to need another expulsion of energy. His lips met my neck.

Let me know if you need me to take more, he breathed into my mind, eliciting goose bumps along my skin.

Thank you.

My pleasure, he responded, a hint of need underlining those two words.

A need that I felt all the way to my throbbing core.

But the clearing of a throat drew me back to my surroundings and the Elemental Fae still standing before us.

I recalled each of their names.

The Fire Fae, Titus.

The Earth Fae Royal, Sol.

The Air Fae Royal, Vox.

And of course, King Cyrus and his Spirit Fae half brother, King Exos.

Talk about a power-circle.

Queen Claire was radiant, wearing a blue dress with silver embroidery that complemented the golden waves of her hair.

She offered me a curtsy, and I responded in kind, praying to the Sources that I could maintain my festive grace. My movements were fluid, as if guided by Festivus joy.

Or maybe they were aided by the touch of my mates, as neither Kalt nor Lark released me.

I sensed Norden tugging on my hair as well, his fingers always finding a reason to touch one of my curls.

Perhaps in this realm, with these men as my guide, I wouldn't be such a klutz anymore.

"Congratulations on your mate-circle and ascension, Queen Artica," Queen Claire said, beaming at me with pride. However, the glimmer in her gaze said that this outcome hadn't surprised her. "I could not think of a more perfect fae for this role."

"Really?" King Cyrus asked, slipping his arm around Queen Claire's small waist to give her a kiss on the cheek. "You mean it wasn't Artica that I heard you and Gina discussing last month?"

"Surely the powerful Fortune Fae Omega didn't foresee this," King Exos added.

"No, she definitely didn't foresee that a Winter Fae Queen would usher in a new era of joy for all the realms," Queen Claire replied. "Nor did she tell me that said queen would be key to all my Interrealm Fae aspirations."

My cheeks heated as the obvious intent of their comments registered in my thoughts. "You... you knew this was going to happen?"

"Let's just say we knew there was a very good chance that it would happen," Queen Claire replied, smiling.

"And we're very glad it did," King Cyrus added, his gaze on Kalt. "Mating looks good on you, cousin."

"Just as fatherhood looks good on you," Kalt returned. "Which, speaking of, where is Prince Ciro?" His question made me want to kick myself for not inquiring about Queen Claire's only child.

I'm really good at this Interrealm Fae internship, I thought sarcastically. *Always remembering key details and all that.*

Well, it's a good thing you have a triad to assist you, Kalt replied in my mind, his icy gaze glittering with delight as he glanced at me. *And a Water Fae Prince who remembers such details for you.*

Queen Claire smiled. "We left him with my mother and Mortus."

"Yes, we've only misted back in for this evening's events. A much-needed date night," King Cyrus said, glancing knowingly at his mate-circle. The smirk twisting

Titus's lips told me they had something planned. Something *hot*.

A few weeks ago, I would have sighed dreamily and wished for my own mate-circle to indulge me in such activities.

But now I had a mate-circle of my own.

"Yes, well, I'm sure little Ciro is giving my mother a hard time," Queen Claire said, her cheeks a beautiful shade of pink as she tried to maintain the previous topic of conversation. "But I promised to bring back a few candy canes if he was good."

"I suggest the blue ones," Kalt said without missing a beat. "He'll love them."

I suppressed a grin. *You're evil,* I told him.

Just paying back my cousin for all his tough love, Kalt replied, the amusement in his tone bringing joy to my heart.

Fae, I loved the sound of him *happy*.

His lips brushed my temple as a silver bell rang through the room.

Lark's father stood at the head of the table with the chair pulled out. "I believe this is your new chair, son. Shall we start the feast?"

ARTICA

Lark led me to the table with Norden and Kalt right behind us. His father smiled, gave the chair a pat, and said, "I'll be at the opposite end with the rest of the family."

"Thank you, Father," Lark replied, embracing him in a quick hug before he skipped—yes, *skipped*—to the other end, where his mates were waiting with giant grins.

He seems rather pleased to be handing over this chair, I thought at Lark.

Yes. It's a symbolic gesture that says he's no longer in charge, and I dare say he's thrilled about it, Lark said, his lips curling a little. *I think that's the real reason he wanted me to ascend early.*

Hmm, no, I disagreed, meeting his beautiful green eyes. *He knew you were ready. You're going to be a remarkable king, my lord.*

He smiled, his palm cradling my cheek. *Only because I have you as my queen, my lady.* He leaned in to kiss me, the sensation of his lips on mine shooting sparks through my veins. He caught them all with his tongue, absorbing my influx of power and grounding me for a moment of peace before pulling out a chair for me.

Do you mind sitting between Kalt and Norden for the feast? he asked me.

I almost said no. Because yes, I did sort of mind. I wanted to be next to him.

Actually, no, I wanted to be beneath him.

To feel all that strength as he drove into me.

To unleash power back into him and finally calm the Sources fighting over my soul.

But I couldn't exactly say that in front of all these fae, so I merely nodded. *Sure.*

He frowned. *Would you rather be beside me?*

I'll be fine here, I told him, taking the seat before he could comment again.

He pressed a kiss to my head, avoiding my tiara. *We'll be discussing this later,* he whispered into my mind. *Mating is all about truth, and you're being dishonest with me, Artica.*

He sounded disappointed.

Well, he could join the party. Because I was disappointed, too.

And frustrated.

And totally acting like a brat.

However, twelve days of playing and he hadn't once penetrated me or let me properly taste him.

Oh, he'd gone down on me several times, but I wasn't allowed to return the favor. And now that my mind was somewhat functioning beyond waves of rapturous pleasure, I wanted to know why.

We'll keep you properly entertained, Sunshine, Norden replied as he settled beside me and placed a palm on my thigh.

Very entertained, Kalt agreed as he took the chair between me and the head of the table, placing him by Lark.

Kalt grabbed my opposite leg, giving it a squeeze.

More power rippled through me at the contact, causing both of them to hum in my mind as they absorbed the excess shocks.

This will be fun, Norden decided, his fingers finding the slit in my dress to touch my bare skin.

Very fun, Kalt echoed, his hand doing the same on the other side.

I know what you're doing, I told them.

Just ensuring you're ready for later, Norden said, his fingers brushing my inner thigh now. *Lark is a fan of delayed gratification, Sunshine. But I think he's hit his limit tonight.*

I followed his gaze to where Lark had just taken his seat, and caught the flare of heat in his pupils.

Heat and a hint of displeasure.

Because I hadn't been honest with him? Or because he was upset with something Norden had just said?

As it was my gaze he held, I suspected it was the former.

I swallowed, my neck prickling. *I'm in trouble.*

Yes, you most certainly are, Lark replied.

Elves hurried all of the guests to their seats, the other side of the table seemingly reserved for the Elemental Fae, with King Exos to Lark's right, and then Queen Claire taking the chair across from me. Vox took the seat beside her, with Sol next to him, then Cyrus, and finally Titus.

I found it a strange order as the elves chittered and started filling everyone's plates with various sweets and frosted delights. And true to Lark's word, there were dishes from all the faedoms as well.

A true depiction of Interrealm Fae relations.

"Are those crab berries?" Sol asked, grabbing a fistful and shoving them into his mouth before anyone could answer.

"*Cranberries*," Vox corrected him as he released an exasperated sigh. "And I'm pretty sure those were just for decoration."

Sol grunted and began piling his plate with various confections, meats, and jams, not seeming to care about the foods overlapping one another.

"There's enough food for everyone," Vox assured him, glowering as a gust of wind glided a serving of enchanted gumdrops and meringue puffs to his own plate.

Well, that's certainly one way to serve yourself food, Norden mused, his gaze sparkling with enjoyment at the banter between Sol and Vox. *The one with the pretty, long hair is an Air Fae, right?*

He'd removed his palm from my thigh to add a spoonful of mince Christmas pie to my plate. Kalt followed suit, scooping up a pile of shredded coconut to add to the top of my pie.

Apparently, the two of them were more concerned with making sure I had food than feeding themselves.

Yes, Vox is an Air Fae, I confirmed. *Sol is an Earth Fae.*

That explains his size, Norden murmured. *And his appetite.*

"This is faelicious," Sol said, pointing to some combination of items on his plate.

Vox sighed. "I don't think you're supposed to combine strawberry jam with spaghetti and meatballs, Sol." He grimaced, avoiding the meatball part of the spaghetti as he carefully added some to his own plate *away* from his helping of strawberry jam.

The two Elemental Fae continued to bicker throughout the meal, amusing Norden greatly.

At least until he noticed the elemental battle going on a few seats down.

Titus brought a cupcake to his mouth, only to frown

when it froze solid, making him clack his teeth against it with a wince.

Growling, he flicked his finger, sending a trail of fire to burst over the surface of Cyrus's brownie, which almost immediately melted.

Norden snickered. *We should double-date with this mate-circle. I like them much more than the Midnight Fae.*

After experiencing Zakkai's chilly greeting more than once now, I couldn't help but agree.

Queen Claire and King Exos seemed oblivious to the chaos happening between their mates, probably because it was a standard affair between the six of them.

They were much more taken by whatever discussion they were having with Lark and Kalt, something I'd missed the majority of, as I'd been avoiding Lark's knowing gaze since sitting down.

Yes, you most certainly are, he'd said.

I wondered what that meant.

What kind of trouble did he have planned for me?

I leaned in a little, catching the latter half of whatever they were discussing.

"The realms have come a long way," King Exos said with a note of pride in his tone as he wrapped his arm around his mate's shoulders. "And we've found them to be much more accepting to Interrealm Fae relations than originally expected."

Queen Claire leaned into King Exos as she rested a hand on his chest.

A multicolored ring caught the light on her finger, glittering with the power of all the Elemental Sources together. It served as a perfect depiction of what a powerful mate-circle could accomplish as a unit.

"Times are definitely changing," she said, eyeing Aflora. She sat about midway down the table with her mates around her. "The fae are becoming more accepting of powerful unions. We're not quite there yet, but change and pure acceptance don't happen overnight."

"No, they don't," King Exos agreed. "But that's why we need to normalize this concept of mingling between the faedoms."

Queen Claire and Kalt nodded while Lark continued to listen in silence.

"Yes, something similar to this," Queen Claire said, tapping her jaw. Then her gaze brightened. "Oh! What if we did something like this every year?"

I quite liked the sound of that. "Like a new holiday?" I ventured, inserting myself into their conversation.

"A holiday would work," Queen Claire replied. "But we would need all the realms to celebrate it, which could be hard."

I nodded, agreeing with that. It was difficult enough to get the faedoms to agree on simple things like an academy for children of mixed fae heritages—formally known as abominations among most of the fae.

I couldn't imagine a holiday would be any easier for them to approve. They'd all want it to be something specific to their own culture, which would defeat the whole purpose.

"What if we did something just like this," I said slowly, thinking out loud. "An Interrealm Fae feast event where we all bring our own famous cuisines for the faedoms to try."

"Mmm, shroomloaves for appetizers," King Exos hummed, his lips curling.

"Selkie candy for dessert," Norden added helpfully.

Lark and Kalt shared a look, their gazes contemplative.

"It's not a bad idea, actually," Kalt put in. "The feast, I mean. The selkie candy might prove... interesting."

"This place is perfect for a feast, too," King Exos

added. "The joy keeps all the faedoms under control. I mean, even the Hell Fae are having fun."

He gestured to the Hell Fae King near the opposite end of the table. His prince sat beside him, his sharp, beautiful features reminding me more of an angel than a Hell Fae, but looks could be deceiving.

"I'm surprised those two stuck around," Kalt admitted, tilting his head at the pair. He frowned, his thoughts analyzing the darker possibilities of what the Hell Fae might have really been up to while in the Human Realm.

Off striking deals with an unsuspecting fae, perhaps? I mused. I didn't know much about the Hell Fae, but I knew the king had a penchant for creating one-sided deals that benefited him more than the counterpart.

Kalt glanced at me. *Perhaps,* he agreed. *But I'm sure any fae in this realm would know better than to strike a deal with the Hell Fae. They're bolstered by joy. What else could anyone possibly need?*

Norden's fingers curled around one of my locks, smoothing the end with his magical fingers. *Oh, I have many needs, Prince Kalt.*

I rolled my eyes as Queen Claire thankfully interrupted our private musing. "Oh, but we need a name for it," she said, her brow furrowing. "Interrealm Fae Food Day?"

"Summer Munchies," Norden put in, making several of Queen Claire's mates smirk. They'd all shifted their focus to our conversation now, the notion of a party clearly grabbing their interest.

"No," Lark said suddenly, drawing the cheer at our end of the table to an immediate halt. "The Winter Fae Queen's Summer Festivus Feast." His tone indicated that wasn't a suggestion so much as an official name. One he had decided on and wouldn't debate. "I'll announce it to the guests, but Artica has to plan it all," he added, his mint-green gaze landing on me.

"Me?" I squeaked, startled not only by the name he'd decided on but by his pronouncement as well.

"Isn't it your dream to manage Interrealm Fae relations?" he asked, arching a brow.

I frowned. *Are you taking advantage of this new bond by searching my mind for my hopes and dreams?*

He met my gaze. *Would you be mad if I said yes?*

I considered him for a moment, my frown drifting upward into a grin. *No, I wouldn't,* I admitted. *But I thought I was in trouble...*

Oh, you are. But we'll handle that privately later. His mouth curled into a smile that promised wicked deeds more than hard punishments.

My thighs clenched in response.

"Consider it done," he announced before picking up his flute to take a sip of the bubbly liquid. Several others followed suit, setting their glasses down in time with his.

"Every year on July twenty-fifth?" Norden suggested. "To celebrate your birthday?"

"So long as the attention remains focused on our queen, I don't care what day it is," my Winter Fae King mate replied. "Her happiness matters most."

"Hear, hear," King Cyrus echoed. "And that's how it's done."

Queen Claire rolled her eyes. "Hush, you."

"Never," he murmured, blowing her an ice kiss that Titus caught in a flame, melting it onto the table.

Queen Claire sighed, shaking her head.

I ignored their antics, my focus falling to the Winter Fae King once more. "It would be my honor to throw you an annual birthday party, my king."

"That is not what I said nor what I called it," he replied, his brow furrowing.

"No, you said my happiness matters most. And that would make me very happy indeed."

He thought about it for a moment, then his lips curled into a genuine smile. "Your happiness is my only desire, so let it be done." *But you're still in trouble*, he added.

I'd been a bit concerned about what that meant before.

Now... now I was intrigued by it. *I accept whatever punishment you wish to give me, my king.*

His lips curled, then he addressed the table, his voice rising as he announced, "As of this moment, the Winter Fae Queen's Summer Festivus Feast will take place annually on July twenty-fifth to bring joy to the realms."

The entire room cheered as a healthy dose of joyous magic fell over the kingdom.

Magic is tied to holidays, Lark whispered into my mind. *You'll bring much joy to our people through this momentous event. They'll love you forever for it.*

My belly flipped at the adoration in his tone. *I thought you were mad at me.*

Disappointed, Artica. Never mad, he corrected. *Now finish your food. I have a surprise for you later.*

Norden squeezed my thigh, his lips ghosting over my cheek. *You're radiant, Sunshine. Positively radiant.*

You're trying to distract me, I accused, my lips curling even as my mind worried over Lark's comments. But Norden's touch was... *Mmm.*

Is it working? His fingers found that slit again, gliding up along my inner leg to the pink lace between my thighs. *Eat your food, sweet Artica. While Kalt and I play for dessert.*

Kalt's hand landed on my opposite thigh as he continued some new political discussions with King Exos and Lark. His expression gave nothing away, but the mate-bond throbbed with knowledge.

Even Lark knew what these two were up to, and the approval practically radiated from him.

I shivered, my hand tightening around the fork as I attempted to focus on my plate.

This was definitely a faetastic distraction.

One I tried not to let anyone see as I chewed and swallowed my food.

But I didn't taste any of it.

My focus was on the two hands beneath my dress. They were taking turns teasing me through the lace.

Then one of them boldly slipped beneath the fabric to stroke my sensitive flesh. I jolted, then cleared my throat as I fought the need to moan.

I shoveled in another bite of something sweet. A custard pie, maybe? It should have thoroughly seduced my taste buds, but the raging fire between my legs was all I could feel or think about.

Another finger slid beneath the fabric, stroking my entrance before penetrating me deep. *Norden*, I breathed, familiar with his touch.

Swallow, Sunshine, before you choke, he whispered back at me.

I complied, then startled as he brought a fork to my lips with his free hand, his other working me skillfully beneath the table while Kalt circled my clit.

You can moan while swallowing this. I'll just tell everyone it's your favorite dessert.

I didn't understand at first, but as the prongs touched my tongue, he curled his finger in a way that instantly pushed me into oblivion.

The fork stopped me from crying out, but it didn't quiet my moan of ecstasy.

Which made Norden chuckle as he used his line out loud about it being my favorite.

A salted caramel cookie covered in cream, I realized, finally tasting it on my tongue as he fed me another bite.

It was so intensely erotic that I nearly came again, but the bolt of power thundering through my veins held me at bay.

Another orgasm would probably make me really explode.

And I truly didn't want to risk whatever magic would happen then.

With my luck, it'd be a hoard of snowballs glittering with strands of confetti or something.

Kalt's touch left my core, his serious conversation continuing even as he reached over to stroke his finger through the cream of my dessert—the same finger that he'd just used to touch me—and brought it to his lips for a taste.

My cheeks were on fire.

Made only worse by Norden doing the exact same thing. "Delicious," he hummed, winking at me.

You all are going to kill me with pleasure, I thought, my legs still quivering from the aftershocks of my pleasure.

Don't worry, Sunshine, Norden whispered back to me. *We'll just revive you with another orgasm.*

Lark cleared his throat, standing once more to address the table. "I want to thank you all for attending our first Mate-Circle Celebration Feast. I hope you've enjoyed the Interrealm Fae cuisine and will join us at next year's first annual Winter Fae Queen's Summer Festivus Feast."

Another round of cheers broke through the air, the joy infectious.

Ideas were already blowing through my mind, reminding me of a blizzard of holiday delight.

"For those interested," Lark continued, "we will be finishing the evening with some hot chocolate in the palace lounge. Otherwise, you are welcome to roam at your leisure. Your accommodations will be complimentary through the end of the week."

He gave a little bow.

More applause followed.

Then he stepped away from his chair, coming directly to me, and held out his hand. "My queen. If you'll join me for the first cup, I've already prepared a mug specifically for you."

ARTICA

All right. Maybe my mother was right. Because this certainly did feel like a fairy tale, after all.

And the decorated mug of hot chocolate waiting for me was positively divine.

Lark had pulled me into a chair with him, the lounger large enough for two more to join us. But Kalt and Norden stood beside us instead with their own cups in their hands.

All of us had Lark's special brew, but he'd prepared each mug with a unique twist—something he admitted now was the real reason he'd left earlier. There hadn't been a Shifter Fae emergency after all. Just Lark wanting to surprise his mates with hot chocolate for after-dinner drinks.

My mug had a dash of peppermint, something Lark suspected I would like.

He was right.

Kalt's drink was spiced with coconut—which he absolutely loved.

And Norden's cup had a touch of salted caramel,

something that seemed to make his eyes roll into the back of his head.

"Thank you," I whispered to Lark, aware now that this was a true gift from his heart. A treat only a Winter Fae King could bestow upon his mates.

"You're welcome," he murmured back to me, his lips going to my ear. "But this isn't the surprise I mentioned, just a bonus."

I shivered, my toes curling at the roughness in his voice.

Several of the fae around us were lost to their own conversations, the tone calming for the evening. Everyone was full, not just of food, but of life, the magic in the air an aphrodisiac that intensified the senses and spread mirth throughout the realm.

My eyes began to drift closed on a sigh as a familiar head of blonde hair caught my attention. I sat up straighter, my lips pulling into a wide smile. "Juniper!" I called, setting my mug down to stand.

She spun around, her sea green eyes widening as she responded with a grin of her own.

I opened my arms as she embraced me in a big hug, her relief palpable and making me frown. "Is everything all right?" I asked, pulling back to look at her.

"I've just been so worried," she said in a rush. "I... I saw..." She glanced around, and I realized she needed a private moment.

I'll be right back, I told Lark, guiding Juniper toward the corner of the room where we could discuss whatever this was softly and somewhat away from the others.

"What is it?" I asked, concerned. "And when did you get here?" She hadn't been here when we'd done our rounds earlier. Actually, none of the Fortune Fae had been.

"I just came back via the portals," she explained. "I had to convince Alpha Oberon to let me come back. He actually said no, but Professor Kamden agreed to escort me." Her cheeks reddened with the name, but she shook her head. "That's not important. I just… I saw you fall, Artica. And… and I owe you an apology."

I frowned. "Saw me fall?"

"Well, pass out, I guess. Against King Lark. After the coronation."

Understanding finally dawned. "Oh, that…"

"Yeah, because of my disbelief, right?" she pressed. "I… I was just so shocked by your new role that I… I don't know. I was worried, Artica. I was worried about what might happen. You barely knew your mates and…" She trailed off, sighing. "I should never have touched the present. I'm so sorry. I didn't realize what it would do. But I shouldn't have spread my disbelief. It just… it just happened. Will you ever forgive me?"

I blinked at her. "You… you think I fainted because of your disbelief?"

"Didn't you?" she asked.

I smiled and shook my head. "No, I fainted from the combining Sources inside me." I'd sensed her disbelief a little when she'd touched the gift, but I'd been so far gone to the magic at that point that her little bit of shock couldn't add more harm to anything. "It's okay, Juniper. I've had my own moments of shock, too."

"You're sure?" she pressed. "I've been so worried!"

"Thank you, but I'm okay. I promise." I hugged her again, meeting Lark's gaze over her shoulder.

Norden had taken my place in the chair, his head resting on Lark's shoulder while the Winter Fae King played with a lock of his hair. Norden must have allowed him the touch after enjoying Lark's hot chocolate gift.

I sighed. Our mate-circle had grown so much in such a short time, and in part because of the challenges we'd been through and the difficulties we'd been forced to overcome.

Kalt joined them in the chair, his icy irises lifting to mine as he winked, the gesture going straight to my heart.

"I'm not mad," I promised Juniper, giving her another squeeze.

Yet somehow my words felt more directed at Kalt. Because I found I'd wholly forgiven him for denying his bonds. Denying *us*. My heart was his fully and completely, and I could feel the echo of that in our mating link.

Juniper sagged in my arms, deflated with relief. "Oh, thank Fae. I've been… a mess. It's why Professor Kamden brought me. He… he knows that I've been distracted."

I pulled away to study her face. "Uh-huh. And who is this Professor Kamden you keep talking about?"

This time her blush went all the way to her neck. "He's… well, he's a professor, so I've really only met him in passing. I know he's not interested in me; I mean, I'm just an intern. But he's…" She sighed. "He's dreamy, Artica."

"I know that feeling well," I told her, glancing at my mate-circle again. She followed my gaze with a giggle. "I'm an intern, too." I frowned. "Or was, I guess." I was a queen now. Which I supposed meant I didn't need my intern credit.

Well, at least all my courses were already done.

But the internship was supposed to be my final "course" at the Academy.

Maybe Kalt will give me a passing grade.

I'll consider it, he replied, a twinkle in his gaze.

"Well, we'll see what happens," Juniper sighed, taking a step back.

I smiled and reached out to give her arm a reassuring squeeze. "Follow your heart, Juniper. It'll never let you down."

She returned the smile, then a strange flutter of magic rippled under my touch as her skin ran cold against my hand. "Juniper?" I breathed, sensing the magic seeping out of her. "Juniper!"

She began to convulse, her bright eyes rolling into the back of her head. I held her upright with both hands, ensuring she didn't fall while my heart beat a mile a minute in my chest. "Juniper," I repeated, her name a whisper as I tried to pull her back from whatever was happening to her.

She froze.

Blinked.

Then stared at me.

Through silver irises.

My lips parted as Lark reached my side, followed by Norden and Kalt. They'd sensed my panic in the bond and were immediately by my side.

Or maybe they'd seen Juniper convulsing.

A few other fae looked our way, concern etching into their brows at the eruption of power.

But it was brief and already complete.

Except I could no longer sense the water magic in Juniper.

And her eyes *glittered.*

A snap radiated from her soul, one that jolted me to my core as I sensed the Water Source releasing her, accepting my blessing that she discover her own fate.

My belief in her heart, I realized, shock rendering me speechless. I'd told her to follow her heart. And... and she'd done exactly that.

Because she'd just transitioned into a *Fortune Fae,* the only race among our kind that could see into the future and interpret it with prophecy.

She shook again, power radiating through her—power

that touched my own and hummed along our skin to Juniper's lips.

"And so all the realms will herald the Queen of Festivus Cheer, her love a beacon to light the path to reunite the fae long lost to their fears

They will be inspired

They will learn to believe

Only one heart remains as cold as stone

A fissure that only a Halfling must remedy

Or all the realms will suffer his wrath and Festivus will be no more."

The room had fallen silent from the display of power, their focus on Juniper's eyes as they frosted over with the silver magic of the uttered prophecy.

Then she slid onto the floor, drifting into a deep sleep.

A muscular male with broad shoulders joined us, dropping to his knees as he pulled her protectively into his chest. His silver-sliced irises and fangs gave him away as a Fortune Fae Alpha.

He glanced up at me from his kneeling position, his long black hair hiding part of his face. "Queen Artica," he greeted, his voice gravelly.

"Professor Kamden?" I guessed, my voice hoarse.

He nodded.

"Is she all right?" Lark asked, concern radiating in his tone.

"She'll be okay," Professor Kamden said, slowly standing while cradling Juniper in his arms. "The transition… was sudden."

Juniper's arm fell, hanging limply at her side.

I lifted it without thinking, setting it on her abdomen.

Which was when I noticed the snowflake imprint on her hand.

My lips parted and the professor's silvery eyes snapped up to mine. "Did you say anything to prompt this?"

"I… I told her to follow her heart," I whispered.

He nodded again, the action clipped. "A blessing of belief."

"One that could only have helped push someone to follow a dream that already existed," Lark added.

"Yes, I know," Professor Kamden replied. "I'll take her from here." He uttered it in a way that said he would not be accepting alternatives.

Not that I had one to offer.

And he started toward the exit without another word.

I followed him with my eyes, gaping at his hulking back.

My influence had certainly assisted this unexpected transition, but I sensed in my heart that Juniper was on the right path.

What concerned me more were her words.

A fissure that only a Halfling must remedy

Or all the realms will suffer his wrath and Festivus will be no more.

What did that mean?

My gaze went to Queen Claire across the room, the only Halfling I really knew. Was she the one Juniper meant? Did Queen Claire have another role to play in the fate of the realms?

Or was there another Halfling we had yet to meet?

And whose cold heart put Festivus at risk?

"Well, a festive blessing," Lark said to the room. "Our queen's first gift to the realms. I cannot think of a better way to end our evening." He wrapped his arm around my shoulders, his smile firmly in place. "I believe it's time for us to depart. Merry thanks to you all, and to all, a festive good night."

LARK

Well, that certainly was an unexpected twist to the evening. But I knew just what Artica needed to help take her mind off the incident.

She'd done nothing wrong other than express belief in a friend.

Something she would understand just as soon as she saw my surprise for her.

Norden, several items arrived back at the suite while we were enjoying the feast. Could you take Kalt with you to unpack them? He'll know what to do, I said.

I wasn't sure how to engage them both in a mental discussion without involving Artica, and I really didn't want to spoil the surprise for her. So I hoped Norden would convey my request to Kalt.

Are you taking her somewhere?

I am.

Where?

I glanced at him as we walked, the four of us near the entrance to my wing now. *To my heart.*

His lips curled. *Talk about a perfect evening.*

Which meant he knew exactly why I intended to take her there.

"We'll meet you both back at the room," Norden said out loud, clapping Kalt on the back. "I promised Frosty here a bath."

Kalt glanced at him, arching a brow. "Are you going to comb my hair afterward?"

"I absolutely am," Norden told him.

The Water Fae grinned. "Then lead the way, selkie."

Artica frowned as they left, her pretty eyes landing on me. "Do you want to talk about the prophecy?"

My lips curled down to match her own. "The prophecy?" I snorted. "No. I really don't."

I'd heard every word Juniper had said.

But I wasn't worried.

If a coldhearted soul wanted to take Festivus from the realms, he'd have to face me and my mate-circle. And I didn't doubt our ability for one second.

We were about to become the strongest mate-circle in the history of the Winter Fae.

Anyone who wanted to test that was tempting fate.

"Not all prophecies are realized," I told her. "Some are just warnings. And I think this one may have been inspired by our mate-circle being not quite complete." I held out my hand for her. "So let's go fix that."

I'd sensed her displeasure with me during dinner, and I knew what had caused it.

But the most important aspect of a relationship was truth.

And she hadn't given me that tonight.

Something I intended to rectify.

She pressed her palm to mine, sending an electric jolt up my arm. The power inside her craved an outlet. I ran my thumb along her skin, absorbing as much of the energy from her as I could through that simple touch.

"You really think prophecies can just be warnings of potential futures?" she asked as we started walking toward the nearest palace exit.

"Prophecies are potential paths in life that will happen under the right set of circumstances," I told her, pausing by the door to grab the coat I had made for her this afternoon. It was white with faux fur along the edges and had a hood to protect her hair. The thin fabric also flowed all the way to the ground to ensure every part of her remained warm.

She slid it on, the silky texture covering her arms in a sheen of magic meant to keep her insulated. A sigh escaped her lips, her cheeks immediately flushing with the enchantment. "Wow," she breathed. "What is this?"

"A coat made for a queen," I answered honestly, brushing my lips over hers. "Don't let the prophecy concern you, sweetheart. It's a potential course, one I am confident we will counter."

"But she said only a Halfling can save us," she whispered as I pulled her out through the door to the sleigh waiting in the snow.

"Our mate-circle will save us from any and all threats," I promised her. "However, you want to know what I really think?" I asked, facing her.

"Yes."

"I think the prophecy wasn't meant for us at all. I think it was meant for the Halfling or the coldhearted one to hear." One or both of whom might have been in the room tonight. "I don't think it has anything to do with us or our mate-circle. And you know why else I think that?"

"Why?" The word came out as a puff of air.

I palmed her cheek, capturing her gaze. "Because I

believe in our mate-circle, Artica. I believe we can handle any and all threats to our kingdom. And I believe we are on our way to enjoying one of the happiest ever afters in existence." I pressed my lips to hers. "Now join me in the sleigh. It's time for your surprise."

She glanced at the sleigh and then back up at me. "How will it move?"

"You'll see," I promised her, helping her into the seat meant for my queen. Then I settled behind her, bracketing her with my legs, and pulled her back into my chest. With my arms wrapped tightly around her middle, I whispered a magic incantation that brought the sleigh to life.

And we shot across the snow.

She squealed in delight, the sound a beautiful kiss to my ears as we sped through the snowy palace grounds and out into the glacier beyond.

Enjoy, Norden whispered to me, his tone holding an edge of amusement that told me he was about to enjoy Kalt before they started unpacking the boxes.

Artica would be able to feel their warmth as well, which explained her shiver of longing. I kissed her pulse, the wind whipping too fast and aggressively by our ears for me to speak. So instead, I chose to whisper into her mind.

I know you're upset with me, my queen, I told her. *But I wanted everything to be perfect and right.*

She didn't reply right away, her mind processing my words. *Perfect how?*

Maybe that hadn't been the right word choice. *I meant the situation,* I tried to explain, my grip tightening as we went down a steep hill at immense speeds.

Her palms went to my thighs, squeezing my legs as though they were handles. But magic kept us in the sleigh.

My magic.

I need you to know just how much you mean to me, I

continued. *Most couples require time and courting to understand their hearts. Yet I've never been that way. I knew you were my destiny the moment I laid eyes on you. Just like Norden and Kalt. And now I'm going to show you how I knew. But first, I want you to close your eyes.*

It wasn't lost on me that I'd just said I want to show her something, followed by a statement requesting she close her eyes.

But she would understand in a moment.

Try to relax, I added in a whisper, noting her stiffness. *I won't let anything happen to you.*

A hum of trust encircled us as she allowed my words to calm her, and I sensed her closing her eyes in kind.

Just in time for our sleigh to slip through the veil of the glacier before us.

To anyone else, it would be a solid sheet of ice.

But not to the King and Queen of the Winter Fae Realm.

Or the heir, for that matter, as I'd been here countless times before.

However, it was my first time bringing a guest. Norden had tried to enter with me once but couldn't. Perhaps he would be able to now that our mate-circle was complete.

The sleigh started to slow as the interior of the ice cave glimmered to life. It reminded me of being inside a diamond, the natural interior light illuminating every crevice and edge. Even in the heart of winter, this place glistened like an icy sun.

Where are we? Artica breathed, her mind filling with wonder at the enchantments unfolding around us.

Five more seconds, I told her, the sleigh gradually coming to a standstill in the heart of the ice cave. "Don't open your eyes yet," I said against her ear. "I'll help you up."

I carefully exited the sleigh first, then reached down to

pull her into my arms and gently set her on a sheet of ice with my hands on her hips. Turning her slowly, I placed my chest at her back once more.

"Okay. You can open your eyes now, my queen."

Her intake of air told me she'd complied, her heart beating so fast I could almost hear it. But I more just sensed it through our bond and the magic of this place. "Where are we?"

"The center of Winter Fae magic," I told her. "This is where the source materials for the belief crystals come from; meaning this is the power that drives the whole creation process. It's the literal heart of our world."

"Oh Fae," she whispered, her adoration tangible. "I can feel the magic on my skin, taste it on my tongue."

"Because it's responding to you as its queen. Which is what I wanted you to see, to understand why I've known from the very beginning that you and I were destined to find each other." I turned her to face me, my gaze dropping to the snowflake pendant at her neck. "That crystal comes from here, Artica. It glows brightly when you're near a compatible mate. Kalt may have enchanted it, but the material is all Winter Fae magic."

"It's a wishing stone," she told me. "That's what he told me, anyway."

"Yes, it's fueled by belief. If you wish for it and believe in it enough, it'll happen. But it's also a pendant that expresses compatibility."

"Yes, Norden mentioned that," she replied. "So you're saying that's how you knew? Because of the pendant?"

I shook my head. "No. I'm telling you that the pendant is made from the magic in this cave, the same magic that lives inside me and has always lived inside me. It's the same magic that lives inside you now, too."

"You're like the pendant," she translated in a low voice.

"Yes. A much more powerful version of it." I cupped her cheek. "My heart sang the moment I saw you. And while I handled myself poorly, it was more a result of frustration that you didn't immediately feel it, too. But I was born to believe in fate. It's who I am. And not everyone is gifted with that same understanding of life."

Her eyes glistened. "I can feel it now. I can feel that you're meant for me. That our mate-circle is exactly what it should be."

"No," I said, smiling. "It's not exactly what it should be. But it's about to be." I kissed her, holding her to me, allowing her to feel the passion and warmth in my heart as I embraced her in the place most dear to my kind.

Magic hummed around us, the cave coming to life in response to the sensations growing between us.

I've waited to touch you, Artica, because I wanted this moment. I wanted you to trust me and know me so completely that there wouldn't be a single doubt in your mind that I was taking you for all the right reasons.

I pulled her toward a bed of faux furs that I'd set here earlier this week for this very purpose, aware of exactly what I intended to do tonight after the feast.

She shivered, her blue eyes filled with tears as she looked up at me. "I thought I did something wrong," she whispered.

"You could never do anything wrong, my queen," I promised her. "Other than not tell me how you truly feel." I pushed the coat from her arms and shoulders, adding it to the pile of fur.

The magic in the cave continued to hum, keeping her warm as I stared down into her eyes.

"If I do something that upsets you, I want you to tell me," I said. "Trust me to fix it. Trust me to understand. Trust me enough to voice your discomfort. And I will do whatever I can to ensure I never make you feel that way again."

"Okay," she whispered, her gaze holding mine.

"Now tell me what you want, Artica." I already knew, but the point was for her to tell me. To trust me, just as I'd requested.

Her lips curled, the tears in her gaze sliding onto her cheeks to form little ice crystals. "I want you to make love to me, my king."

"It would be my absolute pleasure, my queen," I said, kissing the frozen tears away from her skin as I reached around to unzip her dress.

The one from the coronation had been a corset— something that we'd had to cut off her.

I much preferred the zipper on this gown.

It went all the way to her ass, making it easy to push the fabric from her shoulders and let it pool against the ground below. She stepped out of it, completely confident in her nudity, her pert breasts beckoning my mouth. But I knelt instead, wanting to remove the heels from her dainty feet.

She used my shoulders for balance, her touch an electric warmth I could feel through my tuxedo, all the way to my soul.

I leaned forward to kiss the pink lace between her thighs, aware that Norden had requested this color against her creamy skin.

She wore nothing else.

Just the thong.

And so I licked her sweet heat through the material, loving the flavor of the orgasm she'd received during dinner. It made me so hungry for her, my cock already hard and aching behind my zipper.

Her fingers threaded through my hair, holding my mouth to her as I nibbled her swollen clit through the lace.

"Lark," she breathed, her hips moving.

I knew if I kept this up, she would come from the magic and my mouth alone.

But I wanted her naked beneath me, her slick channel hugging my shaft, and her body convulsing against mine as she came.

She released a low whine as I stood again.

However, she quickly quieted as she realized I was stripping.

First my jacket.

Then the vest beneath.

Then the dress shirt.

Followed by the shoes, socks, and pants, until all I wore was my skin.

Because I didn't do any undergarments. Just like Norden and Kalt hadn't worn any, either.

Her gaze fell to my groin, her tongue sneaking out to lick her lips appreciatively.

Then she fell to her knees and took me into her mouth.

I cursed, not expecting that reaction at all, but *frost*, her mouth felt fucking divine against my skin. "Artica," I groaned, my fingers weaving through her hair.

She still had on her tiara—something I'd forgotten to remove.

I took it from her, carefully dropping it into the furs at the side, then grasped her hair properly with my fist.

She swallowed me deep, her tongue working over my shaft in a manner that suggested she'd watched Norden and Kalt over the last week and had memorized their movements.

"Did that upset you, too?" I asked on a pant. "That I

wouldn't let you—*Fae*." She took me all the way to the back of her throat, sucking me down like a woman starved.

I've wanted to taste you all week, she moaned inside my mind. *You kept saying no.*

Because I didn't trust myself not to fuck you, I admitted. *I wanted to wait... until here... until now... but sleigh bells, Artica, I'm going to come if you keep doing that.*

Oh, but I wanted to be inside.

To *feel* her.

To fucking mate her the way I was meant to all along.

I yanked her off me—an act that required severe strength and sheer force of will—and immediately pushed her down into the furs. I fell to my knees between her legs, one palm going to the ground beside her while the opposite cupped her between her thighs.

"Soaking wet," I marveled. I slid two fingers inside her, pumping deep and loving the way she arched into my palm. "You're made for me, for this, for *us*."

She whimpered, her thighs falling to the sides as she attempted to beckon me forward with her luscious offering.

I leaned down to lick her clit again, loving her sweet flavor on my tongue. Then I kissed a path up her body to her throat and slowly removed my hand from between her thighs, replacing it with my groin.

She immediately wrapped her legs around me, the blatant invitation a damp kiss to the head of my cock as I positioned myself at her entrance.

"Please, Lark," she begged. "I need you inside me. I need you—"

I slammed home, drawing a scream from her throat that echoed off the ice chamber. Power poured out of her, the intimate connection awakening both Sources and driving them to battle once more.

But our souls together were enough to tame them.

Something we proved as our bodies began to mate in a furious display of passion and grace.

I kissed her, my tongue engaging hers at a much slower pace than the one happening between our legs.

I made love to her in my own way, devouring her mouth, stealing her very breath, while forcing her to scream again as I drove deep inside her.

Bigger than the others, she panted, the fragment of a sentence ending on a groan of delight.

I'm the king, I told her, aware of my size and certain that she could take it.

But this had been the other reason I hadn't taken her all week.

I'd wanted her warmed up and primed for my cock.

And she was absolutely ready now.

Her ankles hooked together at my lower back as I took her hard against the furs, her nails biting into my shoulders as she cried out for more.

Energy continued to ripple around us, the two Sources engaging in a manner they weren't accustomed to.

It could so easily spiral out of control.

However, our mate-circle *believed*.

And that belief tamed the Sources, forcing them to behave.

Artica's mouth fastened to mine, her tight sheath squeezing as her body began to convulse. The rapturous waves were unfolding around us both, threatening to drown us in fiery power.

But I held the Winter Source close, sucking the energy from Artica via our bond as our bodies moved as one.

"Come for me, sweetling," I whispered, the endearment falling off my tongue. "I want to feel you come against me. I want you to drench me in your pleasure. And I want to hear you scream my name."

She gave me my wish, her body exploding on a climax so powerful that it shook the cave with her expulsion of energy.

I took it all, filtering each biting lash to my spirit back into the Source.

Her orgasm continued on a wave, stretching on and on as the power rippled out of her, her soul giving me everything I could take until I succumbed to the sensations and followed her over the edge.

It fucking hurt.

But I'd never felt anything so beautiful, so blissful, so *addictive*, in my entire existence.

She milked more from my shaft than I ever thought possible, filling her entirely and allowing me to claim her from the inside out. As the quakes subsided, I went down, licking my pleasure from her sex and drawing another convulsive wave from her that made her scream my name again.

Then she pushed me to my back and returned the favor, her mouth sucking me clean as she forced more pleasure from my veins, her throat working as she swallowed each drop.

It was a hedonistic wet dream, observed only by the crystal magic around us.

Until finally our hearts began to calm, our bodies replete for the moment, the power exchange more than complete.

I pulled her up to lie on my chest, my arm wrapped around her shoulder. "I have another gift for you," I whispered against her forehead. *Technically two*, I thought, but I didn't want to spoil it.

Her sleepy eyes glanced up at me. "You do?"

I nodded, pulling the small box from the fur—one I'd

hidden earlier today before making hot chocolate for my mates.

She smiled at the red paper. "This reminds me of the gift Kalt gave me." Her fingertips grazed her necklace.

"Because it's the same paper," I replied, handing her the present. "Open it."

Her pretty eyes twinkled with unveiled delight as her fingers worked through the paper to the jewelry box beneath. A childlike glimmer overtook her features as she pulled off the top, then her lips parted at the dazzling ring inside.

"A crystal diamond to match your necklace," I told her, smiling at the utter joy glowing from her mind. "May I?"

Tears started gathering in her eyes as she nodded eagerly, her thoughts telling me she was speechless.

"It's customary in the Human Realm for mates to wear rings on their wedding finger," I explained, taking her left hand and finding the appropriate digit. "So I had this made for you, and three bands for me, Norden, and Kalt." Bands that they'd already found waiting for them in the suite with a note from me asking them to wear it. "It only seems fitting since we're in this realm." I found the second box holding my ring to show her the crystals etched into the metallic siding.

Power hummed through me as I put it on, the energy telling me that Norden and Kalt had also donned theirs.

Our mate-circle was officially complete.

"I love it," Artica finally managed to say, more of those happy tears falling from her gaze. "I... I love you all." The hesitation was minimal, her mind holding her back only because of time and the way life had always been explained to her.

But she chose to see us all through her soul.

Through her connection to the Winter Source.

By *believing* in our shared destiny.

Which was the best gift she could ever have given me, one I thanked her for with my tongue.

Before taking her again, this time slower, against the bed of furs.

And making love to her with my mind, body, and soul.

My Artica.

The heart of our mate-circle.

Our beautiful Winter Fae Queen.

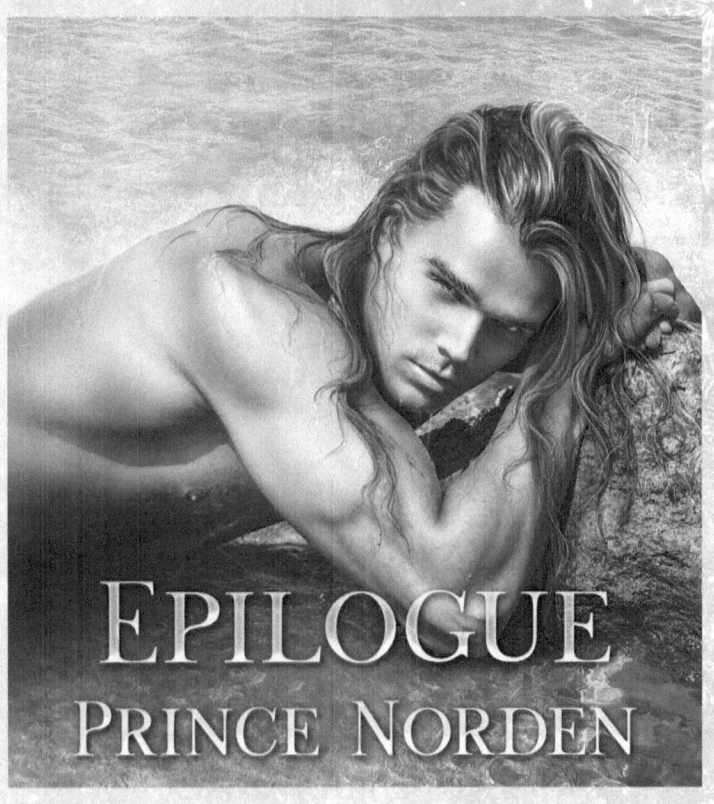

EPILOGUE
PRINCE NORDEN

"They're almost here," I told Kalt, my gaze scanning the suite for anything out of place. "You're sure about the mistletoe?"

"Oh, yeah," Kalt said. "I'm sure."

He grabbed the back of my neck, pulling me into a kiss beneath it just as the door opened beside us.

Artica giggled.

Then she gasped as Kalt pulled her to him, also beneath the mistletoe, and kissed her hard on the mouth. "*That* is how I should have kissed you in your dorm room," he said after leaving her dazed against him.

"Oh," she breathed. "Oh, yes. Yes, please."

Lark chuckled behind her, his shoulder braced against the door frame as he took in our decorating job. "Nice," he said, nodding. "I approve."

"Approve of…?" Artica trailed off, her eyes finally *seeing* the room. Her lips parted, her mind unraveling in a series of excitedly shocked statements.

At some point, Lark had arranged for all her decorations to be shipped here.

With the addition of six or seven more boxes.

Or that was what Kalt had estimated, anyway, because her tiny dorm room certainly couldn't contain this much Festivus cheer.

There were ornaments and horns and water shells and elemental flowers I'd never heard of and wreaths and a live evergreen tree planted in the center of the room. Apparently, it'd been in Artica's dorm room.

So Kalt had called in a quick favor to Sol, who'd promptly replanted it for us in the center of the suite and made it about six times bigger.

Fortunately, the two-story ceilings allowed for that.

Four presents sat beneath the tree as well—which were my and Kalt's additions to the surprise.

We had two for Lark.

And two for Artica.

Kalt's were heartfelt.

Mine were useful.

"Oh… my… Fae," Artica finally said, spinning in a circle of glittery white, her dress miraculously as pristine as it had been at dinner.

Did you not fuck her in it? I asked Lark, somewhat disappointed.

No, I removed it first.

Hmm. I'd have to rectify that, then. Because those slits on the skirt existed for a reason. I'd tried to demonstrate during dinner. Alas, my hint clearly hadn't registered with the king.

But at least he'd finally made love to her.

Something that was evidenced by the glow in her features and the glitter in her blonde hair.

"This is so beautiful," she said, laughing as she continued to twirl.

I caught sight of the ring on her finger, my lips curling in approval. It was a crystal diamond that matched her necklace and the bands Lark had left for us.

Something I still needed to thank him for.

Wandering over to where he lounged in the door, I threaded my fingers through his silky, silvery white hair and kissed him hard on the mouth.

He grinned, his palm circling my nape as he pulled me flush against him.

I missed you, too, he thought at me. *And to think, I left you and Kalt up here naked for so long.*

My lips curled. *You like that, do you?* I'd convinced Kalt to join me in naked decorating, just like he'd convinced me to put the mistletoe by the door.

It was a relationship built on trust and mutual respect, whereby I would pretty much do anything he asked so long as he let me stare at his naked ass all day.

Same rule applied to Artica.

And Lark, too.

"What's in the boxes?" Lark asked.

"Oh, you noticed some presents, did you?" I pretended to be shocked. "And here I thought you didn't like those."

He grinned at me. "Tease."

"Always," I promised, pulling him into the suite by the lapels of his jacket. "Artica gets to open hers first."

She was still twirling around and enjoying the ambience of the room, causing snowflakes to fall all around her. She giggled, radiating pure delight and joy and *sunshine*.

I waltzed up to her, whirling her into my arms for a dance that left her laughing.

Kalt watched with a matching smile as Lark began disrobing.

Naked time? I asked.

Always, he returned, the twinkle in his gaze telling me he'd purposely echoed the word back at me.

I spun Artica into a dip right beside the tree. "You have presents to open. It's our Matemas Celebration." A term I'd absolutely just made up and would now be using annually exactly twelve days after Lark's birthday.

Oh, what fun.

A Winter Queen Fae Feast for Lark's birthday, followed by twelve days of mating, and ending with a festive Matemas.

The perfect existence.

I was destined to be one very happy selkie.

I kissed my queen before standing her upright again. Then Kalt appeared with his gift.

"But I didn't get you anything," she said, a note of sadness in her voice.

"We'll accept blow jobs," I informed her helpfully. "Or fucking in the jacuzzi. Or breakfast orgasms. Or all of the above."

Lark joined us in a pair of flannel pants, the sneaky king having swapped his tux for pajamas.

Cheater, I told him.

Giving you something to take off with your teeth later, he returned.

My mood instantly brightened.

And Artica's eyebrows hit her hairline. "My graduation certificate?" she asked, sounding shocked. "How…?"

"I might have called in a few favors last week during one of your napping sessions," he replied. "Cyrus brought it with them tonight when he misted in his mate-circle."

Artica's gaze filled with tears as she threw her arms around his neck. "Thank you!"

He hugged her back, his lips brushing her temple. "You're welcome, little flurry."

"Well, I suppose you can go next," I decided, handing Lark the gift I'd found for him.

His gaze narrowed.

I merely smiled.

He carefully opened the box like he thought it might attack him. Then he grinned at the brush inside.

It wasn't for his hair.

But for mine.

Something he knew the moment he saw it. *Thank you*, he whispered.

You're welcome. It was a gift that meant he could brush my hair whenever he wanted, which might be strange to most, but it was basically a proposal from a selkie.

Artica kissed Kalt before releasing him, her eyes still glistening with happiness. "I have the best mates in the world."

"It's true," I agreed. "But you still have one more present to open."

I bent to retrieve her box, eager for her to open it.

And use it.

She unfastened the box, her brow furrowing at the jar inside. Then she read the label—one I had requested just for her—and her eyebrows hit her hairline.

"Salted Caramel Chocolate Body Cream," she said, reading the official title. "A BDSM creation for your mating pleasure."

"Edible paint," I said, waggling my brows. "For the morning orgasms, perhaps?"

She laughed. "What am I going to do with you?"

"Paint that paste all over my cock and swallow?" I suggested. "Gives a whole new meaning to 'candy center,' doesn't it?"

She bent over laughing while Kalt retrieved his final gift from beneath the tree and handed it to Lark.

A moment passed between them, then Lark opened the envelope and read the contents inside.

I already knew what it was, having heard the news from Kalt himself.

"Is this a job application?" Lark asked, frowning at it.

"Yep," Kalt said. "I've officially resigned as the Elemental Fae Emissary. So I need a new job. I'll do pretty much anything you want. If you'll have me, I mean."

Lark grinned. "Maybe you can oversee the distribution of Winter Fae magic throughout the Human Realm? You know, to help with adding protective veils to fae activities."

"Yeah?" Kalt's eyes sparkled, the topic one I'd overheard them discussing a few times.

"Among other things," Lark said, shrugging. But I could feel his excitement in the air, the warmth of it a kiss to my spirit. "That's just the first item to come to mind. I'm sure I can think of additional tasks later."

"A lot of tasks," I corrected. "Because I'm worthless at fae politics."

"As evidenced by your clever naming conventions," Lark drawled, glancing at me. "You realize I had to sign off on all of those acronyms, right?"

"You loved it," I told him. "I'm betting the T&A is your favorite."

His gaze went to Artica and the paint in her hands. "I wouldn't mind painting some T&A right now."

"And licking it off?" I suggested, wrapping my arm around our queen's waist.

"Mmm, absolutely," the Winter Fae King rumbled. "It's Matemas, after all, right?"

"It is," I confirmed, my fingers finding Artica's back and the zipper securing her dress. "May I?"

"You may," she confirmed with an anticipatory shiver.

Her dress fell to the ground, revealing her beautiful curves.

No lace.

Because someone had clearly taken those panties as a souvenir.

Not that I could blame Lark. I'd have done the same thing.

"You're stunning, sweet flurry," Kalt told her.

"Absolutely breathtaking," Lark echoed.

"Our alluring sunshine," I added, my lips curling as the three of us surrounded our queen. "Merry Matemas, Artica."

Now close your eyes, I added in a mental whisper. *We're about to make all your dreams come true.*

BONUS EPILOGUE: ARTICA
ONE YEAR LATER...

I drew in a deep breath as Lark and I waited for our cue, standing behind the silver curtain that blocked our view of the rest of the palace ballroom.

I thumbed my masquerade mask, having hoped that the costume theme would help calm my nerves, but I found myself wondering if I had chosen the right colors to complement my mates instead.

My mask was a jewel blue trimmed with frosted silver, a representation of my union between two Sources.

Lark wore a silver mask that made his mint-green eyes blaze with festive heat.

Norden wore an aquamarine blue mask engraved with crystals. And based on the way he kept plucking them off and popping them into his mouth, they were actually selkie candies.

Kalt's mask was a gorgeous green that matched Lark's eyes and made me think of the wrapped presents under the Festivus tree in our suite.

Music thrummed through the air, kicking off the

evening's festivities with the tinkering notes from an array of icicles drifting along the ceiling.

The icicles were a result of my own creation, thanks to my connections to the Water Source and the Winter Source. It seemed appropriate to use my talents to stir up a little festive cheer.

"Everyone will adore you," Lark informed me, his gaze burning with embers of passion.

"They'll adore your *hair,* too," Norden insisted as he tucked a strand behind my ice crown, which Kalt had reinforced against my head with a frosty kiss that had glued it to my hair.

"No one will adore you as much as we do," Kalt promised, brushing my chin with his fingers, stealing a quick kiss before he took his place at our side.

"This isn't about me," I reminded them all as Lark continued to devour me with his eyes, suggesting that this holiday would forever be about my beauty and joy to him.

Welcome to the first annual Winter Fae Queen's Summer Festivus Feast!

Those words rang through my mind before the curtains flung aside and Lark spoke them aloud, eliciting a cheer from the impressive gathering of Interrealm Fae guests, elves, North Pole indigenous species, and fellow Winter Fae.

"Would you like to say anything?" Lark asked me, a glint of delight in his eyes. "This is your day, after all."

I grinned at him because it was *his* birthday, and if he wanted me to speak, then I'd make sure everyone knew it.

Raising my fingers, I called upon the vibrant joy in the room and the lingering snowflakes, forming a fluted glass in my grip that contained pure festive cheer.

It only took me a moment to provide every guest with

their own glass of festive cheer, my control over magic having improved exponentially over the last year.

"A toast to the Winter Fae King!" I said, my voice increasing with confidence. "Today, he turns thirty-three, but I also celebrate our first year as an official mate-circle." I raised my glass to Kalt. "To Prince Kalt, the fae who taught me to believe."

"To Prince Kalt!" the audience echoed.

I moved on to Norden, who'd begun to blush, his mask eaten away enough so that I could see his pink cheeks, the uncharacteristic look on him quite adorable. "To Prince Norden, the selkie who taught me to—

"Scream for my ice cream," he said with his classic mischievous mirth.

"Taught me to find joy in all things and to make all my dreams come true," I corrected him. Although, he definitely wasn't wrong about his *ice cream*.

"To Prince Norden!" the crowd repeated, with the group of selkies singing his name with a note of pride.

I turned to Lark, who held me close to his hip, his arm wrapped around my waist as he lifted his own crystal glass.

"To King Lark," I said, lowering my voice, but my magic still carried my words to the entire room. "The fae who taught me how to love."

My heart thundered at my words, because even now, we had not yet truly spoken our feelings aloud. Not since that night in the ice cave, anyway.

But I didn't doubt his love for me. It just reminded me a bit of the twelve days of our mate-circle bonding where he hadn't touched me, because he seemed to be waiting for the right moment to utter those words to me.

He grinned as the crowd echoed his name. We all drank from our glasses, and then the music continued in a lifted beat meant to inspire dancing.

All of the nations indulged in food and festive cheer, fae accepting dances as the floor quickly filled with a mixture of races.

It was beautiful.

"I couldn't have imagined a better affair," Lark told me, his glass disappearing on a puff of ice, as did mine. He turned to me as he drew me onto the dance floor, guiding me in a practiced dance that involved all of my mates.

I swapped to Kalt, laughed when he peppered my skin with snowy kisses, and then joined with Norden, unable to avoid his infectious delight when he brought his lips to mine.

They moved me around, dipped me, and twirled me until I returned to Lark again, breathless and glowing.

He beamed as he wrapped his arms around my waist.

"I'm so proud of you, Artica. I'm proud of our mates, and I want you to know that you've made me the happiest fae in all the realms." He lifted me with ease, bringing me to him for a kiss that left me dizzy. He pulled me away, slowing our dance to a subtle drift as snowflakes kissed his eyelashes. "And I want you to know that I love you, too."

I swallowed past the thick lump in my throat. "I-I never said I loved you." Well, I said I loved all my mates in the ice cave. But I hadn't repeated the words since.

He grinned. "You tell me every day, my queen. You tell me with your laughter, with your infectious joy, with every kiss."

I smiled as joy filled my heart and tears crested over my cheeks. "I'm sorry I haven't said it out loud more. Because I do love you, Lark. I love all of you."

He kissed me, pulling away so that his reply brushed against my lips. "Never apologize for taking your time. Words are meaningless without actions and feelings, my queen," he replied softly.

He was right.

I didn't need my mates to say the words to know how they felt about me; I could already sense their love in my heart and in my soul.

Because they all believed in me.

And belief was the most wonderful gift of them all.

THE END

HALL FAE CAPTIVE

Welcome to the Hell Fae realm, a place where only the strong survive.

My parents made a deal with the devil, and now I'm a Hell Fae captive.

Enslaved. Owned. Thrown to the Hellhounds and expected to survive.
Because only survivors earn their mates.

It doesn't matter that I don't want to be a bride.
I'm a Halfling. Part Hell Fae and part girl-who-doesn't-give-a-shit.
But because of a bargain, *he* owns me.

Lucifer. The Hell Fae King who created this godforsaken realm.

Also known as the orchestrator of these deadly bride-trial games.

Okay, Luci, I'll play.
By burning this whole kingdom to the ground.

Assuming I don't get caught in the hot Midnight Fae Warden's web first.
Or ensnared by the brooding Hell Fae Commander lurking outside the gates.
And don't even get me started on the Hell Fae King's favored prince. That sexy lunatic won't stop sending me gifts.

No amount of hotness or sensual persuasion will keep me here.
I'm not bride material.
I'm a menace.

You made a deal for the wrong girl, Lucifer.
Prepare for the fight of your life.

Authors' Note: *Hell Fae Captive* is a dark kidnap paranormal romance with four tormented mates and no choosing required. If you like your anti-heroes dominant and sexy, you've come to the right realm—the Hell Realm where the romance is hot and no forgiveness is required.

USA Today Bestselling Author Lexi C. Foss loves to play in
dark worlds, especially the ones that bite. She lives in
Chapel Hill, North Carolina with her husband and their
furry children. When not writing, she's busy crossing items
off her travel bucket list, or chasing eclipses around the
globe. She's quirky, consumes way too much coffee, and
loves to swim.

Want access to the most up-to-date information for all of
Lexi's books? Sign-up for her newsletter here.

Lexi also likes to hang out with readers on Facebook in her
exclusive readers group - Join Here.

Where To Find Lexi:
www.LexiCFoss.com

ABOUT J.R. THORN

J.R. Thorn is a Reverse Harem Paranormal Romance Author.

Subscribe to the J.R. Thorn Mailing List to be Notified of New Releases and Deals!

Addicted to Academy? Read more RH Academy by J.R. Thorn: Fortune Academy

Welcome to Fortune Academy, a school where supernaturals can feel at home—except, I have no idea what the hell I am.